# VOICE IN THE DARK

## CALLING YOU HOME
### BOOK TWO


# KARIN MALLARD

# CONTENTS

# 1

## IRRECONCILIABLE DIFFERENCES

Ren debated long and hard early Tuesday morning, standing in his scrubs near his bed, his arms folded and his fingers drumming along his biceps, staring at Justin. Everything should be ok now. The trial finished yesterday, and Justin's fever had finally broken shortly after. It had been a roller coaster of a weekend, and so many things had changed all at once. But that was over now, and Ren was supposed to be on his way to class. He'd been standing here debating for too long already. Should he risk it? Would it be ok? Probably?

There was such a difference in Justin's rest now. He still kept his hands curled against his chest, though he no longer appeared to be in pain. His breath came easily, deep and sound. For as long as Ren had watched him yesterday and again this morning, he hadn't moved or murmured in distress. No nightmares. No fear. Just a beautiful, dark-haired boy enjoying the pure sleep of a recovering patient. Which meant Ren could very likely head out to his biology class. Ren had almost picked up his backpack and left three times already, but then that damning "what if" made him pause, look closer at Justin's face, and wonder if it truly would be safe to leave him. He'd been with Justin practically every second since bringing him home last Friday. It no longer felt natural to be apart, and it felt especially wrong to leave him on purpose without even telling him where he was going.

And yet, Ren had a lot he was supposed to do today. The biology class was just the beginning. Directly afterward, he was due for a morning shift at the donation center. Then there were two more classes back-to-back in the afternoon, and finally, worst of all, Ren was on-call tonight with the ambulance. A twelve-hour shift that started at six and meant that Ren wouldn't be home longer than a few minutes until dawn tomorrow. Ren guessed that his classes could be skipped, but it meant he would be even further behind. But really it wouldn't help much to skip anything because there was no getting out of the ambulance run. Especially since Ren had asked to be scheduled today to keep his Saturday free for Alek's birthday. He'd known when he switched that he would probably regret moving to a weeknight, but that was when he'd only been thinking about how he wouldn't be able to sleep in the morning after. Now that it meant leaving a recovering Justin alone for the duration of an entire night, it seemed an unfixable mistake.

In the end, when he really should have already been walking to class, Ren wrote a note for Justin in case he woke up before Ren got back. He told him where he was going, what time he thought he'd be home. He explained where he had left Justin's medication with instructions on what he was supposed to take and when, and he underlined the sentence to emphasize that Justin should take every-thing *with food* and he was welcome to whatever he thought he could handle in the kitchen. Ren begged him to take it easy. He reminded him that even though he probably felt better, he would still need a few rest days to get his strength back. North was coming over later to keep him company. Alek had promised to stay close to the apartment today. In case Justin had forgotten, Ren wrote his cell number again, asking for Justin to call him for anything. *For anything!* He'd rather drop everything and come home early than have to pick Justin up in the ambulance later.

Writing that forced Ren to look at Justin one more time, wondering if that could be a possibility. What trouble could Justin get into with his fever finally broken? With his heart medication working and his iron supplement balancing out his anemia, what were the odds that he could relapse at this point? Small, Ren decided, if he didn't try anything too strenuous. Ren wrote it out one more time that Justin needed to *stay down*. Stay in the apartment, stay in bed if he could stand it. *Just stay. Please.*

Ren carefully placed the note on his mattress near Justin's head, then somehow tore himself away from his room without touching Justin. He'd be all right. Ren knew he would. The worst was over, the trial was over, and Justin would only improve from now on. But that wasn't all that was truly worrying Ren. In fact, knowing that Justin was getting better was troubling him more. Because it meant there would be nothing keeping him at Ren's apartment. If Ren weren't taking Justin's temperature, comforting him in the dark, he no longer had a reason to be near him, to touch him. Ren could probably stretch this out for another day or two, but then he knew Justin would pack up his duffel bag, thank Ren for all he'd done, and disappear with North.

Or would he? Maybe they really were friends now? But that was something else bothering Ren. Could he just be friends with Justin? Could he sit with him in class, invite him to Alek's birthday, and then just be casual with him? After he'd held him, carried him through his darkness, now that he'd kissed the back of his neck. Could he pretend none of that had happened? Ren battled with this all the way to biology, not sure exactly which scenario would be worse, then tried desperately not to think about either possibility so he could concentrate. He found it almost impossible and wondered if this was just how it was going to be now. If Justin had somehow broken his ability to think clearly, to focus on anything happening around him. Which, of course, distressed and distracted him even more. He had things to do; he had to be able to pay attention. Still, he focused more on what Justin might be doing at his apartment than the lecture, and then hurried to check his phone the moment the professor dismissed them.

Ren was halfway relieved and halfway disappointed when there were no messages from Justin after class. The good news was Justin didn't need him. The bad news was exactly the same thing. He sent Justin an update text just in case, letting him know he was on his way to work where he wasn't allowed to have his cell phone turned on. If Justin needed him, he could call the donation center directly and ask for him. As he walked through the winter-covered campus, Ren reprimanded himself about keeping his head in the game. Drifting off during a biology lecture was one thing. Not paying attention when hooking a donor to a centrifuge was completely different. He would have to put Justin out of his mind.

He was almost ready to do that by the time he got to the donation center. But then he ran into some confusion that upset the whole concentration thing. He was barely out of his coat and clocked in when one of the newest techs, Brett, suddenly appeared next to him. They had Thursday night shifts together normally, and Ren had done most of Brett's training with him, but it was out of place to see him on a Tuesday morning. It was also strange for Brett to come directly to him; Ren normally had to go find him when they were supposed to work closely together. He needed quite a bit of direction on what to do and when.

"What are you doing here?" Brett asked him, staring him up and down suspiciously, like it wasn't possible for Ren to physically be here, despite the obvious evidence standing directly in front of him.

"Um, working?" Ren replied, caught off guard. What kind of question was that? He could just as well ask Brett the same thing; this wasn't his usual shift time. Brett stood as tall as Ren, but bigger. Broader in the shoulders, in the waist, even his hands and voice were bigger. And no matter what, he always looked like he'd skipped shaving. "What are you doing here?"

"Steve called me in to cover for you," Brett answered defensively, also looking confused and slightly offended. Like he thought someone was trying to waste his time. Ren thought there must have been a misunderstanding.

"Yesterday?" Ren clarified. He'd written to Steve, their supervisor, on Sunday night and let him know that he'd be gone on Monday. He felt sure he'd only asked for one day off; there'd been no need to call Brett in for today. Actually, Ren felt annoyed that Brett had been called in to cover for him at all. They were nowhere near the same level. But then again Ren hadn't given Steve a whole lot of notice for his absence. He'd probably brought in the first person who said they could spare the time. And Ren knew he wasn't being fair since Brett was still learning, but it made Ren tense to even watch him. He was just so big, and he moved so fast, every gesture sudden and choppy. He made Ren nervous.

"Yeah, yesterday," Brett confirmed, still watching Ren in an interrogatory manner. "But he said you'd probably need today off too."

"Well, I don't," Ren heard himself say, then paused. What was he doing? If Steve already expected him not to be here, then shouldn't he just put his coat on again and leave? It'd be an easy thing; Brett was already here. Though he didn't feel comfortable leaving his patients in Brett's novice care. He'd barely stopped Brett from ramming a needle completely through a donor's vein the last time they'd trained together. He wondered how well he'd done yesterday on his own.

"You sure about that?" Brett continued with the annoying questions, staring conspicuously at Ren's face. At the healing bruise that was making its way toward the grotesque yellow, green, and brown color, hanging on to purple still in the center. Ren didn't like the tone or the stare, even though he knew better.

*He doesn't mean it as a challenge*, Ren told himself firmly, forcing himself not to bury his face in his hanging coat. *There is no need to rise to this; he's just asking a question.* The Texas drawl in Brett's accent was making it seem like something more than what it was, and Ren knew that, but he found himself ruffled anyway. *It doesn't matter*, he repeated. *Take this as the opportunity it is and go home. That's three hours you weren't expecting to have today.* Ren looked at his coat for just a few seconds too long.

"Ren, good, you made it." *Hello, Steve, what impressive timing you have.* Ren sighed. "I wasn't sure you'd be working today."

"Apparently," Ren muttered, holding on to his coat sleeves, surprised at his own rotten mood. Steve walked up, shorter than both of them by several inches, and yet he owned all the authority of the group. Steve wasn't a doctor, but he was a skilled phlebotomist, and he'd been running the campus donation center probably longer than Ren had been alive.

"I called Brett just in case," Steve explained the Texan's presence. "But since you're both here, Ren, I'd like Brett to shadow you this shift if you're feeling up to that?"

Now Ren had to turn and look at his supervisor. He was too tired and honestly unmotivated to keep up with whatever was going on here. Brett was going to shadow him? Now? He really should have asked for another day. Or left a little sooner.

"I guess so?" Ren replied, more a question than acceptance. It wasn't up to him what Steve wanted to do with the staff. Steve nodded at him, trying to communicate some information with the gesture.

"Wait," Brett said, caught off guard. "I'm confused. Is this a training or a shift?"

"You get paid the same either way," Steve reminded him, attempting good humor. "But it's a training, for the record. You're just watching Ren this morning. Then before you leave, we'll do a venipuncture test to make sure you've got it."

"On a donor?" Ren asked, wanting to make sure he understood correctly.

"On you," Steve volunteered. Ren did not shift his eyes heavenward, but he wanted to. Today? Really? He supposed he'd known there would be repercussions from taking an entire day off, but he hadn't thought it would mean he'd have to bleed for it.

He felt Brett's eyes on him, not hostile, maybe wounded. This was quite a blow to his ego. He thought he'd already completed training. *He's not a bad guy*, Ren reminded himself. *Steve has a point; if you taught him better, you wouldn't be doing this.*

"Go on and get ready," Steve instructed Brett, doing a great job of ignoring the dark expression on Brett's face.

Brett set off immediately to wash his hands and don his lab coat, stock up his pockets with tape and gauze. Ren automatically moved to follow him, but Steve put a hand on his shoulder to stop him. Ren closed his eyes, waiting for some kind of reprimand about his training.

"You all right, Ren?" Steve asked him, which took Ren by surprise. Maybe because he didn't know. The real world, his normal schedule, seemed suddenly weird and wrong. Part of him was still in his room, watching Justin sleep, thinking about what was going to happen now. He knew it was slowing him down, but he hadn't thought it was enough for anyone to notice.

"Fine," Ren responded automatically, the translated answer for "it's so complicated, we don't have time or energy to get into it." Steve looked doubtful, but since what he wanted was to have Ren and Brett here at the same time, he eased into acceptance of the answer.

"Let me know if that changes," Steve requested before heading toward his office. Ren admired Steve's office. It was the only medical room Ren had ever seen that did not have stacks of paperwork all over it. Steve kept his things tight and orderly. His office, his shifts, his training schedules. Everything in place.

Ren also went to his place, shrouding himself in the white lab coat and getting ready to show Brett, again, how to successfully place a needle. It turned out to be a good thing to have a shadow on his shift. Having Brett at Ren's side kept Justin out of his head. It meant he couldn't zone out; he had to verbally narrate everything he was doing and why. Brett proved a good sport and student, correctly answering all of Ren's questions. But then again, knowing what to do had never been Brett's problem. During the next three hours, Ren took care of twenty-four donors and only had time to wonder how Justin was doing twice. He'd also almost forgotten about Brett's test. If Steve hadn't come to get them shortly before the shift was up, Ren might have said "good work" and "goodbye" to Brett and left without giving it another thought.

"Ok, guys, come on," Steve invited them into the back area behind the cashier's office. There were a few cots back there, reserved for patients who were feeling faint or for this sort of training test. "Let's see how it went."

Ren would feel more victimized by this if he hadn't done it himself when he was new, cannulating his own trainer last year when he'd started working at the donation center. He'd also been on the receiving end of a needle many times for new trainees. It was never a big deal, but Ren discovered that he was nervous having Brett do it even though he knew Steve would be there and nothing really awful could possibly happen with a 14-gauge catheter. It's not like Brett could kill or maim him. Still. He wanted it to be over.

"Show him we know what we're doing," Ren told Brett, trying to sound casual as he positioned himself on the cot and extended his arm. Brett didn't look concerned. He looked like Ren felt — like he wanted to get it out of the way. As usual, he moved too quickly.

"Take your time," Steve invited, not knowing that Brett wasn't rushing because he was nervous. This was just his normal pace. Ren pressed his lips together tightly so he wouldn't say anything. Not that he had time to give Brett any instruction. The Texan was moving almost frighteningly fast through the prep work. Tearing open the cannula kit, ripping off pieces of tape with a surprising lack of grace. It was making Ren twitchy watching him, but there wasn't anything to be said as Brett wasn't doing anything wrong.

Ren bit back a grunt as Brett stabbed him with the catheter, forcing himself not to wince. *Ouch.* He'd hit the vein true, as evidenced by the backsplash that pumped up into the guard, but Ren thought he could use a lot more practice on how to get access without it being torture for the patient. He hadn't collapsed the vein or rolled it, just jabbed into it too hard, like he expected Ren's skin to be more resistant. Despite this, the venipuncture had been a success. Ren looked at Steve for his assessment and saw his expression mirrored Ren's feelings exactly.

"What do you think, Ren?" Steve asked once Brett had reversed the whole process, removing the needle and disposing of it properly. The yanking it out part hadn't hurt, but watching Brett go at it caused Ren to tense up his arm in expectation that it would, an anxious tingling in all the nerves around the puncture site. Ren paused in his answer, pressing a gauze pad to the inside of his elbow.

"He followed correct procedure," Ren allowed.

"But?" Steve prompted, and Ren wondered why he was making him say it.

"But it hurt," Ren confessed, looking apologetically at Brett. "Try slowing down. Pretend you're trying to cannulate a water balloon without popping it."

"That's impossible," Brett scoffed with a forced laugh as though Ren had made a joke. Ren shrugged, ready to leave.

"No, it's not," Steve contradicted authoritatively. "I've seen Ren do it, and I agree. Get yourself some water balloons and polish up your technique. Ren, is that going to bruise, do you think?"

"Too soon to tell," Ren dismissed, though he was almost certain it would. There were so many variables that went into a venipuncture. Sometimes a tech could bruise a donor on one visit, but then have everything go just fine the next time. Basing Brett's performance on whether Ren's puncture site bruised wasn't really fair in Ren's opinion, especially since he knew he'd be working tonight. He decided to take it out as a factor in the decision-making process. Some techs hurt more than others; there was no getting around it except to have them practice. Since Brett had done the steps correctly, there wasn't any good reason not to let him practice.

Though Ren intended to keep Brett away from the more delicate donors on Thursday if he could help it.

"So, do I pass?" Brett asked impatiently.

"Yes," Steve allowed. "But slow it down. I had some complaints about you yesterday, and I'd rather not hear any more."

"Complaints?" Brett said, standing straighter. "About what?" Ren started to get up. He could guess exactly what the complaints had been, but this conversation sounded as though he didn't need to stick around anymore. If he was quick, he could run home to change, eat, and check on Justin before his next classes.

"I gotta go," Ren excused himself quietly between Steve's explanations and Brett's defensive responses. "Thanks for covering for me yesterday."

He didn't think anyone even heard him, but he didn't care. He wanted to get home. Except the place was deserted when he arrived. There was a note on the table from Alek. He said North had come to pick up Justin, who looked pretty decent today, so Alek was out with Denny, but he'd packed Ren a lunch to take on the ambulance shift. He'd also left him a burrito.

Ren stood at the table, reading the note repeatedly to see if there was anything more to it, though he didn't know what he expected. He thought about calling North as he made his way to his bedroom to switch out the books in his backpack and change from his scrubs into his EMT uniform. This would be the last time he'd be home today. He felt let down that there was no one here for it, but then remembered that he'd be the one gone the most today, so it wasn't like he could expect for everyone to just sit around waiting for him to show up.

The note Ren had written for Justin this morning lay open on his desk next to his chemistry book. At least Justin had seen it, though apparently, he was going to ignore Ren's suggestion that he continue to rest. Ren picked up the paper, intent on crumpling it up and throwing it away when he saw Justin had written a reply. Ren set down his backpack so he could hold the page with both hands.

*Thank you*, he'd written. *I'll be with North. We're going to finish the adoption paperwork today, but then I'll be back.*

He hadn't bothered to sign it, but the most important thing about the note was the part where he said he'd be back. Ren shot a glance to the corner of his room, comforted to see Justin's duffel bag still there.

After so much note reading, Ren again had to hurry. He buttoned into his uniform, zipped up his reorganized backpack, and barely took the time to reheat the burrito before bolting it down, eating the last few bites in the hallway on his way out.

Then there was chemistry and early child development for the next several hours, and one last phone check before Ren was back at the hospital emergency room. Dr. Delacroix might have been here earlier, but she'd already finished her shift by the time Ren arrived. He wondered if Officer Geisler had emailed her yet, and if she'd been pissed or pleased if he had. Ren stowed his backpack and lunch in his assigned locker, padlocking them inside. He had to leave his phone there too. He put it in reluctantly after noticing, again, that he hadn't received word from anyone today. Had they all just forgotten him or something?

It wasn't Grayson and Stefany scheduled with him tonight since he'd changed his normal shift day. Today he was with Connor Shaughnessy and Dante Medina — names he knew, people he did trainings with, but they'd never done a shift together, which Connor pointed out immediately upon arrival.

"Hey, Cordero, we never ride with you!" Connor greeted him, fresh and enthusiastic, extending his hand to Ren.

Ren recognized Connor, remembering his heavily freckled face. He also remembered Connor and his wife had recently had their first baby; there'd been a little shower at the last First Responder's meeting, though Ren had never seen the newborn or Connor's wife in person.

"I asked to switch my day," Ren admitted, reaching out to take Connor's hand. Connor gripped him tight and friendly, pulling him close so he could pat him on the back before letting him go. It made Ren feel better about his day and his upcoming night in the field.

"Couldn't take the weekend traffic anymore, huh?" Dante put in as he opened his own locker. "Wanted to try a boring Tuesday graveyard?"

That sounded magnificent to Ren at the moment. He was still so tired from the weekend, from sleeping only a few uncomfortable hours at a time and being on high alert for so many straight days. A boring night waiting around for a call would be the next best thing to sleeping in his own bed.

"I hear you guys have more fun and less bullet wounds," Ren returned, almost feeling playful. *It's ok to feel normal*, he told himself. *Justin's ok. He's coming back. You'll see him tomorrow. You're going to have to figure out how your life works now you can't be with him all the time.*

"Oh? Is that what they told you?" Dante asked, and Ren couldn't tell if the older man was joking with him or not. Dante had run the weeknight graveyard shift for almost fifteen years. Ren had met his wife a few times, a shy woman who had the most amazing smile, especially when she looked at Dante. They had five children, all of them boys. Dante would be the Incident Commander in Charge for tonight, which Ren accepted with relief. He wanted to be told what to do for a while, and hopefully, things really would be boring.

"Dante, come on." Connor shoved him. "You're freaking him out." The way Connor spoke told Ren they both considered him a kid, which made sense on Dante's side, but Connor was barely thirty.

"What, Cordero?" Dante exclaimed with exaggerated surprise. "He doesn't freak out; look at him! He's rock solid." He switched his attention to Ren, becoming instantly serious. "But we do need to go over a few things, because I heard some rumors about you, and I'd like to validate them before we're called out. Fair?"

Ren compelled his shoulders not to slump. Rumors? He couldn't even imagine.

"Fair," he replied, mostly because he didn't have a choice.

"Ok then, true or false. Your face got messed up in a bar fight last weekend?"

Ren choked on a laugh. He still wasn't sure if this was going to end up painful for him, but it wasn't starting off so bad.

"False," he responded, glad he could tell the truth. "It was a combative patient on Friday morning." Or at least truthful *enough*.

"All right. Next question. I heard you cannulated a patient on Saturday, even though you were unauthorized and off duty, is that true or false?" Oh. So that piece of information had made the rounds already? Ren sighed, but he refused to look away from Dante. He'd already endured Dr. Delacroix about this; he wasn't going to be intimidated by it now. Though he could see that this was going south in a hurry.

"True," Ren confessed, which made Connor whistle from his witness position on the sidelines.

"And you ignored protocol and Stefany Lopez's directions?" Ren took another long breath, wondering if it would help if he explained himself. If he could make Dante understand how that had been an anomaly for him.

"Also true," Ren answered simply, judging from the expression on Dante's face that he didn't want excuses or explanations.

"Last one," Dante continued darkly. "True or false. You are not going to be pulling any of that maverick shit on me tonight. You're going to do everything I tell you when I tell you."

"True," Ren said with conviction, staring straight into Dante's dark eyes. Dante held his gaze, gauging his answer, looking every bit like a father with five sons.

"Good." Dante released him, and so the night began.

Ren quickly found there was nothing different between Tuesday or Saturday night. About the same amount of crap happened. They responded to a horrible traffic accident where they took one of the drivers to the ER and left the pieces of the other for the coroner. There were no drive-by shootings, but there was a domestic violence call that required police backup. They went almost to the edge of their area to help a little girl having a seizure and then turned around when a call came in from a terrified roommate who walked in on a botched suicide attempt. There was an obese man with angina pain and a Spanish speaking woman in labor whose husband delivered her baby on the side of the road on the way to the hospital.

Quite a lot going on in the dark cold of a January night when all should have been peaceful and sleeping. Ren was always amazed how many people were awake all night long. How there were always other cars on the road when the ambulance went out. Always lights on in the houses and apartment buildings, in the offices and the gas stations. All the activity that happened after the sun went down. How it all meant that he was not going to get a break.

Between calls, Ren assisted Dante and Connor in taking care of the vehicle. Making sure it was always filled with fuel. Putting things away that had been knocked down or replacing items that had been used. Sterilizing after blood spills, writing up the paperwork in the aftermath. Running, moving, shifting from trying to remember what the date was, before or after midnight, to grabbing his coat and rushing for the door. Through it all, Ren deferred to Dante and Connor. He meekly accepted every request they put to him, a diligent robot, though Dante was kind by protecting Ren from the worst of the traffic accident fatality.

It was also Dante who shook his shoulder somewhere around six in the morning after Ren had fallen asleep sitting up, waiting in the back of the ambulance. He woke up startled at the company and the environment, embarrassed that he'd nodded off when he should have been cleaning.

"Where are we going?" Ren asked, trying to wake himself up, focus on the next emergency. Dante held him still.

"Home," Dante answered. "The next shift is here, and I've already gone over everything with them. Go get some sleep, Cordero. Great job last night. I hope to ride with you again."

"Thanks," Ren slurred, exhausted despite his catnap. He wished he could go home and sleep, but his English class was in two hours.

He'd have just enough time to shower and change, drink some very strong coffee, and then head out again. He checked his phone as he put on his coat and backpack. This time there were a few texts. One from Alek congratulating him on remembering his dinner and wishing him good luck on the run. One from Denny asking if he'd been involved with the traffic accident last night. And one from Justin.

*Are you always this busy?*

Ren smiled through his exhaustion. His impulse was to respond right away, but he stopped himself when he remembered it wasn't even six thirty yet. Also, Justin sent the text last night at nine, so it wasn't like he was still waiting for an answer. It would be better to just get home as quickly as possible.

Ren's body protested the pace he set on the way home through the icy air. His muscles were weary; he didn't even want to look at the place where Brett had pierced him after all the heavy lifting he'd done. His back ached and burned at the same time, making Ren guess that he had been too casual about getting antibiotic on it the last couple days. Mostly, he was just a crushing sort of tired. Like he was every night he stayed up with the ambulance, but this time he couldn't just go collapse into bed and sleep most of Sunday after he hung up with his family.

*You knew you'd regret this*, Ren reminded himself as he slogged through campus on his way home. By the time he'd reached his apartment building, the sun was just making its appearance over the lake, somehow looking different since Ren had also watched it go down the previous night.

He eased himself into the apartment, trying to make as little noise as possible. Alek could sleep through just about anything, but Ren wasn't sure who else might be here. It wasn't often Denny slept over on weeknights, but last weekend had changed a lot about the apartment — particularly the who was there and when part.

The couch was empty of everything except the familiar afghan, meaning Denny hadn't spent the night. However, Justin's coat and boots were in the tangle by the door, which meant he had. Seeing that eased Ren's heart. The table was an endearing mess of electronics again, and the rich scent of coffee saturated the air. Alek had apparently reconciled himself to the coffeemaker and even decoded the timer so it would be ready for Ren the moment he walked in the door.

"Thank you, Alek," Ren murmured as he leaned against the counter, steadying himself to pour the strong brew into the biggest mug they owned. Knowing it was way too hot to try and swallow, Ren did the next best thing and hugged the warmth close to his chest, keeping it near his face so he could inhale the steamy blackness of it, taking it with him to the couch. He had to set it down for a minute so he could undo the laces on his boots, tucking them to the side. Then he reclaimed the mug and stretched out on the couch, sagging sideways into the back of it and closing his eyes. For just a minute. Just until the coffee was cool enough to drink. It was a risk to sit still like this, and he knew it, so he positioned himself so if he did end up falling asleep, he'd douse himself in scalding coffee.

What he really wanted to do was go into his room and check on Justin, but he didn't want to wake him. He'd have to go in there eventually, for clean clothes and the textbooks he'd need for the day. Since he wasn't sure if he could do that without disturbing Justin, he figured he'd wait so he'd only wake him once, if at all. Though it turned out he'd already woken Justin, just from walking in the door.

"Ren?"

Ren opened one eye, too tired to even startle at the unexpected voice. But when he saw Justin standing at the edge of the couch, one hand resting on the wall as he leaned against it, Ren forced himself to a sitting position. He knew it was mostly because he was exhausted and positioned on the couch, but he'd never seen Justin looking so tall.

"Hey, Justin, sorry I woke you," Ren managed, his voice croaky from being up all night. He tried a sip of the coffee, discovering it was the most powerfully delicious stuff he'd had in a very long time. It made him close his eyes again, sighing appreciatively. "Guess I'm used to Alek being a heavy sleeper. How are you doing? Feeling better?"

"I'm fine," Justin dismissed, obviously not wanting to talk about himself, staring at Ren in that unnerving way again. Like he wasn't sure who Ren was, but Justin intended to find out. "Is this something you do all the time?"

"No, just once a month for training." Ren took another careful swallow of coffee, trying to summon more energy for Justin, who had perched on the chair and looked ready to have some kind of conversation. "It was bad timing on this one, but I asked for it."

"How'd it go?" Justin asked gently, as though he weren't sure about Ren anymore. Like something had happened in their day apart. "We heard there was a car accident. Did you have to go to that?"

"Did Denny have her police scanner over here or something?" Ren asked, shaking his head, trying not to make this a big deal. He'd told them before not to listen to it when he was on call. It made Alek worry, and it made Denny ask him way too many questions. Ren gingerly leaned back into the couch, drained, watching Justin nod.

"We were there," Ren finally gave in, doing his best not to picture too vividly how bad that had been. Dante had taken one look on scene and half-shoved Ren into the bay, forcing him to wait on radio until he and Connor brought the surviving driver over to him. He hadn't even wanted Ren to see the other one. Even so, the victim they'd brought to the hospital only barely made it. Ren wasn't sure he'd be going home.

"Hey," Justin called, shaking him from the memory, bringing him back to the apartment. "Why don't you go get some sleep?"

Ren pushed himself up until he was sitting on the edge of the couch, less in danger of drifting off. He took a long swig of coffee.

"Because I can't," he answered, trying to sound more alert. "I've got class in an hour." Technically, so did Justin, but Ren wasn't in favor of Justin walking all the way there in the early morning cold. It was too soon in the recovery period. And Ren hadn't done a stat check on him in over twenty-four hours. Some doctor he was.

"Class?" Justin repeated incredulously.

"Yeah, you know," Ren said, keeping his tone light. "English class? Starts at eight."

"What are you crazy? Just skip it," Justin lectured, and Ren seriously considered it.

"I wish," Ren groaned, drinking more coffee. Such good, happy coffee. "I've got a meeting at the hospital right after that I can't skip, so there's not much point."

"So, when are you coming back?" Justin asked, almost angrily. Ren looked at the ceiling, thinking about the question and the tone.

"My shift at the donation center ends at eight tonight, so however long it takes me to walk home after that. Unless you need me," Ren amended seriously, trying but failing to meet Justin's gaze. "If you need me to stay, I can get out of almost everything except the meeting at the hospital, but that shouldn't take more than a couple hours. So, how are you doing? You were gone yesterday when I came home for lunch."

"North took me to the clerk's office," Justin offered, his voice melting slightly. "We weren't gone long."

"So, you're legal now?" Ren asked. "Are you going to change your name or anything?"

"No," Justin said quickly. "I'm keeping my name, but everything's official."

"Congratulations." Ren toasted him with the last of his coffee. "I'm glad for you. Though I wanted you to take it easy yesterday."

"It took less than two hours," Justin defended himself, but there was something in his voice that told Ren that Justin was pissed at how tiring his small excursion out of the apartment had been.

"Bet it wore you out, though," Ren ventured, and this time Justin full on glared at him. It made Ren pause, remembering how Justin had acted when they'd first met, how wild and fierce he had been. Now that he was getting better, it seemed that part of him was returning. Justin turned his head away, hiding his expression, putting Ren off balance. He thought he was getting to know Justin, but he should have known Justin would be a completely different creature once his fever broke.

"Give yourself a break," Ren tried to fix what he'd just done. "You almost died three days ago. You think you can just jump back into what you used to be able to do?"

"Yes," Justin said curtly. And Ren could hear it. In Justin's mind, he still wasn't completely free, and it was messing with him. The court had freed him. The foster system had freed him. But his body was keeping him a prisoner. And Ren felt guilty that something so frustrating to Justin was something he was taking advantage of. Though he had to admit, he was struggling to find the time he wanted to be with Justin, to experiment on how they were now that he was getting better. It wasn't working the way he wanted; his schedule was too brutal for any extra or new activity.

Ren found himself reaching out to Justin, as he'd done countless times over the weekend, intending on resting the back of his hand on Justin's forehead, a rudimentary gauge of his temperature. To his astonishment, Justin flinched away from him, a gesture that twisted hard in Ren's spirit. It was happening. Justin was pulling away from him, from the experience they'd shared. It had been terrible enough that Justin wanted to distance himself from it. Meaning he didn't want to be here. Didn't want Ren to touch him. He may want to forget about Ren entirely, a remnant from a past he wanted to leave far behind.

"I'm fine," Justin repeated, adamant, though Ren could hear his heart rate in his voice.

"I know," Ren agreed, still wanting to touch Justin but no longer feeling as though he were allowed to. "Can I do a stat check anyway?"

"Really?" Justin asked, frustrated, and this time he sounded tired.

"Please?" Ren pleaded, standing up with the expectation that

Justin would follow him into his bedroom where his notebook and stethoscope were.

"You're unbelievable," Justin huffed, but he got to his feet. Ren noticed with relieved apprehension how much easier it was for Justin to stand, to walk on his own without leaning on the wall. The slight hunch in his shoulders was the only clue that he wasn't at a hundred percent yet. Ren still had a little time.

Justin kept his gaze on the floor all the while Ren took his readings. His blood pressure read normal, as did his oxygen level. Though his heart rate was still slightly higher than average, and his temperature came in at 99.1. Ren was starting to wonder if Justin was one of those people who just ran hot all the time, but he'd need so many more readings over the next week to figure out if that were true.

By the time Ren finished, Justin looked as sleepy as Ren felt. All Ren wanted to do was curl up on Justin's chest and close his eyes too, but that was dangerous to even daydream about. Ren busied himself putting his med gear away, pulling out clean scrubs from the dresser, and rearranging his backpack again. Justin watched him quietly, his expression perplexed and the tiniest bit angry.

"I'm going to take a quick shower," Ren told Justin where he was going. "You should get some more sleep. How's your mouth? Could you eat anything yesterday?"

"Not really," Justin muttered after a long pause, as though he didn't want to tell Ren that information.

"I know it's annoying," Ren admitted, sad that his apartment had become a prison all on its own. "But I'd like you to stay here at least until you can eat normally, all right? Then I'll know you've made a full recovery. Until then, just rest as much as possible. You don't have anywhere you need to be, do you?"

"We're meeting Kelly later," Justin said. "And her friend in finance. There's still a lot of paperwork to get through, I guess."

Ren didn't like the sound of that. North was coming to pick Justin up and take him out again? Didn't he understand that Justin needed to *rest*?

"Try not to overdo it," Ren reminded him.

"Look who's talking," Justin murmured, though he was obediently tucking himself back into Ren's bed.

"Take your meds later," Ren went on as though he hadn't heard. "And don't forget to eat. If you need me, you can call me. I'll come home. Ok?"

Ren could no longer read Justin's expression, though after another long pause, he did nod in agreement to Ren's offer. It was all Ren could do not to smooth the quilt over Justin, run his fingers through his hair. He sighed away his longing and gathered his things, closing the door softy on his way out.

The rest of the day went by in an exhausted blur. Ren sat in the back during English, the place where Justin had been when they'd first met. For part of the lecture, Ren had to stand up or he'd have been the one sleeping through class.

The debriefing at the hospital went almost as Ren expected, though it was Dr. Delacroix who went over the cases with him, going through them one by one, asking him what had happened, if anything had gone wrong, if there was something he would have changed or improved if he'd had the chance to do it over. Only when they'd discussed every call at length did Angelique turn to other topics — like Justin and the trial and if Ren had suffered any delayed panic response to any of the cases on the run. She seemed satisfied by his answers. Justin's fever was broken; he'd been acquitted. Ren hadn't been shaky at all last night.

He lied to her twice. The first time when she asked if he was taking care of the wound on his back. The second when she asked him if he was ok. He could tell she saw right through him, but before she could ask again, he threw her off balance by asking about Officer Geisler. It made her head tilt, and she instantly lost ten years from her eyes as she confessed that yes, they were going to go out on the weekend. Ren wished her good luck and made to leave before she could press him about anything else. She looked startled at the rush but allowed him to go when he said he had to get to class.

Before he knew it, he was back at the donation center. On Wednesday. He worked the floor, without a trainee this time, and thought back to last week when he'd had his first conversation with Celeste about the book she was reading. When they'd made plans to meet and talk about it. When that had been the thing Ren wanted most in the entire world.

Between donors, Ren watched the clock, silently enduring the teasing from his coworkers for paying so much attention to how it was nearing six. He hadn't thought much about it, but now that he was here, he did want to see Celeste. Wanted to secure her to the centrifuge as though nothing had happened between them. Or maybe he wanted to stay beside her to explain exactly what happened, force her to understand that he'd made the right choice.

But then six came and went, and Celeste didn't come. The teasing changed afterward, queries about what Ren had done to offend his pretend girlfriend. Though it wasn't long before all teasing stopped completely, and new questions and apologies started. *Ren, we didn't mean anything. Don't worry about it. Are you all right?*

The last one was repeated so many times that Ren got frustrated replying to it. Yes, he was fine. He was just tired. So, so tired. The disappointment was nothing compared to the ache of exhaustion. It took so long for six o'clock to turn into eight, for Ren to retrieve his coat and backpack, shield himself as best he could, and head finally toward his apartment. To Alek and Denny. Maybe Justin.

When he walked through the door after the long, cold trip, his apartment was full. Dinner was on the table, though just one serving that Alek had saved for him. Denny had her laptop on the couch, her feet up on the coffee table, reading something to Alek as he tended to his herb garden on the kitchen counter. And North sat at attention, his elbows on the table with his fingers pressed together, just touching his lips. Justin was nowhere to be seen, but Ren noticed his coat in the pile on the camp chair.

"Ren, you look like a zombie," Denny interrupted herself to

comment, which brought Alek's attention from his miniature rosemary bush.

"It's been a long day," Ren defended, hoping not to sound too sharp. He slumped into a chair across from North and stared at his plate.

"Yeah, your day is at what? Thirty-eight hours and counting?" Denny closed her computer. Ren dragged his eyes over to glare at her. She knew why he'd changed his ambulance schedule. They'd planned the whole thing. It was up to her to keep Alek out of the apartment so Ren could cook and get ready for birthday festivities. His pointed look seemed to jog her memory, and she stopped smirking.

"Where's Justin?" Ren changed the subject, absently picking up his fork to sample whatever Alek had made for him. Not even noticing if he were hungry, but he knew he must be.

"He's lying down," North answered, speaking for the first time but not moving. "He was waiting for you but had a hard time staying awake. Now that you're here, though, we can get going."

"No, don't," Ren protested, swallowing his bite without chewing. "Let him sleep. He's fine where he is."

North blinked with exaggerated slowness, carefully lowering his clasped hands onto the table. "Ren," he began, and Ren knew exactly where this was going. *It doesn't make sense for Justin to stay here anymore. He's taking your bed, and you definitely need it.* Both excellent points, but Ren didn't want to hear them.

"Could he eat today?" Ren cut North off. "Was he dizzy or breathless at all?" *You know, when you took him outside against my advice?* Ren may be dragging this out, but North was rushing it. North took a deep breath, locking eyes with Ren.

"He ate," North disclosed, as though giving an official report. "But it was a struggle. And you're right, he was getting dizzy and breathless toward the end of our meetings today."

"Then he should stay here," Ren decided, adamant. North's mouth twitched.

"For how long?" he demanded. Because as much as Ren wanted Justin to stay, North wanted Justin to come home. He was Justin's family now, legally. Ren was nothing. Though Ren did wonder why Justin had been waiting for him. Maybe to say goodbye like North suggested?

"Until he's fully recovered," Ren said, then decided that he respected North enough for a better answer. He couldn't be selfish about this. "When he's strong enough that a simple meeting doesn't exhaust him to the point where he's in bed asleep before eight at night. When he can eat like a normal person."

"Then I guess we'll wait until you give the ok for him to be officially discharged," North said, lightly enough, but Ren felt wounded. Like he was keeping Justin here against his will, but he didn't want to believe it. "I'll come by tomorrow to check on him again. Will you be here?"

Thursday. Ren's longest day of the week. He was never home on Thursdays. Justin was making him realize he was hardly ever still at all.

"If Justin needs me," Ren promised. "I'll be here."

North looked worried, conflicted. He got up gracefully from his chair, said good night to Alek and Denny, thanking them for dinner, company, and their help with Justin. Ren's friends responded cordially, exchanges happening over Ren's head as he stared at the uneaten food on his plate that he hadn't wanted much in the first place and knew he couldn't finish now. He was so tired.

Ren tried to stand up to see North out, but North put his artificial hand on Ren's shoulder, keeping him in his chair. Ren only had enough energy to stare at North's shoes.

"It'll be all right, Ren," North told him, making Ren's breath catch in his throat. How did he know? Sure, it would be great for him. He and Justin were family; nothing could take that away from them anymore. Ren just nodded as if he believed it, and North disappeared into the hall.

He'd no sooner closed the door than Alek and Denny were at the table with Ren, staring at him in concern and curiosity. He didn't want to talk to either of them.

"Sorry, guys," he apologized, this time succeeding in standing. "I just want to sleep, ok?"

"Makes sense," Denny allowed.

"You can take my bed," Alek offered. "I can sleep on the couch tonight." Ren smiled at his roommate, genuinely touched.

"Alek," he said. "There's no way you can sleep on the couch. I'll be just fine on the floor. But," he amended as he saw Alek droop at being refused. "If you wanted to do that magic coffee timer thing you set up yesterday, that would be amazing."

"Coffee?" Alek said, confused.

"You know, you fixed the timer, so it was ready when I came home? That was the best coffee I've ever had."

"That was Justin," Denny volunteered when Alek still looked lost. "He made the coffee. He set it for tomorrow too."

"He did?" Ren repeated, wrapping his head around that. "Huh."

Ren turned toward his room, but Denny called one more question after him.

"So, Ren? It's Wednesday. Were you able to talk to Celeste?"

"She never came," Ren replied, his head hanging, not turning from where he stood facing the hallway. He also didn't wait to hear anything more; he hurried into the warm darkness of his room where Justin slept quietly in his bed.

Ren plopped into his desk chair, too tired to move, watching Justin. That broody punk had just sat there and watched Ren drink his coffee without saying a word about it. What the hell did that mean? Did it mean anything?

The only thing Ren knew for sure was his time with Justin was coming to an end. And even though he was exhausted, he sat there with his eyes open for much longer than he should, watching Justin breathe, wishing he would wake up so he could talk to him. Wishing he knew what Justin wanted. Wishing it was the same thing Ren did.

"*No me dejas,*" was the last thing Ren remembered whispering.

# 2

# LIABILITY

For the next hours of darkness, Ren found himself waking repeatedly. His conflicted emotions, weariness, and worry tangled together in a manner hardly conducive to rest. All through the night, he struggled to find a position of comfort on his bedroom floor, though it got better after he tossed the contents of his clothes hamper out, making himself a wrinkled laundry nest. But even after he'd settled physically, he found himself shaken awake continually like something was wrong. Like the emergency pager was going off. He'd jerk awake, unnerved to find that he was shrouded in dark, neither in his bed nor in the ambulance, taking longer each time to figure out why. Once he was oriented, he'd look at Justin. Then, satisfied that Justin was still sleeping and hadn't disappeared, he'd put his head down and close his eyes, frustrated that he couldn't just fall asleep and stay that way.

*You're being dumb*, he'd remind himself, shifting to accommodate the slope of his shoulder, the angle of his hip, rearranging his clothes underneath him as his constant movement would slide them out from under him. *Everything's over*. Still, every tiny thing woke him. A car driving outside the window. Soft murmurings or stirrings from Justin. Images kept floating to the surface of his subconscious. The driver. The failed suicide. The lights of the ambulance, the burning ache of his back. North's eyes.

It was almost a relief when morning came, and Ren could stop trying to rest. He got up before he needed to, stiff and heavy, gathering his laundry mattress and shoving it into the hamper. Then he slogged into the kitchen to see if Justin's coffee would be as amazing this morning as it had been yesterday. The strong scent of it lay thick in the apartment, just the smell doing the job of easing Ren's muscles, helping his senses turn on again. And somehow, today it tasted even better, so Ren gratefully guzzled half of it as he got ready for his biology lab and selfishly poured the rest in his travel mug. Then, feeling guilty, he cleaned everything and started a fresh pot for Alek and Justin when they woke up.

Ren began writing another note for Justin, which was full of words that had nothing to do with what he really wanted to tell him. Instead, he wrote most of the same things as yesterday. And an apology for not being home much. Though Ren confirmed that Thursday would be the last busy day. He'd be home around eight. Unless Justin needed him. Ren really wished Justin still needed him. Not that he wanted him to still be sick, but there were other ways to be needed. Better ways.

He wasn't finished when Justin once again surprised him from the hallway. Ren never heard him; he just appeared in the early morning shadows of the apartment, standing at the junction where the living room split into hallways. Justin leaned there in Ren's pajama bottoms and hoodie, his hands hidden in the front pocket, the light from the kitchen illuminating only parts of his face, putting an interesting sheen over his black hair. Ren felt an urgent tug deep in his stomach, both from the start of seeing Justin somewhere he hadn't expected him to be and from how much better he looked.

"We're going to have to get you a bell or something," Ren said, forcing himself not to stare, trying to hide all the emotions Justin stirred up in him. "Are you feeling ok?"

"Ren," Justin began, a crease appearing between his eyes, his tone full of wearied patience. He shook his head, as though changing his mind about whatever he'd been about to say. "I'm fine." There came another pause as Justin studied the coffee table. "Not so sure about you, though," he murmured to the floor.

"Me?" Ren tried to scoff but discovered his voice was sticking on something in his throat. He cleared it, trying again. "I'm good. Running a little late, but —" he trailed off, unable to continue because Justin was staring hard at him again. "What?" he asked.

"What are you late for now?" Justin asked him combatively.

"Biology lab," Ren disclosed, trying not to falter under Justin's glare. "It lasts all morning. Then early child development and chemistry. I'll be home for a couple hours after that, but then I have the last shift at the donation center." He heard his tone drop as the list went on, noticing there was new pain in Justin's face, deepening as he talked. Was he sure he was ok?

"Are you always this busy?" Justin repeated the question he'd texted Ren two days ago.

"This week is kind of special," Ren started, but then realized his answer was going to be misunderstood when Justin stiffened.

"Because of ..." Justin ventured, the question sharp.

"No," Ren assured quickly, wanting Justin to understand that Ren's intense schedule had nothing to do with Monday. "Alek's birthday is on Saturday, so I changed my ambulance run. That's all I meant. But my Thursdays are always long."

Justin mumbled something else, this time too low for Ren to hear, looking with hostile shame at the floor again. Ren took a small step nearer, close enough to feel Justin's heat.

"What'd you say?" Ren asked, noticing Justin had shifted away as he'd stepped closer. "I didn't hear you."

"Just that I get it now," Justin answered tersely, pulling his shoulders back. "Why you'd get so pissed when I couldn't meet up for that assignment."

"I'm sorry about that," Ren apologized immediately, hating how he'd behaved. "I had no idea what you were going through. I was being —"

"Would you shut up," Justin snapped, and Ren obeyed, closing his mouth so quickly his teeth clicked. Justin sighed, leaning moodily against the wall. "I'm the one trying to apologize," he finished, soft again.

Now they both stood quietly. The space between them filled with unasked questions, unspoken and confusing sentiments, undeserved desires on Ren's part. He felt he had to break the silence, needed to put his coat on and leave.

"Tell you what," Ren offered, voice as level as possible, easing the situation. Humor, as always, acting as his best defense. "Tell me how you've been making this amazing coffee, and we'll call it even, deal?"

"Oh," Justin didn't sound sure, though the corners of his mouth twitched slightly, as though he were fighting a smile. The tiny change in expression snapped something loose in Ren, though not in a helpful way. "I just ... make it? Like everyone?" The systems part of Ren that was ready for a recipe, or at least a measurement, slumped at this explanation. Apparently, the method for preparing Ren's new elixir of life was going to remain one of the many mysteries that made Justin who he was.

"In that case," Ren said flippantly. "I'll just have to keep you here forever."

"Ren." Justin's eyes met his, full of question and tolerance, a glimmer of a future Justin knew but wasn't telling. Ren felt his mouth fall open, realizing what he'd just said. Out loud. No wonder Justin was looking shocked.

"I've ... got to go," Ren changed the subject, dragging himself away from Justin, from his heat, his eyes. "Text me if you need me."

"Ren?" Justin called him as he busied himself with separating his coat from Justin's on the camp chair, pulling it on, hiding his embarrassment at what he'd said, at what he wanted Justin to say back.

"Justin?" Ren returned, forcing himself to stand still, to hear what Justin wanted no matter what it was. He stood where Ren had left him, his fists against his chest, like his pulse was racing. "Is your heart all right?" Ren checked him, monitoring the posture. Justin's face hardened, tensed into something that looked like annoyance.

"Would you just —" Justin broke off, deliberately lowering his hands. "Do you ever stop? You can quit worrying about me, all right? You're the one who looks like shit."

For some reason, likely the lack of sleep, Justin's words stung. Ren wasn't ready to stop worrying about Justin. Wasn't ready for that to be over, even though he knew it was messing with him. Ren knew he looked as bad as Justin said. The healing bruise on his face had merged disturbingly with the bags under his eyes. He knew he was wearing his weariness like a too-heavy bag, but if he stopped, he'd fall so far behind he would have no hope of catching up. He could already feel it, the shadow of a wave bearing down on him. He also knew Justin might just be sticking around because he was waiting to tell Ren goodbye, and he just wasn't *ready*.

"It's my thing," Ren quipped, trying to deflect, ignoring the comment on his appearance. "Ask anyone." If Ren didn't leave, he was going to be late. Still, he hesitated at the door, pleading silently with Justin. *I'll stay if you want me. If you ask me to stop everything, I'll make it happen.* But somehow, he needed Justin to be the one to ask. He needed Justin to give him permission to break from his routine, to want something he knew he shouldn't. He needed Justin to want it first.

"I'll see you tonight?" Ren said, more question than farewell.

"I guess," Justin answered. Ren nodded, as if that answer had been in any way satisfying. He put on his backpack and picked up the warm travel mug.

"Thanks for this," Ren said in parting, holding up the tumbler. "It really is the best coffee ever." Justin just shrugged him off, looking as though he were headed back to Ren's bedroom as Ren shut the door. Ren would watch Justin turn away from him in memory for the rest of the day. And he would hate that it would be all he could remember.

His concentration was so damaged by Justin wearing his hoodie and his own growing exhaustion that he spent most of his time forcing himself awake or reorganizing his focus. He mangled the pig fetus he was supposed to be dissecting to the point where the lab TA declared it a lost cause and took it away from him, joking harshly that it was a good thing the poor animal was already dead.

"This isn't like you," the TA declared, scrutinizing Ren.

"I'm sorry," Ren apologized, a theme that began at lab and would continue for the remainder of the day. "It was a rough weekend."

"It's Thursday," the TA said dryly, sighing and shaking her head, as though the weekend were so far in the past it was no longer a valid excuse. "Now come to my station and identify the main arteries of the heart so I don't have to give you a zero on this."

And so it went all day. He dozed off during child development. He gave an answer in chemistry that was so wrong his professor kept calling on him, torturously, as if trying to give him a chance to redeem himself. And then there was the other question that persisted, no matter what classroom he found himself in, no matter who he was with.

"Are you all right?" Chelsea Wheaton asked him as she poked him awake in child development.

"Ren, you good?" Simon Daines, who sat next to him in chemistry, after he'd physically reached over to open Ren's book to the correct page for him since Ren had spaced out and missed the instruction.

"Wow, Ren, you getting better or worse?" The last was Brett as he held the door open for him upon his arrival at the donation center. By this point, Ren was sick to death of being asked this, so he growled in response. Not only was he tired of making the point that he was fine, but he was also nursing his own disappointment that the apartment had once again been empty when he'd gone home after chemistry. He'd known it would be empty; he'd received texts from Alek and Justin telling him where they'd be. Alek and Denny were picking up their results from taking some amateur ham radio licensing test, and Justin was once again with North and Kelly, going over financial recommendations.

Ren switched out his books in solitary silence. Looked at how Justin had made his bed. He tried to do some of his homework but ended up falling asleep at his desk and waking up excruciatingly groggy with just enough time to run across campus in order to not be late for work. And no one knew he had been home at all.

"Seriously, are you still sick?" Brett pressed him without any kind of social grace.

"No," Ren denied, donning his lab coat over his scrubs, moving to the sink so he could wash his hands, wishing he'd never told that lie, never knowing how it would come back to irritate him. But Brett stopped him, one of his huge hands blocking Ren at the shoulder.

"Well, you still look it," Brett told him, and Ren bit back several responses. He wanted to tell Brett he could still outwork him. He wanted to snarl that at least he knew how to shave. But he swallowed all those words because Brett was looking at him with friendly concern, without any sort of rivalry or malice. *Brett's not a bad guy,* Ren told himself, and then felt even more guilty about his angry thoughts when Brett offered him one of those tiny five-hour energy shots from his backpack.

"I better not," Ren declined. "I don't know what those would do to me, and now's probably not the time to find out. But thanks."

"Ok," Brett accepted Ren's decision, but let him know it was available in case Ren changed his mind. Ren pushed against the venipuncture Brett had performed on him, pressing hard against the bruise there to wake himself up for what felt like the hundredth time today. He just had this one last thing to do. Just three more hours until he could go home. And by that time everyone else would be home too. Justin would be home.

But then what was he going to do? Sleep on the floor again? That wasn't working so well. He'd have to figure something else out; he couldn't keep going like this. It was hurting his schoolwork; it was making people ask him annoying questions. And honestly, Ren knew he wasn't sick, but he didn't feel great either. He felt heavy and slow and inexplicably angry. The TA from this morning was right; this wasn't like him at all. But the alternative to getting his bed back was for Justin to leave, which somehow seemed worse.

Ren decided it was better not to think about it.

He went through the motions, deliberately not thinking about anything other than what was right in front of him. It was easy to do, most everything in his periphery was hazy. So, he carefully cannulated donors without making eye contact, without saying anything other than what was legally required at the beginning and ending of donations. He tightened his procedures so he could stay on autopilot, and it felt surprisingly good. Despite everything, this was the most mental rest Ren had gotten in almost a week.

Ren pulled the next chart from the wall without looking at it, enjoying a comfortable numbness in his chest, flipping the folder open as he walked toward the waiting area, scanning the top for the name. But as his eyes focused on the words, he found himself stopping dead in the doorway, all the numbness sharpening like the spike of an icicle. He almost dropped the file.

Celeste Lyons.

But that wasn't right. She wasn't supposed to be here. Not today. He wasn't ready for her today. Not knowing how he dared, Ren lifted his head from the file and there she was, on a Thursday, sitting regally in one of the plastic chairs, her coat and bag on the floor at her feet. Her long white-blonde hair covered her shoulders in soft waves, almost obscuring the Nordic patterning on the yoke of her navy-blue sweater. He fought off a shudder. He'd almost forgotten how beautiful she was.

As he stared, her folder open in his hands, she turned towards him as though she'd felt the weight of his gaze on her. Their eyes met, and then Ren watched, wounded, as her face contorted into shock and dread, into embarrassment. She looked away, her hand nervously clawing her hair behind her ear, fussing with her stuff as though she were seriously considering just picking it all up and running for the door. And that's when Ren knew. Before this second, he could have thought up a dozen different reasons why she'd needed to break her tradition of coming on Wednesday, but upon watching her reaction to seeing him, Ren dismissed them all. The truth was obvious on her face, in the sudden tenseness of her body.

She hadn't come yesterday because she'd been trying to avoid him.

Ren heard footsteps behind him, a heavy, long stride, and he calmly closed Celeste's folder, watching as she peeked painfully from under her extraordinary lashes to see what he would do. She looked like she wanted to leave, like she'd rather be anywhere but here with him. For some reason, it made Ren think of Justin and how he'd leaned away from him this morning, how he'd flinched from under his hand the day before that. The icicle in his chest wedged deeper, colder, the stab of rejection. It hurt so much that Ren forced himself furious in defense. It was going to be like that, was it?

"Hey Brett?" Ren addressed the Texan as he also came into the waiting area, a different folder in his hands. Ren let his gaze shoot back and forth between Brett and Celeste as he deftly and unapologetically switched folders with the less experienced tech. "Trade me on this one."

"Uh," Brett floundered, taken off guard by Ren's behavior. Brett didn't know about Celeste; he'd never worked a Wednesday. He had no idea all the nuances happening here. But Celeste knew. She met Ren's eyes, realizing what he was doing. She didn't exactly soften, but she stopped fidgeting, a different expression rearranging her face, though Ren couldn't figure out what it was anymore. Was it relief? He tried to hold on to his anger.

"Why?" Brett asked, still trying to figure out Ren's angle, though now the concern had returned to his face.

"Just take care of her for me," Ren quipped, no longer able to look at her gorgeous inaccessibility.

"Ok," Brett agreed, though Ren hadn't given him a choice. Ren nodded, wounded, and then he called the name in Brett's folder, leaving Celeste in Brett's choppy, ungraceful hands.

By the time he'd seated his new patient, Ren regretted what he'd done. *That's not like you*, the TA repeated in his head, and he knew it. He wasn't petty like that. Was he? He wasn't really going to let Brett hook Celeste to the centrifuge? She was strong and not in the least bit squeamish, but since when had Ren wanted her to get hurt? No matter what she'd done to him or thought of him. And yeah, it was obvious she hadn't wanted Ren to be the tech assigned to her, but that was because she had zero experience with anyone else.

But she'd learn quickly. In just a few minutes, Celeste was going to understand that not every lab technician at the donation center was as gentle or careful as Ren. That was something Ren could live with. The part that chilled him was how Celeste would realize that Ren had *given* her to Brett. He'd hurt her on purpose. And somehow, he didn't think she would see it any other way. She'd forget she was here on Thursday to avoid him, that she had almost left rather than donate if it meant he would be her tech. All she would remember was Ren had her folder in his hands and then given it to someone else who was probably going to stab her.

Ren swore suddenly under his breath, causing the donor in the chair to startle, as though Ren had screwed something up on him.

"I'll be right back," Ren told him wearily, holding up a hand. The donor looked confused, but he didn't have time to say anything as Ren pivoted away from him, hurrying across the floor to where Brett was violently ripping off pieces of tape and sticking the ends to the top of the centrifuge. Good. He hadn't got to the needle part yet.

"Brett," Ren joined them quietly, holding back, knowing this was going to look psychotic, but he just couldn't let this happen. Celeste physically shrank into the chair at his approach, but since Brett had already secured her blood pressure cuff, she couldn't go anywhere.

Brett turned, abruptly as usual, and now Ren had both his hands up, thinking of how he was going to do this without hurting anyone's feelings.

"Ren?" Brett prompted him when he didn't say anything, studying him up and down. "You ok? Change your mind about that shot?"

*Brett, you big, dumb hero. That's perfect.* "Yeah, I did," Ren lied. "I'll finish up here if you wouldn't mind grabbing it for me?"

"Sure thing," Brett said, looking pleased to be of service. Ren managed a partial smile for him, sorry he was sending him away because he didn't trust him. "Be right back."

And that's how Ren found himself alone with Celeste, faster than he wanted to be. He still didn't know what he wanted to say. He was still hurt, still angry. It didn't help that she looked horrified and trapped, eyes following Brett desperately, as though she wanted to call him back. Ren pulled a donor kit from the drawer on the centrifuge cart, thinking he'd just get this over with.

"Ren," Celeste fumbled, starting to force some kind of conversation to banish the awkwardness. Hearing her talk made something inside his chest twitch. Her accent. The lilt in his name.

"You don't have to say anything," he told her, surprisingly terse, but if he didn't keep things tightly reined in, it was likely to get messy in a hurry. He was just here to hook her up safely. "I'll be done in a minute."

She stopped, her lips coming together in a straight line. Ren focused his attention on her arm, though he did notice her turning her head away from him. There was a tenseness in her; Ren could feel it in her muscles.

"Relax, Celeste," he commanded. "I'm not going to hurt you." *I came all the way over here specifically so I wouldn't be responsible for hurting you.* "Trust me; I'm doing you a favor."

"A favor?" she repeated, with some of her typical strength. It sounded like a challenge.

"Yes," he snapped. "Not that you deserve it."

He watched her eyes go huge before he let his gaze slide off to the floor. *Don't be so bitter*, he lectured himself. *It's not her fault you're a mess.*

"What makes you think," she started again, but he really meant the part where she didn't have to say anything. He wasn't going to defend himself anymore. Especially since this was just like last time where Celeste was making assumptions about what Ren was doing without having all the information.

"Don't," he said, unwilling to hear her out. "Keep still. You'll feel a sting here." She clamped her mouth shut as he inserted his needle in one smooth motion, quick and painless as usual. Then he left without looking at her again, disliking how his conscience didn't seem all that clear.

Brett caught him on his way, handing him the five-hour energy bottle. Ren thanked him, taking it. He still had no intention of drinking it. He sensed Brett staring at him as he walked away, but he offered no explanation about what he'd just done. In fact, he thought it would be easiest to go back on autopilot. He had less than an hour before he could go home.

He and Brett walked past each other across the floor, engaged in their various tasks. Each time Ren felt he had to give him something. So, he would nod to him, tell him he was doing a good job, but please keep it slow. No need to rush. In return, Brett blossomed under the praise, took it upon himself to do the low-ranking restocking and cleaning jobs no one liked, and he continued his vigilance on Ren, popping up at his elbow occasionally when Ren had truly zoned out to make sure he was doing ok.

Ren wasn't sure. Something hurt inside him, but he couldn't tell if it was a physical or emotional wound. Though he suspected it had something to do with Celeste and Justin, how both were distancing themselves. It made him feel unwanted and misunderstood, and he hated it.

"So, Ren, is that your girlfriend?" Brett asked him when they found themselves at the sink together, washing their hands again. Ren shook his head, more to clear it than to answer.

"No," he said, voice more bitter than he'd wanted it to sound. "She's not interested."

"You sure? She's been watching you. She looks worried."

"Brett," Ren began, but he had no hope of explaining the situation. There was too much. And despite how cool Brett had been this shift, Ren didn't feel like being that open with him. He was relieved to hear an alarm go off, a clotted line. He grabbed a paper towel, grateful to leave this conversation, but Brett once again stopped him with a hand on his shoulder.

"I'll take care of that," Brett offered. "Go talk to her."

"She doesn't want to talk to me," Ren dismissed.

"I think you've got it backwards," Brett contradicted, giving him a small shove in Celeste's direction. "Go on and straighten it out. Whatever it is. Because if you slump anymore, you'll be dragging your knuckles on the ground."

Without giving Ren another chance for protest, Brett headed off to the station where the alarm was going off. Ren watched him sidle up to the cot and start pushing the buttons to get things quiet first before he started in on the problem. Ren recognized the donor, Makayla Walker, a good-natured girl who made hesitant attempts to shyly practice her Spanish with Ren sometimes. Her face looked up at Brett questioningly. She'd never had a second's trouble with a donation before and obviously didn't understand what had happened. Ren hoped Brett would explain that clots just happened sometimes, and it wasn't a big deal.

Brett caught him still standing there watching, so he jerked his head over to Celeste, lifting his eyebrows in a not-so-subtle command. Ren looked across the walkway from Brett and locked eyes with Celeste, who apparently had been watching him just like Brett said. As soon as she'd been caught, Celeste quickly turned away, embarrassed. There was no book on her lap today. What was that about?

Fine. Maybe this would be good. Maybe they could get everything straight, have one real and final conversation in this weird, quasi-friendship they'd kept going for months. Then maybe Ren could get some closure about her.

"Everything ok over here?" Ren began with the question he always asked her, those days when all he wanted was to have an excuse to come to her station to talk to her. Across the walkway, Brett smiled as he worked on Makayla, pleased that Ren was taking his advice.

"I don't know," Celeste admitted, her voice hesitant. Her answer made Ren check the machine, her blood pressure, her color, finding them all normal. The donation was going perfectly, just like always. Whatever she wasn't sure about, it had nothing to do with plasma.

"Then what's up?" Ren asked her honestly. He didn't know what he was doing standing here when he knew she didn't want to see him. But then why was she staring at him? Not reading?

"How is your friend?" Celeste asked, picking at an invisible piece of lint on her jeans.

"He's getting better," Ren answered, easier now that he was speaking about Justin. "But it was rough. I had to take him to the ER." He stopped short of saying "he almost died." That seemed too much to tell Celeste and not enough to do it justice.

Celeste licked her lips nervously, her mouth opening and closing as she searched for something to say. Ren didn't even know if she believed him but found it didn't matter anymore. He knew what happened, and he wouldn't change anything if he could do it over again.

Ren was still waiting for what Celeste would say next when a lightning strike of emergency hit the donation center. It happened so fast it took several seconds for Ren to even register what was going on. His first clue was Celeste. Her mouth dropped open, and she uttered a harsh "oh!" of shock. She lifted her hand, covering her face for an instant before she began pointing across the walkway, trying to get Ren to look. It wasn't until Ren started turning that he could hear the screaming.

Confused, Ren stared, taking in the scene at the station opposite Celeste, where Brett had been clearing Makayla's line. It had changed in a dramatic way that didn't make sense at all. Brett now stood helpless, his head jerking around, trying to see in all directions at once. The alarm from the centrifuge was shrieking in cadence with Makayla, who was staring at where the needle had once been secured in her arm. Where blood seemed to be gushing out, splashing on the floor, dripping from the plastic mattress. Shit.

Ren took one more second to lock eyes with Celeste, and they communicated better in that look than they had in all the previous months of Ren trying to talk to her.

"Out of the way," Ren directed Brett, who was too overwhelmed to be any help here. As Brett tried to take a step backward, Ren saw what happened. Somehow, Brett had gotten tangled in the tubing, and when he'd tried to walk away, probably too big and too fast, he'd ripped Makayla's needle out, at the wrong angle, tearing open her vein and the skin of her arm. *Damn it*, Ren growled in his head, but knew better than to say anything out loud. Makayla was screaming, terrified at the blood draining out of her arm. What's worse, she'd been on a return, so her filtered blood was also draining at an alarming rate from the centrifuge, spilling messily onto the floor from the unsecured line.

"Shut off the machine!" Ren shouted at Brett, who still stood helpless. But for Ren, this was the first time all day he'd felt absolutely, perfectly awake. He ducked down to pull an absorbent pad from the bottom of the cart. Instead of throwing it on the floor, he wrapped it tightly around Makayla's arm to stop her bleeding first.

"Lift your arm," Ren directed her, no longer shouting, but keeping an authoritative clip to his words, knowing Makayla's mind needed firm instruction as it was reeling right now. Her normally calm face was full of panic and losing color. She was almost hyperventilating, though her screams had turned to little moans of terror.

By this time, other techs were swarming toward them, as many as could be spared from the other donors.

"Get her feet up," Ren instructed someone standing at his elbow.

"Ren, I'm sorry," he heard Brett beginning to apologize.

"Not now," Ren growled at him. Someone put a hand on his knee, and he realized his other coworker, Ian, was crouched at his feet, trying to put more pads down to cover the blood on the floor to minimize the risk of slipping. Ren took a careful step to allow him to get at it before turning all his attention to Makayla.

"You're ok," he told her, hugging her blood drenched arm tight to his torso, keeping pressure on the tear, his fingers clamped down into the inside of her elbow, making sure she wasn't using any of her own strength to keep her arm lifted.

"Look at me, Makayla," he encouraged her, keeping calm for both of them. "It's not bad." Ian was back with warm, wet towels, and Ren once again shifted out of his way so he could lay one across Makayla's forehead and around her throat. Ren paid attention to the wound under his fingers. He could no longer feel it throbbing, couldn't tell if more warm blood was pumping out of it in synch with Makayla's heartbeat. He wondered how much she'd lost. The centrifuge pulled out a pint at a time, but she'd been on a return. She might need to go to the other side of the hospital and receive a transfusion. Or maybe there was less than a pint in the machine and on the floor, though it looked like gallons.

Ren started asking Makayla questions, easy ones. "What day is it? What's your name and birthday?" He started easing her into talking more. "What did you do last weekend? What's your favorite class? You're doing so great; keep looking at me."

Superstar Ian brought the center's first-aid kit and settled it on the cot near Makayla's hip, then silently stood ready for whatever Ren might need. Ren didn't know where Brett went.

As Makayla's breathing eased and her arm relaxed against Ren's chest, he changed topics to ask her harder questions, monitoring her for shock with each one. "Does anything hurt? Are you feeling faint or nauseated?"

After a very long time, Ren felt safe to start the second part of treatment. He made sure Makayla's feet were still elevated on a pillow. He had Ian bring him more warm towels to replace the ones cooling on her. This time he instructed Ian to put one over her eyes, forcing her to keep them closed. Then he began cleaning her up.

First, he cut the excess off the pad, cut it into a neat square that covered the wound, having Ian help him by keeping pressure on it. It might be overkill, but he wasn't taking any chances on the bleeding starting up again. Somewhere he asked if Steve had been notified. Steve was a nine to five kind of guy, but this sort of thing required him to come in after hours. Ian said he was on his way.

Ren sat with Makayla as she came back from shock. He kept her injured arm, holding her wrist and supporting her elbow, keeping her off his scrubs, which were now soaked. Steve came in and started asking more questions, which Ren and Makayla answered back and forth. Steve called the ER to have them send some of their techs and a gurney over, but by the time they arrived, Makayla was calmly sitting up and drinking a Capri Sun. She thanked Ren several times, signed some forms for Steve, and then she was wheeled away.

That's when Ren noticed Celeste was still sitting in the chair opposite the scene, watching him intently. Her machine was quiet, her bottle of plasma filled and finished. Ren brought it to Ian's attention that Celeste could be taken off, but Ian just shrugged.

"I tried a long time ago," he confessed. "She said she wanted you to do it and didn't care how long it took."

Ren checked with Steve, who nodded, preoccupied with the mess he was going to have to deal with. Ren still didn't know where Brett was hiding. Maybe Steve had already fired him. Ian handed Ren a plastic cover, a huge tarp-like gown that went over his head, down to his wrists, and far past his hips. Another precaution since his scrubs were now contaminated by biohazard fluid. Ren removed his bloody gloves, replacing them with fresh ones after washing his hands again. Then he put on the cover before going to see Celeste. She stared at him, a new expression on her face.

"Sorry about that," Ren apologized for something he hadn't done. "You ok?" Because sometimes watching traumatic incidents like that put people into shock too. But surely Ian would have checked her for that already. Why had she waited for him?

"That was horrible," she said, her voice far away, as if she could still see it. Ren wondered what it had looked like from her perspective, trapped to her donor chair by her own needle and blood pressure cuff. She could have closed her eyes, but somehow Ren didn't think she had.

"Yeah," Ren agreed. "It shouldn't have happened. I don't know how many times I've told him to slow down."

This made Celeste's eyes widen as something seemed to click with her. She looked at Ren with a deepening understanding of the evening. Ren busied himself with disconnecting her, more pressure, more arm lifting. No lost blood here.

"That could have been me," Ren heard Celeste whisper. *No*, he wanted to assure her. *I didn't let him. I couldn't.* But he had thought about it. Because he'd been hurt first and wanted to give it back to her, however passively. He'd been so angry at her. He was so ashamed of that now.

"That's why you —" Celeste continued, staring at him in fear and something else Ren didn't have the energy to identify. He didn't think he could screw up anymore when it came to his relationship with her.

"Come on," Ren interrupted, throwing her tubes into another biohazard receptacle. "You're done." He picked up her plasma bottle, walking her over to the cashier like this was just another day. Because for him, this was just another day. He had to be prepared for things like this all the time. And he also had to be prepared for it to take him away from conversations, from people he loved. He had to prepare himself for the lifestyle he'd chosen to keep him alone, because how could he expect anyone else to just sit by the sidelines and wait for him to finish? To watch him cradle another girl's arm against his chest and just wait? Wait for him to come home, not even knowing when that would be? It wasn't fair to even ask. Not fair for Celeste even though she had sat and waited for him tonight. Definitely not fair to Justin who was still trapped and waiting in Ren's apartment, thinking he'd be home by eight. Ren couldn't ask anyone to wait for him anymore.

"Ren?" Celeste asked as they stopped in front of the cashier. Ren placed her bottle on the counter to be added to the others.

"Thanks for donating," Ren told her, ending the conversation, just wanting it to be over. "And for future reference, if you don't want to see me, come in on Monday or Friday nights. That's when I'm off."

Celeste blinked in surprise and embarrassment. She looked like she wanted to say something, but Ren had no desire to continue. He was more than done. The weariness was returning now that the drama was over. Ren could feel himself starting to crash from the adrenaline rush. It was going to be evident very soon how much it had taken out of him. Not that he'd had a whole lot to start with. He looked at the clock, realizing his shift had been over for twenty minutes, the center was in closing mode, but he knew he couldn't go home yet. He had to clean every nook and cranny of Makayla's centrifuge. Mop and disinfect the floor, the mattress, every bolt and joint of the cot. Steve would want him and Brett to debrief in his office. It would take hours. He felt Celeste's eyes on him as he turned away from her, but there was no longer anything to say. Ren felt his emotions shut down, autopilot returning as he went down on his knees to start gathering the pads Ian had set on the floor. He didn't see Celeste leave.

Honestly, he didn't see much of anything. Just red splatters in front of his eyes that he methodically wiped clean with bleach. People walked behind him for a while, the last of the donors finishing up and leaving the center for the night. The techs cleaned the other stations and then they too were gone. Steve brought Ren and Brett into his office as expected and asked them questions about the incident, filling out form after never-ending form. Ren could barely keep his eyes open at this point, even though he knew it was important.

"Ren," Steve said, for what could have been a second or third time according to the tone he used when he said it. Ren shook his head clear, trying to focus. "Get your stuff."

"Ok," Ren said automatically. Whenever he closed his eyes, he could still see the blood he'd cleaned, the splashes on the floor, the mattress, the centrifuge. He hoped Makayla was ok.

Ren got his coat and bag and stood waiting while Steve said some last words to Brett. Something about being put on probation. Which meant he wasn't fired. For some reason, even after everything, Ren was glad. Brett wasn't a bad guy. He could use another chance.

Steve had to pull on Ren to get him moving, and Ren thought he was still asking questions, but it was like it took too much effort to translate English anymore, so Ren didn't bother answering. He closed his eyes and saw Celeste turn a page. The blood splattered on the white floor. He blinked and realized Steve was shaking his shoulder. He was sitting in Steve's front seat, and Stony Island was just outside. He didn't remember telling Steve where he lived. Didn't remember getting into the car.

"Get some rest, Ren," Steve instructed, watching him worriedly. "You did a great job today. I'm really glad you were there, but if you need some time, take it." There was a pause where Ren thought he should probably be doing something but couldn't pin it down. "Ren, I can't tell if you're like this because of what happened tonight or if something else is wrong. You've been off all week, so if you need something, you can talk to me, all right?" Another pause where Ren realized he wasn't moving yet; he was just sitting here staring at nothing, not responding. He heard Steve sigh. "You need help getting inside?"

It was so weird to be on the receiving end of these questions. Especially when Ren knew there wasn't anything wrong with him.

But he couldn't make the effort to tell Steve that. He just shook his head. He thought he mumbled a thank you, but he wasn't sure. He thought Steve told him one more time that if he needed another day off to just email him. Then Ren blinked again, and he was standing in front of his apartment door. *Thank you, autopilot.*

He stood there looking at the doorknob, not bothering to reach for it because he was concentrating too hard on the voices he could hear on the inside. He could distinguish Alek easily, the comforting rumble. Also Denny. Then a raised voice, one he didn't know so well. At least, not when it was strong like this. Justin?

"I thought he got off at eight. It's almost eleven; where is he?"

"Justin, calm down. He's late sometimes." That was Alek.

"I'm going to go look for him."

The apartment door tore open before Ren had caught up. He felt an electric jolt go through him at the sudden change in the door's position, at the light pouring into the hallway, at Justin standing there with his coat half on. Ren blinked.

"Oh my God," Justin exclaimed, startled to find Ren just standing there outside the door. He shed his coat in a smooth motion, dropping it onto the camp chair and then immediately reaching for Ren. "How long have you been ... What the hell happened?"

What did happen? Ren tried to focus, tried to keep his balance as Justin dragged him through the door. He registered movement, lots of movement, too much movement all around him. Alek and Denny on the periphery and Justin's hands on his coat sleeves. Everything was going extremely fast. Ren tried opening his mouth to answer because he thought he remembered being asked a question, but only a strangled half-laugh came out and then didn't stop because everything was so bright in here and moving and how was he supposed to answer a question when he couldn't remember what it was?

"What are you — are you laughing or crying?" Justin asked. Ren felt his knees quaking and decided to just drop onto the floor. That would make it easier to take his shoes off anyway. "Are you drunk?"

Justin demanded, and that made Ren laugh harder, doubling over on the floor so forcefully Justin had to let him go.

"Ren doesn't drink," Denny pointed out. "He gets like this when he's exhausted."

"You damn idiot," Justin snarled at him, which helped Ren stop with the crazed giggling, made him realize it was Justin's hands, not his, undoing his shoelaces for him. Justin pulled off his shoes and started on his coat, tugging his backpack off his shoulders.

"Stop," Ren told him, ineffectively brushing at his hands. "Calm down." Wow, his words did sound slurred. No wonder Justin thought he'd been drinking. But still, he needed to get it together. Justin sounded upset, and Ren remembered that wasn't a good thing. "Your heart —"

"To hell with my heart; you're covered in *blood!*" Justin's tone picked up speed and ferocity as he succeeded in undoing Ren's coat, revealing the plastic gown cover and the stains splashed all over him.

"What?" Alek's suddenly high-pitched voice from somewhere behind Justin's shoulder. "Blood?"

Something urgent pricked at Ren, enough to get him back on his feet. Something about Alek. Something about Alek and blood.

"It's ok," Ren soothed, trying to focus on Alek, who was staring at him with his mouth open, completely freaked out. "Alek, chill. It's not mine." Justin somehow succeeded in relieving Ren of his coat, even as Ren started walking away from him, toward Alek.

"Ren, stop," Denny intercepted on Alek's behalf, pausing Ren for a second as he considered her. Didn't she know he was just trying to help? Alek's face was changing color as Ren came closer to him, and with the next step, he turned away from Ren completely, headed for the kitchen sink, making desperate little gagging sounds.

"Alek, it's ok," Ren entreated him again while Denny followed Alek, putting her hands on his back as he leaned over the sink.

"Ren, back off!" she shrieked, which did make him pause, suddenly hurt. What was going on? "You can't help right now; you are literally covered in the problem. Justin, get him out of here, will you? Get him cleaned up."

"Right," Justin said from somewhere behind Ren, his agreement turning tangible as he firmly grabbed on to Ren. "Come on."

Still confused, Ren allowed Justin to drag him away, then began walking himself to the bathroom. Justin might be talking to him, but all he noticed was the heat from Justin's hand on his shoulder. It reminded him he needed to tell Justin something. He had to explain that Justin didn't have to wait here for Ren anymore. He could go because it wasn't fair.

"What the hell is this thing?" Justin spoke to himself as he stripped the plastic cover from Ren. For some reason, that question got through to Ren, and he found himself rambling in response.

"It's a biohazard protection cover. Ian gave it to me, but I probably didn't need it. I'm sure her blood's clean; I think she's a Mormon or something."

Justin was staring at him with a strange expression on his face. Like he wasn't sure what to do with all the random information. He bundled the plastic, compressing it as small as it would go before ramming it into the trash can by the sink. Ren noted they'd have to take it outside before Alek came in.

"Take that off," Justin directed, gesturing at Ren's scrub top. Then he paused, leaning closer to Ren. "Shit, it's in your hair. Do you think you can handle a shower on your own?"

"Sure," Ren agreed, slowly looking over to the tub. A shower sounded wonderful, because now that Justin mentioned it, Ren felt cold all over.

"Ren!" Ren blinked, wondering why things kept skipping. Justin had moved very suddenly. He wasn't standing in front of Ren anymore; he was kneeling. He was on the floor because Ren was sitting down. Ren didn't remember sitting down. Justin had both of Ren's shoulders gripped tightly. He was staring at him. "What's wrong with you?"

"I'm cold," was the only thing Ren could think of to say, the only thing he could think about now that Justin had brought it up. "The shower will help." He moved toward it, completely numb, and started the water, hardly noticing Justin hovering at his side.

"Maybe don't stand up in there," Justin suggested worriedly. "I'll get you some clean clothes."

"Thanks," Ren said absently, focusing on the water. Something was nagging at him, telling him he was being too casual about what was going on, but he didn't know how to fix it. He just wanted to get out of his sticky, bloody scrubs and into the water. He wanted to be clean and warm. "My room is down the hall."

"God, Ren, I know. Are you ok?"

"Yeah," Ren assured. Justin hesitated at the door, but eventually pulled it shut. Ren stepped into the shower with his clothes on, the fabric immediately vacuuming to his skin. When the water running down the drain turned bloody, Ren's mind revived slightly. The events from the donation center came back to him, not in order at first, but by the time he'd peeled the scrubs off, he thought he had everything sorted. Poor Alek. Ren couldn't believe he'd tried to chase after him. He hoped Denny remembered what to do.

He began scrubbing. First his hair and then his face, rubbing everything hard, the last blood cleanup of the night. He had to wake up, stay awake for a little longer. He had to tell his friends what happened to him, so they'd know he wasn't losing his mind. Had he really just told Justin how to find his bedroom? That was funny. And really horrifying. He watched the blood running down the drain. So much blood.

Ren stopped the water, drying off. The roughness of the towel hurt his back. His whole left arm ached as he moved the towel over his body. He'd have to clean everything up before Alek came in. He pulled his soaking wet scrubs out of the bathtub, transferring them to the sink. He wrapped the towel around his waist and then stood with both hands clinging to the sides of the sink basin. Like Alek in the kitchen.

He held tighter to the sink as his hands started shaking. This was familiar, but bad, but not unexpected. His clothes were staining the sink. He needed to scrub them clean. How did he make his hands stop shaking? There was a trick. Portable, mindless. How did it go?

"Ren? I've got your clothes." Ren turned his head slowly toward the door because it was saying his name. No, a gorgeous, raven-haired boy coming through the door was saying his name. Justin. The wolf with the colorless eyes who slept in Ren's bed but didn't sleep with him, which was something Ren wanted but also didn't want to want. Justin looked so good, but so scared entering the room. He rushed at Ren, confusing him all over again. Why did he have to move so fast? "Shit, you *are* sick. I knew it! Come on; sit down. Damn it; this is my fault."

The only reason Ren didn't fall onto the toilet lid was because Justin eased him down onto it. Ren stared at him silently, amazed at how animated he was. He fussed over Ren, exclaiming over each discovery. Justin hadn't seen Ren with his shirt off for a few days.

"Fuck, Ren, your back. I thought you were taking care of it. And what happened to your arm?" Justin was on his knees again, and he had stretched Ren's arm into the light to inspect it better. Ren dragged his eyes over to it too. He hadn't seen what Brett had done to him yet but understood Justin's reaction when he saw the bruise wrapped around his forearm, almost to his wrist, an enormous aching internal hemorrhage. The damage was impressive.

"I'll get Alek. We'll get you out of here. Man, you're shaking so bad."

Ren's mind zeroed in on Justin getting Alek. Somehow that idea lit up the very last of his energy. Alek couldn't come in here; the scrubs were still in the sink. He grabbed on to Justin to stop him from leaving or calling out, forcing Justin's attention.

"I'm not sick," Ren told him, even as he tried to gather however many words it was going to take to explain. He closed his eyes, saw splashes of blood behind his lids.

"Pretty sure I said the same damn thing," Justin quipped, but he did return to Ren's side. "Where did you put that antibiotic the doctor gave you?"

Ren reached for his clothes — certain Justin would take him more seriously if he weren't wearing just a towel, but Justin wouldn't hand them over until after he'd applied more ointment to the infected wound on Ren's back.

Ren tried to explain as Justin worked over him, faltering badly on the details. He backed up several times, overlapping the events from tonight with stuff that happened on the ambulance run. He couldn't seem to put details together very well; he could tell he was all over the place, but he kept losing his train of thought. He told Justin about delayed panic response and Dr. Delacroix and knitting with pencils. Then he explained about Brett and how he did venipunctures as though he were plunging vaccines into livestock.

"And I almost let him," Ren half moaned in regret as Justin took both his hands, trying to still them. "I was so mad; I was going to let him touch her. I'm the only one who should ever touch her."

"Ren, you aren't making any sense," Justin told him gently. "Let's get you in bed, ok?"

"Justin? What are you guys still doing in here?" Denny asked as she came up behind him, taking stock of the situation. Ren jerked his hands away from Justin, tugging the sleeves of his shirt over his fingers and tucking them under his arms. Justin tilted his head at him.

"How's Alek?" Ren asked, watching Denny's face soften.

"He's fine. I got his head down and did everything the way you told me to. What the hell were you thinking, chasing him down like that?"

Justin blocked Denny from getting any closer to Ren, putting a hand up, protecting him. She looked at him questioningly.

"Leave him alone," Justin demanded. "I think he's sick."

"I'm not," Ren protested again. Couldn't they tell? Denny came closer, placing one cool hand on his face and her arm around his shoulders. He leaned into her automatically, feeling the room swoop under him as he rested his head against the softness of her hoodie.

"I don't think he has a fever," Denny said reassuringly to Justin. "We'll check after we get out of this hot room, but I say, he gets like this sometimes when he's been pushing too hard. He just needs some sleep." She bent down to catch Ren's eyes, focusing him. "Real sleep."

Denny continued talking as she straightened, motioning for Justin to help Ren stand. "I answered your phone for you, Ren," she said, though Ren didn't know if he was picking up all the words. Sometimes it seemed a few got lost in the middle as Justin slipped an arm around Ren's waist. He was so warm. "Your supervisor called to make sure you're all right and said there are resources available if you need ... oh, never mind, you can't even hear me, can you? I'll have to tell you later." *No, I got it*, Ren thought but didn't say. He was paying too much attention to walking.

"Did he tell you what happened?" Justin asked as they made their way down the hall.

"No, he can't tell me anything like that; it's illegal."

"He tore the needle right out of her arm," Ren volunteered, the strength of the memory vocalizing almost on its own. "There was ... there was blood everywhere. I told him. I'm always telling him —"

"Stop, Ren," Justin commanded gently, tightening his hold as Ren's knees shook. "You don't have to say anything."

"I shouldn't have let him touch her," Ren continued anyway as Justin eased him onto his own bed for the first time in a week. His pillow smelled like Justin. "But she wasn't supposed to be there. Not today. No one should touch her but me."

"Wait, Ren, what are you saying?" Denny was close to his face. Justin was pulling his quilt over him. It felt so good. "She came today? What do you mean tore a needle out of her? Is she hurt?"

"Don't," Justin ordered. "Don't make him talk right now."

Blood all over the floor, the mattress, his sheets. Ren whimpered, and Justin shushed him.

"It's ok, Ren."

"There's blood everywhere," Ren moaned. "Alek can't come in."

"I'll take care of it," Justin promised. "Denny, do you know where he keeps that thermometer? He's just ... he must have caught whatever I had."

"He has like three in his med bag; hang on."

"Justin?" Ren called, and heat was suddenly all over him. He could feel it near his abdomen, his shoulder, circling his wrist. "I can't take your bed."

"It's *your* bed."

"Your heart —"

"My heart's fine," Justin reassured. "I'm worried about *you*."

"Found one!" Denny crowed triumphantly. "Ok, let's just make sure." Something cold and metallic swept across Ren's forehead. Denny taking his temperature. "Yeah, he's normal, no fever. See? He's all right. Just tired. Come on, let him rest. You're not going to get anything rational out of him before tomorrow."

Lights dimmed, a quiet darkness settling into the room. Ren's muscles melted into the bed, the ache in them not leaving but changing in a way that was a relief. The warmth didn't move, neither did the pressure Ren felt on the covers, the place near his hip. The circle around his wrist.

"Justin? Come on; we'll figure out somewhere for you to sleep too."

"Don't worry about it. I'm going to stay here for a while and watch him. Oh, but Denny? He left his scrubs in the sink so be careful. I'll get the blood out of them soon."

"Thanks, Justin."

Ren tried talking to them. Tried to say he'd take care of his own scrubs; no one had to clean up the mess for him. Tried telling them he was fine.

"Shhh." Justin's voice in the dark. "Stop talking, Ren; I can't understand anything you're trying to say. Why can't you just relax?"

Because he was in the wrong bed. And Justin was so much

stronger now. And if Ren fell asleep, he might wake up in a world that didn't have Justin in it anymore, and he wasn't ready. He wanted to hold on to this a little longer. Even though it wasn't fair. But none of those words made it past his lips. He could only think of one thing.

"Don't disappear." He wasn't sure if he said it out loud until Justin answered him.

"I won't if you won't."

# 3
# DEGREES OF SEPARATION

The Friday Ren woke to was almost completely unchanged from the Friday before. At first, all Ren could do was cuddle under his quilt, staring at the sunlight peeking in from between the blinds, making connections. He'd forgotten what it felt like to be comfortable and rested. Flipping over, Ren hugged his pillow, shoving his face deep into it and inhaling Justin. His pillow still smelled like Justin. Which reminded him.

Where was Justin? Where had he slept? Because all the options in the apartment that weren't Ren's bed were awful. Ren knew. He'd tried them all. And even though waking up alone in his room was normal, it filled Ren with dread. He wasn't supposed to be waking up alone here. He *knew* if he fell asleep that Justin would leave. Ren threw off the quilt, searching his room for Justin's duffel bag, disappointed to find it gone. He thought he remembered Justin promising not to disappear. This certainly looked like disappearing, though apparently not without a trace.

Getting up and dressed in new scrubs brought to Ren's attention all the other differences in the room besides Justin's missing bag. Ren's backpack was sitting on the desk. His scrubs from last night were draped over his chair, dry and spotless. Ren could also smell coffee brewing; Justin must have put that together last night too.

Ren paused, returning to sit on the edge of his bed, elbows on his knees and his face in his hands, coming to terms with last night. There wasn't much to work with, only a few images and sensations. Blood down the drain. Disjointed voices. Heat. Ren groaned in embarrassment. He'd been so out of it. No wonder Justin left.

As Ren made his way through the apartment, he didn't find Justin, but he had certainly left his mark on the place. The scrubs on Ren's chair were just the beginning of what Justin had done while Ren slept.

Ren's coat and shoes had been picked up and set out neatly on the camp chair and entrance rug. Justin's medication was gone from the kitchen counter. The antibiotic ointment balanced on top of the coffeemaker — an obvious indication that Justin meant for Ren to take care of his back before drinking any. But for that, Ren would need help; he just couldn't reach, so he poured a cup of coffee and took it to the table, blank and confused.

He was still sitting there when Alek joined him.

"Hey, Ren, you're up. How'd you sleep?" Ren's roommate also helped himself to Justin's coffee, pulling up the other chair and looking over Ren with friendly interest, his open face free of judgment, just sincere one-hundred-percent Alek.

"Alek, I am so sorry," Ren apologized, remembering coming home last night drenched in Alek's kryptonite. "I was trying to help you yesterday if you can believe it."

"No sweat. At least you're back to speaking in complete sentences," Alek dismissed, absently picking up the antibiotic. "Justin says I'm supposed to help you with this. And you could have asked me earlier, you know."

"How?" Ren asked, trying to figure out how Alek could even look at the wound without getting woozy. "Apparently, I'm a mess."

"I'll be quick," Alek said casually. Like it was no problem. "Let me see."

Ren groaned, mostly for show, and slipped his scrub top up around his shoulders, leaning forward over the table to give Alek easy access. Alek whistled through his teeth, then it seemed he held his breath, proving good on his word as he hurriedly began applying antibiotic while Ren did his best not to squirm under his hands. The ointment was unexpectedly freezing, and Alek's fingers felt different from Justin's. Though Ren knew his roommate was being gentle, it didn't feel that way. He suspected Alek wasn't looking at what he was doing. As Alek worked, Ren tried to distract them both, finding a good opportunity when he saw the radio on the table. It looked different than before, upgraded.

"Is this almost finished?" Ren asked, refocusing Alek's mental awareness to something that wasn't his scraped up, infected back. "It looks like you did more stuff to it."

"I think it's done," Alek mused, his voice still strong. Maybe this chat was working. Or maybe he had his eyes closed, who knew? "Guess we'll find out tomorrow. We worked on it yesterday while we were waiting for you. Justin put the new dial in."

Ren immediately turned the radio so he could see the dial. It wasn't elegant by any means, but it did look complicated. Huh. Getting blood stains out of clothes, making coffee, engineering dialing mechanisms on amateur radios. Justin was a man of many talents.

"I didn't know Justin could do that," Ren commented, staring at his handiwork without fully comprehending how it was done.

"Oh yeah. It's completely different now that he can sit up for more than five minutes at a time," Alek answered. "He's a cool guy. Kind of broody, but cool."

"Too bad he left," Ren huffed, unable to hide his disappointment.

"Dude, it's not like he's gone forever," Alek countered, tugging down Ren's shirt. "It'll probably be like with Denny, you know, in and out. I invited him and North over for dinner tonight and tomorrow, and you'll see him at class, right?" Ren jerked upright.

"Class! What time is it?" He snatched his phone to check.

"Hold up! Justin said I'm not supposed to let you leave."

Ren somehow found this more frustrating than endearing. "Oh yeah? He asked you to babysit me? What else did Justin say? And where is he? What happened after I fell asleep?"

"Come on, don't be mad," Alek soothed, still cool and relaxed at the table. "You know you've been killing yourself ever since Justin got here. I tried to get him to stay, but he said he didn't want to be in our way, and we were kind of out of beds. I think it bothered him to see what he was doing to you."

"What?" Ren interrupted. "He's not responsible for that." That was the weeknight ambulance run more than anything. Staying several hours after closing time at the center didn't help much either.

"You can tell him next time you see him," Alek returned smoothly. "Maybe it'll mean something coming from you, but Denny and I weren't getting anywhere. Can't really blame him; you should have seen yourself last night."

"So, he didn't stay here?" Ren moved on, scowling. The only details he wanted from last night weren't about him.

"No. North took him back to his place."

"They were supposed to wait for me to do that," Ren complained, not liking it, knowing North had been waiting to take Justin away. He also knew he was being selfish trying to keep Justin here, but he was hoping for more time to find some sort of balance. Like joint custody?

"Bro, you haven't been home, so you haven't had a chance to see, but Justin? He's fine. His fever broke, what, Monday? He's been ready to go for a while. And your face says you knew that already."

"Yeah, fine," Ren moped. Alek rolled his eyes, making Ren want to take a jab at him even though Alek had a point.

"Anyway, Denny and I were wondering," Alek changed the subject. "You were all over the place yesterday, but it seemed like you said Celeste got hurt at the center? Is that what happened?"

"No," Ren corrected his own ranting. "It was someone else. I know her, but you guys don't. Celeste was there, though."

"On Thursday?" Alek mused from behind his coffee mug.

"She switched days to avoid me," Ren admitted bitterly.

"Wow, that's cold," Alek sympathized. "Sorry, man."

"It doesn't matter," Ren said, as if it were true. As if it didn't still hurt his feelings. Celeste going out of her way to avoid him. Justin vanishing before Ren woke up. All that embarrassing crap that happened last night when Ren was too tired to make coherent sentences. It smacked hard into Ren's soul that he didn't appear to be desirable to anyone but Genevieve down the hall. And even that might have been something Denny told him in the moment to make him feel better.

"Ren? Why don't you go lie down?" Alek broke into Ren's self-piteous thoughts, jerking him into motion again.

"No, I'm headed out. Class starts at eight, and my shift starts right after," Ren explained as he headed toward his room for his backpack. "I'll be back a little after noon like always."

"Justin wanted you to say here," Alek protested.

"Well, he's not here to stop me, is he?" Ren shot back, dropping his bag near the door so he could put on his winter gear. "He told me he wasn't going to disappear."

Ren fought with his coat zipper, angry and hurt about so many different things. Even if he wanted to, he'd never get back to sleep now. He felt Alek's eyes on him. But Ren didn't want to be pacified. He wanted to be distracted. Which meant movement. Which meant getting out of here.

"Ren, what's up? It's not like you're never going to see him again."

Except that was exactly what Ren was afraid of. North had come and taken Justin home with him, and Justin never answered his phone. But even if he did come back, it was going to be different. Justin didn't need Ren anymore.

"I've got to go, Alek. I don't want to be late," Ren said in parting, refusing to be comforted by Alek's words. He just didn't understand what was happening here. Not with Justin. Not with Celeste.

He had no idea how Ren's world was turning into such a lonely place.

"Whatever, I'm not your mom, but if you come home again like you did last night, there will be an intervention," Alek said, shaking his head from his place at the table, surrounded by his familiar wires and radio pieces. Ren remembered as he walked down the hall that it was Alek's birthday tomorrow. He'd have to get his emotions together by then. It wasn't fair to Alek for Ren to be moody like this, especially after all he'd done to help Ren lately. Tomorrow, Ren was going to be happy. It's not like there wasn't plenty to be happy about. Ren had great friends. He was going to talk to his family on Sunday. Justin was healed and free and honestly, Ren had a lot going for him. Things he needed to stop taking for granted.

He tried. All the walk to English class Ren did nothing but list things he was grateful for. The cold, icy path didn't make the list, but there was so much else that did. He was even starting to feel better, the crisp air clearing the rest of the fatigue from his head, the sharpness of it fresh in his lungs. He snapped a couple photos of the gothic architecture of the campus in the snow to send to his family. He smiled as he thought of what their reactions might be, almost at peace as he entered the classroom.

But then Justin didn't come again. The lesson was not in any way interesting, and not just because Ren was distracted as he continually looked behind him toward the door just in case Justin came in late as he had last Friday. Ren had purposefully sat in the back row, keeping the seat on the end open, but no one came to claim it. It wasn't true, or at least Ren didn't know that it was true, but it felt like Celeste all over again. It felt like Justin was avoiding him.

Denny called as Ren walked from class to the donation center. She wanted to check up on him too, make sure he had gotten enough rest. She asked some random questions as though she were testing his mental sharpness. They spoke briefly of Saturday and how many people Ren should expect to feed at what time. Denny also asked about Celeste, so Ren had to explain it all again. And then he found himself back at the door of the donation center where he had to put away his phone. No new messages. *I won't disappear.*

"Sure," Ren muttered bitterly to himself.

Steve met him less than two minutes after he'd walked in, looking surprised to see him. He forced Ren to look him in the eye and asked him questions, more testing of his lucidity. Ren didn't blame him. Steve didn't look like he could handle more emergency paperwork caused by an employee mistake.

But Ren was good in here. This was his space. He knew every inch, every button. He may not have been as chatty as normal with the donors today, but it wasn't because he was tired. It may have been an effort to smile, but he did everything correctly, as usual. So, it caught him off guard when Steve met him at the cashier's window.

"Go ahead and clock out, Ren," Steve invited pleasantly, and Ren narrowed his eyes at him. Noticing his concern, Steve went on. "Your roommate is out front waiting to pick you up."

"My roommate?" Ren checked, not understanding why Alek would do something like that. He'd never come to get Ren before. Was this more babysitting? Because Ren was totally fine now and didn't need it.

"He said he'd wait, but you've put in more than enough hours, so you can go. I'll see you Monday."

Distrustful and puzzled, Ren watched Steve return to his office. He didn't want to leave yet, not if this had anything to do with the intervention Alek had threatened him with earlier. Ren marched out to the front desk, intent on explaining to Alek, with as much force as necessary, that he didn't need to be picked up and he was going to finish his shift.

But then he stopped short in the doorway, because it wasn't Alek waiting for him.

It was Justin.

He stood near the entrance, hands in his coat pockets, leaning against the wall and staring outside, an apprentice-in-training for the kind of stillness North had mastered. He wore a slouchy charcoal-colored hat today, and one of his pairs of black jeans. And Ren's hoodie. It had been a while since Ren had seen Justin in daylight. He looked so mesmerizingly handsome that Ren wondered how it was possible not to have noticed Justin before last Friday. He took a deep breath and began crossing the waiting room floor.

"Justin?" he called out before he got too close. He had to speak first, his nerves wouldn't allow him not to, though he wasn't sure what to say beyond Justin's name. That wasn't quite true; he had a million questions, just none he felt comfortable asking. What was Justin doing here? Where had he gone? What were they supposed to do now? Would Justin hate him if he knew how much Ren wanted to take his hands out of his pockets and wrap them around Justin's waist?

Justin turned unhurriedly, smiling as he recognized Ren, his eyes scanning him up and down, taking in the scrubs and lab coat. Ren had to stop moving since he wasn't so certain about his knees holding him up while Justin was looking at him like that.

"Why do you even have real clothes?" Justin asked, shaking his head.

"So I can loan them to you," Ren quipped. Justin glanced down at himself as if he couldn't remember he was still wearing Ren's sweatshirt.

"I'll get it back to you," Justin promised guiltily, brushing his hands over the lettering as if that would suddenly make it unrecognizable to Ren as something that belonged to him.

"Don't worry about it," Ren tried to backtrack. He didn't even want the shirt back, because if Justin had it there was still something keeping them together. An excuse. "No rush or anything; it looks good on you." Ren closed his eyes, wishing he hadn't said that, then decided to move on quickly to minimize the damage. "What are you doing here?" His question froze Justin, turning him somber and uncertain. He shrugged, like his being here wasn't unprecedented.

"You didn't answer your phone, so I went to check on you. Alek said you were here."

"*You're* checking on *me*?" Ren asked, surprised. Was that something it would be safe to be happy about? Maybe not, considering how dark Justin's expression had turned in the last few seconds.

"Yeah," Justin challenged. "You were supposed to stay home and rest." He paused, frustrated, shaking his head. "Why is that so impossible for you?"

"It's not impossible, just unnecessary," Ren dismissed, trying to figure out if he felt threatened, unsure why Justin sounded so mad. Because he was fine now. Surely, Justin could see that. "I've got a lot of stuff to do. What about you?"

"What about me?" Justin pressed.

"You didn't stay home either." Ren hadn't meant to say that. He just hoped his tone didn't sound so betrayed in real life as it had in his head. "Never mind," Ren sighed, wondering if they were ever going to get anywhere. Justin's face had turned complicated, too many emotions overlapping at once.

"That's not my ..." Justin paused, as if he were unable to say the word home. "Ren, I can't keep staying there. It's messing you up. I mean, you were a complete wreck last night. I had to leave."

Ren closed his eyes, embarrassed. He prepared himself for what was coming next, expecting a thank you and goodbye. Justin had taken his duffel bag away with him. Everything he owned was now probably in a dresser at North's place.

"Ren, I didn't mean ... Shit, I suck at this," Justin growled, sounding exasperated. Ren timidly lifted his head to find Justin with one arm folded across his waist, his face dropped into his opposite hand. "Let's just go back to why I'm here, ok?"

"Sure," Ren agreed, needing to just get it over with. "Why are you here?"

"When do you get off?" Justin asked instead of answering.

"I'm done," Ren responded, suddenly glad that Steve had told him to clock out early. "I just have to get my stuff."

"Ok," Justin said, nervous. "Do you have time to grab a coffee or something?"

"My next class isn't until three," Ren said, amazed and unbalanced listening to Justin. What was going on here?

"So," Justin trailed off, looking at his shoes. Ren wondered why Justin suddenly seemed unable to look at him anymore. He used to stare without blinking at Ren. What had changed besides his temperature? Other than Ren's weird behavior last night.

"Coffee sounds great," Ren supplied, watching tension visibly leave Justin's shoulders. "Let me get my coat."

Ren hesitantly began backing up, eyes still on Justin as if expecting him to vanish if he turned away. Justin made eye contact for a second, one of his brows lifting along with one corner of his mouth.

"I'm not going anywhere," Justin promised, but Ren wasn't sure. Justin had options now; he was definitely going somewhere. But not right this second. Right this second, he was with Ren, and they were going to get coffee like regular people. Like friends. And Ren was going to enjoy it like it was the last time they'd ever see each other. A shiver ran over him as he pulled his bag over his shoulders. He wasn't going to think about it.

Waving farewell to his coworkers, Ren made his way back to Justin, who'd been true to his promise and hadn't moved until he saw Ren. Then Justin pushed the front door open to let Ren out into the cold first.

They started walking, and Ren felt weird about how clumsy they were at it. His first steps were way too close to Justin, almost touching him, barely stopping himself from reaching around his waist to support him as he moved. Justin no longer needed assistance to walk, but they had never walked anywhere without Ren physically supporting him. He overcompensated, stepping away and almost tripping off the sidewalk. Justin grabbed his coat sleeve, pulling him closer before releasing him, as though setting the new standard of how much space should be between them.

"You ok?" Justin asked, some of the worry of last night creeping into his voice again.

"Yeah," Ren answered promptly, maybe too fast. He caught Justin staring sideways at him and almost tripped again. He was going to have to figure this out in a hurry; he was acting crazy. "I just realized I've never really walked next to you before."

And just like that, Ren made Justin overly aware of his own natural gait to the point where he paused on the sidewalk, letting that sink in. "Shit, you're right," Justin whispered. He looked so adorably befuddled by this realization that Ren had to laugh about it. Justin looked at him, trying to figure out if he were being made fun of, but when he saw Ren's face, he hesitantly snickered too.

"Come on," Ren invited, Justin's quiet laugh helping him feel better, like they were going to be ok.

"I can't remember how I walk now," Justin told him, still unmoving on the sidewalk.

"I think it works best if you don't think about it," Ren advised. "And anyway, it's not like I'll know if it's different than usual."

Ren started walking, forcing Justin to take some steps to keep up with him, though it looked as though Ren had made it awkward for him.

"Justin!" Ren burst out, still laughing. "Just walk!"

"Ok!" Justin returned, though he didn't sound mad. "But where do you want to go? Who makes your favorite coffee?"

"Uh, you do," Ren said seriously. Justin seemed stunned before shaking his head.

"Your second favorite then," Justin amended, glossing over it. They were walking side by side now, naturally, close but not touching, no longer overthinking it. Ren figured that was probably the best way to play this. Do not overthink. But he really didn't have a second favorite coffee.

"I don't know," Ren answered honestly. "I don't buy coffee; I just bring it with me. Where do you usually go?"

Ren watched Justin debate the pros and cons of the coffee options they had within walking distance. Actually, the way Justin scanned their surroundings made it clear he might be more familiar with the university grounds than Ren was. He suddenly wanted to ask Justin to take him to all his favorite places, wanted to see the university from his viewpoint. He couldn't think of anything better than that.

Justin made up his mind with a visible jerk of his head and began leading Ren through the grounds. When they hit the east side, Justin turned left into the Eckhart Library, but didn't stop. Ren divided his attention between watching Justin and looking around their path as the library transitioned into the math department and then into Mandel Hall.

"Justin? What's your major? How long have you been a student here?" Ren asked as Justin sped him along through the hallways with the ease of someone who had obviously done this many times.

"I'm actually not," Justin answered vaguely, pulling Ren up a flight of stairs to the front of a café called Hallowed Grounds, a sketched ghost holding a tiny coffee mug printed on the door. Ren hadn't even known this place was here.

Ren entered the café first as Justin's statement came to the front of his focus. "What do you mean you're not? You're not a student?" Because how could that be right; they had a class together. Justin lived in the dorms. Except North said that wasn't his apartment. Now Ren was confused. Again. And afraid. If Justin wasn't attending university here, that was one less reason for him to stay.

"I didn't finish high school, Ren," Justin confessed, looking like he didn't really want to talk about it.

"Justin," Ren began, though he didn't know if he wanted to ask for more information or apologize for bringing it up. He probably should have known. If Justin had been put into a correctional facility at sixteen, it had definitely messed up high school for him. But then why did he attend Ren's English class?

"Get us a seat?" Justin asked, more a request to postpone whatever conversation Ren had just started than worrying they wouldn't be able to find a table. The café was busy, but Ren could spot a place for them on the far wall, past the trio of pool tables that dominated the center of the room.

"I — all right," Ren agreed, unwillingly separating from Justin to hold the table. He slipped past a group at one of the pool tables, noticing the line of couches for the first time as he walked around them. The whole café was painted cream and black. There were hanging lights of two varieties, lamps with green shades and long strings of patio bulbs. They were all turned on, though Ren could hardly tell since the room was so full of natural light from the arched windows lining two of the walls, broken only by an enormous alabaster fireplace. Ren picked a table close to it, setting his backpack in one of the wooden chairs for Justin, then settled into the one across from it, thinking about what Justin said.

Sometimes Ren thought he knew Justin, but he'd just been hit hard how he knew almost nothing. Ren remembered that he and North hadn't talked about the time after North had transferred as Justin's social worker. Ren knew Justin hadn't stayed at the group home; he hung out at that one bookstore because it stayed open until midnight. Had Justin pretended to be a student to cover being homeless?

Ren thought how easy it would be. It was almost perfect. If you were quiet and resourceful, everything to live was available here. Ren wasn't sure that's what Justin had been doing, but it made a sad sort of sense; Justin could have lived here, sneaking in after faculty luncheons and parties where he hadn't been invited to pick up food. Dodging into dorm rooms by pretending he'd forgotten his key card in order to use the resident showers and laundry facilities. Ren suddenly wanted to rest his head on the table — the weight of his thoughts pulling him down.

"Hey," Justin's voice behind him, right next to his ear. Ren hated that he jumped. He turned toward the voice, but paused halfway, sensing Justin's heat covering him, too close. "I forgot to ask what you wanted."

"I'm good," Ren said, thinking of his travel mug already in his backpack and how he couldn't possibly let Justin buy him anything after all his new speculations.

"Ren, you saved my life. Let me buy you coffee," Justin pleaded, still bowed over Ren, mouth near his ear, one hand resting on the back of Ren's chair. Ren tried not to shudder; he had to fold his hands together tightly under the table so they wouldn't shake. "What do you want?"

There were about twenty things Ren could think of right now that he wanted, and none of them had anything to do with coffee. He wanted to lean backward and pull Justin closer. He wanted to kiss the soft place under his jaw, breathe him in deeply. Wanted to settle against Justin's warmth and beg him not to go anywhere, that he wanted them to be together from now on. He clenched his hands.

"Whatever you usually get," Ren croaked, his voice doing weird pitches, eyes fixed on the decorative carvings on the fireplace mantle.

"Ok," Justin accepted, not moving from behind Ren. "What about lunch? Did you want a sandwich or anything?"

"No," Ren answered quickly. Having Justin buy him food was too much. He had his lunch already packed in his bag. "I'm all set. Really."

"Be right back," Justin said, at last standing straight. Ren felt Justin's hand slide across his upper shoulders as he pulled away. Or maybe he'd imagined the touch; it had been so light. Now that Justin wasn't right on top of him, Ren found he could move again. He turned in his chair, watching Justin return to the line, ready to cut his gaze to the bulletin board on the far wall at any moment if Justin turned back. He didn't want to be caught staring.

And there was plenty to stare at. Ren watched Justin move, healed and healthy. He didn't quite have North's grace, but there was a certain elegance to his movements. He dipped a shoulder and slipped between a group of students who were carrying their coffees toward the couches. Ren could see how he had maneuvered through the university, never casting any doubt that he was part of it. Ren was beginning to understand how he'd never noticed Justin before. But he'd never be invisible to Ren again.

By the time Justin returned, Ren mostly had himself under control, though he still hadn't decided how he wanted to proceed. Part of him wanted to tell Justin everything, lay all his emotions out and see what happened. The more sensible part of him repressed that idea, reminding him about his family, about his lack of time for relationships, and how unfair it would be to ask anyone to walk that path with him. And then there were the sharp memories of the past few days with Justin — how Justin had been pulling back from Ren, flinching from his touch. Remembering that made Ren realize he wasn't ready to be crushed. He thought it would be best to keep quiet.

Ren moved his backpack while Justin set down two cups of coffee and a wrapped sandwich on the table.

"I know you said you didn't want anything, but we can share this," Justin offered, taking the newly cleared chair.

"I'd rather watch you eat it," Ren replied honestly, keeping his hands under the table, not trusting himself not to spill the coffee if he reached for it. "It won't hurt your mouth?"

"Not enough to stop me," Justin answered, picking up the sandwich and taking a bite. The flavor of something that wasn't completely free of salt made Justin close his eyes in appreciation. Ren smiled, relieved to see him able to eat.

Ren pulled out his phone, a sudden idea coming to him. He waited for Justin to finish a bite before calling his attention.

"Hey, Justin, let me get a picture," Ren suggested, then explained when Justin looked flustered and confused. "My family wants me to send more pictures home, and they've never seen you."

"What do they need to see me for?" Justin asked, uncomfortable, almost hiding.

"Because you're my friend," Ren told him, reaffirming it was true, as though he wanted to remind Justin that they had something between them. "We'll have to turn, though. The light needs to be coming from the other side."

"Ren," Justin hesitated, unsure, not turning. "I need to talk to you."

Something closed in Ren. The way Justin was talking sounded final. He looked almost upset. Ren decided to stall. "About what? The lights or my family?"

"No, Ren, listen. I've been thinking about it for a couple days." *Wait, Justin, don't say anything. I don't want to hear how it was great and thanks so much, but you're going to be staying with North now and leaving campus because you were never a student to begin with.*

"Here, Justin, turn your face this way," Ren interrupted. *Because this might be the only way I can keep you. Keep us right here in this coffee shop with your hair and my hoodie and your eyes.*

"Oh!" Ren exclaimed as Justin finally gave up and turned the way Ren wanted. "Justin, your eyes!"

Justin didn't look like he knew what to do with that. First, he widened them, then closed them. "God, Ren, what about them?" Ren could tell Justin was frustrated that Ren wouldn't listen to him, but Ren needed a few more minutes before everything changed. Because after Justin laid it all out, they wouldn't be able to come back to this. Once Justin decided to reveal anything, Ren couldn't pretend anymore. He stared at Justin's eyes, trying to get a better look at them even though Justin was now studying the table.

"They're violet," Ren told him, amazed, finally seeing their color for the first time when Justin turned toward the light. Justin rubbed his hands over his face.

"They're gray," Justin corrected, muttering. "Ren, can we —" But something caught Ren's attention over Justin's shoulder. Something that blurred Justin's words into the background music.

"Oh no," Ren murmured, distracted, lowering his phone from where he'd been trying to capture a photo of Justin. "I don't believe it. Crap." His new position gave him a perfect view of the café entrance through the camera app. He quickly shifted back to his original chair, hoping he'd been quick enough.

"What now?" Justin asked, extremely flustered. Ren understood he'd been all over the place the last few minutes. Moving chairs repeatedly, going on about photos and lighting and the color of Justin's eyes. Which were not gray, but now wasn't the time. Justin turned to see where Ren was looking, but Ren grabbed his arm. "Ren, what the hell?"

"Don't look," he hissed. "It's *her.*"

"What?" Justin asked again, ignoring Ren and shifting slightly in his seat to look toward the entrance where just a few seconds ago Celeste Lyons had come through the door with another girl Ren didn't recognize. "Who?" But then revelation snapped his features tight. "Wait, you're kidding — *her*? That's your girl?"

"Never see her anywhere but work until she's trying to avoid me, and now she's everywhere she's not supposed to be," Ren said under his breath, forgetting he was the one in this café for the first time. Celeste might come here every day for all he knew. Then it hit him in the next instant how rude he was being. "Sorry, Justin. Is it ok if we go? Maybe back to the apartment? Then we can talk."

Because he wouldn't be able to handle it if Justin were to give him bad news here at this table while Celeste sat chatting with her friend in the same room. It was bad enough that both were unavailable.

"Which one?" Justin asked softly, watching Ren carefully, ignoring Ren's request to leave, making it seem like he'd asked the most important question ever. Ren risked a quick side glance toward where Celeste stood with her friend in line. He didn't know the other girl. She was beautiful, not as gorgeous as Celeste, but still very pretty. She had golden blonde hair pulled into a long ponytail, fair skin. They were extremely close, laughing with each other, shoulders touching. It hurt Ren to see it, how this girl was obviously Celeste's best friend, but Ren didn't even know she existed until this moment. "Ren? Which one is yours?"

"Neither," Ren answered bitterly, but softened as Justin glared at him, demanding an answer. "The one in the white coat," Ren admitted, wondering why Justin sounded so earnest. What difference did it make which one?

"Oh," Justin sounded relieved. "Why would she be avoiding you? She's not still mad at you even after you helped her yesterday?"

"No, Justin. She was there, but not involved. I'll explain later; just keep your head down for a second. Maybe they aren't staying."

But Justin was doing the opposite of keeping a low profile. He'd pulled his arm out from under Ren's hand, standing up. "Justin!" Ren whispered furiously at him. "What are you doing?"

Justin looked down at Ren, half smiling, his violet-gray eyes full of warm pain. What sort of look was that? "I'm giving you a thank-you present," he said, and then he slipped away, leaving Ren unsure of what to do. What just happened?

Ren watched, horrified, as Justin marched right up to the girls. They had their attention on the menu board as he silently joined them, but it didn't stop him. He reached out and gently tapped the blonde girl on the shoulder.

"What on earth?" Ren murmured to himself, shocked, as both girls suddenly threw themselves at Justin. Celeste wrapped her arms around Justin's neck while her friend slipped hers around his waist. Justin lowered his dark head between their bright ones, putting an arm around each of them, and for a second, they just stood there embracing as if they were all alone.

They didn't separate until the barista pointed out they were holding up the line. Celeste's friend kept attached to Justin's arm as Celeste ordered and paid. All the while, Ren was reeling. They knew each other? How?

It appeared he was about to find out. Once their coffees were done, Justin began leading everyone back to Ren, who didn't know what to do. What was Justin thinking? What kind of thank-you gift was this supposed to be?

"Come sit with us," Justin invited, coming within earshot, using his free arm to shepherd Celeste closer to the table. Unable to cope with this, Ren found himself jerking to his feet, not sure if he wanted to stare at Celeste or Justin. Celeste's eyes doubled in size as she recognized Ren, and she pulled her coffee closer, holding it with both hands.

"This is my best friend, Ren," Justin introduced him casually to the girls, as though he had no idea Celeste and Ren had history, as if he wasn't noticing how they had shied away, awkward as hell. As though he couldn't tell he was killing Ren right now. "Ren, this is Celeste and Sheridan. They're …" Justin paused, all his smoothness coming to a stop as he tried to figure out how to explain his relationship with the girls in simple language.

"We're Justin's friends too," the blonde girl who must be Sheridan supplied, gazing fondly at Justin. Extremely fondly. Ren tried to stifle a gasp as information came together in a rush in his head. He'd seen the name Sheridan before. In the case file. Sheridan was the name of the girl Justin saved. That meant Celeste … Celeste had been the friend in the parking lot that night.

"That's great," Ren forced out, trading a desperate look with Justin before trying to summon his courage to look Celeste in the eye. Sheridan easily put out a hand to shake Ren's, the only one in this group who had no idea what was really going on. Could she not feel the tension that was closing in tight around them?

"Should we sit?" Sheridan invited, smiling innocently, reminding them all they were still standing awkwardly at the table.

"Actually," Celeste spoke up, hesitant, and Ren realized she was about to excuse herself. "Sheridan, I just remembered …"

Sheridan's lips pursed slightly as she sent a heavy stare at Celeste. The expression was clear. She did not want to leave yet; she wanted to stay with Justin. Ren didn't blame her but was starting to feel jealous about how easily Sheridan had attached herself to Justin's side.

"No, sit down," Ren heard himself speaking, still looking pointedly at Celeste, feeling that icicle stabbing into his heart again, freezing him inside. "Catch up. I'll go." Because this couldn't get any worse, could it? Staying here at the table trying to drink coffee as he watched Sheridan snuggle with Justin, watched Celeste trying to look everywhere and anywhere but at him.

"Ren," Justin froze him to the spot. "Stay."

He swallowed, pulling a chair out for Celeste, trying to prove he could mind his manners. She hesitated, but then took the seat, allowing him to push it in. Ren sat down across from Justin and next to Celeste, picking up his coffee mostly to have something to do.

"So, Justin, how are you?" Sheridan asked, her features somber. Ren thought he should tell Denny that Sheridan wasn't as carefree as she'd accused her of being. There was still guilt on her face. She knew she'd done irreparable damage to Justin's life. It bothered her. "Is everything over now?" She risked a glance over at Ren as she asked, probably thinking Ren might not know what had been going on recently.

"Yes," Justin said. "On Monday; I'm clear. Thanks, both of you, for testifying for me."

Ren almost choked on his coffee. *Chaotic*, Celeste had said when he'd asked her how her week had been before any of this started. He'd wondered what that meant.

"Thank goodness," Sheridan sighed, drenched in bad memories. "I'm so sorry you had to go through that."

"Ren got me through the worst of it," Justin responded. "I really owe him."

Ren set his coffee down gently as everyone's eyes settled on him. He decided the safest place to look was at Justin, who looked right back, resigned and unflinching as usual.

"I didn't do much," Ren muttered, but Justin wouldn't allow him to be humble about it.

"You saved my life," Justin emphasized, and Sheridan stiffened.

"What do you mean?" she squeaked. "What happened?"

"I got really sick," Justin said, too casually for how bad it had been. "I had to go to the ER in an ambulance. If Ren hadn't been there taking care of me, I probably would have died."

"Oh my God," Sheridan breathed, staring at Justin worriedly, placing a palm on his chest. "Are you ok now?"

"I'm still on medication, but yeah, I'm better." Justin pierced Ren with another stare. "Thanks for canceling your life to stay with me."

Ren thought his heart would break, but then he heard a strange sound to his right, where Celeste was sitting. He risked a glance at her, shocked to discover she had her face in her hands. Was she crying?

"Celeste?" he checked her, surprised. Timidly, he reached over, barely touching her sleeve. She peeked out from between her fingers, her eyes wet and shining.

"Celeste, don't cry," Sheridan comforted, stretching her hand across the table. "Everything turned out all right." But Celeste was shaking her head.

"Ren, I'm so sorry," she wept, covering her eyes again. The ice in Ren's heart didn't melt at her apology. It felt more like it had finally cracked his ribcage in half. Now she was sorry?

"I wasn't lying," Ren told her, probably unnecessarily now.

"I knew that," Celeste cried. "I knew it before you hung up. I can't *believe* the things I said to you."

"Wait," Sheridan said, realizing. "*Ren*?" Celeste jerked her head up from her hands, her eyes daring Sheridan to say anything else. Justin quietly stood, pulling Sheridan gently with him.

"I think you guys need to have a talk," he instructed. Celeste nodded, biting her lip, staring at the table. "I'll take Sheridan home."

"Justin," Ren pleaded, but he didn't know what he wanted him to do. Not leave. Definitely not leave with Sheridan. Justin dipped his chin toward Celeste. There it was. Ren's thank-you gift. A chance to work it out. But Ren didn't know if that's what he wanted anymore. Justin hadn't even had a chance to tell Ren what he'd wanted to talk about. They weren't finished. "I'll see you tonight, right? Dinner?"

"No," Justin responded, handing Sheridan her purse. "North's meeting his military friends for dinner tonight. They do it every Friday, and he wants me to go."

"But tomorrow?" Ren pushed, feeling things coming apart at the seams. He couldn't let Justin out of his sight without some sort of promise for a future meeting. "The party?"

"I wouldn't miss that," Justin promised, soothing Ren. "Now." He very pointedly shifted his eyes toward Celeste again, who sat wringing a napkin in her hands. Sheridan bent over her before she left, giving her a tight squeeze of encouragement before taking Justin's arm again.

"He *is* cute." Ren thought he heard her murmur to Celeste. "Good luck," she said more audibly.

Both Ren and Celeste turned to watch Justin and Sheridan leave, knowing they were being abandoned in awkward. Ren thought about letting Celeste off, telling her that he accepted the apology and that was that. He wouldn't bother her again. But part of him was curious. If she had known he wasn't lying, then why hadn't she texted him her email address? Why go to such extremes to avoid him? He thought, now that Justin had given him the opportunity, he would like an explanation.

"So," he began, hoping his tone was gentle. Celeste lifted her eyes from the table, contrite, ashamed. The ice in Ren's chest started to melt.

# 4
## LOGISTICS

"You knew I was telling the truth?" Ren repeated, mostly to process, lifting the very top layer from this deeply tangled mess that had become his sort-of relationship with Celeste. A relationship that was somehow more complicated now they knew they had a mutual friend. The friend Ren was already missing. He understood that Justin wanted to give them some privacy, but what Ren thought this conversation needed most was a referee. Or at least someone who could back him up. He had never been good at talking to Celeste.

"Yes?" Celeste didn't seem sure of her answer. She stared at her coffee, held tight to the mangled napkin. "Certainly by the end of the call. You'd never spoken to me that way before."

"You could have sent me your email address," Ren prompted, trying to keep any hardness out of his voice. If he wanted answers, he couldn't shut her down before he got them.

"No," Celeste denied, apparently mortified by the thought. "I'd just treated you abysmally. I called you a liar for needing to help your friend, to help *Justin*. I most definitely couldn't ask for your help, for a *favor*, after that."

"Can I ask what happened?" Ren ventured, hoping Celeste would know what he meant. Because really? Where had they gone wrong? If she was sorry, why hadn't she felt safe enough to say so? "I know we weren't exactly friends, but I thought we could be."

Celeste turned shy now, her hands clenched in her lap, eyes sinking further from the table to the floor. She didn't look capable of answering him. He wasn't sure she understood the question. Maybe they couldn't effectively communicate after all.

"I was looking forward to it," Ren disclosed bluntly but not harshly, trying to show her by example what sort of information he wanted, astonished at the ease of the confession, how quickly it unstuck from his throat. "My roommates had been pushing me to ask you out for months, so it was a huge deal." This was the first time he'd ever felt so completely in control with Celeste. And while he didn't like how unsettled she seemed to be, he was enjoying the freedom to say what he'd always wanted to say. "It was supposed to be a breakthrough where you could finally see me outside of work. I was so excited to finally talk with you without being interrupted by a machine. Where I wouldn't be in scrubs." He paused, looking down at himself and sighing, remembering Justin teasing him earlier. "Though apparently I'm always in scrubs," he said, wilting slightly. The comment curved the corner of Celeste's lip, the tiniest of sorrowful smiles.

"I planned my outfit for an hour," Celeste said in surrender, still unable to look at him, but the ghost of a smile strengthened, as though talking were getting easier for her as well. "Something I'd never wear to donate plasma. Something I'd never wear to study either." Ren thought it best to keep silent. He wanted to see every nuance of her expression for these words, as though he needed visual confirmation of the truth.

"Sheridan did my makeup," Celeste continued, laughing in a soft embarrassed way, laying herself open and vulnerable. Maybe she did trust him. "I had her do this fancy braid in my hair. I told my parents I'd be staying the night with her. They didn't even want me to go to class that day. They were worried about the drive and the storm. Remember it was a blizzard last Friday?"

"Yes," Ren vocalized, knowing he'd likely never forget the lightning on the lake, the thunder crashing into the base of his spine, Justin's secrets just beginning to bleed into his life.

"They didn't want me driving in it. I almost had to beg, and in the end, they only let me go because they knew I wouldn't even try coming back. I only had one class that didn't cancel, so I spent the rest of the day at Sheridan's apartment, nervous and excited and watching the clock. The hours were just dragging interminably. And then you called."

"And ruined everything," Ren lamented, though he couldn't regret his decision. Nervous? When was she ever nervous? He made her *nervous*? Ren looked at her posture, her hands. She was nervous right now. He hadn't expected that. Maybe all this time she'd used her silence and her book to hide it. She'd done a spectacular job. He'd never seen a hint of anything other than poised sophistication from her.

"I'm the one who ruined everything," Celeste corrected.

Ren continued to monitor her, noticing her long hair had fallen over her shoulders, obscuring her face. Feeling irrationally brave, he leaned closer, pushing the hair back. It was every bit as soft as he'd always daydreamed it would be. Celeste didn't move, which Ren couldn't tell was a good or bad sign. He actually wasn't sure about any of this. What he wanted from her. Where he wanted this conversation to go.

"I was so disappointed," Celeste continued. "But that's no excuse for how I behaved. I think I stood in Sheridan's room with the phone in my hand for twenty minutes after you hung up. I thought of calling you back immediately."

"Why didn't you?" Ren probed, and as he asked, she raised her eyes to his at last. Her shiny, pale-blue, crystalline eyes.

"Sheridan asked me the same thing. I've asked myself the same thing, and the answer changes every time so it must not be real.

Sheridan told me all weekend to just get over myself and call you, like I couldn't do it because of my own pride. And I didn't want that to be the reason, but the longer I waited, the more impossible it became until it was Wednesday and I just ... I'm really not who you thought I was, am I?"

Ren sighed, ignoring the open invitation to insult her.

"If you're not, that's more my fault than yours," Ren mused. "But you know, there is a solution."

Celeste tilted her head to the side, intent, humble, coming to terms with her own arrogance and how it had almost taken something from her. Ren found himself smiling, remembering a time, such a short time ago, when he would have given anything to be with this girl. He offered her his hand.

"I'm Ren," he said, as though they were meeting for the first time.

"Celeste," she responded, her slim hand taking his steadily, the first time they'd touched without the barrier of gloves.

"Nice to meet you," Ren expressed, watching as Celeste's shoulders rose and fell, as though a weight had been lifted from her.

Their conversation moved forward from there. Celeste asked Ren questions about Dr. Farley, his childhood growing up outside the US, his major, his schedule, and his plans for the future. He asked her the same things, getting all the requisite preliminaries, setting the foundation of getting to know someone. Celeste studied political science. Her father was the CEO of a manufacturing company; her mother taught dance to children as a hobby and was involved in several charity organizations. Celeste had no siblings compared to Ren's four. She'd been accepted at Columbia but decided not to go that far from home for college.

Ren noticed as they spoke that Celeste wasn't nearly as confident as she had always appeared. Her aloofness was part of her protection. If no one really knew her, she could maintain a nearly perfect façade. Their misunderstanding made more sense to Ren now. Channeling her disappointment about their missed date into an accusation of his character was something she regretted but somehow couldn't take responsibility for. She found it easier to pretend it hadn't happened, which meant not seeing Ren anymore, not having him remind her of how she'd behaved. A lie to herself that he'd forced her to admit by working Wednesday and Thursday nights, by following Justin into this coffee shop.

Though it was obviously good for her, apologizing, acknowledging that she'd made a mistake. She no longer clenched the destroyed napkin. In fact, she laughed as she scattered the shreds of it across the table, feeling better, like she could be herself. They talked easily, without expectation or worry about how they were coming across. It was better than how Ren had pictured their first date would go. He found himself remembering all the things he had once admired about Celeste — things that were still there to be admired.

"Ren, can I ask you something?" Celeste asked. They'd been asking each other questions for a long time now, but this one felt different. She'd gone shy again.

"Sure," he invited, open, surprisingly grateful to Justin for forcing them into this. It felt so much better to have all the inhibitions regarding Celeste broken. It was such a relief to look at her and just see a girl. A beautiful girl, but still, a real, breathing, mistake-making human. He liked her better this way.

"It's about Justin."

"Ah," Ren said neutrally, taking a deep breath as something in his chest tightened. He hadn't forgotten about Justin, not for a second, but somehow, he wanted to keep Justin and Celeste separate in his head. "Ok," he said anyway. There was no reason he couldn't talk to Celeste about Justin. He wasn't dating either one of them. He'd probably never date either one of them. This was not a big deal.

"I wouldn't normally pry like this," Celeste prefaced, watching Ren for signs of disapproval. "But you're his best friend, so I wondered ... has he brought up Sheridan to you recently?" The question came so hesitantly, as though Celeste thought it rude to ask. Ren also knew the answer wasn't for her; she was asking for Sheridan.

"He told me what happened," Ren admitted. "Nothing more than that."

"Oh," Celeste sighed, disappointed. Ren knew why. He'd seen Sheridan's face as she looked at Justin, saw how quickly she'd gone to him, how close she tried to get.

"He was really sick," Ren heard himself explaining, wondering what he was doing. Why was he giving her this? Why encourage them? "On top of everything else that's been going on."

"I'm sure," Celeste granted, nodding to herself. "I'd just hoped. It's been so hard for her, you know?"

"No?" Ren said doubtfully. What had been hard for her? Did Celeste even know what hard was? "In what way?" He didn't mean to sound confrontational, but he didn't know if he succeeded. Justin had ruined his life for her. What sort of difficulties could she possibly have?

"I've known Sheridan my whole life. We grew up together," Celeste told him. "All of us. David, Sheridan, and me. She lived in the house next to mine, and we were always going back and forth. But after what happened with David, she hardly ever left her house. She didn't come to class anymore; her family started homeschooling her instead. And as soon as she was accepted here, she moved out, came to campus where no one knew her."

"Why?" Ren asked, intrigued. Celeste gave him a sad, indulgent smile. Ren had seen this expression on Denny before. It meant he was being stupid, but he couldn't help it because he was a boy.

"It was so terrible," Celeste went on. "The Hunts blamed her for everything, of course. She and David dated for a year before she finally realized she didn't have to let him control every piece of her life. He told her what she could wear, what she was allowed to eat, how much make up she could put on, and what events she could attend. Everyone always told her how lucky she was to be his girl-friend, like it was something special. That's probably why she put up with it for so long, thinking there was something wrong with her because she wasn't happy. When she broke up with him, it was bad.

He refused to leave her alone, which is, as you know, how Justin got involved."

Ren kept quiet, sensing there was more to be said. Celeste gauged him, watching him for something. To see if he believed her? To see if he understood the injustice here? Whatever she was looking for, she seemed to find it. Celeste continued explaining how David had ruined more than one life.

"Then after David came back from the hospital, after Justin was sentenced, everything got so much worse. No one would even listen to the truth. Somehow the story got out that Sheridan was cheating on David with Justin. The girls we went to school with started calling her the most horrible names, shunning her, stealing from her. They blamed her for David getting hurt. And Mr. and Mrs. Hunt didn't help. They started poisoning the whole neighborhood against Sheridan. In the end, I think I was the only friend she had left. Sometimes she'd ask me what really happened, as though she'd heard the lies so many times she'd forgotten the truth."

Ren exhaled hard; he'd never even thought about this. Probably because it was so wrong. And yet, knowing what he did about the Hunts, he wouldn't put it past them to be so unkind.

"That's terrible," he acknowledged, feeling sorry for Sheridan for the first time since he'd found out about her.

"It was getting better once she moved to campus, away from everyone," Celeste said, trying to brighten her tone. "She's made some new friends here, good ones. Real ones. She was starting to move past it, even starting to finally let go of Justin. But then we were called in last week for Justin's trial, and it brought everything back to her. The poor thing. The Hunts' lawyer was so cruel to her, too. I think the only way she got through it was because Justin was with her. He never took his eyes off her the whole time, as though he were holding her together from where he was sitting."

Oh. So Ren wasn't the only person who Justin stared at that way. He knew that shouldn't hurt his feelings, but it still did. He thought of Sheridan grabbing on to Justin when she'd seen him, the relief in her face, the contentment as he leaned his head over hers, how he'd held her. The familiar gesture of him pulling her from the table, handing over her bag.

"She's in love with him," Ren said.

"Of course, how could she not be?" Celeste questioned, and Ren tragically agreed. How could you help but fall in love with the person who came out of nowhere and saved you? "She's been completely infatuated from that night he helped her. She wrote him letters while he was in the facility, called him every day to check on him. She even went to visit him a few times. I was worried at the beginning. I mean, the first time I'd ever seen him he was … you know, and Sheridan had already been through one abusive relationship. But Justin has always been very gentle and sweet. Well, you saw. I thought for sure they'd get together once he was released, but she lost touch with him. It's like he vanished completely."

Ren glossed over this, knowing that part of the story already. The lost years of Justin Kittrick when he was never where he was supposed to be. Where he'd been thinking no one wanted him, despite the growing evidence to the contrary. Ren had already heard about that. He was more fixated on the most important thing Celeste had said so far about Justin and Sheridan.

"They were dating?" Ren clarified.

"Well, sort of," Celeste answered. "They couldn't really go anywhere, but they *were* close. Sheridan was devastated when he disappeared. Before Justin, she'd never been with anyone except David. And she hasn't been with anyone since. I've been trying to get her to move on forever. I was horrified by the situation that brought him back to her, but awful as it sounds, I was happy they'd found each other again. Don't you think they belong together?"

"I don't know," Ren stuttered, put on the spot. Was he really sitting here with the girl he'd fantasized about, making plans to create a relationship for the boy he was suddenly infatuated with? Or was it recreate? They'd already been together. Funny how Justin had forgotten that part when he'd explained it to Ren earlier. Ren hadn't even thought to ask if Justin kept in contact with her.

"Oh, is he seeing someone?" Celeste changed direction as she monitored Ren's expression, crestfallen at his lack of enthusiasm for her idea.

"If he is, he didn't tell me," Ren said, all the ease of their chat falling apart at this new direction, thinking of Justin and Sheridan. Together. Her hands around his waist, burying her face into his chest. "But it's really up to them, isn't it?"

"I suppose that's true. I guess we'll just have to see what happens," Celeste said, shrugging, disappointed but not daunted. "At least they've found each other again, and everything is finally over. It might work out wonderfully well."

Ren swallowed, swirling the last few sips of his coffee around the bottom of his cup. It had gone cold a long time ago. *Wonderfully well,* she said, though Ren was struggling to see Justin and Sheridan together. Though she probably had a better chance than he did, what with her having a longer history with Justin. Oh, and being a girl probably helped a *lot.* God, Ren was so stupid. He might be the only idiot in the world who could confuse being vulnerably and deathly ill with being gay.

"Ren?" Celeste called, bringing him back to where she was still seated next to him at the table, the sun glinting off her white hair. She had reached forward to touch him; he just now noticed. Her hand was resting carefully on his arm.

"Yeah?" he asked, wondering if she'd asked him a question he hadn't heard, feeling so helplessly ungrateful. How long had he wanted to be with Celeste? And now she was touching him, talking with him, and he was barely paying attention. What was wrong with him anyway?

Celeste pulled back, noticing him staring at her hand. "Nothing," she stated. "You just seem sad all of a sudden."

"No," Ren contradicted, not wanting Celeste to even suspect why he might be sad. "Just tired. It took a long time to clean up last night."

"Oh," Celeste said, her eyes losing focus momentarily as that scene replayed in her memory. "You were absolutely brilliant, by the way. I meant to tell you, but somehow, we just didn't — Do you know if she's ok? The girl?"

"She's fine," Ren confirmed, liking the change in topic. He didn't want to talk about how perfect Sheridan and Justin were together. He was going to have to think about that later, when he was alone and could process it properly. "Brett's been reassigned to the front desk, though."

"I have questions about that," Celeste hinted, and Ren understood why. Looks like Celeste wasn't the only one who was going to have to admit to screwing up today. "You gave my file to him."

"I was … I shouldn't have done that," Ren let her know. "I didn't know I was holding your folder. I wasn't expecting to see you; it wasn't your normal day. And when I saw your face, I knew you didn't want to see me, so I decided to let Brett take you back."

"You looked so angry," Celeste said, sounding sad, knowing he had every right to be angry. Even though angry wasn't the right word.

"More hurt than angry," Ren corrected her. "I figured you were still mad at me. But I shouldn't have switched folders. Not with Brett."

"Why do you say it like that?" Celeste speculated curiously. "Like you knew he would hurt me."

Ren hesitated before deciding to show her what he was talking about. He pulled back his sleeve, displaying the dark bruise covering the inside of his forearm, all the way to his wrist and halfway up his bicep. Celeste gasped and reached out, as if unable to stop herself from softly resting her hands over the damage. Ren's muscles tensed, but her touch was too gentle to hurt. Her fingers were cool as they rested lightly against him. She stared at him with her mouth slightly open, concerned and horrified at the same time.

"This is how Brett does venipunctures," Ren explained.

"How ... Ren, I didn't even know this was possible. How can he work there if he does this kind of damage consistently?"

"Well, that's the thing. It's not consistent; it all depends on the person. Brett's not a bad guy," Ren defended him. "But he's not very gentle. So yes, I knew he'd hurt you. That's why I sent him away."

"You were protecting me?" Celeste asked, her voice warm, touched, and guilty. Ren slipped his arm carefully out from under her hands, tugging down his sleeve again.

"Yeah," Ren said, wondering where to go from here.

"Ren, I don't know what to say," Celeste fumbled. "Thank you. I'm so sorry."

"So am I," Ren replied, picking up the pieces of the shredded napkin and stuffing them into his cup. Their conversation felt as though it were coming to an end. Ren wanted to start moving, processing everything that had happened this afternoon. When he stood up, Celeste also rose with graceful speed, as though afraid he was abandoning her forever.

"Ren, wait. I know I don't deserve it," Celeste began quickly, wanting to get it out before he left. Ren paused in the process of picking up his bag. "You've already been more than gracious, but do you think you could give me another chance?"

Ren met her gaze, looked hard into her face, and thought about what she'd just offered. A week ago, he'd been a stuttering disaster at the very idea of being with her. Now he wasn't sure. But if he couldn't be with Justin, and he'd known that wouldn't work even before he'd learned about Sheridan. Since he couldn't be with Justin, why shouldn't he give Celeste a chance? He'd wanted her once, and he knew if he turned her down this time, there would never be another opportunity.

"Ok," he heard himself agree quietly, reserved. "I'd like that," he finished, willing it to be true. Being with Celeste was a better choice logistically anyway. It was a match that would be more acceptable to his family. It was better for his own protection, really. Justin was unpredictable and unobtainable on so many levels, and the sooner Ren got that into his head, the healthier he would be.

Celeste beamed at him, and he smiled softly back at her. She took it as an invitation and stepped closer. Ren opened his arm almost on instinct, allowing her to embrace him, folding her against his chest with both arms. They'd never been this close. She had a floral scent to her hair; he could feel the sculpt of her shoulder blades. She fit into him as perfectly as he'd always fantasized she would. *It's right,* he told himself, forcing his heart to believe it.

"Thank you," Celeste whispered, close to his ear.

"Thank you," Ren echoed, stepping away from her. *This is good. This is everything I've always wanted.* He found her hand and purpose-fully interlocked their fingers, leading her out of the coffee shop, wondering if they could cross the threshold and not have everything burst apart, like waking from a dream.

But no. Even in the corridor of Mandel Hall, Celeste still stood beside him. Ren held on tighter as they walked together outside, back towards the Quad, waiting for the part where this would feel real.

"So, what do we do now?" Celeste asked him.

"Well," Ren speculated, trying to sound like he knew exactly what they should do now, as if he were completely in control and not half-dizzy in confusion as to how the world had suddenly rearranged itself in the last few hours. "Right this second, I have to go to Spanish."

"Ok," Celeste accepted, smiling. "Maybe I can see you after that?"

"I have one more class right after, but I'll be done by five. We can," Ren paused, wondering what an acceptable proposal would be. He thought of his apartment, how Alek had already planned on extra people for dinner tonight, how that might be the best start to what-ever this might turn into. He wanted Alek to meet Celeste, that would be the most reliable test of her character. If Alek liked her, then it would be ok.

"Do you want to come back to my place for dinner after class?"

Ren suggested, sounding surer of himself now. "You can meet my roommate."

"Well," Celeste started, looking worried. "I'd love to, but I'll need to drive home before dark. I didn't bring anything with me this week to stay the night with Sheridan."

"Oh," Ren said, disappointed. This was harder than he'd thought. Celeste laughed.

"Don't worry," she assured him. "I'm sure we can find somewhere in our schedules to pencil each other in."

"Celeste, I think ... before we go any further, we should talk about that," Ren said as he stopped walking. He just wanted her to understand what this might be like. He wanted her to have all the information before he disappointed her again.

Celeste turned serious, studying him.

"I don't think I'm going to be the easiest person to date," Ren confessed. "I'm not home much. I just want you to understand that situations like last week can happen again. I may have to cancel plans, sometimes at the last minute, especially since I'm considering being mentored by someone in the ER, and she's ... well, she'll probably own my soul if I agree to that. But the point is it's not fair to ask you to wait for me, and I won't be offended if you change your mind about starting something with me now that you know."

Ren wasn't sure what he expected after disclosing all of this. Maybe Celeste would agree with him, shake his hand, and wish him luck in his loneliness. But when he turned his head to look at her, she was looking back with a soft kindness in her eyes. A new patience.

"I appreciate the offer, but after watching you yesterday, I think I have a better understanding of what being with you means. I know I handled last week badly, but I promise I will never do that again. I'll be satisfied with whatever moments you can give me. I want to support you."

"Celeste," Ren began, wondering how long this promise could possibly last when the reality of what she'd just agreed to hit her. But at the same time, what right did he have to tell her she couldn't keep her promise? How could he tell her she would fail him when he'd never given her a chance to try?

"Go on," Celeste released him, nodding toward the door. "You don't want to be late for your class."

"What are your plans tomorrow?" Ren asked, a sudden burst of a question as Celeste turned to leave. "It's my roommate's birthday, so we're having a party. If you're free, maybe you could come? Bring Sheridan." He didn't know why he said that. Maybe he thought it would be a good way to test himself, or maybe he just wanted everything to hurt all at once. Or maybe it was a last, weird, and desperate attempt to keep Justin in his life. If Ren were going to date Celeste, and Justin was dating her best friend, then they could all stay together. Maybe it was a normal Ren could get used to.

"That sounds perfect," Celeste agreed, coming closer.

"It'll go until after dark," Ren warned her, thinking of her winter restrictions.

"Then I'll go home with Sheridan," Celeste answered smoothly, showing him that she could be available. It would take just a little forethought is all. "Text me your address?"

"Sure."

Celeste had tucked herself up against him, looking into his face, smiling with that serene sophistication he'd admired for so long. Ren timidly brushed the back of his hand down her cheek.

"Then I'll see you tomorrow," Celeste promised, and Ren realized her hands were wrapped around his waist. *This is a good start. This is good. This is what I wanted.*

"You are the most amazing girl," Ren told her, reminding himself that this was the truth. His words made her break eye contact, like she didn't believe him, her head tilting downward as she looked at the slush at their feet. "Drive safe, ok?"

She nodded, turning her face up. Ren felt her lift and her arms tighten around him. As soft as a snowflake, she kissed the corner of his mouth. He took her elbows before she took a step away, recovering from the surprise. He bent down, giving her a longer kiss, her lips smooth and wonderful. *We can do this. This is going to work. I'm going to do right by her. I'm going to make this right.*

He wasn't sure about his kissing abilities, it wasn't like he had a whole lot of practice, but Celeste seemed dazed and extremely pleased when he pulled back. She squeezed his hand and then deliberately gave him a little push, making it clear they couldn't keep standing here saying goodbye. Ren had to get to class, and even though he knew that, he watched her walk away for a few more seconds.

By the time he'd made it to his apartment, the sun had set, and so had his resolve. He'd almost convinced himself he was truly happy about how things had worked out. It was going to be fine. He was smiling as he opened his door.

Though it slipped from his face as he entered, feeling immediately that something was very off in these rooms. There were no lights on, no music.

"Alek?" Ren called, closing the door and pulling off his mittens. "Anybody home?"

He glanced at the table, surprised to find it clean. Not so much as a stray bit of wire to be seen. Where was the radio? Where was Alek?

"Alek!" Ren repeated, louder this time, making his way to the back, down the hall to Alek's bedroom. Here at last, he could hear something. Music playing inside the room. Metallica. Oh no. Ren knocked for the politeness of the thing, but he was already opening the door before he'd finished. "Hey, big guy, how's it going?" Ren greeted as he peeked inside, worried by what he might see.

Alek was sitting morosely on his bed, a stack of computer games by his desk, random piles of clothes and tools all over the room. Ren carefully picked his way through to get to Alek's desk chair, inviting himself to sit. Alek hid his face in his hands.

"A Metallica kind of bad, huh?" Ren asked, hoping that would break Alek open into explaining what had brought this on. Alek groaned in response, which got them nowhere.

"I'll, um, order us a pizza, ok?" Ren offered, waiting for Alek to get it together enough to tell him what happened. Or maybe he should call Denny. He might have better luck getting information from her. Unless she was the reason Alek was so unhappy. They did bicker a lot, but it never went anywhere near a real argument. "What do you want on it? Pineapple?"

"I'm not hungry," Alek murmured, deepening Ren's worry. He couldn't remember a time when Alek had turned down pizza. This was serious.

"Aw, buddy, pizza fixes everything," Ren said softly, unconvincingly, all thoughts of Celeste and Sheridan pushed aside for the moment so he could prioritize Alek. He was thinking back to this morning. Had Alek been normal this morning? What had changed? Or had Ren just not noticed. It could have happened so easily. He'd been so distracted lately. "Can you tell me what happened?"

Instead of answering, Alek pointed to his computer, where he'd set his screensaver as a series of gears turning in never-ending circles. Curious and overwhelmed, Ren jiggled the mouse to wake up the machine, the last webpage Alek had been looking at brightening enough to read.

It was the JPL website. The one Alek checked multiple times a day, waiting for the outcome of the internship. They'd still received no word. Ren scanned the page for what was so upsetting. The title of the position was at the top, right under the official logos and seals. The required credentials for applicants were there along with the deadline for submissions. But there was new wording on the page today.

*This position has been closed.*

"Oh, Alek, I'm sorry," Ren breathed. "Does Denny know?"

"Yeah, she was here when I brought it up," Alek managed, still distraught.

"Should I go get her?" Ren offered, wondering what sort of shape she was in if Alek was this low.

"She said she was going to stay home and play the most violent video game she owns," Alek said, and Ren's soul eased about Denny.

Being pissed and taking it out through a first-person shooter game seemed better than how Alek was taking this. Ren felt horribly guilty about being so relieved. If they hadn't been accepted, it meant they weren't moving. They weren't going to leave him. He was sad that Alek was so upset, but Ren didn't know what he'd do if he found out he'd lost Justin, Alek, and Denny all in one day. There wasn't enough Metallica or pizza in the world.

"Alek," Ren repeated helplessly, clicking the webpage closed and trying to figure out where the music was coming from. He wanted to turn it off but decided not to. He'd have to let Alek process his own way, but that didn't mean he couldn't encourage him. "I'll be in the living room, ok? Come out when you're ready."

He patted Alek encouragingly on the shoulder as he left, mentally preparing the bait that would lure Alek from his own despair. First, he ordered the pizza, the one with the weird toppings Alek liked best. He'd just finished when his phone rang. Justin's number.

"Justin?" Ren answered, surprised to hear from him. When had Justin ever called him?

"Hey. How'd it go?" Justin asked, getting straight to the point. "Did you work everything out with Celeste?"

"Well, everything is a tall order, but she's not mad at me anymore." Ren decided that he loved the sound of Justin's voice. It had a richness to it now that it wasn't slurred with fever, and Justin had a tendency to linger over vowels, opening them more than Ren was used to. *Damn it, Justin.*

"Good," Justin quipped, sounding satisfied.

"You could have told me you *knew her*," Ren accused.

"If you'd ever said her name, I would have," Justin defended himself, and Ren knew he was right. He paced around the living room, trying to figure out the correct cords and remote buttons Denny and Alek had rigged to the television.

Ren heard someone on the other side of the line call to Justin, and he knew it was North. It was time for them to go and meet with

North's friends from the Air Force. Ren found he could be happy about that.

"North's waiting for you," Ren said.

"Yeah, I've got to go," Justin said. "I just wanted to check on you. You're home now, right? Nothing crazy going on?"

"I'm home," Ren confirmed, looking around the empty front of the apartment. He wished he had time to talk to Justin about the crazy, but he was busy. And Justin deserved to have a night where everything was perfect for once. "Have a great time tonight, ok? I'll see you tomorrow." If there was still going to be a tomorrow. Alek might not feel like celebrating anything, not even his birthday.

"See you, Ren," Justin said in farewell, hanging up before Ren could respond. His three-word goodbye strangled Ren around the throat. He was going to have to get tighter control over this if he was going to hang out with him tomorrow. *Practice*, he admonished himself. It was just going to take practice and getting used to.

Alek stayed in his room while Ren tried to guess which Star Wars movie might be his favorite. Eh, if he got it wrong, Alek could distract himself by re-educating Ren about the correct sequence. Ren started one up, setting the volume high enough that Alek could hear from the bedroom. Then he grabbed his backpack, spreading his homework out on the coffee table to work with the movie playing in the background. Though he hadn't made it very far into his child development reading when the pizza showed up.

Ren took a minute to have a slice of it, remembering as he ate that he hadn't texted Celeste his address yet. Except he'd no sooner sent it then he wondered if he should have waited. The scent of the pizza and the dramatic ascending leitmotif of the Star Wars soundtrack wasn't bringing Alek out of his room yet, which meant this funk could last a while. Which meant Ren could be canceling on Celeste again without ever having a real, successful date. He was the worst boyfriend ever. Man, was it always going to be this complicated? He thought he'd better call her, at least get it all out in the open so if there did end up being no party, at least she'd know sooner.

"Hi Ren," Celeste greeted him. He wished he had a better reason for calling her. "I was just texting you. Should I bring anything with me tomorrow?"

"No," Ren said quickly. "You don't have to bring anything. I'm not sure if the party's still on." Ren looked over his shoulder toward the hallway.

"Is something wrong?" Celeste seemed to be getting better at reading Ren's voice, as though she were learning his tones like a second language. Ren was impressed.

"My roommate got some bad news today. I'm trying to cheer him up, but if he doesn't want to see anyone tomorrow, then I'll postpone the party for a better time. We can still do something together, though," Ren offered, almost as an afterthought, though he wasn't sure what they would do. "I'm not going to cancel on you again, promise. But we might have to alter the plan." Maybe he could talk her into coming over and doing their classwork together on the couch? Or should he take her out somewhere? But should he really leave Alek in his misery like this? That didn't seem right. Especially after everything Alek had done for Ren just this last week.

"Let's wait and see how things go tomorrow," Celeste offered graciously. "I'm sure you'll have him feeling better soon. What sort of bad news was it?"

"He wasn't accepted into the internship position he'd been hoping for," Ren explained. "Which doesn't make sense. They must have had some incredible candidates if Alek and Denny didn't make it in."

"You have two roommates?" Celeste hesitantly asked, and Ren realized he was talking to her like she knew all about them. He may have gone on at length about Celeste to Alek and Denny, but he'd never told her about them.

"Alek is my roommate," Ren reiterated. "Denny is his, um, partner? They do everything together, and they're the smartest people I know. I thought for sure they'd get in. You know they just finished building a radio? Supposedly, they can use it to talk to the space station. They were going to test it tomorrow. Oh! What'd he do with it?"

Ren stood up, scanning the apartment for the newly completed radio that had lived either on the table or in the cardboard box next to it for weeks. He hoped Alek hadn't decided to do anything he'd regret, like smash it with a hammer or throw it from the balcony. But it definitely wasn't here anymore.

"Do with what? The radio?" Celeste tried to keep up. The double question forced Ren to hold still, closing his eyes so he was only focusing on one thing. The phone in his hand. The patient girl on the other side of it.

"Yes," Ren confirmed, slowing himself down. "He put so much work into it. I hope he didn't decide to take it apart, but I'll look for it later. How was the drive home? Ok? It takes you what? Half an hour?"

"A little more than that," Celeste said, a nod in her voice. "I get a lot of reading done in the car, what with going back and forth every day." Ren smiled with his eyes closed. Even when she was driving, she was reading. This girl.

"What are you listening to right now?" Ren asked.

"Napoleon Hill's *Think and Grow Rich*," Celeste answered promptly, passion in her voice. "It's positively mind blowing. Or mind altering? Anyway, it's not anything like I thought it was. I'm enjoying it very much."

"That's not your normal genre, though, is it?" Ren ventured, trying to picture a book like that on the same shelf as Jane Austen and the other books Celeste normally brought to her donations. "The last one I saw you with that wasn't homework was *Gone, Girl*, wasn't it?"

"Oh, that," Celeste scoffed. "I didn't pick that. My book club did. I bring those fluffy things to donations because they don't take much concentration to get through. I love the girls in the club, but their taste in books is somewhat ... well, I'm sure they think the same about me. The last time it was my choice I made them all read *The Seven Habits of Highly Effective People*. I'm surprised they haven't kicked me out yet."

For some reason, Ren found this intensely funny. "There really is a book club?" he managed to say, struggling to get the words out because he was laughing too hard. That's what Denny had always called it. Ren's stalker book club.

"Yes," Celeste said, guarded. "Is that so amusing?"

"I've read every single book you brought in," Ren confessed, softening into snickers as he realized she might think he was making fun of her. "I thought it would be a good way to get to know you." Nope, no good, it was too funny. "I stayed up all night reading *Pride and Prejudice*!"

"Oh, God, I'm sorry! I *hated* that book!" Celeste burst out, and Ren could hear she was laughing too. Ren leaned against the wall, weak from laughing. All those books, and she hadn't even picked them. "You'll have to come to the next meeting. You've read more of the selections than two thirds of the girls, so we simply must have you as an honorary member."

"They wouldn't want me either," Ren said teasingly. "The last book I read for fun was the *Outdoor Emergency Care Guide*."

"No, now I insist you participate," Celeste encouraged with mock authority. "After a book like that, they'll be begging for my self-improvement titles. Oh, but please don't be offended. I think it's incredible that you put so much effort into learning."

Ren huffed, calming down, smiling. She really was amazing. He felt genuine affection taking root in his chest, replacing the icicle that had been there yesterday.

"I do what I can," Ren admitted humbly. "Just like you."

"Hmm," Celeste hummed, pleased.

"And right now, I'm going to go do what I can for Alek," Ren followed up, drawing their conversation to a close. "I just wanted to let you know that tomorrow is a little sketchy. But I'm *not* canceling. We'll figure it out."

"Thank you, Ren," Celeste said, gratitude thick in her voice. "I'll see you tomorrow one way or another."

"Right. Good night, Celeste."

There was a pause after the final word, and Ren knew she was waiting for him to hang up first. He thought about waiting, but in the end, he shook his head and clicked the red button on his phone. He would see her tomorrow, and right now he was concerned about Alek's missing radio. Ren knelt in front of the cardboard boxes, beginning to carefully pick through them to see if he could find it.

"Ren?"

Ren jerked his head up, relieved to see Alek leaning against the opening to the hall.

"Hey, Alek, want some pizza?" Ren invited, trying to be bright. Alek was staring at him strangely, his arms folded across his broad chest, eyes narrow and calculating.

"Did I just hear you saying goodbye to Celeste?"

"Oh, yeah," Ren said, realizing Alek had no idea what happened this afternoon. "That was her on the phone. We were talking about books."

Alek let his arms drop, staring around the apartment, confused. Like he'd fallen into an alternate reality. "She's talking to you? You're laughing about it?"

"Yeah. We're, um, we're sort of dating now?" Ren didn't know why that came out as a question. Maybe because it didn't feel real yet. Maybe he wanted Alek's approval first before it could be a real thing. He watched Alek's eyebrows shoot up to his hairline.

"Ok, that's literally the last thing I thought you were going to say," Alek accused. "What is it with you lately and the dramatic revelations? Oh, hey, this stranger I brought home who almost died in our living room is on trial for murder, but he didn't really do it, and by the way, I'm dating the girl who wouldn't speak to me yesterday. How does that even work?"

"You better sit down and have some pizza for this one, buddy," Ren warned him, and Alek obediently perched on the couch near the food, staring at Ren, who figured this was probably a welcome distraction for him. So, Ren talked. Told Alek all about Sheridan and Justin and how they were all connected and how Ren and Celeste had worked out their misunderstandings and now she was his girl-friend ... sort of ... maybe. They were working on it.

"Wait a minute," Alek interrupted him. "What about Justin?"

"What about Justin?" Ren repeated, stiffening, knowing that even if he successfully tricked every other person, including himself, he'd never get it past Alek, who was looking at him scoldingly for playing ignorant about his question.

"The way you two have been acting, I was expecting your dating announcement to be a little different," Alek replied, putting it tactfully.

"Justin's not like that," Ren blurted out, staring at the carpet. "He and Sheridan dated after he saved her."

"And you were head over heels about Celeste before you met Justin," Alek pointed out, undaunted. "Who's to say Justin's not the same as you? Did you even talk to him about it?"

"God, no. How am I going to bring up something like that?" While Ren was grateful that Alek wasn't acting so depressed, he wished there had been a better way to get him out of it.

"Easy. You look at him and say," Alek stuttered, deflating. "You say —"

"You can't even say it, and he's not even here!" Ren exploded, and Alek shrugged in defeat. Ren decided to move on, softer. "Celeste thinks Justin and Sheridan are going to get back together. And I want him to be happy. He freaking deserves it. So no, I'm not talking to him. I'm dating Celeste like I wanted in the first place, and Justin is going to date her best friend, and I am going to be ok with that. Ok?"

Alek looked extremely skeptical. "You're going to be ok with that?" he repeated, as sarcastic as Ren had ever heard him.

"Yes," Ren said emphatically. "Celeste is fantastic. She's better than I even imagined her. It's so perfect it's like it's not even real."

"And there it is," Alek said smugly.

"Alek," Ren pleaded. "Justin and I can't work out; there's nothing there to work with. It might have looked like something, but only because he was *sick to death*. The past couple days, he didn't want me to even touch him. He flinched the last time I took his temperature. *Flinched*. I want him to stay in our lives, so I'm going to support him through however many girls he wants to date whether it's Sheridan or whoever."

"I still think you should talk to him," Alek advised, grating at Ren's heart.

"I don't think so," Ren denied, unwilling to talk about it anymore. He slouched dejectedly onto the couch next to Alek, his eyes pulled toward the television where he had no idea what was happening in the movie still playing in the background. "What's even going on in this?" he asked, just to switch topics.

"Let's shut it off," Alek suggested. "It's not the movie we need anyway."

"Fine," Ren agreed immediately. "What do we need?"

Alek's normally soft brown eyes had a sharpness to them as he turned to look at Ren. "Something violent," he said, pushing a button on his remote without breaking eye contact. Ren was willing; he'd rather watch than talk. Though he had one thing left to say.

"Hey Alek? Promise me something?"

"I'm not going to say anything to Justin," Alek said, knowing exactly what Ren was going to ask. "But if you want to be fair to everyone involved, and I gotta say, the body count on this is getting high, then you should."

They stopped talking as a movie started, but Ren didn't think either of them watched it.

# 5
## GRAVITY TURN

At a quarter to seven, Ren had already been awake a long time, though he hadn't moved from his bed. He lay there, hands behind his head, watching the shadows in his room dissipate as shards of sunlight speared their way from his window, across his desk, along the carpet, until they finally hit the closed door on the other side. He'd eased himself onto his back, a position that had stopped being painful thanks to Justin's and Alek's dedication to keeping antibiotic on the long wound from the coffee table.

Worry had kept rest at bay for a long time last night. After Alek helped Ren with medicine before quietly and sadly drifting back into his room, the worry had turned into one of those nights filled with excruciating dreams, as though Ren's subconscious was waging war with his decisions. In one, he kissed Justin just as Celeste walked into the room. She burst into tears, and Justin shoved him back with a growl, as aggressive as the first day they'd met. In another, Ren watched Alek destroy his radio more than once, asking Ren if he was happy, until Ren finally woke up and stayed that way. The scenes remained, but at least now he could sort through them.

What shook him the hardest was everything that was happening right now had been his deepest desire. He'd desperately wanted Celeste to be his girlfriend. With almost the same fierceness, he'd wanted Alek and Denny to stay here in Chicago. Now he had both, but he couldn't enjoy either. And the guilt was crushing him under his quilt as though he'd been the one responsible for denying the internship application, as though he'd done something unethical to trick Celeste into liking him. And there was the other guilt, the darker one that made him involuntarily lock muscles all over his body, his jaw, his hands, his core, and shoulders. The feeling of self-ishness for not appreciating how he'd just gotten everything he'd ever wanted. How could he not be *grateful?*

Because Alek was miserable, for starters. Probably Denny too, but Ren hadn't spoken to her yet. The weird, knotted thing that was Justin and Celeste was too complicated to touch, so Ren was avoiding it. Now that the sun was up, he could settle into his best avoidance strategy — keeping as busy as possible. It wasn't hard; he had plenty to do. Homework, birthday preparations, which included a trip to the nearest Latino grocery store for plantains. Then, of course, today was laundry day. No time left to think at all, really.

In the quiet of the early morning, Ren kept mostly to his room, leaving it only to make coffee and use the bathroom. He wanted to let Alek sleep as long as he liked today. He was going to do every-thing to make his birthday as good as it could be, despite JPL.

While Ren waited for Alek to wake up, he wrapped the gift he'd asked his mother to send from the Dominican Republic, a native blend of spices Alek had tasted in a restaurant once and then contin-uously tried to replicate without success. He was constantly coming at Ren to try a new experimental combination, never quite getting it, asking Ren all the time whether he needed more or less of one thing or another. Ren knew what the spice was, but growing up eating something and knowing what was in it were very different things, so he asked his mom to mail the authentic mix almost four months ago, figuring it would take forever for something like that to make it through customs. It didn't help that, as usual, Eva overdelivered. Ren had asked for 200 grams. Eva had sent a two-kilogram brick. Before he sealed it with tape, Ren reserved a couple tablespoons to use when he cooked dinner later.

Somewhere between Ren's chemistry and biology assignments, he heard movement in the kitchen. Cupboards opening, mugs clinking together. Alek was up. Ren finished the last couple sentences of his chapter before heading to the table to keep Alek company. It was a relief to see Alek wearing his apron over his pajamas, steaming coffee mug on the counter by the sink, a bowl and wooden spoon in Alek's hands.

"Hey, there he is! Happy birthday," Ren greeted cheerily, making himself at home at the table, watching Alek carefully, trying to gauge his mood. Just because he was awake and baking didn't necessarily mean anything good.

"Thanks, man," Alek replied, smiling down at the contents of the bowl. Ok, so borderline on the despair. It looked like Alek was trying to pretend yesterday had never happened. Ren was more than prepared to run with that plan.

"So, where's Denny taking you?" Ren moved them forward with the question, knowing too long of a pause would be like disappointment quicksand. "Somewhere special?"

"The museum," Alek answered, placing the bowl on the counter so he could rummage through the cabinets for one of his large skillets, checking if the oven had preheated.

"Yeah? That'll be fun." Ren tried to sound excited, but really, Denny and Alek went to the museum at least once a week. They knew everyone who worked there and could probably give the tours themselves. He'd thought Denny would have stepped it up for a birthday, but then again, maybe it really was their favorite thing to do.

"Not that museum," Alek corrected Ren. "The Field Museum. Denny wants to introduce me to Sue." Ren must have looked confused when Alek resurfaced above the partial wall with the skillet. "It's the T-Rex skeleton," Alek explained. "They named her Sue.

Denny says there's a ton of stuff there. I don't think we can look at everything in one day, but we're going to try. You want to come with us?"

Ren couldn't think of anything he wanted to do more than go look at dinosaur bones with his friends. It had been one of the most magical days ever when Denny dragged them both to the Museum of Science and Industry for the first time. They spent all day there and then went out for gyros afterward. Life had been easier then.

"That sounds awesome, Alek," Ren told him, meaning it. "I wish I could."

Alek's face crumpled, so he hid his disappointment by being extremely dutiful in scraping batter from the bowl to the skillet.

"Maybe you and I can go later," Ren suggested hopefully. "Or maybe I can finish my stuff and meet you there for a couple hours this afternoon. It's not far away, right?" Ren went through his calendar and to-do list as he spoke.

"That would be great," Alek said with so much conviction that Ren felt compelled to make it happen. "Just like old times."

"I'll hurry," Ren promised just as Denny let herself in. Her inquisitive eyes took in everything in an instant, and she jumped into the conversation as if she'd been there all along.

"No, Alek needs to hurry," Denny chastised, pulling off her coat and making a shooing gesture at Alek at the same time. She shifted into a lecture. "Come on. You're not even dressed, and they open in twenty minutes! If we're going to have the best day ever, I'm going to need some cooperation here."

"Best day ever?" Alek echoed like he had no idea what Denny was talking about. Or maybe that such a thing wasn't going to be possible.

"Yes," Denny said, rather manically. "Starting from the dawn of time, there were about five trillion things that had to go exactly right to put you on this earth, and so the anniversary of all that success simply must be celebrated with the best day ever — damn the admittance committee *to hell*." Denny spoke faster and faster until she got to the end where her throat seemed to close up on her, Ren's first and only indication that she was suffering as much as Alek was. He made the mistake of watching her too hard and with too much sympathy, causing her to jerk her head down. Ren's instinct was to go to her, but he knew touching her right now was a bad choice. He looked instead at Alek, who was normally more receptive to comfort, but Alek was fixated on Denny, immobile and rigid. Ren saw a delicacy between them, something that had cracked along with Denny's voice, and Ren understood they were both going to force themselves into a good day for each other's sake.

"Pull out the skillet if the timer rings before I get back," Alek instructed Ren as he detached himself and disappeared around the corner to follow Denny's directions. Meanwhile, Denny angrily dragged her arm across her eyes, plopping down at the table across from Ren.

"You all right?" Ren bravely asked.

"Shut the hell up," Denny returned. "It's the best fucking day ever."

Ren took a long swallow of coffee, suddenly glad he'd excused himself from going with them. He wondered if they'd make it out of the apartment, much less up Lake Shore Drive. He also wondered how he was supposed to comfort Denny without getting snapped at. He silently judged her reaction to different phrases like "they have no idea what they're missing" and "I hate them for you" but decided in the end that the safest thing would be to just keep quiet. When Denny was ready, she'd start talking.

"You're all set for when we get back, right?" Denny finally initiated conversation again, the snarl gone from her tone, knowing Alek would return any minute.

"I will be," Ren promised. "Dominican comfort food for twelve."

"Twelve?" Denny checked. The last time she'd given him a head-count, the number had been lower.

"Uh, yeah," Ren confirmed, hoping he hadn't just gotten himself in trouble. "There's your five physicist friends, then the three of us, then Justin and North, and Sheridan and Celeste?"

"Ren, really," Denny warned him around a tight jaw and shoulders that were suddenly up around her ears. "I don't know if you've noticed, but I am in no mood for —"

"Sheridan is the girl Justin saved, and Celeste's her best friend," Ren explained quickly before Denny tightened to the point where she exploded. He thought he might have broken her anyway since she paused, her head tilting and her eyebrows scrunching together, her lips flattening into an incredulous line. He heard her take an exaggerated breath.

"You're joking," she said, all emotion gone from her voice. As though she still had to say that line even though she already knew he'd never joke about something like that. Her face went slack. "It's like your whole life is a movie."

"I just found out yesterday," Ren continued, not sure what his words were going to do to help but something shivery in his chest was forcing him to speak. "Justin and I were in this coffeeshop when Celeste came in with Sheridan and —"

"Stop talking," Denny cut him off, disgusted. "That's ridiculous." Ren obediently clicked his teeth shut. Denny had her head in her hands now, elbows on the table, a portrait of a long, frustrated night followed by too much reality distortion from Ren this morning. Ren reminded himself that he absolutely should not put a hand on her shoulder.

"So," Denny breathed, talking to the table. "You discovered you all knew each other yesterday, Justin probably talked Celeste into forgiving you, and now you're telling me that you purposefully asked for Justin and Celeste to be in the same room with you at the same time?" Denny lowered her shoulders incrementally as she thought about that. "At Alek's *birthday party*?"

"Well, when I invited them to come, I thought it would actually be a party," Ren defended himself and simultaneously put himself into new danger. "I can call and cancel if you want."

"No, no," Denny said, shaking her head as she lifted it, spreading her hands out across the table. "I think I want to be there for that. And here I thought *we* were being masochistic today." Ren heard her murmur the last bit under her breath. The timer rang before he'd decided if he were going to say anything about it, forcing him out of the conversation to pull Alek's skillet out of the oven, a beautiful, fragrant pastry bubbled up high in the middle of it.

"Was that the timer?" Alek brought himself back into the room just as Ren was coming out of the kitchen with the skillet.

"Ack!" Ren exclaimed, watching as the gorgeous puff popped open in a flush of steam and deflated in his hands before he'd had a chance to set the thing down on the table. He froze lest he cause more damage, eyes wide in guilt as he watched Alek's reaction. "Alek, I'm sorry! What did I do?"

Whatever he'd done to the pastry, it rewarded Ren with the first genuine smile from Alek. And he heard Denny snickering from the table too. Ren didn't trust himself to move, afraid he would break whatever was going on here.

"It's a German pancake, Ren," Alek explained, nodding toward the table, an invitation for Ren to put it down. "You didn't do anything; it's supposed to sink like that."

And even though Denny had been in a rush when she arrived, she didn't say a word as Alek doctored the pancake with berry compote and powdered sugar. She held her peace as he dished it up with eggs and sausage on the side. And she ate every bite on her plate with dedicated enjoyment while Ren watched them both. If he didn't know about yesterday, he could have pretended this was an ordinary Saturday. One like the dozens of others where the three of them sat at this table and ate breakfast together, or dinner, or worked on homework or electronics or a crowded combination of them all. He hoped the JPL thing wouldn't sour any of the future memories they would make together. He hoped their disappointment and his relief would level out sometime in the very near future.

When breakfast was over, Ren ushered his friends out the door with the assurance that he didn't mind cleaning up. He exchanged a meaningful look with Denny as she was leaving. She was going to give Alek the birthday he deserved if it killed her. And Ren already knew Alek would pretend to enjoy it if it killed him. And hopefully, at some point, they would both not need to try so hard to make it happy. But until that happened, Ren intended on doing what he could to help them.

He thought about his own dedication to other people's happiness as he washed the dishes. How he was preparing to settle himself between Justin and Celeste as a best friend and boyfriend and how it might take some getting used to, but with time and effort, he thought it would be the same as Denny and Alek getting used to not going to JPL. And someday it would feel as though it could not have turned out any other way. Ren had known something big was happening. And he was going to run with it, just like everyone else was doing around him. But first he was going to wash sheets.

Well, he was going to wash Alek's sheets at least. His still smelled like Justin, and even though Ren had firmly decided on moving forward for the sake of everyone including himself, he didn't see the harm in holding on to just that tiny thing for a few more days, or however long the scent lasted.

Ren stripped Alek's bed and threw all the laundry together into one of the big mesh bags they used for transport. Then he indulged in kicking the floppy bundle all the way down the stairs instead of carrying it, his inner ten-year-old enjoying the sight of the amoebic mass flipping over itself through three entire stories.

He regained his maturity on the first floor, scooping up the bag and carrying it properly into the laundry room, where he sighed at the sight out of the windows. It wasn't snowing, but it was yet another gray and dreary January day. Windy, of course. Probably the bitter kind of cold that would partially freeze his blood while he walked, making his legs feel weird and tingly for hours after he got back. The closest grocery store that had what he needed was still almost six miles away, and the more Ren thought about that, the more convinced he became that he had to find a ride somehow for the sake of time and potential hypothermia. Alek's car was gone already, six miles in a different direction. Celeste had a car, but Ren thought it would be too much to ask her to come to a party almost nine hours early so she could drive her stranded boyfriend to the grocery store. He'd have to use a service even though he wasn't keen on the idea of strangers picking him up. But it would be warmer, and he wouldn't have to carry everything so far. And it might get him home early enough that he could meet up with Alek and Denny at the museum.

Tucking the laundry detergent under his arm, Ren dashed back up the stairs to get his wallet and phone. He'd already written the list of what he'd need, but he went through it again in his head as he walked down the hall from the stairwell. Plantains, but he needed bananas too, chicken, they already had the rice. He'd have to double check the flour and sugar since it was normally Alek who kept tabs on pantry staples.

Distracted, he let himself in to the apartment, nodding as he ticked off each ingredient, murmuring them out loud as he stepped through the door, where he stopped dead and dropped the detergent, shocked to find someone in his apartment.

"It's just me!" The movement and voice came together into an image of a dark-haired boy in black jeans and a maroon sweatshirt, hands extended in peaceable fashion, and eyes that were too large on his face.

"Justin, you scared me to death!" Ren squawked, his heart rate downshifting.

"You left the door unlocked," Justin said, as if that were an explanation. "I didn't mean to scare you." As he talked, Justin walked toward Ren, glancing at the detergent on the floor, but Ren darted too quickly and picked it up before Justin could.

"It's ok, right?" Justin pressed, and Ren saw him as he must have looked when he realized he'd have to move again, that whatever foster family he was staying with had made the decision they couldn't handle him anymore and wanted him gone. He stood uncertainly, awkwardly between the front door and the table, wondering if he'd made some kind of unfixable mistake. Ren took another breath, knowing Justin was misinterpreting Ren's surprise, because being unwanted was Justin's default setting.

"Of course, it's ok," Ren told him, rearranging his features so he could smile, taking the final steps into his apartment and closing the door behind him, needing to reassure Justin that this was one place he would always be accepted. "You're always welcome, Justin."

His words made Justin smile, a rare and beautiful thing. Ren forced himself to swallow, then move, trying to be natural in his own environment. *Justin is welcome here. So am I. And we can coexist here together; we've done it before.*

"So, where's North?" Ren asked Justin, just so they could talk, so they wouldn't be standing there staring at each other. Ren made his way to the hall closet to replace the detergent, grabbing a couple dryer sheets while he was there so he could take them down with him later. Natural. Justin followed him to answer the question.

"He's working today," Justin said, sounding suspiciously guilty. "There's a pile of stuff that needs to get done since he missed so many hours last week." Oh, that's where the guilt came from. Justin was still feeling bad he'd forced so many people to rearrange their lives for him. The emotion didn't stop as Justin made eye contact with Ren, only deepened. "You probably have a ton to catch up on too, don't you?"

Ren shrugged it off. "No more than usual, but that's tomorrow's schedule," he dismissed lightly. "Today my biggest worry is getting to Mi Mexico grocery store on 59th and Rockwell."

The response puzzled Justin. Ren could see him process both the name and the address, but it did the trick of calling Justin's attention away from his unwarranted guilt. "You know anyone with a car?" Ren asked him.

"Yeah," Justin responded, straightening, coming back into himself. "I've got North's. Do you — I can drive you, if you want."

"That would be great, if you have time," Ren acknowledged, relieved and happy. This was a million times better than a taxi. Justin shrugged.

"That's why I came over," Justin said. "To see if you needed any help." For some reason, Ren didn't think Justin was telling the whole truth here. Not that he was lying, just that he was holding something back. Ren suspected it had something to do with the prospect of staying alone in North's apartment all day while he was at work, how that would be too new, lonely, and strange. Ren knew he'd feel like that if he were in Justin's position. He'd want any excuse to not stay home alone too. And now neither of them had to be alone, and Ren could spend the entire day with Justin. Perfect. Sort of.

"I need all the help I can get," Ren told him gratefully. "This birthday really needs to go well, so I'm glad you're here."

"Huh?" Justin asked, looking confused again, but no longer self-conscious or worried. Ren slipped his phone, wallet, and list into his pockets before grabbing both their coats.

"I'll tell you on the way," he promised.

As Justin drove, Ren filled him in on what happened last night, starting with the internship position itself and how much work his friends had put into their application. He went through it all, the Metallica, the missing radio, how both Alek and Denny were forcing themselves to keep going like it hadn't affected them. How he felt like such a jerk for being relieved they wouldn't be moving away.

Ren hadn't really meant to put in that last part. His feelings about the internship weren't important, but Justin was so quietly attentive through the whole thing that it seemed so safe to tell him. And it made Ren feel better to finally confess, sitting there in the passenger seat of the Altima. Justin drove North's car with casual ease, eyes on the road, but Ren still knew he held Justin's complete attention. He continued to listen as they walked through the icy parking lot of the store, silently grabbing a cart for Ren.

"How awful is that?" Ren burst out at the end. "I shouldn't be happy about this when they're so upset."

"That's not it," Justin told him, looking around the unfamiliar aisles of the store. "You aren't happy because they're disappointed; you just wanted to stay together. But I see your point on making the party extra special. What's the plan?"

"I'm making dinner," Ren started, then realized how completely boring that sounded. "It's just this thing my mom made all the time, but it's one of Alek's favorites, and I don't make it very often. Then we somehow have to convince Alek and Denny to go through with their radio test. They were so excited and went to all that trouble to get their ham radio licenses. But we'll have to look around for the radio. I can't find it, and I'm worried Alek took it apart yesterday. Do you think you could put it back together if he did?"

"I," Justin paused, overwhelmed.

"Alek said you put the dial in," Ren reminded him.

"Sure, the dial. They did all the hard, technical stuff," Justin protested. Ren was ready to let it go; they didn't even know if the radio were in pieces yet, and he didn't want to push Justin too hard. He added canned pineapple and Sprite to their cart, moving on to the produce when Justin seemed to make up his mind about something.

"I'll try," Justin said, with such determination in his voice that Ren melted. The way Justin spoke reminded Ren that having friends was a relatively new thing for him; he wasn't sure how it worked, and he wasn't used to any of this.

"That's more than enough," Ren emphasized, wanting him to understand that it was the attempt, the thought, that would be appreciated even if he didn't succeed.

The rest of their shopping adventure was slightly less intense, and extremely enjoyable for Ren. He showed Justin the difference between bananas and plantains as he put both into the cart. They debated how many chickens it would take to feed twelve people — Ren's generous "everyone needs to have enough to eat" combating Justin's more conservative "six chickens is way too many. When was the last time you ate an entire half a chicken?" They settled on three, though Ren was certain that Alek could eat half a chicken and Justin was certain they still had one too many.

They paused in the baking aisle when a tiny woman stopped Ren, one look at him sufficient for her to assume correctly that he was both tall enough for what she needed and could speak her language well enough for her to ask. She needed help reaching a bottle of almond extract high on a top shelf. Her Spanish was languid and sweet, as rich as chocolate to Ren, and he smiled as he handed her the extract with a fond, "*Aquí tienes, abuelita,*" knowing that even though she wasn't *his* grandmother, she wouldn't really mind if he called her that.

She responded in kind, calling him her son, "*Gracias, mijo.*" She patted his arm before going on her way, and Ren watched her for a second before returning his attention to birthday candles. Though he noticed Justin staring at him oddly.

"What?" he asked, feeling heat rise in his face for no other reason than Justin was looking at him. He quickly turned toward the candles, deciding on whether he wanted the regular kind or the ones that wouldn't go out no matter how hard Alek blew on them.

"Nothing," Justin said, unexpected warmth in his tone. "It's just cool, watching you do stuff like that. I like hearing you speak your own language."

Ren made a strange huffing sound. It was weird to be admired for something so simple, especially by Justin.

"Did you know her?" Justin wanted to know, almost as if he could tell how embarrassed Ren felt.

"No," Ren said dismissively, reaching for a pack of normal candles. *Be normal.* He began pulling the cart away.

"Oh," Justin sounded surprised. "It looked like you did."

"It's a Latino thing. You could walk up to anyone in this store and call them grandma, or sister, or cousin, and they'd probably just go with it." Ren hadn't meant the statement to have the impact it did, but Justin stopped walking, grabbing on to the cart as if he needed something to steady him. Ren realized what he'd said, what it meant for Justin who had grown up without anything even close to a family.

"You too," Ren reminded him, which made Justin turn toward him, looking wounded and hesitantly hopeful. "You're part of our family now, like it or not."

Justin gave a little bark of a laugh that had too much of a different emotion in it. And even though Ren knew he shouldn't, he reached out to put a hand on Justin's arm anyway, making sure Justin understood that Ren meant what he said. Justin stared at him, eyes unquestionably violet, and huge, surprisingly innocent even after all Justin had been through.

"Ren?" Justin began, though Ren had nothing to communicate in words here. Having a hand on Justin spread warmth all down that side of his body, and he fought with himself on taking another step closer. *Only friends*, Ren told himself, removing his hand with dedicated effort. *If I want him to stay in my life, we have to keep it at friends. Don't make it weird.*

"Come on," Ren invited, pushing the cart toward the frozen aisle. "Let's see what kind of sherbet this place has so we can make punch."

By the time they'd gathered everything on Ren's list and were placing it on the belt at the cashier, Justin was shaking his head and making little frustrated noises to the point where Ren had to look up from double checking that he'd remembered everything to see what was going on.

"What's up, Justin?" he asked, slightly concerned.

"Nothing," Justin denied, but then decided he was going to say what he was thinking anyway. "How the hell were you going to get all this back to the apartment?"

"Carry it?" Ren answered, but his voice tapered off as Justin gestured to all the groceries, looking at him with one eyebrow raised as though he were patiently waiting for Ren to realize there was no way one person could carry three whole chickens, five liters of soda, a gallon of sherbet, and all the other little pieces of birthday that lay scattered among the larger items.

"Six miles in the snow?" Justin forced the insanity of his plan onto him.

"I was going to get an Uber," Ren defended himself, not particularly sure he was pronouncing Uber correctly.

"Next time just call me," Justin instructed, as if that were the most obvious thing in the world. As if Ren had ever called him and actually got him to answer. But he wasn't going to point that out while Justin already looked insulted about it.

"I will," Ren promised, which seemed to satisfy Justin.

Together, Justin and Ren managed to get all the shopping bags through the snow, into the elevator, and up to the apartment in one trip. Though Justin muttered the entire time about how Ren was incapable of asking for help, and what was up with that anyway? Ren pretended he didn't hear him. If he'd really needed help, he would have asked for it. But the "need" threshold was so high. He was used to just figuring things out on his own.

They separated only for a few minutes so Ren could run down to the laundry room to switch the sheets over to the dryer. When he came back, he showed Justin some of the pictures Alek and Denny were sending from the museum. It reminded Ren that he hadn't taken a photo yet of Justin, a problem he remedied on the spot by snapping about five of Justin emptying out the contents of the grocery bags onto the table.

"What are you doing?" Justin demanded, blinking at him.

"Pictures, remember?" Ren said, grabbing one more now that Justin was looking at him. He checked the phone, curious to see whether Justin's peculiar eye color would show up properly in photos. Disappointingly, it seemed not to. "My family wants me to send more pictures."

Justin shook his head, still unconvinced anyone would want to see a picture of him. Ren just smiled, wishing he could tell him how important he was, what he meant to Ren. But that was taking things too far, and Ren did not want to ruin the good vibe they had going. So he went to work. There were chickens and sweet potatoes to roast, a cake to bake, and a radio to find.

Through all the prep, Justin remained an arm's length away. Sometimes at the table, watching Ren do one-person jobs. Other times he fetched and carried, holding tape for streamers, blowing up balloons. They put on some music, ingredients disappearing from the table as Ren transformed them into their final forms. They finally found the radio, stuffed in a box underneath Alek's bed, thankfully still in one piece. Ren set it up as the centerpiece on the table, on top of a galaxy-themed tablecloth.

They talked as they worked. About Alek, who Justin didn't know much about but wanted to know more. About music, which Justin also didn't seem to have an opinion on. The boy was like a blank page, ready to accept Ren's commentary on just about everything. They texted pictures back and forth with Denny, and Ren noticed their expressions seemed less strained as the day went on. They looked to be truly enjoying themselves, though Ren had to be careful not to let Justin see some of the things Denny texted once she found out Ren was alone in the apartment with Justin.

Breaks happened as both Ren and Justin had to pause to accept phone calls. Kelly contacted Justin, giving him an update on how things were going with his financial paperwork. Justin pulled Ren into the conversation for a few minutes to discuss Justin's health and when it might be appropriate to have a medical exam performed. Ren had no idea what Justin's blood-work had to do with finance, but he said it would probably be best to schedule this after Justin was finished taking prescribed medication. That conversation ended with Kelly promising to take Justin to lunch sometime soon, and Ren speculating that if North hadn't beat her to it, Kelly would have adopted Justin herself.

Ren's call came from Dr. Delacroix, who informed him that she had spoken with Dr. Taneja, and they were both going to talk to the provost about letting Ren shadow at the ER for credit if that was something he wanted to do.

"Yes!" Justin hissed at him, though Ren remained undecided. He stood in the kitchen in the middle of shredding three chicken carcasses. Could he really handle the pressure of the ER? Ren glanced at Justin, who nodded encouragingly to him. "Do it," he mouthed.

"Lorenzo?" Dr. Delacroix checked to make sure he was still there.

"Ok," Ren burst out, wondering if this was something he could back out of once he'd started. Somehow, he didn't think so. Justin flashed him that knee-buckling smile as he agreed, which meant Ren only barely heard the rest of what Dr. Delacroix said. Something about a schedule. He'd have to confirm by email later.

"How come everyone thinks I can do this except me?" Ren wondered out loud, surprised he sounded breathless.

"I don't know," Justin mused as he poured Ren the cup of coffee Ren had begged him to make. The good, rich black stuff that tasted like lightning and home and something else Ren hadn't bothered placing yet. "Because when you found me half-dead, you seemed pretty damn confident about what you could do and you saved my life, so it doesn't really make sense, does it?"

Ren braced himself on the counter, overcome by Justin's encouragement. He wished they could still touch each other the way they once had, so easily, so often. Right now, all he wanted to do was lean his head against Justin's chest. He was standing close enough to do it. He was right there.

"Ren?" Justin said his name questioningly. He did it a lot, that unasked question that started and ended with Ren's name. It probably meant something different every time he did it, but lately it sounded too much like an invitation, and Ren needed to move away quickly before he did something he would regret.

"I'll be right back," Ren excused himself, knowing that even if Justin thought he was acting weird, it was nothing compared to how he could embarrass himself if he didn't take a few minutes out of this room. "I'm going to check the mail. Then we'll do the cake, ok?"

"Sure," Justin said, backing off, and Ren felt something slip between them. He awkwardly escaped to the hallway, bringing his phone with him so he could ask Alek to tell Denny that Ren was dating Celeste now so she could knock it off with all the images she was putting into Ren's head of how he and Justin could be spending their time alone together right now. Then he rubbed his hands over his face to scrub his mind of those exact, tempting images. He even leaned against the cold of the metal mailboxes for a moment, gaining his composure for both returning to Justin and joining Dr. Delacroix in the ER. What *had* happened to her last student? He wondered if she'd even tell him if he asked.

He grabbed the contents of the slot without looking at it, jogging back up the stairs. Justin looked up from where he was cleaning the counter of chicken juices but didn't say anything as Ren joined him. Ren smiled at him before thumbing quickly through the mail. There was never a lot. On Saturdays, a huge clump of coupons for the local restaurants and things showed up without fail, and for a second, Ren thought that was all. But no, there was one envelope in the chaos of loose-leaf flyers.

"Oh my God," Ren whispered in astonishment, recognizing the NASA logo in the top left corner. It was addressed to Alek, his real, full name typed formally in the exact center. It looked so strange to see Alek's true name, apostrophes and all.

"Ren?" Justin noticed that Ren stood shocked in the entryway, and Ren tightened his grip on the coupons so he wouldn't drop something else in front of Justin today. "What is it?"

"It's from JPL," Ren tried to raise his voice enough to be heard, but it was hard to say anything while his insides were twisting up so violently inside him. "A letter for Alek."

"An acceptance letter?" Justin checked, hurrying over to inspect the envelope himself. "Do you think Denny got one too?"

"Probably. It was a team application," Ren spoke words he didn't even hear himself say. "You're late," he scolded the unobtrusive, plain white envelope, his voice infuriatingly choked up. "You caused so much trouble."

"Should we open it?" Justin speculated, but Ren didn't need to. The unsuccessful candidates had been notified via a postscript at the bottom of a website, unworthy of the cost of postage. Ren knew what this piece of paper said. *Congratulations. You're a wizard. We're bringing you into our program and your boring roommate can't come.*

"No," Ren denied quietly, leaning the envelope against the radio on the table. "I'm not opening someone else's birthday present."

"Ren, you ok?"

"Of course, I'm ok," Ren said fiercely, but he needed to make himself believe it. They were going to be so happy. They were going to be over the moon, almost literally. Ren had to be happy along with them. Justin placed a hand on Ren's shoulder, too gently. "I'm such a jerk."

Justin pulled Ren closer, and Ren let him do it. "That's not true," Justin told him, and Ren tried to nod, to accept that, but was finding it difficult. "You're allowed to be happy for them and sad for yourself at the same time." The sophistication of this answer surprised Ren, momentarily distracting him from focusing on his upcoming separation. It made him realize that Justin was holding him; Ren was folded up against him. It was so warm inside his arms. Ren closed his eyes and let himself enjoy it for just a few seconds. He let himself pretend. But he couldn't stay here. The truth was too heavy and dominating.

Reluctantly, so very reluctantly, Ren pushed backward, forcing himself to smile at Justin. "Thanks," he said gratefully. *Thanks for that memory, that heat, that moment.* "Let's make a cake, yeah?"

Ren decided to wait to tell Alek about the letter. He seemed to be genuinely enjoying himself at the museum now, and Ren knew if he said anything about it, they would come rushing home. And he didn't want that yet. He wanted to stay with Justin a little longer in this strange bubble, before he knew for certain what was going to happen. Before everything shifted again. He complimented Justin again on the coffee. They made a huge mess with Alek's electric mixer, and Justin teased Ren about the metric system and how it wasn't on any of Alek's measuring cups.

As far as Ren was concerned, the afternoon could have lasted for the rest of time. Then he'd never know if he were going to be a disappointment to Dr. Delacroix. He'd never know what it felt like to help Alek pack his things to leave. It would be just Justin, here with him, skeptically dumping an entire can of crushed pineapple into the cake batter, asking him questions about dinner, his family, his country.

But just as with the court case, time didn't care about Ren's opinion of how fast it should move. All too soon, Justin was pulling on his coat because it was time to pick up North. The text came from Alek that they were on their way home. In less than an hour, this apartment would be filled with a dozen people.

And in less than a month, Ren would be the only one here.

# 6

# INTERSTELLAR COMMUNICATION

Ren would forever classify that night as the last evening his life was as perfect as he could have hoped for. The dark still pressed against the windows, a draft of the future howling on the balcony, but at the beginning of the evening, the music and light inside the apartment overpowered it. Dinner spread over the counters, piles of napkins, plates, and cutlery next to pans of food. Alek's largest stock pot held all the Sprite with fizzy dollops of sherbet floating inside.

At the last second, Ren removed the NASA letter from the table. He'd decided somewhere after Justin left and before anyone else came that Alek should read it in private. Ren tucked it underneath the wrapped spice blend on his desk to wait until he'd decided about when the best time would be to tell Alek. Then he went to answer the door.

Two of the physicists arrived first, and even though Ren asked and received their names, he almost instantly forgot them again. These two could have been new to the apartment, or they could have been over many times. Either way, they stood awkwardly in the entryway until Ren ushered them inside with plain, simple instructions on where to leave their coats and wet shoes, inviting them to help themselves to punch. They each ladled up a cupful, and then they all stared at each other in strained, uncomfortable silence.

Fortunately, Alek and Denny's arrival less than two minutes later bridged the communication gap. They burst through the door in a gust of banter, and if it struck them in any way to see the radio pulled out from under the bed and returned to its position of glory in the middle of the table, they pushed right past it, talking nonstop about the museum and how Ren really needed to join them the next time they went, and "hey, how's it going, good to see you" at the guests. Alek did pause long enough to sniff at the air, his face breaking into joy as he recognized the scent of what Ren had cooked. He sped toward the kitchen while Denny joined their friends at the punch, and they all began talking unique physics jargon that was more a feeling to Ren than speech. It hummed around his ears like electricity, just the way he liked. He let himself relax, making sure to savor how it sounded and felt to have everyone here like this. He let it sink in until it started to hurt, that slight tearing deep inside him as he remembered these times were going to be over soon.

Ren was about to join Alek in the kitchen to pull him privately into his room where they could talk about the letter, but another knock on the door forced him to postpone. He left the scientists to do what they did best while he fulfilled his role as host and opened the door to the next guest. No, guests, not astrophysicists this time, but they still rendered Ren practically speechless.

"Oh, wow," Ren exclaimed involuntarily right before all the English words he knew went right out of his head, taking in the scene and forgetting about parties and space stations, letters and spices. Celeste clasped her hands demurely, bowing her head as Ren pulled it together enough to realize he was rudely standing in the doorway, staring at her.

But how could he not? Her hair plaited back from her temples in what must have been the complicated braid she'd spoken of before, the one she'd worn for their failed date. The dress could have been the same one she'd intended for last week too, a pale blue, simple thing that gained elegance just by being on her person. It buttoned down the front and flared out at her knees, and she wore navy leggings under it that matched her boots. Dangly shooting star earrings hovered at her jawline, swinging with her every movement, and the moment she stepped past the doorway, she would break the record on the amount of makeup that had ever been in the room at once even though she wasn't wearing all that much.

Celeste was so captivating that Ren barely registered Sheridan standing next to her, even though it was no surprise they'd arrived together, and Sheridan was also a lovely girl. Her outfit was a different kind of simple, a pink-ish turtleneck and dark blue jeans, the kind with beaded patterns on the back pockets. She'd done her makeup with slightly heightened dramatics. Ren thought there might be something glittery on her cheekbones.

"Ren, who is it? Are you going to let them in, or are you waiting for a password or something?" Denny yelled from somewhere behind him, voice thick with sarcastic goading, breaking him into motion.

"Right, come in," he managed, shepherding them inside. He noticed Sheridan scanning the room hopefully, searching for Justin, practically going up on tiptoe as if that would help. "I'm glad you made it."

"You sure?" Celeste asked, removing her famous white coat. Ren took it from her while he decided what his face should look like in response to her question. "You looked so surprised to see us I thought maybe you'd changed your mind about your invitation."

Satisfied Justin wasn't hiding under the dining room table, Sheridan mentally returned to Celeste's side, watching the exchange with renewed interest. Ren wondered if Celeste had told her everything about him yet. From the way she stared, critically sizing him up as he reached for her coat, he thought so. He felt as if he were being graded.

"I don't normally open my door to this much beauty," Ren

explained, thinking he may have gotten an upper hand somehow as his comment caused Celeste's eyes to seek out the carpet again, smiling.

"Hey!" Denny squawked indignantly behind him, but he didn't give her the satisfaction of looking at her. He kept his eyes on Celeste, waiting for the moment when she'd lift her head again.

"Oh, don't pretend to be insulted," Ren called carelessly over his shoulder to Denny, who frequently, passionately, and disgustedly ranted about girls at the university who spent more time in front of mirrors than on their homework. She felt they were a waste of resources, and if Ren had ever dared to suggest that Denny was beautiful, she would have groaned, laughed, or punched Ren in the arm. Probably all those reactions, actually, in that order. However, he thought he'd better smooth over what he'd said in case he had hurt her feelings somehow. "I don't open the door for you; you let yourself in."

A possessive arm twined around Ren's as a tiny body leaned against his side. Denny had come over to protect him while she determined what was going on. Sheridan wasn't the only one gauging character references here. Denny was on high alert, studying every detail about the new girls with the precision of Sherlock Holmes. Ren felt it best not to move. He wanted to see how Celeste and Denny would mesh. He'd never be comfortable if they didn't get along, but he hoped Denny wouldn't be rude on purpose. She'd already had a long day forcing herself to be at her best for Alek, which might sharpen her tongue and temperament more than was fair for anyone.

"Denny," Ren invoked her name as an introduction and a plea. "I'd like you to meet Celeste and her best friend, Sheridan."

Celeste smiled, nodding her head like a princess as she was introduced, sophisticated and just the sort of charming that usually made Denny pretend to gag. Sheridan also smiled, though less artistically. Denny pressed tighter into his side, staring critically at the taller girls.

"Huh," Denny exhaled, unblinking. "So, you really do exist after all."

"Pardon?" Celeste began, her beautiful features tugging together into confusion. Ren used his proximity to Denny to give her a slight warning jab with his elbow. He felt Denny tense, but not for very long.

"The way Ren described you, I figured you were imaginary." Now Denny took a step away from Ren so she could turn her face up toward him. He looked down to meet her eyes, half afraid until he saw them.

A bit of tension released inside Ren, and he used the sudden relief to pull Denny tight against him again. *Thank you*, he said with the squeeze.

"Let me take those," Denny offered, freeing Ren of both the girls' coats to add them to the growing pile by the balcony door. The guest count for tonight meant they needed every chair, including the desk chairs in their rooms and the camp chair that normally held the winter gear. Plus, the heap of warm things by the balcony helped block the draft. "Go say happy birthday to Alek and get some food. Ren made it."

Sheridan and Celeste were holding hands now, unsure in the new environment, watching Denny shuffle away with the coats. Ren felt as though he suddenly had permission to get close to them. As he took a step, Celeste turned toward him, looking bewildered but not angry.

"Denny?" she repeated the name, not unkindly. Ren nodded, his gaze following Denny around the coffee table as she went to rejoin Alek. She seemed to need physical comfort today as she stepped right into Alek's personal space. Without even looking, Alek put an arm lightly around her shoulders.

"She's like my sister," Ren explained, hoping this information would let Celeste know everything she needed to about their relationship and why Denny acted the way she did. "But she's Alek's girlfriend."

"Ah," Celeste answered with the sound, letting Ren know she did understand. At least, he thought that's what it meant.

"Did you want some food?" Ren offered just for something to do besides stand here at the door.

"It does smell amazing," Celeste granted, crystalline eyes twinkling. Sheridan nodded.

"Come on," Ren invited, taking the hand Sheridan wasn't holding. He thought the girls would separate, but it seemed Sheridan gripped tighter as they began moving toward the kitchen. He wanted her to let go; he could barely handle Celeste right now, but how was he supposed to ask for that? The only person she knew in this room was Celeste, and honestly, Celeste was in a new space too. New apartment, new people, new boyfriend. It was all strange. It looked like Ren would have to take care of them both for the foreseeable future and do his best not to make it awkward. Something sarcastic inside him wished him good luck.

Even though Alek was the guest of honor at this party, he'd automatically taken up the serving station in the kitchen. The scientists had already been supplied with food and were seated at the table when Ren brought Celeste and Sheridan to the kitchen doorway. Behind him, there was another knock on the door, but Denny went to answer it this time, leaving Ren free to see what Alek would think about meeting Celeste in real life instead of listening to Ren talk about her.

"Ladies, meet Alek," Ren declared, making sure to say Alek's name louder than necessary to draw his attention. "Engineer, astrophysicist, winner of the best roommate award two years running, and officially the oldest resident of the apartment."

"Hey," Alek said as he turned, the exclamation phasing from good-natured welcome to confusion as he saw Ren attached to two girls. Ren told Alek their names, making sure Alek could tell which was which. Ever gracious, Alek set down his serving spoon momentarily to shake hands, smiling warmly at everyone, all the melancholy from yesterday either dissolved or pushed down too far to notice. He expressed how nice it was to finally meet Celeste, and he took Sheridan's hand in both of his, encasing her in some kind of wordless exchange that seemed to make sense to them. It eased Sheridan enough that she didn't feel it necessary to latch onto Celeste the moment Alek let her go. Ren thought he'd like to ask about that later, though it was likely some kind of empathy trick only Alek could do.

Together, Ren and Alek filled plates and set the girls up at the table, exchanging pleasantries the entire way. Comments on the food, gentle questions about how everyone in the apartment fit with each other. Meanwhile, Denny escorted the next group of scientists, now free of coats and hats, toward the kitchen. Ren hoped there would be enough for everyone. He knew he shouldn't have let Justin talk him out of that extra chicken.

The front of the apartment was growing crowded now, brightly lit, and full of people, music, and scent. It was starting to look and feel like a party. Almost. Ren still felt unnaturally out of place and unbalanced. He didn't know the scientists. He barely knew Celeste, and still wasn't sure how he should act around her. Sheridan just made him uncomfortable. And underneath was the pressing ache of how it was all ending, changing in a way he hadn't wanted and wasn't ready for. That knowledge forced Ren to focus on all the little details. Denny's laughter. Alek humming along to the music. Ren stretched his consciousness as wide as possible to fill himself with these memories, collecting them like a harvest to last for an indefinite social winter. He moved about the room with his phone, snapping pictures the same way he'd seen children dart for a coin dropped on the street.

He caught one of Alek standing at the table, one large hand resting gently on his custom-built radio, a soft, pensive look on his face, and he decided he shouldn't keep the letter a secret anymore. Before going to Alek, Ren tucked his phone into his back pocket and dipped his head between Celeste and Sheridan, knowing he should probably be sitting next to them but not able to bring himself to be still yet. He softly placed his hand on Celeste's shoulder, leaning close so she would hear him over the music and physics chatter.

"Doing all right here?" he asked, just like he always did when he checked on her at the donation center. Celeste delicately set down her fork to reach up and place her cool hand over his, turning so she could see him.

"It's wonderful," she acknowledged. "I had no idea you were such a good cook."

"Don't be too impressed," he warned, though part of him was pleased she was enjoying it. "I'm a one-dish wonder. Alek usually does all the cooking around here, but seeing as it's his birthday, I gave him the night off."

"How is he doing, by the way?" Celeste elegantly shifted topics, keeping her hand on his, splitting his attention between her words and the smooth sensation of her fingers. "It seems you were able to cheer him up."

"He's putting up a good front," Ren revealed. "Denny too. I was actually going to steal him away for a few minutes to talk to him about it, but I didn't want you to think I was abandoning you."

"No, of course not," Celeste accepted his plan. "Please do take care of him. We're all right, aren't we?" She leaned in closer towards Sheridan, including her in the conversation.

"Sure," Sheridan responded, not as energetically as Celeste. Her lower lip twisted slightly after she said it, her teeth pinning it that way as she looked at the table. Ren understood the expression and took pity on her.

"Justin *is* coming," he answered the question Sheridan obviously wanted to ask but didn't want to be rude about. "He was here earlier to help with the party prep, but he had to go pick up North from work. I'm not sure how long that's supposed to take, but he's coming."

Sheridan's sky-blue eyes lifted to Ren, full of a sudden acceptance and gratitude. Ren tried not to hate her.

"North?" Celeste questioned, thankfully breaking Ren away and reminding him that up until quite recently, Justin was the only person who called him that.

"Elias?" Ren threw out his real name. "Tall guy with the scar on his chin?" And a perfect robotic arm. But Ren didn't have to go that far; he could see Celeste knew who he was talking about now.

"Oh, Mr. Kaplan," she breathed, nodding as she remembered. "That's right. He was — what was he?"

"Justin's case worker," Sheridan supplied readily, proving how well-versed she was about Justin's life and acquaintances. Ren couldn't help himself.

"They're family now," he revealed, dedicatedly not looking at Sheridan as he said it. If he was going to one-up her in this weird game of "who knows more about Justin," he'd better keep his gaze away to not appear too arrogant. Especially since she could probably best him in two sentences. "The adoption paperwork went through earlier this week."

Sheridan's whole face opened in surprise. She blinked it away, and Ren felt bad for some reason. He decided he'd better leave before he did something damaging.

"You can congratulate them when they get here," Ren offered, squeezing Celeste's shoulder to let her know he was leaving. At the last second, he quickly kissed her cheek, causing her to raise her shoulder and lean her head toward him. "I'll be back as soon as I check on Alek."

Celeste's hand slipped away from his, letting him go, as patient as she had promised she would be. He'd barely stood straight before Sheridan leaned in for some private conversation. Ren wondered what she had to say but wanted to talk to Alek more than he wanted to find out.

Luckily for Ren, Denny was deeply engrossed in an explanation to her science friends about the future of trans-atmospheric remote-controlled devices, so it was easy to pull Alek away without her noticing. With Alek, all he needed to do was pat him on the arm and jerk his head toward his bedroom. They both slipped to the back without anyone even looking at them.

"What's up, Ren?" Alek asked as Ren closed his bedroom door, shutting out the noise in the other room. "Oh, hey, congrats about Celeste by the way. You were *not* kidding; she is gorgeous." The air was still here, noticeably cooler. Alek stood near the door, hovering as though he were being pulled. Ren knew they shouldn't stay here long, but it was nice to be alone with Alek for a moment, the way it had been at the beginning. Before Celeste. Before even Denny. "But, uh, where's Justin?"

"Coming," Ren said, though he wondered if that were true. Where were they? He'd call if he thought Justin would answer. What if something happened on the way here? Or worse, what if Ren had done something today that made Justin decide he didn't want to come? But one thing at a time. Right now, it was just Alek. "I just wanted to give you your birthday gift before you do your radio test."

"Dude, you already cooked my favorite thing." His words may have been protesting, but Alek looked flattered and pleased that Ren had something for him.

"Yeah, well," Ren snatched the wrapped package and letter from his desk. "I thought you could use this." He handed over the spices first while concealing the letter behind his back. "I asked my mom to send it."

Alek accepted the package with almost reverent care, particularly after Ren mentioned where it had come from. He seemed to recognize the feel, the weight, and shape of it. "You picked it up for me last weekend," Ren affirmed. "It just made it in time."

"What?" Alek began the question but didn't finish as he gently folded back the wrappings. "Is this what I think it is?" He held up the tightly packaged, dense, dark red brick.

"I took some for dinner," Ren admitted, but Alek obviously didn't care.

"*That's* why it tastes like that!" he exclaimed, holding the spice blend up to his face to see if he could smell it through the plastic. "Here I thought you'd been holding out on me."

"Now you can make it whenever you want. That block should last you, oh, I don't know, the rest of your life probably. Mom went a little overboard."

"This is awesome. Thanks so much."

Ren smiled, content that his gift had been well received. But now it was time for the other one. The one he wasn't so sure about. "That's not all," Ren said, not meaning to have his voice come out so quiet.

"Looks like your mom isn't the only one going overboard," Alek said, his tone heavily implying that Ren had gone too far. "This is too much, Ren. Dinner, the party, that *cake* I saw in the fridge." Alek stood with the spice block in both hands, as though he wouldn't accept anything more, so Ren took it back so it could be swapped out with the letter.

"No, I think it's just what you deserve." Ren managed to sound like he meant it. Because he did. Alek did deserve that internship. He deserved to go to JPL and live out his dreams. Ren had already done it, left his island, left his family, the people who loved and missed him, to fulfill his dream of attending a US college and med program. He knew what opening a letter like this felt like. How nerves and hope could burst and then melt into almost overjoyed, excited relief. Now he'd get to know about the other side. What his family and friends at home had felt while watching him read.

"Ren," Alek whispered, rubbing his thumb against the NASA logo on the envelope. He sounded confused and apprehensive.

"It just came today," Ren told him. "I don't know what it says, so I thought you could open it in private. If you want, I can —"

"Stay here," Alek commanded. Alek's hands slid around the edges of the envelope, and it looked so tiny in his grasp. With the delicacy that came from years of turning miniature screwdrivers, Alek tore neatly into the envelope, slipping the pages from it in the worst slow motion. Ren found himself leaning forward as if that would either speed things up or let him see well enough to read. He swallowed as he watched Alek's eyes scan the first page.

"Well?" The statement shot out of him as Alek sank onto his bed, his hand over his mouth. He couldn't stand it anymore. Was he losing his friends or not?

"We made it," Alek choked out, and Ren could both see and hear all Alek's faculties slam to a stop and reverse. If he'd just skipped that one day looking at the website, if the mail service had been just a little bit faster, all that Metallica-coated misery could have been avoided. Alek handed over the pages so he could put both hands on his knees, curling over, his shoulders shaking in some strange mixture of laughing and trying hard not to cry. "We actually made it."

Ren's own vision blurred over the paragraphs, but he blinked enough that he read the important parts. Congratulations. Awarded the Jason C. Albright Fellowship. Relocation to the Pasadena area by the first of March. A salary number and offer of tuition remission at Caltech. A phone number and website to acknowledge receipt of the letter and to formally accept the position. Ren took a shuddering breath. *That's it, then.*

"Good for you, buddy," Ren wheezed, hoping Alek hadn't heard him since his voice sounded so strangled. "Denny too," came out in the tiniest of whispers.

"Don't tell her yet," Alek recovered enough to say, proving he had heard, eyes wide and plunging deep into Ren. He reclaimed the letter from Ren's stiff hands, secreting it away into his back pocket. "I want to." His face broke into a wicked grin, the tendrils of a plan curling Alek's mouth.

"Sure," Ren agreed. It wasn't news he trusted himself to give properly anyway. He could barely keep his eyes off the floor, so he'd be certain to taint their triumph if he tried to tell her about it. Without looking, he could feel Alek settle, pulling in his focus until it turned into a hand on Ren's shoulder.

"Why don't you come with us, bro?" Alek invited. "USC has a great med program." But Ren was already shaking his head.

"Scholarship," was all he could say, reminding Alek about the only reason he'd even been allowed into the country. Ren had to stay in Chicago.

Alek's face had twisted into conflict, and Ren perked up so he wouldn't ruin this for him. He absolutely was not going to make Alek feel the way Ren's brothers sometimes made him feel. "But when you get where you're going make sure to invest in a longer couch because I am going to visit you all the time," Ren instructed, knowing his words had done what he wanted them to as Alek's broad smile returned, and he shook Ren's shoulder.

"You'll have your own room. We'll go to the beach," Alek promised, flooding Ren's brain with bright skies and salty winds, the memory so strong Ren tried to take a deep breath of it.

"I can't wait," he replied honestly. "But for right now, maybe we should get back to your party."

"Oh, yeah," Alek said, as if he'd forgotten there were eight people in his living room. Ren couldn't blame him. That tiny piece of paper had certainly changed the entire tone of the evening. Alek hurried to the door, as if he'd suddenly decided they'd been gone too long and needed to make up for it. "Sounds like Justin's here," Alek said over his shoulder, leading the way down the hallway, but his casual comment froze Ren to the spot, his internal organs liquifying as he pictured being in the same room with Justin and Celeste simultaneously. Which was his original plan, but now that it was happening, he'd changed his mind. How was he supposed to do this?

He spent the next few seconds folding all his emotional laundry, separating it and smoothing it, crisping the corners on his expectations. Ren was going to walk down the hall. He'd greet Justin the way best friends do, a method he was going to figure out somewhere on the way. He would shake hands with North. He would watch for how and when Alek told Denny they were going to California, and he was going to be the one who began the applause about the news. He would not impede Sheridan's and Justin's relationship. He would stay near Celeste and make sure she had a good time. He was going to behave exactly the way he was expected to. And no one would know any of this might be difficult for him.

By the time Ren rejoined the others, Justin and North had already added their coats to the pile. North had taken up a sentry position standing between the couch and the balcony door, arms folded, eyes contentedly fixed on Justin, who was excitedly helping Alek tear into a large box on the table. Sheridan and Celeste had finished eating and disposed of their dishes. Sheridan, naturally, was also staring at Justin, standing as close as she could without getting in his way. Denny sat with her arms around her knees at the table near Alek, waiting to see what was coming out of the box. The scientists filled out the empty spaces with their graphic T-shirts and tilted, inquisitive stances. Celeste noticed Ren first and with an almost relieved look on her face she picked her way through the crowded apartment to be at his side.

Ren stepped away from the hallway to join her, taking her hand and pulling her gently over to stand near North since the couch was covered with scientists and Ren didn't think he wanted to sit down right now anyway. Standing let him move the way he liked when he wasn't sure, and it allowed him a better view of all the party participants.

"North, hi," Ren said, twisting into position, back to the wall, amazed that he sounded breathless. "Thanks for coming."

"Hello, Mr. Kaplan," Celeste also greeted, slightly timid, exceptionally polite. Ren tried to picture their first meeting, how it had gone. In a courtroom undoubtedly, when Justin was sixteen and his life was falling apart. "I'm not sure if you remember me, but I'm Celeste Lyons. I ... was a witness," she started to falter, and Ren didn't know what to say to help her. Fortunately, North held up a hand, allowing her to stop.

"I remember you," he said, smiling to reassure her, letting her know he harbored no hard feelings. "And I'm glad to see you again in a friendlier place. I wasn't aware you knew Ren, though." He shifted his gaze between them, deliberately noting their joined hands, the scar through his eyebrow wrinkling as his forehead creased.

"Celeste donates plasma at the center where I work," Ren offered. "We've known each other for over a semester."

"Isn't that something?" North murmured, filing away those details, coming to his own conclusions about the information he'd been given. He shook his head slightly before returning to his watch over Justin. After a moment of quiet observation, North sighed softly, a pleasant sound. "You know, this is what I've always wanted for him," he confessed.

Justin and Alek lifted a piece of equipment from the box, pulling free the wires and what looked like a mouthpiece, the kind police use. Now that Ren was paying attention, he could hear what they were saying.

"It doesn't work," Justin told Alek with a rather hopeful apology. "I figured you might want to —"

"You bet I do!" Alek exclaimed, taking the black box from Justin and turning it over in his hands so he'd be able to look at it from all angles. "Thanks, man."

"What is that?" Celeste asked innocently.

"It's an old CB radio," North answered. "Otherwise known as the reason we're so late."

"Alek is going to have a blast fixing that," Ren put the statement out there to make sure everyone knew a broken radio was a perfect gift for Alek. Really, a broken anything would have been good, he took such pride and pleasure from calculating strategies of making things functional again. An internal smile warmed Ren down his neck and into the small of his back, proud of Justin for being so thoughtful.

"Thank you," North said suddenly, tearing his gaze away from Justin to penetrate Ren with a gratitude that almost hurt. "I can't tell you how much I appreciate what you've done for Justin. He's never belonged anywhere, never been included like this."

"Well, he's stuck with us now," Ren said, trying not to sound too emotional. He watched Justin stand with Alek and Denny, pointing out the details of the radio, then watched him smile uncertainly at Sheridan when she put her hand on his back, coming close to ask him a question. That smile damaged the mood, poked sharply into Ren's side, something more than jealousy stinging him when he saw it. He told himself he was too invested, that he was looking for things that weren't actually there. He knew it shouldn't matter if Sheridan touched Justin, and so what if he smiled back at her when she did? Didn't Ren want the same things for Justin that he wanted for himself? A future. The affection of a good-natured, loyal girl. Ren had promised himself he would do nothing to interfere, but something in how Justin looked at Sheridan forced Ren forward to do just that.

"Hey Justin," Ren called him, probably interrupting Sheridan, but he wasn't thinking too much about it. He just wanted to separate them, or at least include himself with them. Even though he knew this was counterproductive to his plan.

Justin's head snapped up, eyes scanning the guests until he found Ren in the crowd, causing his whole face to soften in recognition and causing Ren's heart to beat hard in his throat. He had to clear it before he could talk again.

"Come get some dinner." He gestured for Justin to meet him in the kitchen, looking back for only a moment at North. "I'll bring you a plate," he promised. North nodded in acknowledgement, an interesting expression on his face, questioning, almost puzzlement, like he didn't quite understand the true significance of what had just happened, but he was going to work it out. Ren decided he'd worry about what North thought later. Right now, he wanted to be with Justin. Ren kept hold of Celeste's hand, pulling her with him across the living room. Justin was on his way too, coming to a space where Ren could have more control of the situation.

They all came together in the small kitchen, Ren and Celeste from one direction and Justin and Sheridan from the other. Ren let Celeste go in order to start serving. Though he hesitated briefly before handing a plate to Justin, too many thoughts running through his head at once. What if he didn't like it? What if he couldn't eat it?

"It won't be too spicy for you, right?" Ren double checked, trying hard to ignore how possessively Sheridan stood next to Justin. Reminding himself that dropping the plate so he could grab Justin around the neck and kiss him full on the mouth would cause more hurt than it was worth. It was extremely hot in this kitchen.

"Just give me the plate, Ren," Justin commanded, stepping so close Ren almost gasped, and Ren decided he would say nothing else tonight that would give Justin any suggestion that Ren might be fussing over him or his health. He knew Justin had grown tired of that, and the impatience was strong in his voice. "I've been waiting all day to try this."

"It's really good; Ren did a fantastic job of it," Celeste offered her opinion, drawing Justin's attention. Ren saw his eyes flash freeze, until they really did look gray for a moment, a hint of tightness around his mouth and jawline. He hid it by studying the food as he took it from Ren. When he looked up again, he'd smoothed all trace of whatever that had been from his features. Ren wished there was some way he could ask him about it. Instead, he dished up a serving for North while Justin managed one bite of his own. But after the first taste, he set the fork down, holding the plate awkwardly and still.

Ren almost asked him about this too, worried he really didn't like it, before he remembered that Justin felt uncomfortable being watched while he ate. Especially if he was the only one eating. Ren passed over North's food to Celeste, asking her if she'd mind bringing it over to him. Then he filled a third plate, which was a good thing. He'd been so caught up in everything else that he'd forgotten he hadn't eaten yet either. He raised his fork to Justin, a weird toast, but Justin relaxed immediately, returning to his meal with such dedicated purpose that Ren no longer worried about him liking it.

The chairs in the room were already full, so Ren and Justin leaned against the counter, hips touching in the small space, and ate together while Sheridan and soon Celeste again, stood beside them. He felt Justin lean into him slightly, an almost imperceptible touch that could have happened on accident, but the warmth of it eased Ren.

The music continued around them, as did the talk, small groups chatting, switching, talking some more. One of the scientists, Ren thought his name might be Noah, stood in the center of a small cluster which included Denny. The animated way he moved his hands indicated he was in the middle of his most passionate conspiracy theory, but it must have been truly extraordinary since Denny was staring at him in rapt concentration with an almost impressed expression on her face. Closer to him, Ren heard Sheridan ask Justin what he was planning to do now.

"Study," he replied, sounding humiliated, hesitant to give out this information. "I'm scheduled to take the GED in two weeks."

"That's great," Ren broke in just as Sheridan said something extremely similar. He didn't spare her a glance; he'd barely heard her over the pride that coated the inside of his chest at Justin's decision to finish his high school education. He really was moving on, in such a good direction. "I can help you if you want," Ren offered, a split second before Sheridan this time. In his peripheral vision, he saw Celeste's wry smile at how they were speaking practically in synch. Glad someone could find it funny. He dared to shoot a quick look at Sheridan this time and discovered her glaring at him. But whatever. He was Justin's best friend. Justin said so.

Justin blushed between them, looking as though he wished he'd lied in response to Sheridan's question. "Actually," he said apologetically to both of them, "Alek's going to help me."

Ren must have looked stricken because Justin continued, explaining his decision defensively. "You have so much going on." And that hurt because it was true. Ren wasn't even sure where he was going to fit Celeste into his already cramped and demanding schedule. But he would have figured it out, would have turned the world upside down if Justin had just said something. At least he was getting help from Alek. That meant he'd be at the apartment often in the next two weeks. That was good. Or maybe it wasn't.

"Alek's a great choice," Ren complimented, smoothing it all out. "He's less likely to emotionally damage you." Now Justin looked confused enough that Ren had to expand his answer. "I had Denny help me study once," he explained.

The party progressed mostly as planned. Ren finished eating and took out his phone, keeping himself from worrying about Justin, Sheridan, Celeste, and upcoming separations by focusing on pictures. He took one of Alek blowing out his candles. Another of Denny with one of the biggest pieces of cake. North and Justin standing together, North's arm around Justin's shoulders as they laughed over something Justin had said, looking very much like they were related. He couldn't bring himself to take a picture of Justin and Sheridan together, though he had ample opportunity. Sheridan kept close to Justin, almost constantly touching his arm or back. Justin never touched Sheridan first, but he quite often took her elbow so he could scoot her a pace away. He was always gentle, treating her as if she were made of glass, but Ren began to wonder if he truly enjoyed having her so close to him. Celeste didn't seem to notice anything amiss going on, so Ren tried not to think about it. It could very well be that he was seeing it only because he desperately wanted to.

Ren spoke more with Celeste, who stayed almost as close to Ren as Sheridan did to Justin, filling her in on details of the day, telling her things about Denny and Alek, speculating on whether the signal from their homemade radio could breach earth's atmosphere. Sometimes Sheridan and Justin joined them; Justin's eyes fixing on Ren's with untranslatable emotions that Ren despaired about because he couldn't read them. Whenever they came, Ren did his best to keep Justin close, but something always split them up. And each small distraction was enough for Sheridan to drift away with Justin, creatively disappearing in the tiny space of the apartment and reappearing as far from Ren as she could get. Ren wasn't sure if she was trying to just have Justin to herself or if she specifically wanted to keep him away from Ren, and he wished he could talk to Celeste about it, but he didn't want to say anything bad about her best friend, even if she was getting on his nerves. Ren was starting to wish the party could be over.

It seemed he wasn't the only one. Ren noticed Justin had stopped smiling at some point, even for North. He kept holding his left bicep, his right arm tight against his ribcage. He stood hunched, a position of pain. At first, Ren thought he was imagining it; he knew he was watching Justin too much, too intently. But then he saw North pull Justin aside, hand on his shoulder, concern on his face, and Ren knew what he was seeing was real enough for others to notice too.

"Would you excuse me for a minute?" Ren requested of Celeste, knowing it was probably in bad form to leave her to see about Justin, but he was acting strangely enough that Ren wanted to investigate. If his left arm hurt, it could be heart related. "I need to talk to Justin about something."

"Certainly," Celeste acquiesced, the memory of the promise she'd made to wait for him mixed into the word. It made Ren smile, tracing a finger down her cheek, wondering if he even deserved her, wondering how many times he would have to touch her, to see her looking at him, before it began to sink in that they were really together.

"I'll be back soon," he assured before ducking through the guests to the other side of the room, almost physically pushing himself past Sheridan with the same request to her as he'd made to Celeste. Though phrased less politely. *Can you leave us alone?*

"Come with me," Ren ordered, tugging on Justin's sleeve, who submitted so quickly Ren thought he'd been waiting for someone to give him permission to leave. Ren's worry deepened as he led Justin to his bedroom, not saying anything to North as he followed them. Ren wanted quiet and privacy for whatever conversation was going to happen, and he didn't want anyone near Justin, though he knew he'd have to make an exception for North. Ren pulled Justin into the room, waiting just long enough for North to slip inside as well before shutting the party out, allowing his focus to sharpen in the soft, familiar stillness.

Justin automatically sat down on Ren's bed, some of the rigidness leaving him already now that he was out of the crowded room, back in an environment where he was more comfortable. He hung his head, closing his eyes, breathing deeply as though Ren had just pulled him from a boxing ring.

"Can you tell me what's wrong now?" North began immediately, worry making him blunt. "And don't say nothing because Ren could see it all the way across the room."

"Are you feeling ok?" Ren asked on top of North, dialing down the questions to be more specific as Justin continued to stare at the floor in silence. "Is it your arm? You've been holding it for a while now. You took your heart medication on time, right?"

"You watched me take it," Justin shot back heatedly, frustrated, and Ren internally chastened himself. He'd made a promise not to fuss over Justin tonight, but that was before Justin started acting like he was in the beginning stages of a heart attack. He was still rubbing his arm even after Ren had mentioned it. "And it *is* nothing."

North sat down next to Justin on the bed, which seemed to force Justin off it, pushing away, testing boundaries again. Something must be stressing him out if he'd started behaving like this. Ren stationed himself in front of the door, blocking the only exit. What happened? Where was the boy laughing with North over cake earlier? The boy who looked so happy to give Alek a broken CB radio? When and why had the guarded wolf part of his personality returned with such force?

"Justin," Ren entreated, knowing better than to go any closer with Justin all wound up and distant. "It's just us." But Justin was shaking his head, still trying to deny anything was wrong.

"Do you want me to take you home?" North offered, and Ren saw a tremor shudder all down Justin's body at the word. He wished Justin would allow him near, would still let Ren touch him. He wanted to put his arms around him, hold him until whatever was troubling him went away. He wanted him to feel safe.

"No," Justin said curtly, but then wavered. "Maybe." Maybe? Was it the party? Maybe it was too loud, overstimulating. While Ren enjoyed it when the apartment was full, he knew Justin preferred things quieter, that he didn't like so many strangers or so much attention. Maybe it was wearing him out to be around so much noise. Maybe he was getting tired of Sheridan hanging on him — oh!

"Is it Sheridan?" Ren questioned, hoping he wouldn't regret saying it out loud. He braced himself for both North and Justin to look at him strangely, so ready to be wrong about what he thought he'd seen between them that he was stunned by the actual reaction.

Justin flinched, his body language flashing bright red guilt as he returned to the previous posture that had caused Ren to bring him back here in the first place. Right hand clenched tight over his bicep, the arm pressed hard against his ribs, shoulders hunched, and head drooped. A stance Ren had never seen until tonight.

"Sheridan?" North echoed, confused even though it was obvious Ren was on to something. "Justin?"

"I'm sorry," Justin murmured automatically, which made all the acid in Ren's stomach curdle, suddenly too hot. It always made him so sad when Justin apologized that way. "I know I'm ruining everything."

"Now wait a minute," North began, reaching entreatingly for Justin, who shrank against the desk.

"Nothing's ruined," Ren contradicted, verbally attempting to hold on to Justin, to the shredding pieces of his trust, trying to figure out why he would say something like that. Also wondering what it would take to help Justin stand straight again, if he was experiencing real physical pain or if this was something mental, a memory of a wound.

Justin raised his eyes just enough to stare into Ren's, and this time some things were strong enough for Ren to decipher. There was remorse glistening there, the guilt Ren had seen before, and some kind of wish. Justin's ribcage collapsed as he exhaled harshly, and Ren decided to risk it. He stepped forward, reaching out deliberate and slow to put his hand against Justin's chest, over his heart. It exploded in a rush at the contact, punching into Ren's palm, and Justin gasped again, but then it slowed, steadying, as Justin mimicked Ren, at last removing his hand from his arm and creating that Josephson junction Ren had taught him in the emergency room.

Emboldened by his success, Ren took one step closer, feeling Justin shudder, feeling North's eyes on them. Justin leaned his forehead against Ren's shoulder, and Ren forced himself not to move. He didn't want to disturb this. Whatever this was.

"I can't do it," Justin confessed to Ren's shirt. "I thought I could, but —"

"Ok," Ren accepted, soothing, though he was becoming increasingly confused. "What do you think you can't do?"

"I know it makes sense," Justin began, and Ren held his breath so as not to shift him, not give him any reason to stop what he'd started. "It'd be perfect, wouldn't it? You and Celeste, Sheridan and me. I know that's what she wants, too, but God, every time I look at her." Justin pressed his face closer into Ren's shoulder, and Ren noticed they had stepped even closer to each other. He felt Justin's fingers clench into his shirt.

"Oh, Justin," North breathed outside their circle. Not a sound of sympathy or pity. There was an understanding in it, like North knew exactly what Justin meant. "That's nothing to be sorry for."

"Will it stop?" Justin asked North, who looked haunted. "Or am I going to feel him stabbing me every time she touches my arm?"

Oh. Ren closed his eyes, turning his head away. Why did it have to be Sheridan who was Celeste's best friend? Why did it have to be that they'd met that way, in that dark parking lot, before Ren had come into any of their lives? Justin's posture made sense now. He'd been covering the scar from David's knife. That's what Denny had said. He had a knife. He sliced open Justin's arm, cracked one of his ribs too. Psychosomatic pain from the memory of the night Justin met Sheridan. When he'd shattered pieces of himself onto the ground that he might never put back together. Those shards of trauma cutting into him now, triggered by Sheridan's face, her touch, her scent. Getting worse the longer he forced himself to stay next to her. But he'd felt the expectation to try and pretend there was nothing bothering him.

"I don't know the answer to that," North responded, voice full of something more than what they were talking about. Drenched in his own demons that Ren hadn't even thought of. He looked over to North just in time to see him slowly clench his artificial hand. Ren had no idea that his room could be this full of pain, and he would have no way to heal it. There was nothing in his med bag for this. "But it's not fair to you to force yourself to have feelings for someone. Not fair to her either."

Justin retreated, at least physically, from Ren, his breathing ragged now as he struggled with what to do. He stood open and vulnerable in front of them, shaking his head.

"I wish I could," he said, again apologetically. "I tried talking myself into it. She's a sweet girl. She deserves to have someone take care of her, and there's really no reason not to like her, but I just … I can't do it. I can't get past it. I'm sorry, Ren."

"No, it's fine," Ren protested, not knowing why Justin felt he needed to apologize to him for this. "Justin, really. North's right; you can't force yourself." But what was going to happen now? Even though Ren was speaking words of assurance to Justin, he felt like he was losing something important here. "But you should probably tell Sheridan. She does deserve that."

"What's going on?" The feminine voice, the innocent question, slipped into the room a little ahead of Sheridan herself. Celeste was with her. Ren felt his mouth drop open, felt himself begin stammering some kind of explanation that would protect Justin from having to answer until he was ready. Nothing was coming to him.

"They're starting the radio test in a couple minutes," Celeste explained their presence, entering with a hesitancy, gauging the expressions on all their faces. Ren felt weighed down with guilt and sorrow and something else that didn't even have a name. It was astonishing to him that just down the hallway there was still a party going on. "Is everything ok? You all look so serious."

Ren tried to smile, but his heart wasn't in it. Celeste clearly felt it keenly, as she stepped close to him, holding on to his arm the way Denny had done earlier. He covered her hand with his free one, looking desperately to Justin, who was obviously doing his best not to shy away from Sheridan. Ren could see the struggle now that he knew it wasn't in his imagination. Justin could barely look at her.

"You wanted to tell me something?" Sheridan said to Justin, trying to engage him, trying to catch his eye, and Ren took a deep breath as though his bedroom was going to plummet to the ground floor.

"Yeah," Justin acknowledged, eyes fixed on North for strength as he spoke. Ren waited, urging Justin to just get it over with. It would be bad, of course. Sheridan might storm off in a fit of tears. She might take Celeste with her. They might not ever want to talk to Justin or Ren again. It might indeed ruin everything, and Ren steeled himself for that possibility. He didn't want Justin to suffer anymore, especially for something like this. He shouldn't have to pretend because it was convenient. Because he thought it was what he should do or feel.

"I'm leaving," Justin said abruptly, and Sheridan stiffened in surprise. Ren tilted his head. That wasn't what he thought Justin was going to say. Even North looked startled.

"Leaving?" Sheridan repeated as a request for more information. "Like right now?"

"No, I'm ..." Justin faltered for a second, taking a deep breath. "I'm joining the Air Force. Once I get my GED, I'm going to Texas for boot camp. The next class starts in the spring."

Ren bit his tongue to prevent himself from shouting out. *What?!* Justin was going to what? No. That was so much farther than

McKinley Park. He might never see him again if he did that. The Air Force? Where had that even come from?

"Justin," North said warningly. "I thought we were going to —"

"No, it's the right choice," Justin protested. He shifted his huge eyes to meet Ren's. There was resolution in his face now that he'd apparently finalized his decision. "It's what I've always wanted," he said softly, as if in explanation to Ren for what he was doing. And even though it killed Ren to do it, he nodded in what he hoped was an encouraging way. Like with Alek and Denny, if this was something Justin wanted, Ren was going to support him.

"The Air Force?" Sheridan clarified, her voice seeming to echo somewhere from the very pit of her soul, where Justin had likely dropped her heart. Justin took her hands in his, mostly to remove them from his body, pressing them firmly towards her before releasing her completely. "How long will you be away?"

"Years?" Justin guessed, looking again at North, who nodded. "Training only takes a few months, but then I'll be stationed somewhere."

Stationed. Oh, God, where would they send him? Somewhere far? Dangerous? What was even going on in the world right now? Ren didn't know; he'd been so micro-focused for so long. Ren felt Celeste's hands on him tighten, as though she were preparing to catch him if he fell over. He grounded himself by focusing on where she touched him. Near his ear, she sighed in pity and disappointment. In shock. Because they all knew what this meant. Justin had removed himself from any kind of availability. Ren felt as though the very foundation of his life were crumbling out from underneath him.

"Ren, get out here!" Denny called from the doorway, sharp, immediate, stabbing into the tenseness of the situation and exploding it open. She paused, taking stock of what she'd walked into for maybe two seconds before shaking it off and sternly addressing Ren again. "We have a window; we can't wait for you."

"Yeah," Ren acknowledged, breathless, like Justin had just punched him in the stomach. "We're coming."

Denny took pity on him. While she could have no idea what had just happened here, she could read him well enough to know how to help him best. Darting forward, she firmly took hold of Sheridan's and Celeste's wrists, pulling them with unquestionable authority out of the room. Sheridan looked too stunned to protest, but Celeste glanced back at Ren before Denny dragged her away.

"Right behind you," Ren assured, though he wasn't certain he could move. Not sure if his equilibrium could take it if he tried to walk out of here. North was on Justin immediately.

"Are you sure this is how you want to do this?" North pressed him, the voice of experience. The voice that knew exactly what Justin was signing up for. "Because once you've committed, this isn't something you run away from. And it's not the solution for avoiding a difficult conversation."

"That's not what I'm doing," Justin emphasized, his posture much stronger now. He glanced over at Ren, and he caught the tiniest hint of regret on his face. "It's better this way."

Ren opened his mouth, a "how can you say that?" brimming at the back of his throat that he never got to say because Denny yelled at him again from the hallway.

"Ren, come on!"

They all looked toward the door, even though it was only Ren who was being summoned.

"All right; now isn't the time to get into it," North said. "Did you want to leave or stay?"

"Stay," Justin decided forcefully, with so much conviction that Ren wanted to ask him why he thought he had to join the Air Force if he wanted to stay so much. Did he really want this? Was it only because he wanted to get away from Sheridan? But no, Ren remembered Denny had said he'd tried to join before but had been turned away because of the assault on his record. Now that it had been wiped clean, he had a second chance.

"Ren," Justin called him, and he realized they were leaving him standing frozen in the middle of his bedroom floor. He spoke softly, easing Ren up and out of his shock, persuading him to leave it be for now. "Let's go see if my dial works."

"Ok," Ren said, forcing his stiff limbs into motion. North patted him sympathetically on the back as he passed him, as they silently tabled the conversation about this huge, sudden decision to a better time. But even if they talked about it later, Ren knew Justin wouldn't change his mind. He'd officially lost him in every way possible. *Damn it, Justin.*

Almost everyone clustered around the radio as Ren came back to the party. Alek had David Bowie's "Space Oddity" playing on his phone while Denny compulsively checked the time. The physicists stared intently at the radio, willing it to connect to the cosmos. Having them all flocked to the electronics had left the couch free, so Ren sank into it. So much had happened and was still going on that he felt numb, except for the warm place to his side that bloomed up as Justin sat next to him. North perched on the arm of the couch, his robotic arm gripped to Justin's shoulder. Sheridan looked over at them, but it seemed as though Denny had set a guard over her. The astrophysicist, Noah, held her in conversation. She looked torn, but after a moment of staring at Justin where he didn't look back, she submitted to Noah, allowing him to continue whatever lengthy explanation he'd started. Ren knew he owed Denny for this. She'd even picked the scientist she respected the most to distract Sheridan. A strange compliment.

Celeste had no bodyguard restraints, however, and she quickly came to Ren's side. The couch was too short, but Justin and Ren shifted enough so she could squeeze in, putting Ren in the middle. Ren lifted his arm, easing it gently around Celeste's shoulders to make more room, and she nestled into his side.

"You ok?" she whispered into his ear. "I take it that news was a surprise to you too."

"Yeah," he whispered back, answering both questions at once, and she nodded, picking up on his tone. They were going to pretend everything was ok for tonight. He'd untangle the knot in his chest later. "Is Sheridan ok?"

"She's too stunned right now to feel anything," Celeste confessed.

"I bet," Ren said, though he knew exactly what Celeste meant. He felt that way too. Justin shifted next to him, and he felt every point of contact along their shoulders, hips, and thighs, heat radiating from each place. Celeste stretched her arm out from where it was caught against Ren's side, resting it along the top of his leg and curling her elegant fingers around his knee. They switched their attention to Denny, who repeated her call sign into the receiver, paging the space station.

"This is KK6EJK," she told the universe. "Calling ISS. Do you copy?"

Nothing but static on the line, nothing but held breath around the table. Denny handed the receiver to Alek, who tried with his own sign. The song played on repeat in the background. Alek fiddled with Justin's dial, trying to fine-tune the frequency. The guests began to fidget, doubt spreading like a disease among them.

"This is KK6EJK," Denny pleaded into the receiver, more than one kind of disappointment tainting her words. "Does anyone copy?"

"We hear you," came the invisible voice at last, distorted but decipherable. Justin sat forward next to Ren. "Hailing from ISS."

A cheer erupted around the table, and Alek crashed into a chair. Denny flapped her hand at everyone, demanding quiet so they could hear. Ren heard himself huff in surprise and appreciation. So, they'd succeeded after all, initiating a conversation with an astronaut two hundred and twenty miles above the earth's surface. That tiny, cobbled-together box on the table enough to bridge that gap. Incredible.

Denny and Alek quickly told their story. Who they were and how they'd built the radio and gotten their licenses specifically so they'd be able to talk to ISS as they drifted over Chicago. They asked the astronauts a few questions, and they were gracious in their answers.

"Congratulations on your radio," ISS personnel expressed kindly. "That's so impressive you built it yourselves. Maybe you should join our team at NASA."

Denny's face fell, and Ren realized that Alek hadn't told her about the letter yet. It looked as though he'd been waiting for this exact moment because he dashed forward, snatching the receiver out of her hand.

"We had the same idea," Alek told everyone in the room and in space. "You're talking to the newest recipients of the Jason C. Albright Fellowship award. We will be joining you very soon." The room gasped collectively, and Denny almost dropped to the floor.

"What?" she half-shrieked. Alek produced the acceptance letter from his back pocket, handing it over. A chuckle filled the room from space.

"Well, how about that?" the captain said good-naturedly. "In that case, I'm looking forward to hearing from you again. I'm sure you'll have a lot of good things to contribute to the program. Take care now, and happy birthday!"

The static intensified as the space station continued on its path, out of range. Celeste breathed out an exclamation of amazement, words Ren could feel on his neck more than he could hear. The physicists were beside themselves, more animated than Ren had thought possible, hooting and laughing, shaking Alek's hand, and slapping a disoriented Denny on the shoulder. Alek closed the communication, neatly switching off the radio before Denny flat out attacked him.

"Holy Stephen Hawking," Denny shrieked, the letter clenched tightly in her hands. "Alek, you monster!"

"It came today!" Alek called out his defense. "Don't kill me; I just found out too!"

Denny screamed out another frustrated, emotional noise, covering her face. Alek waved off some of the attempts to comfort her, doing it himself by shielding her in his arms.

"We did it," Denny sobbed. "We're really going."

Ren tuned so far inward he couldn't hear the celebration

anymore, Denny's last words rattling around in his head. Celeste whispered in his ear, more talk that had no meaning for him. She pressed her hand on his knee, and he registered with surprise Justin doing the same thing on the other side. He bowed his head, grabbing them both, almost clenching his hands over theirs, sandwiched between them. It felt like he was falling through the floor, the walls of the apartment tearing from the frames, rearranging in a new and frightening way. How was he supposed to move forward after this?

# 7
## SEPARATION ANXIETY

"So let me get this straight," Denny began as though they were in the middle of a conversation, even though Ren hadn't seen or spoken to her all day, and she made the comment as she strode purposefully and non-apologetically into Ren's bedroom. A shadow at the doorway let Ren know Alek was right behind her, though he at least carried an offering, a plate with a steaming mug and a grilled cheese sandwich. Ren wanted to turn away from them both. He didn't feel like chatting, and he knew for a fact that grilled cheese was near the top of the American comfort food list. This was some kind of good cop, bad cop intervention thing, and he wasn't up for it. But apparently Denny had been revving up for a confrontation, not hesitating at all to call Ren out on his attitude today. "Are you sulking or pining?"

Denny sprawled across Ren's bed, ensuring she had his attention, though she ignored his glare. Alek deposited the plate on top of Ren's open notebook and then took a position to the side, leaning against the wall with his arms folded, watching like a referee.

"I'm busy," Ren returned, monotone, pulling his notebook from underneath the plate. He wasn't lying; there had been a long list of things he had to catch up on today. Homework assignments, repacking his disheveled med bag, talking to his family early that morning. Then Ren had prepped for another full week, though this one would be free of ambulance runs, birthday parties, and hopefully spending the night in the ER.

"Nope," Denny countered rapidly, eyes sharp and scrutinizing. "Busy is when you're eating standing up in the kitchen or when you wear your scrubs to class because you won't have time to come back and change. What you're doing here is hiding."

Ren turned to Alek, who simply put both hands up, palms out and head shaking.

"Don't look at me, buddy," Alek deflected, unwilling to come to Ren's defense. "I'm with her." Ok, so no good cop.

"Fine," Ren huffed. "Hiding, sulking, pining. Call it whatever you want, but at least my homework is almost finished."

"No!" Denny yelled, obviously unwilling to play mind games, and Ren tried to summon the energy to deal with her. What did she care what he did with his Sunday? What did it matter if he spent it in the living room or his bedroom? She wasn't even going to be around for much longer, so she didn't get to have an opinion. "Ren, come on!"

"What?" he managed, feeling picked on. What did she want from him? Didn't she understand he was in here because he didn't want to damage their triumph? He didn't want to rain on any parades, and he didn't trust himself to keep his disappointment under control. So he was keeping to himself until he could. If he was hiding, it was for her sake.

"Don't you 'what' me like you don't get what's going on. You're just going to give up without even trying?" Denny sat up as she spoke, perching on the edge of the mattress, her face broken open in an unsettling mix of compassion and fury.

"What are we even talking about?" Ren asked too quickly. His soul cooled as he realized he probably knew exactly what they were talking about, and the conversation was about to go spinning into an even worse direction than how much time he'd spent alone today.

"Justin," Alek volunteered quietly from the sidelines. Ren felt himself crumpling and tried to hide it by rolling his eyes. Yeah, of course. Justin. Who left last night with North and started an ache inside Ren that was close to homesickness, but without a location attached. Just a sense of loss and a desperate hunger for something he could never have. A hurt that drove Ren to bed earlier than he'd intended and imprisoned him in his room all day, suppressing any desire he might have had for food or company, knowing there was nothing in the apartment that would truly satisfy him.

"There isn't anything to say," Ren said, shrugging, willing them to drop it.

"I disagree," Denny hissed, staring pointedly at him, watching him for every tell-tale nuance in his expression that he wouldn't be able to hide from her no matter how he tried. "I think you've got plenty to say, and you'd better do it fast, or you are going to lose him forever."

"Wasn't that what you wanted?" Ren threw out, vicious, defensive, unwilling to cooperate with her. She didn't understand. Not really. It just wouldn't work. "For him to disappear forever?"

"Don't you dare twist this," Denny challenged, frustrated. "My goal then is the same as my goal now; I'm trying to keep you from making a mistake."

"What am I supposed to do?" Ren asked desperately, his volume raising as the intensity of how much he wanted that question answered exploded into the room. He saw Denny's shoulders raise as she drew in a long breath, her mouth dropping open to explain to him in minute detail exactly what she thought he was supposed to do and what she thought of his intelligence for having to be told to do it. Ren's lungs splintered in his next inhale, his whole nervous system stinging in preparation.

"Talk to him, Ren," Alek rumbled gently from the sidelines before Denny could say anything sharp. "Celeste too."

"See, now that would be a mistake," Ren emphasized, wishing they could see that as plainly as he could. Denny growled something under her breath, reaching forward and snatching his notebook away from him, flipping it open to a clean page.

"Let me spell this out for you," Denny suggested through gritted teeth, on the verge of being completely condescending. But when she started drawing a flow chart in his own notebook as she spoke, she pushed it to insulting. "You have this awkward infatuation with Celeste for months where you worship her from afar and never talk to her because you're afraid of what might happen. Enter Justin," Denny drew their names in little circles and began attaching arrows to key words like rejection, pining, fear, and a few more Ren didn't want to see.

"Justin's different than Celeste," Denny continued. "He needs you, and you love that. He's a hurricane of drama, and you pour a week of your energy into him and manage to wake up his emotions without sabotaging yours. You spend every waking minute with him being your helpful, sweet self, and that's good. It's leading some-where good too. Until you think he doesn't need you anymore. Until you start thinking you need him more than he needs you. Then that freaks you out, and you pull back, which makes him think you aren't interested, and *he* pulls back."

Denny drew an arrow from Justin pointing to the emotions that connected Ren and Celeste, illustrating how Ren was treating his relationship with both of them the exact same way, with a hesitant fear of future rejection that would cost him both. Then she created another circle, another name. The arrows and circles getting increasingly messy.

"Enter Sheridan," she went on mercilessly. "Who turns your weird love triangle into a tight and perfect quad." Denny crossed out all the circles and moved to the bottom of the page where she drew a rendition of a Punnett square, Ren and Celeste on the top, Justin and Sheridan on the bottom. "Except it's not perfect because everyone with eyes can see that Justin couldn't be less interested in Sheridan, and you are trying too hard with Celeste because you wanted the quad to be the solution that kept you close to Justin." Bold lines scrawled in, separating Sheridan and Justin, but then also Ren and Justin, and Ren and Celeste. "Since Justin doesn't want to be with Sheridan, and he doesn't want to ruin anything he thinks is going on between you and Celeste by rejecting her best friend, he is breaking himself out of the whole thing and running away into the military. If you want to stop him, you will have to take a chance and tell him how you feel about him."

Denny wrote the word CONFESSION in all capital letters to the side of the square, drawing arrows toward Ren and Justin. Ren shook his head, done with all of it. He pulled the notebook back, tearing out the page.

"Justin's wanted to join the military since he was thirteen years old," Ren protested. "And he's only just been given the opportunity to make that happen. For the first time in his life, he's free to make choices for himself. He's not ready to be in *any* kind of committed relationship, and even if he were, it wouldn't be with me." Ren's throat tightened, remembering how Justin pulled back, flinching from under Ren's hand. How Ren's relationship with Celeste was only because Justin had brought them together, a parting thank-you gift for Ren's help. How could his friends not see this? They were confusing Justin's gratitude for something much more.

"Ren, why aren't you getting this?" Denny pressed him, no longer sounding angry, just fiercely trying to get her point across. "*You* are making decisions for him. *You* are taking choices away from him."

"I'm staying out of his way," Ren argued. "It's not fair for me to ask him to give up on his dreams just because I want him to stay here."

"Ren," Denny started again, but Ren jumped on top of her.

"I'm not doing it!" he yelled, startling her. "I left my family so I could come here and become a doctor, and they all hate it, but they are supporting me in my choice. If I'm allowed to be selfish like that and stay here because it's something I wanted for myself most of my life, then I sure as hell will support anyone else in what they want to do, no matter who or where it is or how I feel about it."

"Renzo," Alek interjected, still quiet, still gentle, but Ren was speaking too fast and too hard to stop now.

"I got what I wanted," Ren said decisively. "I got my scholarship. I came to America. I got the girl. And now it's my turn to stay behind while you all go fulfill your dreams. And I cannot be selfish about it. I'm not taking that away. Not from you and not from Justin. That's not fair."

Denny deflated during his tirade, her head tilting as it usually did when a new idea struck her from out of nowhere. Ren had never meant to tell them how hurt he was that they were leaving him behind, but it had pushed itself out in the heat of that moment and he couldn't take it back now.

"Ren," Denny said, looking at his quilt, ashamed. He hadn't wanted to do that. Why couldn't they have just left him alone? "We don't want to leave you."

"I know," Ren allowed, full of remorse. "But I can't come with you, so you have to. And so does Justin. I get it; I did the same thing."

"But why can't you —" Denny stressed but stopped when Ren's phone rang, Dr. Delacroix's number appearing on the screen. Unusual.

"I have to take this," Ren excused himself, though neither Alek nor Denny moved as he answered. Alek blocked the doorway, so Ren had no choice but to stay and talk to the doctor right there in front of them. He clicked the button, staring at the floor.

"Lorenzo?" Dr. Delacroix began before he'd even said anything. "Are you busy? Can you come to the ER?"

"Right now?" Ren asked, wondering and worried. Why would she want him after dark on a Sunday night?

"Yes," Dr. Delacroix answered briskly, and Ren decided he'd better stop asking stupid questions and start putting on his coat. Obviously, this was an emergency. "I need you to set up an IV for me.

The only other nurse I would trust to do it is off for the weekend, and I can't get him to answer his phone. Will you come?"

"I'm on my way," Ren assured, though he looked up at his friends as he said it to make sure they understood that he was leaving this conversation. "Give me fifteen minutes."

"Less if you can manage," Dr. Delacroix requested before hanging up. Ren couldn't help but feel relieved that he now had a good excuse for getting out of here, though it came at the expense of whoever the patient in triage needing an IV happened to be.

"I've got to go," Ren explained, standing up and beginning to slip past Alek, who hesitantly stood to the side for him, his expression apprehensive and curious. "Dr. Delacroix needs me in the ER."

"I didn't know you were on call for the ER," Denny said, put out, not liking that Dr. Delacroix had interrupted their discussion.

"I didn't either," Ren responded, calmer than he felt. "But she wouldn't have called if she had anyone else."

Denny gave a frustrated huff, shaking her head. "When are you going to learn?" she muttered under her breath as Ren left the room. He didn't understand what she meant. If this was still something about Justin or if she was just frustrated that he was getting out of any lecture she had remaining to give him.

Alek didn't say anything, hadn't said much this whole time, but he watched Ren get into his shoes and coat with sad, brown eyes. Whatever Ren had thrown at Denny would have hit Alek harder, and Ren knew he owed him an apology, but it would have to wait until later.

"I'll be back soon," Ren promised, though he had no idea what he was leaving them for or how long it would take to return. "Save my sandwich for me?" That seemed to pacify Alek because he gave Ren a small smile and a nod, which was good enough for Ren to leave on.

He hurried through the bitter cold of the almost abandoned campus, most of the students snuggled into the warmth of their apartments at this time of night. He wanted to run but didn't trust himself not to sprawl flat on the concrete if he hit any ice, so he kept at a brisk walk, wondering what was waiting for him at the ER, if this was the start of something that would happen often. Wondering if he wouldn't be grateful for that once he was alone in his apartment after everyone had gone their separate ways.

The lines on Denny's page kept jumping into his head as he hurried toward the hospital. The arrows pointing at Justin and Ren from the huge commanding CONFESSION. Denny might not have noticed, but Ren had. There were two arrows, which meant Ren wasn't the only one who could confess. Justin could have done it too. Justin could have told Ren if he'd been interested. But he hadn't. Nothing about a future together, no hint they were anything more than new friends. He'd even gone out of his comfort zone to get Ren a *girlfriend*. Which meant, of course, that there was nothing on Justin's end to confess in the first place, and Ren risked losing him if he were to freak him out with any kind of suggestion about it. Better to leave it as it was. They were friends, which was good enough. Celeste was with him, and that was also good enough. Dr. Delacroix needed him in the ER, and that was going to be good enough too.

Flickers of memory shivered against Ren's throat, making him swallow. Remnants of nondescript but very real pain watching Justin and Sheridan together last night at the party. Ren understood now there was no future there, but he would somehow have to prepare himself for when it happened the next time. Undoubtedly, Justin would find someone else, someone he did want to be with. And if Ren were his friend, well, that was another choice he was going to have to support no matter what. He wanted it for Justin at the same time he never wanted to see it.

Ren didn't have any more time to go over it now, however. He'd reached the ER, entering the welcome warmth through the ambulance doors and throwing his coat into that little office where he once sat with Dr. Delacroix going over a testimony proving Justin's innocence that had never been used.

The doctor herself met him halfway to the central nurse's

station, a lab coat for him in her hands. He hadn't taken the time to change into scrubs, so he tossed the coat over his jeans and sweater.

"Thanks for coming," Dr. Delacroix said, motioning for Ren to follow her, wasting no time. "We've gone through two techs already to get this going, and the mother is understandably upset, so the next stick has to be the one that works."

"Mother?" Ren broke in with the question, gently prodding Dr. Delacroix into remembering that she hadn't given him a single piece of information about what he was walking into. Except now he knew he'd be working with a minor.

"Right," Dr. Delacroix quipped, pausing in front of a triage door, the twist at the corner of her mouth impatient that she had to take the time to explain this. But it wasn't like Ren could read her mind or anything. "The patient is a three-week old infant with symptoms of RSV. I have him on oxygen already, but the IV set up is proving delicate and complicated. Which is why I asked for you."

Ren heard himself inhale all that information, startled. RSV. *Three weeks old.* And Dr. Delacroix had called for *him* to do this? Suddenly he felt that staying in his apartment and listening to Denny would have been the easier thing to do this evening.

"Me?" Ren whispered, as if there had been some mistake. Ren still didn't know exactly how he'd been able to successfully place Justin's IV in that ambulance, and if that was the event that had made her call him then he'd better give her the full disclaimer right now. "Dr. Delacroix ... I've never ... not on a baby."

"This is the ER," Dr. Delacroix responded flatly, unmoved in her decision that Ren should be the one to do this. "You'll encounter something you've never done on a daily basis. I wouldn't have called you if I didn't think you could do it better than anyone already in the building. Now let's go." She pushed through the door without waiting for a response, leaving him with no choice but to follow her.

This triage room seemed much bigger than the one Ren had stayed in with Justin, but that was probably because there was no bed in here. Instead, a small, plastic bassinet on wheels dominated as the focal point. A frightened, tired-looking woman sat pulled up close in the uncomfortable waiting chair, guarding her baby, one arm at an awkward angle so she could keep a hand on the infant's head. Her other hand covered her face as she slumped against the crib cart. She might have been a little older than thirty — or worry and exhaustion may have added eight years to her posture, forehead, and eyes.

The baby, Ren noticed as he walked close enough to see, remained motionless under the blanket that had been brought in to keep him warm. His tiny chest fluttered in and out as he struggled to breathe through his inflamed airway, that one activity wearing him out too much for him to wiggle or cry. Ren involuntarily drew a deeper breath himself as he watched.

The woman raised her head as Dr. Delacroix approached with Ren, all her movements slow and sluggish. Out of the corner of his eye, Ren saw Dr. Delacroix put out her palm toward him, an indication that he should stop and wait for her to explain. His gaze kept pinning itself on the baby, his miniature clenched hands. Any one of Ren's textbooks probably outweighed him.

"We're getting a room ready for you," Dr. Delacroix told the mother in place of a greeting. "Someone will be in soon with the hospital admittance paperwork, but before that, I called in a specialist to place your son's IV."

Ren felt the mother's dark eyes settle suspiciously on him, and he did his best to appear as though he wasn't completely shocked to be called a specialist. He tried to radiate calm, professional capability.

"Again?" the woman asked, her voice a waterfall of tears barely held back by the dam of her pride. There was worry there, and guilt. Pain that she hadn't been enough to help her son, that she'd had to bring him here to a strange, uncomfortable room where she had no control, where two techs before Ren had poked her baby with needles, hurt him when he was already suffering, and both times it hadn't even worked.

"Only one more time," Ren heard himself promise, the Incident

Commander in Charge. Dr. Delacroix sent him a sidelong look, but Ren wasn't sure what she meant by it.

"Are you even a doctor?" the mother questioned Ren, a hint of helpless frustration layered over the words.

"No," Ren replied honestly, knowing he didn't look like any kind of specialist, or reliably competent, standing there in his jeans and sneakers, not even old enough to drink legally in this country, but Dr. Delacroix cut in before he could say anything else.

"He is a qualified EMT and extremely talented at placing IVs in unconventional situations," Dr. Delacroix edified Ren, sounding as though she had said the same thing to countless other mothers, that she called on Ren all the time. "I understand your hesitation, but your baby needs help, and he is the best we have. I called him from home to do this for you."

"Only once?" the woman repeated what Ren had promised earlier, caving in, knowing the IV needed to happen, even though she was having a hard time trusting in Ren despite anything Dr. Delacroix said about it. He couldn't blame her. After all, she had seen two other people, older and more professional, fail already tonight. Ren made solid eye contact with her again.

"Once," he said, practically vowed, and she sighed in defeat even as she half-nodded in consent. Dr. Delacroix also nodded at Ren, a signal to get started. He went to the sink to wash his hands thoroughly before gloving them and pulling the smallest cannula kit from the drawer. Purple, 28-gauge, for neonates.

He took his time, looking carefully at the infant as he readied the tape and his nerves. So small. Such a small, weak little guy with smooth, black, beautiful skin. The veins in the hand and arm were out of the question. He may be lying still now, but that kind of stillness wouldn't last for long once the medication started helping. Ren didn't like the idea of placing the IV in the foot either for similar reasons. No, for someone this tiny the best vein would be the superficial temporal, which ran under the scalp, along the side of the head. It would look disturbing, but it would be safest and easiest to place.

"Do we have a razor?" Ren asked Dr. Delacroix, who silently retrieved it from the stock cabinets and handed it over along with a tube of gel, which Ren squirted first onto his fingers to warm it before smearing it gently against the baby's head.

He shaved as little of the baby's tight, dark brown curls as possible, just above his right ear. Then he asked Dr. Delacroix to reposition the light, even though he knew already this was something he'd do better with his fingers than his eyes. He ran the tip of his ring finger around the patch he'd just shaved, searching for the vein. Now he couldn't sense the women in the room at all, neither the mother nor Dr. Delacroix. He scrubbed the area sterile, removing any hair or gel residue. The infant didn't like any of the foreign attention. He squirmed weakly. Ren tried to speed up to minimize the effort. Using the same finger as a guide, Ren neatly tapped into the vein with the smallest possible catheter. The baby whimpered but did not move as Ren taped the apparatus in place, ready for whatever tubing Dr. Delacroix may want to plug into it.

He heard a small exhalation close by, the first stimulus to break into his concentration. Ren lifted his gaze to see the mother staring at him, eyes weary and troubled but grateful. She had removed her hands at some point before Ren started his procedure, but now she had them both hovered over the bassinette, as though she were afraid to touch her son now that he had a needle taped against the side of his head. Ren didn't like that. Somehow, it reminded him of his own mother, how she must have looked sitting at Amayah's side in the hospital before she died, helpless, afraid, and separated.

Without deliberating too much about what Dr. Delacroix might think of what he was doing, Ren carefully rewrapped the boy in the blanket in such a way that the IV site was covered. Then he lifted him, oxygen tube and all, so he could place him into the warm safety of his mother's arms. A position that would soothe them both.

"He needs you most," Ren told the woman, a truth he knew inside his heart, a shared understanding as another boy who missed his mother's arms.

"Thank you," she whispered, barely able to get the words out as she instinctively cradled her baby against the warmth of her chest, sighing in relief to have him back again, though they still had a long recovery process ahead of them. Ren could only nod a response, then had to turn away, fumbling at removing his gloves.

"The nurse will be in with the IV medication soon. It will get better from here," Dr. Delacroix promised, resting a sure hand against the small of Ren's back like a grounding wire, steering him out of the room. He let himself be pushed into the hall, then followed Dr. Delacroix obediently to the back office where she sat him purposefully down to study him in the aftermath.

"Is he going to be ok?" Ren asked, looking at his coat on the desk but seeing only the baby wrapped in the blanket and tubing, the rapid, tiny movements of his breath.

"His chances are good," Dr. Delacroix replied, her voice even, staring at Ren critically. "And how about you? How are you doing?" She sounded serious, almost worried, completely changed from when she'd commandingly pushed Ren into the triage room. "You look stunned; let me see your hands."

Ren slowly lifted them as commanded, fingers extended, everything solid and steady. No trembling even as the world sped up to its normal pace around him.

"Good," Dr. Delacroix breathed approvingly. "That was ... well, I hesitate to say this so early in our working together, but that was perfectly executed, Lorenzo. I'm very impressed."

"Thanks?" Ren replied, not intending to make the statement sound like a question, but he was reeling from both the situation and the compliment.

"I appreciate your coming in on such short notice," Angelique repeated, though her tone had changed. This time it sounded more like a dismissal, which felt as abrupt to Ren as the original summons. That's it? He'd come all the way over here for a procedure that took less than ten minutes? Granted, it had been an essential procedure, but knowing what was waiting for him at home, Ren wasn't ready to leave yet.

"No problem, what's next?" Ren piped in before Dr. Delacroix could officially tell him goodbye or leave the room without him. She looked confused.

"For you, nothing," she said with a half-shrug. "I've already interrupted your night." Ren tried not to squirm at the thought of all the uncomfortable questions that would slam into him the second he walked through his front door. It was different here. Everything ran on smooth, efficient protocol. The scenarios here had only a fraction of correct answers. And now Ren understood how he could push back what he was trying to avoid in his life by being focused here. With the concentration he'd just needed, there had been no opportunity to dwell on how Alek, Denny, *and* Justin were all leaving.

"Could I please stay?" Ren asked, voice on the edge of begging. Angelique folded her arms, leaning back, her eyes narrowed as she unashamedly looked him up and down. Ren watched the word "why" form on her lips, but she pressed them together without ever saying it. She could tell; Ren knew he wasn't good at hiding things, especially not from her. She knew his request had more to do with circumstances outside the hospital than anything that could need him inside of it.

"Fine, but we aren't making a habit of this," she warned, and Ren bit back a too-triumphant grin, jumping to his feet. He held the door for her, keeping silent as she shook her head on her way out, muttering under her breath. He thought he heard the phrase "death of me" as she passed him, but he quickly dismissed it. There was nothing wrong here.

The ER quickly became Ren's defense and coping mechanism. The presiding dean and provost consented for Ren to trade hands-on hours in the hospital for some of his class credits, and despite Dr. Delacroix's warning about habits, she never turned Ren away when he asked to shadow her, and she stopped being surprised to find him waiting for her at the nurse's station at the start of her shifts.

Over the next month, he reorganized his entire schedule, feeling the pull of both places. He wanted to be home so he wouldn't miss any of these last weeks with Alek and Denny. On the other hand, he didn't want to be there to see how Alek had gifted his herb plants and sold some of his bulkier equipment pieces. Denny stripped herself out of the apartment in a single weekend, which hurt like hell, but at least Ren hadn't been there to watch her carry everything out as he'd escaped early in her packing to watch how Angelique handled multiple gunshot wounds.

He ghosted in and out of the place, no longer quite happy there as it constantly changed and shrank around him. But at least for the moments he *was* home, his friends were becoming increasingly too busy in their own business to have time to lecture Ren about his. All talk of Justin and what Ren should do about him ceased. Instead, Ren would come into the apartment to find them researching housing in faraway places, making pro and con lists for each location, or on the phone with the records office to get copies of transcripts.

On the best and worst nights, Ren would open the door to find Justin and Alek sitting together at the table, studying for Justin's GED test, and on these evenings, Ren found every excuse he could to linger near them for as long as he could despite how much it hurt. Sometimes they even allowed Ren to participate, especially for English questions. As the non-native speaker, Ren knew more grammar rules than both of them put together. Or when they didn't need him, he would drag his homework to the coffee table, sitting on the floor cross-legged in front of the couch, watching surreptitiously as Justin ran his hand through his hair, his gaze unconsciously zooming up and to the right as if all the answers he struggled with could be found written on the ceiling in that direction. But Ren learned quickly that he could only look for a few seconds. Justin always knew when Ren stared too long and would return his gaze, forcing Ren to dive into whatever textbook he'd brought out with him, hoping he wasn't visibly blushing. Because no matter how often he explained the impossibility of the situation to himself, looking at Justin was a pleasure and a warmth, an indulgence worth the pain.

When he wasn't at the ER, or work, or class, or watching Justin take practice tests, Ren struggled to make time for Celeste. Between his commitments, her schedule, and the fact that she lived off campus and most often needed to drive home before dark, the only times they could successfully get together seemed to be at that coffee shop in the early afternoons and on Wednesday nights at the plasma center.

Celeste had returned to her normal day and time, and Ren noticed money change hands among his coworkers the first evening she came in and greeted him with a kiss. Sometimes they talked about Sheridan. Apparently, Noah had asked her out to the observatory for a late-night meteor shower viewing and had put together a picnic dinner on the floor near the telescope. Celeste mentioned how much fun Sheridan had, how safe she felt with Noah, and hinted strongly that if Justin didn't get his act together, he was going to lose her.

Ren gently shrugged this off, knowing that Sheridan finding happiness with someone else was exactly what Justin wanted. And as far as Ren could tell, scientists were some of the purest souls alive, a beautiful combination of innocence and intelligence. So, despite being thrown together at a party because of Denny, if Noah had looked down from the heavens long enough to put that kind of effort into sharing his world with Sheridan, it would probably be best to let that run its course. Though hearing about Sheridan's fancy date put some pressure on Ren. He hadn't done anything like that for Celeste, didn't even know where to start. He didn't do anything cool like study constellations, and it certainly wouldn't be romantic to show her the inside workings of the hospital. They were barely able to have coffee together, though he did call her every night to make sure she got home ok, ask her questions about how her day had gone, and try to find the next space in their lives where they could fit each other into them.

They did come together for one last small party, weeks after Alek's birthday. They celebrated Justin's success in passing the GED, his temporary diploma displayed proudly on the table. They celebrated Alek and Denny's farewell. All of their physical presence had been carefully removed from the apartment, sold, gifted, or packed away. In the morning, everything would be loaded into Alek's car, and they would start the long drive to California. Justin had purchased his plane ticket to Texas.

Just like the last one, this party brought new and rather disturbing information as North revealed that he'd quit his job in order to follow Justin south. Apparently, the military wanted North to return in a non-combat position. They'd been requesting a timeline for when he thought he'd be able to come back as an instructor almost from the first day North left the hospital with his new hand. Now that Justin was settled and decided on becoming a pilot, North felt the time had come to get back into it as well.

Ren couldn't help but squawk out a protest about this revelation. Is this how Americans worked? Where Ren grew up, families lived and died within a small circle of where they were born. Ren had been the anomaly, leaving the island, and it had been the biggest upset in his village for months. Actually, it probably still *was*. So, it amazed him how casually Americans seemed to roam their immense country.

Celeste was the only outlier. She'd been born and raised in the Chicago area and seemed content to remain. Ren found himself holding her hand tighter as he processed this, glad that Celeste at least was staying.

They worked through it, the bittersweet nature of their last get-together. Ren forced himself to smile, extending the promise that he'd still be here if they ever wanted to return. Alek hovered, never asking if Ren would be ok, at least not out loud, but the question came in every glance and gesture as if he'd spoken it. Denny and North kept their distance, as though their hearts were already somewhere else. And just like last time, Ren found himself pressed in the middle of the couch with Justin and Celeste at his sides, his arms thrown casually around both their shoulders. Except it didn't feel casual to him. It felt as though they were the only things holding him together. North snapped their picture as they sat there that way.

No one said goodbye that night, though they somehow parted to their separate houses and rooms, much later than anyone had planned.

Ren made coffee early that morning. He numbly helped Alek carry the last of his boxes to the car. He helped Denny fold up the blankets and sheets from the couch one more time and didn't shed tears over it. He swallowed them into an increasingly large knot in his throat, which made it hard to talk to his family for very long that Sunday morning. Alek and Denny politely waited until he had finished, drinking their coffee, having one more breakfast together. But Ren could tell they wanted to get going.

Alek grabbed Ren hard and tight, murmuring gratitude for being a wonderful roommate. He offered an open invitation for Ren to come stay in California whenever and however often he wanted, which Ren appreciated even though he doubted he'd ever be able to go.

Denny allowed herself to be held too, surprising Ren by suddenly and fiercely clinging to him, pressing her face into his chest. Ren bent down so he could put his palm against the back of her head, their cheeks touching, amazed that a soul so feisty could exist in such a small vessel. He remembered all their many arguments and teasing, and all the times they had wordlessly made up from them, how they spoke most often without saying anything.

"You're still my brother," Denny told him authoritatively. "Doesn't matter how far away you are."

"Good," Ren tried to return, but his voice sounded husky and flat.

"And I'll be there to put you back together," Denny promised. "When the time comes." He almost asked her what she meant, but she made a sudden leap so she could hug him around the neck. He barely managed to balance them without tumbling over backward, holding her tight.

"You're so stupid; I love you," she said in a rush, and Ren smiled even as he lost control over the tears that he didn't want to show them.

"Love you too," Ren whispered, but that was all Denny could take. She ripped herself away and dashed for the door. Alek gripped Ren's hand one more time, promising to call often, promising to write, promising to send pictures, promises and more promises that this was not the end of their friendship. Ren was already familiar with how much effort it would take; he'd been doing the long-distance relationship thing with his family. But he was more than willing to add Alek and Denny to that list. Even if he had to single-handedly keep the communication up, he was ready for it. He wouldn't let them grow apart, though he did let Alek go.

He counted the minutes in his head after Alek shut the door behind him. Ren paced through the apartment, staring sadly at Alek's empty bedroom, restored to the sterile, un-personalized nothing all the bedrooms in this building looked like before a student breathed life into them. Ren couldn't look at it for long. He realized faster that he couldn't look at the kitchen either. No bread rising on the counter. No plants taking up space near the wall. The missing boxes of electronics made the whole place bigger; it almost echoed with the emptiness of what was now gone.

Ren counted the minutes he thought it would take for Alek and Denny to get downstairs to the car. How long it would take for them to pull out of Stony Island parking for the last time. He counted minutes until he couldn't take the quiet anymore. Then he changed into pale blue scrubs and threw on his coat, heading for the hospital.

No one expected him there, but he'd become such a regular that no one denied him as he made himself useful. He tidied filing. He put together trauma kits and restocked the cabinets in the triage rooms. He threw himself into every job no one wanted to do. Dr. Delacroix wasn't even scheduled to work today, and he'd known that before, though he thanked every nurse for telling him she wasn't coming in, and then he continued to stay anyway.

He probably would have slept in the ER, on the floor in that back office, but one of the nurses interrupted him at the station where he was testing all the available pens at the desks, throwing away the ones out of ink.

"Your ride's here," she told him, plucking the pen straight out of his hand and scattering all his thoughts at the same time.

"Huh?" Ren asked, confused, drifting. What did she mean his ride was here? He hadn't called for a ride. He hadn't even told anyone where he was, so how could anyone be here to give him a ride?

"Don't ask me," the nurse said, shrugging, deliberately returning the pen to the holder on the desk, untested. Ren felt a twitch in his jaw about that but knew he'd look obsessed and weird if he picked it up again. "They asked for you and said they were here to take you home."

"Who are they?" Ren vocalized, mentally shaking himself.

"I don't actually care," she said slowly, spacing out the words and emphasizing each one, smiling mostly to show her teeth. "Provided they get you out of here. Now. *Step away from the pens.*"

Ren must have resembled a kicked puppy because she sighed as he stood up, grabbing his elbow before he turned away from her. "Look, try to have a good night, ok?" she said as an attempted patch. "I'll see you later. Hopefully when you're more ... you. Now, shoo," she scolded, giving him a little shove.

Ren had no idea who would have bothered to look for him. It made the exit look bigger, and Ren feel small and lonely. He pushed the doors open anyway, surprised by their weight, and half-stumbled into ER reception.

Ren noticed that all the glass doors and windows of the waiting room were black. Night had fallen outside in the world while he'd trapped himself inside the windowless horseshoe of the ER. Despite the blackness, he felt himself squint as though walking out into a too-bright space. It wasn't bright, but it was too big. And cold. He tugged at his coat, shivering.

"Ren, you ok?" came familiar words from a familiar voice, and Ren twisted from the entryway to see Justin standing a few feet away. North stood with him, both still in their coats. They'd been facing each other, but now that they'd seen him, Justin broke away toward Ren, eyes large with their strange quality of being sharp and gentle at the same time.

Ren inhaled to answer, but the words got tangled by the sudden, dramatic reappearance of that enormous knot in the back of his throat. Immediately upon seeing Justin, Ren's eyes were stinging, and he had to pause, frozen just outside the doors to the triage rooms, closing tears behind his eyelids, clenching his teeth together to make sure he stayed quiet. He took two blind, blurry, and staggering steps toward Justin before he felt Justin's steadying hands circle around his arms. Ren let his head sag, relieved and tormented when his forehead came to rest against Justin's shoulder.

"You idiot, have you been here all day?" Justin chided him, not letting go. "Why didn't you answer your phone? Why didn't you call me?"

*Because you never answer.* The words shot through Ren's head, though he wouldn't have said them if he could.

"How'd you know I was here?" Ren managed instead, leaving his head resting against Justin. It felt good, safe, warm. Justin smelled like heat and detergent.

"Fritz," North answered, joining them, putting his strong and soothingly weighted robotic hand on Ren's shoulder.

"Officer Geisler?" Ren repeated. He lifted his head but didn't step out of the comfort of the circle. He wanted the touch, wanted to bury his face in Justin's neck and throw his arms around his waist. Wanted to keep him forever. "How?" he trailed off, trying to figure out a path where that would even make sense.

"One of the nurses called Dr. Delacroix wondering why you were here when she wasn't," Justin supplied the connections. "Then she asked Officer Geisler to call us to come get you."

Justin paused, his eyes dropping to the floor, suddenly guilty, still holding tight to Ren. "We should have thought to come look for you sooner," he admitted. "I knew today was going to be rough on you. I did try to call, but you never answered."

"Sorry," Ren muttered, realizing that he'd left his phone on his desk. After he'd spoken to his family, he hadn't even thought that anyone else would try to call him.

"Alek and Denny said they made it to Nebraska," Justin continued, an effort to be bright threaded through his normally dark voice. "It's a boring drive, but they're ok."

"That's good," Ren said, trying to mean it. By this time, North and Justin were steering him toward the exit, and he was walking automatically between them, glad to relinquish any of his thought or free will into their hands.

"Ren, did you eat anything today?" North asked, and Ren felt the gaze of a trained social worker fall on him.

"Doesn't matter; he's coming with us anyway," Justin spoke up when Ren didn't. Though it made him think he should probably be curious on where they were going. He'd follow Justin just about anywhere right now, but he maybe should ask about their destination.

"Where?" he put out there, just for the principle of the thing, hating how he could only put one or two words together at a time.

"To get you some food," Justin let him know, tugging him out into the parking lot. "And to get your stuff. You're staying with us tonight."

"Justin?" North broke in because this was obviously news to him. Apparently, Justin often made spur-of-the-moment decisions without consulting his adopted father.

"He can't be alone," Justin pointed out, which caught Ren up on the whole situation. They felt like they were *rescuing* him? Justin thought he needed a chaperone? Well, if that were the case, why hadn't they thought of that before they'd all made the decision to leave the state?

"I better get used to it," Ren interjected between North and Justin. He tried to make his tone playful but wasn't quite able to keep all the bitterness out.

"We're still here, Ren," Justin reminded him. "Come on; come with us."

"No, it's ok," Ren protested, wondering what he was doing. He was deliberately excusing himself from time with Justin? He barely had any time with him left! What was he thinking? That he didn't want to be pitied, for one. He didn't want Justin to spend time with him only because he thought Ren was having a nervous breakdown. "Thanks for coming to get me, but you can just drop me off at my place. Alek left enough food in the fridge for the next five days, easy. I don't want to waste it."

"Ren, are you sure?" North pressed him, both his tone and gaze heavy, giving Ren one more chance to save himself from a long, lonely evening. And he wanted to say he'd changed his mind, wanted so much to go with them. "You're welcome at our place."

"Yeah, I'm sure," Ren said, because sometimes it was better to just get things over with. "I'll be fine."

He felt Justin staring at him, all the dark drive to his apartment. Ren did his best not to look at him, not trusting himself to walk away from North's car if he did. Justin's eyes would melt his resolve; he knew that. Not only would he stay with them for the night, but he'd probably end up saying something he shouldn't. Something that might ruin the events already in motion. He'd already said things to Alek and Denny he regretted, that damaged the excitement of the next chapter of their lives. He wasn't going to do that to Justin.

Ren thanked them again for the ride as he forced himself out of the warmth of the car and out onto the icy curb in front of his dark apartment. No lights on up there. No music. His table would be uncomfortably cleared of gadgets and wires. He was just in the process of closing the door behind him when Justin unexpectedly flashed out and grabbed his wrist, holding him still. Ren snapped his attention, meeting Justin's eyes, which glinted in the winter dark.

"Answer your phone," Justin admonished him, almost a threat. He sounded mad; he was practically growling.

"Ok," Ren stuttered, which was enough for Justin to release him, though by this point, Ren felt weak and wasn't sure he could walk.

"Last chance," Justin told him, making the cement underneath Ren seem to tilt and sway. Maybe he shouldn't go all day without eating again. "Go get your toothbrush; we'll wait. Or I can come up with you."

*Oh my God, yes, please come up with me. There's an actual bed you can have now; Alek isn't using it anymore. You bring **your** stuff back, Justin. Your dumb duffel bag and your three pairs of jeans. Wear my hoodie. Make coffee. Move in. Please, don't leave me.*

"You go on home," Ren said, though how he managed to get the words out or make them sound so calm, he had no idea. "You guys have a lot to do without babysitting me. I'm good."

Justin looked wounded. But this was for the best. Their relationship had been weird from the very beginning. Now was the time to smooth it out into something sustainable. It wasn't up to Justin to take care of Ren, even though Ren suspected Justin thought he must owe him something.

"I'll check on you later," Justin said, a comforting promise he made somehow frightening. Ren seemed to specialize in pissing him off, but at least Ren was able to close the car door now. Then turn around and begin walking toward the apartment entrance. He didn't look back, but he knew from the sound that North and Justin didn't leave until after he was already inside.

Ren only saw Justin once after that. He gave Ren a heart attack. Ren was just getting home from his shift on the ambulance, another long night behind him. Ren was more careful about it now, spreading out his time between the library, the ER, the lounge downstairs, or just walking around campus for as long as his Dominican blood would allow him to be outside in the cold so no one would suspect he just didn't want to be at home by himself. He answered his phone when Justin called to check on him and lied to him every time about how he was just fine, just keeping busy, then turning the conversation as quickly as possible to what Justin was up to, how preparations for Texas were going. He called his family. He called Celeste every night. He felt himself growing numb inside but preferred that to the ache he felt when he thought about the day Alek and Denny left and the rapidly approaching day when Justin and North would do the same thing.

He tried so hard to prepare for when they would be gone that he was shocked to find Justin casually sitting on his couch when he walked in the door at six thirty in the morning after being out all night with the ambulance. He'd closed the door behind him, dropped his bag and keys, and removed his coat and boots before he even noticed Justin sitting there. Good thing Ren was too tired to scream.

"God, Justin!" he burst out instead, grabbing on to the back of a chair to steady himself. He was too exhausted for surprises like this.

"Denny gave me her key," Justin explained, standing up, watching Ren uneasily. "You ok? How'd it go last night?"

Ren didn't want to talk about last night. There'd been three fatalities and none of them had been pretty. Ren and his team had cleaned up after an accidental drug overdose, a homeless man who had been hit by a car while riding a bicycle, and an old man who passed away from a heart attack before they could get to him. It wasn't the old man who haunted Ren, but the trauma in the eyes of his new widow whose reality had been torn out from under her at eighty-six years old. Not to mention the other stuff he'd responded to where no one had died, but the suffering still clung to Ren like the scent of smoke on his uniform.

"Last night was rough," Ren allowed, still gripping the back of the chair.

"You look it," Justin agreed, sounding validated. Ren tested his resolve by lifting his head to look at Justin, amazed anew at how beautiful he was, relishing the way he moved, a fierce sort of grace.

"Yeah, well, kind of in the job description," Ren said, trying to be dismissive about how awful it had been. Time for his normal trick of switching topics before his heart grew any heavier. He might end up just tipping over. "So how are you doing? Did you need me for something?" Except packing. Ren wasn't sure he could bring himself to help Justin pack. It had been hard enough to do it for Alek. Still, there must be some reason Justin had let himself into the apartment before dawn on a Saturday.

"I'm here to make sure you rest today," Justin said, smiling the way he did when he thought Ren was being ridiculous. "Since last time you almost killed yourself, and I'm not making that mistake twice."

"What — serious?" Ren managed after a long pause where he just stared at Justin with his mouth open. Justin took the opportunity of the question to completely close the distance between them, taking Ren's arm and pulling him toward his bedroom.

"Yes," Justin responded, matter-of-factly, and Ren didn't have enough resolve to resist him. He allowed himself to be dragged toward the hall, all his muscles compliant for whatever Justin wanted.

"Can't I shower first?" he begged, but Justin shook his head.

"Sleep first," he maintained, unmoved, and Ren decided to give up. He was tired. He had been pushing himself hard since his roommates left. And if Justin could stay a while, maybe it would be ok. Maybe his apartment wouldn't feel so desolate. Maybe he could rest.

"Justin?" Ren started as Justin physically settled him under his covers, still in his uniform.

"You can fight if you want, but I'll win," Justin argued without hearing what Ren had to say. "Whatever you think you need to be doing right now can wait. Lie down."

Ren's mattress had never felt so good before. The perfect temperature, the smoothness of the pillowcase. His eyes started closing by themselves, though he didn't want to sleep yet. He had Justin in his bedroom, all to himself. How could he waste that by falling asleep? The tension of the ambulance suddenly snapped loose, so abruptly he winced at the release.

"Hey," Justin said gently, his voice close. Ren wanted to open his eyes to talk to him, but they were too heavy. He hadn't relaxed like this in days. "It's ok; you're home now." Justin spoke like the only other person in the world who could know what it felt like to be spinning out of control and then come to a sudden, heart-wrenching halt. How the transition to peace and rest could hurt, how images and feelings could flicker like flaming nightmares on the sidelines. How they could still burn after they were over.

"Thanks, Justin," Ren whispered, almost whimpering. He twisted his face against his pillow, trying to hide his eyes, squeezing them closed. He reached out with one hand, finding Justin's sleeve and holding on to it, desperate to keep him close. Justin allowed the contact, using his other hand to carefully brush against Ren's cheek before resting his palm on Ren's shoulder. Ren shuddered.

"Go to sleep," Justin encouraged, but a sudden thought jumped into Ren's brain, shaking him awake, forcing him upright. The last time Justin had put him to bed, he'd disappeared while Ren slept. Ren didn't think he could handle that again. His abrupt shift in energy startled Justin.

"Shit, Ren! What the hell?" Justin burst out, confused.

"Please don't leave," Ren begged, knowing he sounded pathetic and needy, but he just couldn't stand it. He was panting with apprehension that he would go to sleep and wake up alone. "Please."

Justin softened, eyes full of understanding. He returned his warm hands on top of Ren, gently pushing him down, pulling the quilt over him.

"I'm not going anywhere," Justin assured him. "I'll be here when you wake up." This time. Today. But it would have to be enough. Ren allowed himself to melt into the mattress again, allowed all the adrenaline in his system to bleed into it. "Shhh," Justin whispered. "I'm here."

Ren had no choice but to let sleep overtake him, his hand clinging to Justin's sleeve. His room got hazy, the bed seeming to pivot underneath him, rocking like the back of the ambulance until Justin's hand on his head stilled everything, quieted it down.

"Who's going to look after you?" He thought he heard Justin breathe the question, but it could have been part of a dream. He remembered nothing else after that.

He woke to the rich scent of coffee, and he smiled, relieved, as he hurried out of his room and toward the table. The position of the sun told him he'd probably been out for at least four hours, maybe more. He rushed past the hall, slowing only when he saw Justin sitting at the table.

"You stayed," Ren said, humiliatingly out loud. Justin looked sheepish, knowing he didn't always stay.

"I promised," he returned, busying himself with pouring Ren his own mug of coffee. "I can't cook," Justin admitted, handing it over, "but I did make this for you."

"It's all I want right now," Ren said, gratefully accepting it with both hands. It felt like years since he'd had Justin's coffee. Justin pulled out a chair for him, and for a little while they both sat there quietly together, sipping coffee as sunshine poured into the room from the sliding balcony doors.

"Sorry I left you alone so long," Ren finally said, wondering what Justin had done with himself while Ren slept. "I crashed hard."

"You needed it," Justin dismissed.

"So," Ren began, trying to make conversation. "You all set for Texas?"

"Yeah," Justin answered, staring at the table. "Flight leaves tomorrow morning."

Ren took another long swallow of hot coffee to melt the ice suddenly freezing his stomach. He'd known what day Justin was leaving, but in the sad blur that was his life now, he'd sort of lost track. "Oh," was the only thing he could think of to respond. They sank into silence. One minute. Two.

"Come with me," Justin shot out suddenly, turning his whole body toward Ren at the table, his face open and eager. Ren blinked, dazed at the invitation.

"What?" he checked. What did Justin mean, come with him? Surely, he didn't mean to Texas?

"Join the Air Force with me," Justin clarified. "A guy with your skills — they'd love to have you. They'll pay for you to finish your doctorate, so you won't need your scholarship. We can do boot camp together."

"Justin," Ren began, not even the heat of the coffee able to melt his insides now. It sounded good. It sounded perfect.

"Let's do it," Justin pressed, caught up in his idea.

"They won't take me, Justin," Ren let him down gently, hating how his words deflated Justin immediately. "I'm not a US citizen, remember? If I want to stay in the country, I have to stay here." But what did it mean that Justin wanted him to come?

That question stayed with Ren the rest of the day, just like Justin did. They hung out, like friends do, and Ren even agreed to stay the night at North's, knowing it would be his last chance to be with Justin, possibly for years.

He spent the day and long into the night drinking in the sight of Justin, watching how easy his relationship with North was, watching how far he had come from the scared and friendless person Ren had found alone in the Snell-Hitchcock apartment. He was doing so much better now, had so much going for him. Ren was happy for him, really, even though it hurt to look at the clock and see how time was running out. He thought often of his notebook page, the way Denny wrote the word confession, all capital letters, arrows pointing to the two of them. He thought of how Justin had wanted him to go to Texas, but knew it was too late. Even if that invitation had been anything close to what Ren hoped it was, it was just too late.

And it continued to grow later as the sun came up, as Ren drove with North to Midway airport. And finally, time ran out as he allowed himself to hold Justin tight, hug him close in the few moments before he stepped through security and out of Ren's life. Justin still wore Ren's hoodie, the straps of his duffel bag over his shoulder. Ren pressed against him, enjoying his heat for a few seconds more, wanting to beg him not to go.

"Don't forget me," Ren said instead.

"Impossible," Justin returned, releasing Ren so he could look him in the eye. "You're my best friend. I'll never forget you. Take care of yourself, ok?"

"You too," Ren repeated, allowing North to also hug Justin goodbye. North needed a few more weeks to put his affairs in order, but then he too would be gone. He stood with Ren, hand on his shoulder, watching Justin pass through security and up an escalator out of sight. He offered to stay with Ren if he needed some company, offered his assistance anytime Ren might need it. He emphasized he was Ren's friend now too, and he made Ren promise to come to dinner with him next Friday night, just as Justin used to do. Then North dropped Ren off at his apartment, alone again.

He woodenly removed his coat, stared sadly at the coffee mugs from yesterday morning that he'd left in the sink. What was he going to do? He shook his head, staring at the apartment, knowing he'd have to get used to this somehow. *People figure out how to be by themselves,* he lectured himself. *There are millions of people on earth right now who somehow prefer it.* But he didn't know how to turn himself into one of them.

He paced as he thought, trying to keep the creeping loneliness at bay when someone knocked on his door. Confused, but happy to be interrupted, he almost pounced on it.

"Celeste!" he exclaimed, surprised to see her standing in the hallway, keys still dangling from her fingers. "What are you — I thought you had an event today?"

"I do," Celeste said, cool and calm, smiling at him. "But not until tonight. I thought you and I could sneak off and do something fun together for a change." Ren's smile faded into suspicion.

"Justin called you, didn't he?" he asked, and she let her eyes float to the ceiling, caught.

"Does it matter?" she returned, pretty in her guilt. "You *do* look like you just lost your best friend, and I happen to specialize in helping people get over Justin Kittrick. Besides, we've both been so busy; we deserve a day for ourselves, don't you think?"

Ren leaned down and kissed her. It made the ache in his chest swell hard to do it, but damn, she was sweet and wonderful and so very *present* there in the hallway. She smelled soothingly of lavender.

"I'm all yours," he told her, trying to shut out everything else, lock it up tight. Her smile sliced into his throat.

# 8

# PROXY

"So where are we going?" Ren finally asked Celeste, seated in the front of her shiny blue Toyota Rav4. The sun seemed to be trying its best to break through the clouds, but mostly everything looked watered down, dismal, and dirty at this point of the winter. Ren could hardly believe he'd just sent Justin off to Texas, and now he was going somewhere mysterious with Celeste. He wondered if anything would ever seem real to him again or if he'd continue to live his life as though he'd wake up any second and it would still be January.

Still, if this was a dream, it was monstrously convincing, detailed down to the jar-shaped air freshener dangling from Celeste's rearview mirror and the stack of books she had apologetically moved from the passenger seat.

Celeste drove with the confidence of someone who had grown up here, who spent a decent amount of her time behind the wheel. She wasn't as timid as Alek when driving on snowy or wet roads, but she wasn't quite as smooth as North. She drove with both hands, concentrating enough Ren thought he might have to repeat his question about their destination. Not that it mattered. Provided Ren wasn't home alone in his apartment, he didn't care where she wanted to take him. He'd asked just so it wouldn't be so quiet in the car.

"The place I always escape to when I can't bear another gray, winter day," Celeste responded cryptically, surprisingly perking Ren's interest. Was there a place in Chicago that wasn't gray, smeared, and battered with the almost archeological landmarks of ice that melted, got snowed on, and refroze over and over? And if so, could it also be used as an escape for other things?

As they drove, banners appeared along the sides of the street, advertising the featured exhibits of the Field Museum, Adler Planetarium, and Shedd Aquarium. Three major attractions of the area all tucked neatly together with a shared parking garage. Celeste pulled her Toyota into a reserved space, reaching across Ren's lap to pull out a placard from her glove box shaped like a sea turtle, which affirmed the aquarium was where they were headed today. She really must come here a lot to have her own space and parking tag.

He followed her, silent and curious, as she made quick, sharp decisions about which direction they should take from the parking spot. She led him into an elevator and across the street to the columned front of the aquarium, long crimson and purple banners swaying gently between the pillars at the top of the steps, each one printed with a different word. Under. Water. Beauty. Ren hadn't even known this place was here, but now that he was on the stairs, he desperately wanted to go in. It was full of life and color in there, movement, distraction. Warmth and water.

They took five steps into the front entrance where Celeste didn't even bother looking toward the ticket counter, and Ren realized at that instant that he knew nothing about Celeste's life. He used to think he did, but now he remembered with embarrassment how he thought he knew what sort of girl she was from the books she'd bring to the center. From the few words they had exchanged during that hour on Wednesdays where their worlds had met. Ridiculous. And even now, though they'd been dating several weeks, he still didn't have much of a grasp. Because she always came to him, he realized. She met him in his space — the plasma center, the campus, his apartment. He never went the other way. Looking around, he thought perhaps that might not be possible. She was more out of his league than he'd ever been teased for.

"Welcome back, Miss Lyons," an employee appeared suddenly at their side out of nowhere, greeting Celeste by name with friendly familiarity and unclipping a maroon velvet rope, beckoning her away from the entering crowds toward a partially disguised door marked with a Private Entrance sign. "How can we make your visit exceptional today?"

Ren glanced behind him at the tide of people they moved away from. Other couples like Ren and Celeste. Moms with small children. Groups of school-age kids wearing brightly colored T-shirts over their clothes. People waiting to purchase tickets, which apparently Ren was not going to do.

"Just looking around today," Celeste responded to the employee as they walked further away from the main door, through the entrance to a private room where Celeste began hanging up her coat with familiar grace. And no wonder. Her name was engraved on the wall. Amazing. "It's Ren's first time visiting."

"That's wonderful," came the answer as Celeste took Ren's coat too. "Please let us know if there's anything else."

"Thank you, I will," Celeste dismissed, obviously acclimated to this sort of treatment, taking Ren's arm and ushering him into the aquarium proper. "Don't look so shocked," she whispered at him, giggling as they left the worker's side.

"How am I not supposed to look shocked?" Ren whispered back. "You have your own coat hook!"

"It's nothing," Celeste dismissed, studying her surroundings as she debated where to take him first. "Try to get used to it, please. I have a lot of places I'd like to show you where someone will be taking our coats."

"What? Is it like this everywhere you go?" Ren asked her quietly, leaning into her, trying to focus on the pressure of her hand and shoulder. She pulled him into a dark exhibit, thick glass on all sides, flowing color all around them. Saltwater fish. Ren's heart felt like it was shrinking, pulling away from the sides of his ribs. It had been so long since he'd seen anything like this. They were so beautiful. It was so warm here. Why couldn't he feel it the way he was supposed to feel it?

"Not everywhere," Celeste replied, staring around her as if this were her first time at the aquarium too, borrowing Ren's wonder and seeming to enjoy it immensely. "Just the art museum, Orchestra Hall, Harris Theater, of course, and oh, there's a few restaurants. I've had a Guardian membership here since I was twelve." She listed these impressive places as she slowly walked up to a large tank where a zebra shark languidly swam past just over her head. Ren had known Celeste's family was wealthy, but in a detached sort of way. It was different walking next to her and seeing first-hand what the word meant in the real world.

For today, though, it seemed Celeste didn't mind behaving as though they were the same as all the other visitors. She brought Ren to her favorite exhibits, gauging him carefully and noticing when Ren wanted to spend any extra time in certain places. Ren wasn't sure if he was enjoying himself or not. He felt split in half, like this was all too much glamor for him, like he was wasting it by not being enough in the moment, like part of his soul had followed Justin onto the plane.

Ren thought about Justin regularly, the pressing question of what he was doing now repeatedly resurfacing in Ren's mind, even as he purposefully pushed it aside. Justin was gone, and Ren was walking with Celeste in this fantastic place. Justin was busy, probably being transported to the training facility. Being assigned a bunk. Having all his hair buzzed short.

Oh jeez, Justin's hair. Ren winced when that occurred to him, trying to picture Justin without the raven-colored waves, a grimace that didn't escape Celeste, and she pulled him deeper into the aquarium where everything felt as though they were underground, walking through close caves. He breathed her in, determined to focus on the details. Her soft hand in his. The color all around. She kissed him in front of the dolphins, and he was relieved that it blurred the edges of his brain.

He could have stayed there, in that world full of movement but somehow outside of time, for the rest of the day, the rest of the season. He wanted it to be summer when he left this place, but Celeste reminded him that she had an event she'd promised to attend, and she needed time to get ready.

When they reached the private room they'd started in, he chivalrously took down her coat, the perfectly white coat, and held it up for her to slip into, putting his arms around her as she settled back against his chest.

"Thank you, Celeste," Ren told her. "Today was fantastic."

"It doesn't have to be over," Celeste hinted, though it was already fading. There'd been hardly any sense of time passing while they toured inside, away from all windows, covered in darkness, but apparently hours had gone by. The sun had weakened into its tired, late-afternoon dimness as Celeste led Ren back onto the street toward her car.

"How so?" Ren asked, holding to Celeste's elbow as they walked to prevent her slipping on any ice.

"Well," Celeste began, unsure of herself now, as though she were regretting that she'd brought it up. "I was thinking about the event tonight."

The elevator doors closed on them as they descended underground. Celeste turned shy. Ren turned doctor protective. And concerned about what she may be hinting at.

"What about it?" Ren persuaded, amazed at her behavior. She shrugged, looking at a corner on the floor.

"Well, it's not as amazing as the aquarium, but I thought, if you didn't want to be on your own tonight, maybe, you could come with me?"

The elevator doors opened, and Celeste stepped out leaving Ren standing alone, thinking about what she'd just said and not noticing that he was going to get left behind in an elevator. He scurried to her side before the doors closed on him.

"I," he started, now unsure himself. He didn't even know what kind of event it was, but he was certain it was black tie. Or white tie? Was there a difference? Whatever — it was formal. Not something you could wear sneakers to. Not a place where he would be welcome. Because angels could come down to earth whenever they wanted, but it was quite a different miracle for a mortal to go up the other way.

"It's a silly, little celebration dinner at Everest," Celeste continued, her voice ruffled, though still quite cool. Was she nervous? It was always so hard to tell with Celeste. Though her words seemed to speed up as she continued. "You could meet my parents."

She'd thought this through. This wasn't a spur-of-the-moment invitation. The whole day had been carefully planned. Justin might have called her to ask if she'd keep Ren company today, but she'd already been prepared before that. As though she'd been waiting for Justin to leave, waiting her turn.

"Celeste," he began again, though he wasn't fast enough with his protest before she interrupted, and this time he could tell she was nervous because she fumbled her car keys. But what was making her nervous? Was she scared he'd say no? Or that he'd say yes?

"I just thought it would be good for you to meet them, my parents. I mean, we've been dating for weeks, and this seemed like a good opportunity now that —" the keys hit the ground, and Ren reached out to pause Celeste before she could bend to retrieve them. She was tense. Why was this so hard for her? Was she worried about him meeting her parents? Worried about what he'd think of them, or what they'd think of him? Both? To be honest, he shared her concern. He was less worried and more terrified about meeting her parents. He probably was nothing like what they'd envisioned as a match for their poised and perfect girl. Still, if this was his life now, if this was something she wanted, he probably should go. Because it *was* her turn, and she'd undoubtedly earned it. But there was a problem. He stalled as he picked up the keys, unlocking the driver's side and opening the door for her himself. She made no move to get in, just stood staring at him with a hopeful, worried expression, waiting for his answer without finishing what she'd started to say.

"I think you're right," Ren said, though he didn't sound convincing to himself. "I should meet your parents." It didn't matter, though. He wouldn't be meeting anyone tonight. Not at a celebration dinner, not even a silly, little one. "But," he added quickly, stopping Celeste's relieved smile before it had a chance to take over her features. "I don't think I can go with you *tonight*. I mean, I don't have a suit or anything."

"Don't worry; it's already taken care of," Celeste told him, and now she really was smiling. Relieved. Pleased and playful again. Ren felt his eyebrows shoot up in surprise. What did she mean? She gestured toward the car. "Get in."

Not sure how much more he could take, Ren had no choice but to obey her. This time she took them to a nearby hotel, relinquishing her keys to a valet and rushing Ren inside, mentioning something about being right on schedule. Ren didn't know why he was surprised, but it still took his breath away for a minute as he realized she already had a key card for a room. When had she done all this? Renting a hotel room, planning the aquarium trip?

Getting him a suit.

"Celeste, how? When did you do all this?" Ren sputtered as Celeste playfully opened the door, revealing a pleasantly decorated room with one enormous bed and the table lamps turned low, casting warm light on a brand-new, navy, pin-stripe suit laying crisply draped over the bedspread. A tie the color of the ocean in moonlight sat in a box beside it, and a pair of shiny, black dress shoes had been set out on the floor.

"Do you like it?" Celeste asked instead of answering his question, standing behind him, watching him study the disembodied suit on the bed. Ren kept his hands carefully clasped at the small of his back, afraid to touch anything. Because it was too much. His silence forced Celeste to continue. "I hope you don't mind. I checked the uniforms in your closet to get your size. We'll of course get it tailored for you, but it should do for tonight."

"What were you going to do if I hadn't said yes to coming?" Ren asked her, genuinely curious about the answer. She'd put a lot of faith into his being able to come. What if he'd had to go to the ER? What if he'd just wanted to return to his apartment? This sort of work meant she'd anticipated his agreement, which could mean a couple of things. Either she knew Ren better than he thought she did, or she was extremely used to getting her way.

Celeste shrugged prettily, as though the thought of him not coming hadn't occurred to her. Except it must have. She'd been tense at the car. "I would have saved everything for the next time. You'd have to agree to come at some point," she said thoughtlessly, carelessly. "There are two bathrooms," she went on, all business now. "We've got about an hour before we have to go."

Ren barely glimpsed a bit of dark blue fabric on the mirror as Celeste disappeared into one of the bathrooms, leaving him alone with the suit on the bed. For some reason, it seemed sentient to him. Something that could take over his will if he put it on. He stared another moment at the closed door where Celeste was doing whatever girls did to transform themselves for formal occasions. As if she could do anything to improve her appearance from the near perfection she already was. And if he was going with her, he'd have to at least try to do this justice. Ren inhaled long and slow, wiping his hands up and down his jeans several times before gingerly slipping his palms beneath the expertly woven fabric and lifting the whole suit as if it were a sleeping child.

Once inside the bathroom, Ren stood helplessly searching for a place to set the ensemble down so he could change into it. While everything in here looked pristine, it felt odd to lay out something so new and expensive on any of the surfaces. Feeling ridiculous, Ren settled for draping it over the edge of the enormous, jetted tub. Looking around brought to light even more of Celeste's prep work. She'd laid out an entire toiletry kit on the sink — razor, shaving cream, aftershave. There was soap and a tube of something Ren guessed was meant to go in his hair. He exhaled longer than he'd inhaled. This was so out of his league. But Celeste would be waiting for him. He'd already said he'd do this for her. He started the water, thinking he'd just begin with the things he knew. The razor, the new toothbrush. One thing at a time.

He smiled bitterly at himself in the mirror, thinking how strange this all was, how he couldn't really believe it was happening. Thinking of how he and Justin were both doing new things, experiencing a new life. Separately. Ren checked himself in the mirror again. The bruise Justin had given him way back in January was long gone now, only a memory. And if Ren let it happen, the memories would fade just like the bruise. He shook his head, reminding himself that Justin was gone and Celeste was in the next room and it was like that because of choices he had made himself. Choices he was going to have to live with. He plugged the sink and picked up the razor.

Forty minutes later, Ren tried to sit still on the office chair in the hotel room. He sat on the very edge of it, not sure what to do with his hands, keeping his back straight and posture rigid. He didn't dare sit back; he didn't want to mess up any of the sharpness of what he was wearing.

When the opposite bathroom opened, he jumped up in relief. He needed something familiar, and right now Celeste was all he had. Though as she daintily swished out into the main room, closing the door softly behind her, Ren froze with his mouth open, his hands dropping limp at his sides. Even she had changed to the point of being unrecognizable. Almost.

Celeste saw him staring and tucked into herself shyly, a hand smoothing an invisible piece of hair back into place behind her ear. The dark blue fabric Ren had glimpsed earlier turned out to be velvet, with tiny beads sewn in constellations all throughout. It clung to Celeste down to her knees where it unexpectedly flared out in shining waves. There were no sleeves, just a couple more swaths of something that looked weightless, though it was somehow holding up the weight of the dress on Celeste's shoulders. She'd tamed her long, wavy hair into a tight twist that must have been held in place by thousands of pins, but the only ones Ren could see were obviously ornamental; it looked as though she had sapphires fastened elegantly all over her head. She sparkled magnificently, though her dress, jewelry, and hair did not come close to the crystalline shine of her eyes as she stood there studying Ren, waiting for one of them to say something.

"Silly, little dinner, is it?" Ren whispered, breathless, his brain fogged with the incessant, insistent question of his reality.

"For them, it is," Celeste assured him, and even her voice sounded different in this space. Like cool, flowing water. Rich and lovely as a brook. "For us, it's special." She started walking toward him, the dress undulating with her movements, making it appear as though she weren't really walking at all. Ren swallowed hard and jerked his fist up between them, brandishing the ocean-blue tie she'd bought him.

"I have no idea how to put this on," he confessed to her abruptly, reminding her, whether consciously or not, that he was a stranger here. He didn't really belong. She didn't seem to notice.

"Allow me," she offered, gently pulling it from his fingers and stepping close enough to drape it around his neck. With deft motions, she successfully knotted what turned out to be a bowtie. Ren hadn't even known that; he'd been going about it all wrong. "There, you're finished."

They left the lamps on low. Celeste tucked her phone, key card, and lipstick into an elegant wristlet bag made of the same material as her dress.

"There is a chauffeur waiting for us," she informed him, pulling on a fluffy, white capelet to protect her bare arms from the cold. "My mother would rather I not try to drive in evening gowns."

"Ok," Ren said stupidly, pulling himself away from the room and his familiar clothes he'd left folded on the bathroom rug. He guessed they would return here after the dinner was over so he could get them back. Despite having more clothes on now than he did before, it felt like less. The suit was warm wool, but soft, with a silkiness he didn't think was possible. Instead of taking his hand, Celeste looped her arm through his, forcing him to lift his elbow like he did in his ballroom dance classes. Formal. Stiff. Though it seemed he would not be leading this particular dance for quite some time.

Celeste walked without hesitation through the front entrance and right up to a white limousine parked so close it was practically in the lobby. A middle-aged man with an impressive mustache opened the door for them, and Celeste thanked him by name. Ren mostly just blinked, his limbs stiffening tighter at every extravagance. Chauffeurs. Limos. What next? No, wait, he didn't want to know what was next. He hadn't had enough time to process what there was already. He could barely look around the interior of the limo as he settled into the plush seat.

Instead, Ren looked at his hands, which were stiffly cupped over his knees. They weren't visibly shaking, but he felt shaky inside. On unsteady territory. An imposter. And one who was about to be found out and exposed for what he was any second now. What was he doing here? How could he introduce himself to Celeste's parents when he didn't even know what sort of tie he'd been given? What should he say? What if he offended them? He was working himself up about it so much that when Celeste brushed her fingers over the top of his hand, he jumped so high he almost hit his head on the limo's roof.

"Sorry," he burst out, though he didn't know what he was apologizing for. Past, present, and future mistakes all in one. Celeste carefully pulled his hand over to her lap, folding it between her soft palms.

"Ren, relax," she entreated him. "It really is just a dinner; there's no need to hyperventilate."

Words clamored up his throat to challenge her on that. Because really, it was so much more than dinner. And she had no idea. No clue as to how Ren had grown up. His house didn't even have consistent electricity. His family had to walk into town and pay by the minute to use a computer to send him an email. They lived off low-paying jobs and anything extra came from selling mangoes to tourists. And now Ren was in a limo wearing a suit worth more than he could make on the playa in months. He didn't think he would even be able to tell his family about tonight. It was so far from who he was that it was almost a betrayal.

"Celeste," he said, the only word he was sure about, hoping it would open a communication link for all the other feelings he wasn't sure about. "This is ... I just ... I don't know."

She put a finger against his lips to stop him, forcing him to make eye contact with her. The crystal in her gaze was cracked with disappointment.

"Could you please try and enjoy yourself?" she asked, an innocent question that stung hard. She'd put so much work into making today a magical experience for him. It wasn't her fault his emotions were torn to the point he couldn't recognize them. He wasn't being fair to her. It was going to take getting used to, but he could speed things up by following her recommendation — he could try harder.

Ren delicately pulled his hand out of Celeste's, raising it so he could brush his thumb across her cheekbone. She leaned into his palm readily. *She is your choice*, he reminded himself. *And no one in the entire world could look at where you are right now and say you'd made a bad one. Don't ruin it.*

"I am enjoying myself," he confirmed, to her and to himself. "This is all just so ..." Oh, it was so. So overwhelming and humbling and practically incomprehensible. Celeste waited for him to finish his thought. "It's amazing," Ren said honestly. "But it's nothing like my apartment." Or Cabarete in the Dominican.

"I love your apartment," Celeste told him earnestly, almost too quickly. "It's so warm and comfortable there." Ren sighed, thinking of the couple of times Celeste had been at his apartment for longer than a few minutes. When she was there, it meant big things were happening, big parties, large events. It was normally full. But she hadn't seen it lately. Didn't know how much it had darkened. How quiet it was. How cold.

"I wanted to return the gesture," Celeste continued as Ren lowered his hand again. She looked out the window as the limo pulled up to the entrance of another tall, rectangular, concrete building. Another hotel? "Show you what my life looks like."

Though Ren had no real idea what he was doing or what he was getting into, he did know enough to get out of the limo before Celeste and hold his hand out to assist her exit. There was way too much fabric around her ankles, and he didn't want it to catch on her heeled shoes and trip her. The limo driver opened and closed the door for them, and Celeste gave him a guess as to when he would need to pick them up. He bowed his head to her before leaving.

Celeste took Ren's arm again, taking a deep breath for him and steering him toward a set of doors, seeing as Ren was completely bewildered as to where they were. He tried getting a sense from his surroundings, trying to map it out from his rounds in the ambulance, but in the end, he got his answer off a walkway next to the skyscraper with the words Chicago Stock Exchange on it.

"Stock exchange?" he mused aloud, letting Celeste lead him through the doors into the warmth of the entryway. They served dinner at the stock exchange building? Maybe he didn't actually know what a stock exchange was.

"Yes," Celeste confirmed they were in the right spot, nodding to an employee at a security counter who apparently already knew her, and heading toward a large elevator that looked incredibly old, and yet somehow sophisticated. A well-preserved historical artifact that still served a purpose. The clicks of Celeste's heels echoed in the lobby, contributing to the vastness of the space. "The restaurant is on the fortieth floor."

"Did you say forty?" Ren choked as once again Celeste moved

forward without him, though she stepped onto the elevator this time. This old contraption, however elegant, was really going to carry them up forty floors? The doors closed on Ren, and he wouldn't have been at all surprised if they opened on the moon. Maybe this had been a bad idea. He fidgeted with the buttons on the cuffs of the suit, trying to rehearse what he should say to Celeste's parents when he was introduced to them in a few minutes. He couldn't let this first impression be like his first meeting with Dr. Delacroix; he winced thinking about all the varied ways he could accidentally spill something on Celeste's mother. Or say the wrong thing. Or just —

"Ren?" Celeste said his name questioningly, watching him fussing with the unfamiliar parameters of his clothes. The necktie seemed to be knotted too tightly.

"Let me just apologize in advance for how I'm probably going to embarrass you tonight," Ren blurted out, watching the dial above the doors slowly but steadily climb to forty. "Dressing me up isn't going to hide it for long."

Celeste's hands shot forward, frighteningly fast, and yet she put her palms on either side of his face quite gently, holding him still and focused. He could barely feel the edge of her fingernails against his skin.

"Ren, let me make something extremely clear. I am not in the least ashamed of you — your background, your manners. And I think I know you well enough by now to be sure you won't embarrass either one of us. *If you can relax and just be yourself.* I didn't buy you a suit to hide who you are; I mostly did it so you wouldn't feel out of place." Ren opened his mouth, but she wasn't finished yet. "Because you should *not* feel out of place. You are in no way worth less than anyone you meet tonight. Do you know why they're here? To congratulate themselves on a successful fundraising year. It's a night where they get together and talk about all the good they accomplish in the world. And they can do that, they *are* doing good in the method they know best. But *you* — you stay up all night every month on that ambulance, you study more than anyone I've ever seen, work so hard. They give a lot, but you give *everything* to make the world better, and you deserve to be here. I know you'd probably have an easier time walking onto the scene of a car accident than into this restaurant, and I *respect* that about you. I'm glad you came with me, but please ... I promise I am not going to treat you any differently once we get off this elevator than I would in your apartment. And I hope you'll show me the same courtesy. Are we in agreement?"

Ren let his hands fall to his sides, chastised and encouraged all in one. Celeste let go of his face, breathing hard after her short tirade. The elevator continued to climb as silence settled between them.

"Good speech," Ren credited her awkwardly, not really knowing what to say. She tucked that imaginary piece of hair behind her ear again, smiling at the floor. "I needed it, thanks." He took her hand softly in his own, showing her his answer, swallowing his nerves, waiting for the dial to hit forty and the doors to open. Until a thought suddenly struck him.

"What do you mean you 'mostly' got me a suit so I wouldn't feel out of place?" Ren asked, focusing on that one word. "Was there another reason?"

Celeste's smile deepened, and Ren could see Celeste's smile was more of a protection than anything. She smiled when she was nervous. She smiled when she felt shy. He suspected she even smiled when she was furious. He wondered if he'd seen a genuine smile on her yet. Though as she turned her face toward him, eyes shining, he thought maybe he had.

"I thought you'd look good in one," Celeste stated, keeping her voice completely flat, practical, which made Ren smile. He smoothed his free hand down his side.

"And?" he pressed, teasing. "Do I?"

Celeste rolled her eyes, shoving him gently with one shoulder. "Of course, you do," she said. "I have excellent taste."

He laughed, which felt so good, breaking up the tension in his chest, loosening the stiffness between his shoulders. His mirth proved contagious as Celeste joined in, both of them laughing, happy, and carefree for the last few seconds before the elevator pulled to a stop on the fortieth floor. The tiny ding quieted them both down in an instant. The doors opened as Ren offered Celeste his arm in proper escort. He wasn't going to treat her differently, not really, but being on his best behavior wasn't really different. He was simply enhancing the respect he already showed her.

"You look wonderful," he whispered as they stepped into the restaurant. He couldn't believe he hadn't thought to say that until just now; he'd been so caught up in other things. The pressure of her fingertips along his inner elbow deepened in non-verbal response, and that was the last thing Ren remembered before being overcome with the elegance of the room. He stared, keeping his jaw locked so he wouldn't gape open-mouthed at things, while one of the restaurant employees asked Celeste for her wrap.

Golden light flooded the dining floor, bouncing off several large sculptures. Regularly spaced, white columns turned the area into a grid, and made the ceiling seem lower, though it felt more intimate than crowded. Small parties of diners in formal attire sat at ease around the room, delicately holding wine glasses or smoothing napkins in their laps. Every table had a different bronze sculpture as a centerpiece, and each and every item in the place seemed to have been set in its location with meticulous planning and care.

"This way," the employee entreated, gesturing for them to follow. "Your party is waiting for you."

Celeste had to give Ren just a slight tug to get him moving forward. They were led through the tables, toward the opposite wall where an enormous, silvery white curtain separated this piece from the rest of the establishment. The host elaborately pulled a portion of it aside to allow them entrance. Ren had the distinct impression he was about to fall down a rabbit hole. But a well-furnished, clean, and elegant one.

The greetings began almost immediately as the host dropped the curtain behind them, sealing them in with the other occupants of this private dining room. Instead of the long banquet table Ren had expected, this room was set with many circular tables where no more than six could be seated at a time. Though no one seemed to be seated, which meant they weren't that late. No, everyone was up, paused in their conversation by Ren and Celeste's arrival, and it seemed to Ren as though everyone turned to them at once, the room blooming with exclamations.

"Celeste!"

"You made it!"

"Oh, it's been so long, dear. Come give us a kiss."

There were other statements, but Ren couldn't really pick them all apart in the tumult their appearance had set off. Celeste elegantly acknowledged all who spoke to her by nodding to them or clasping at hands as they stretched out to her on their way through. Ren mostly clung to her and tried not to make direct eye contact with anyone. He thought they'd likely make the rounds of the room at some point tonight, but no matter the country or culture, the first priority was to introduce Ren to Celeste's parents.

Ren spotted them rapidly, mostly because Celeste's mother looked exactly like her. Same white-blonde, thick, wavy hair, same skin, same crystalline eyes. Age was just beginning to touch her face, but in a pleasant way, the sorts of wrinkles that grace those who are kind and find pleasure in their days. She stood with her arms extended to receive them, taking a step forward, her pale pink, silky evening gown gracefully tracking her movement. Ren felt encouraged as she smiled at them.

Meanwhile, Celeste's father stood at his wife's side, his blue eyes piercing and analytical. His hair wasn't white so much as silver gray, though it looked lighter because of the perfectly white suit he wore. Whiter perhaps than even Celeste's peacoat. Ren wasn't sure, but it looked as though his bowtie matched the blue one Celeste had bought for him. It made Mr. Lyons' eyes vibrant, but hard.

The conversational chatter started up again around them, but Ren became extremely conscious that the timbre had changed. He had the terrifying thought that everyone in this room was now talking about him. He made sure to keep his head up, remembering what Celeste had said. *You deserve to be here. It's not like you weren't invited.*

"Hello darling, did you have a good day?" Mrs. Lyons greeted her daughter, embracing her easily and gently kissing her cheek. "It's wonderful you could join us, Ren," she continued, extending her hand to him, gloved in satin the same color as her gown, in a gesture Ren only recognized from watching movies with Denny. Fumbling slightly, he slipped his fingers beneath hers and bent over her hand, kissing it with the gentlest pressure he could manage. He wasn't all that sure she'd enjoy this — his lips were sandpaper dry right now and caught momentarily in the satin.

"Pleased to finally meet you," Ren managed, hoping he was telling the truth.

"Yes, we've been hoping Celeste would bring you round. I understand you're studying to be a doctor," Mr. Lyons prompted, putting effort into sounding casually interested, though Ren felt bluntly and quickly judged. Maybe that's just what fathers did. Fathers with daughters. Fathers with extraordinarily bright, beautiful, and talented daughters.

"That's right," Ren confirmed, shaking hands with Celeste's dad, hoping his grip was firm enough. It had been a long time since he'd worked in the mango orchards; he'd been more focused on gentling his hands, on making his touch almost imperceptible to his donors. "I've got a long way to go, though."

"All good things to those who work for them," Mr. Lyons said, nodding appreciatively.

"But not tonight," Celeste's mother cut in, resting one palm on her husband's chest. "To everything there is a season, and in that spirit, our table is right over there."

Mrs. Lyons somehow managed to turn both her body and her husband's without seeming to move at all. Ren felt some of the rigidness in his own muscles relax at the thought of sitting down. Standing in the middle of the room felt too exposed.

"Felicity, now, don't sit down before introducing us. We're all dying to meet Celeste's friend."

Celeste stepped closer to Ren, almost possessively taking his arm, and he tried not to shrink into her side. This was starting to feel uncomfortable again. He knew he'd be under scrutiny from Celeste's parents — but all of their friends too? There were way more people here than he'd bargained for.

"Certainly, Charlotte," Celeste's mother returned, well-practiced at this sort of thing, though Celeste took it over.

"I'm pleased to introduce Ren Cordero," she said, giving his arm a squeeze before continuing in a rather bold tone, almost a challenge. "You're likely to see more of him, as we've been dating for weeks now."

"He's studying to be a doctor at the university," Mrs. Lyons volunteered, as though she wanted that point clearly understood. Ren watched Charlotte's smile pinch at the information, though he couldn't tell if she were pleased at the introduction or the gossip. He wondered if it would have made a difference if he'd been studying art history, or computer science. Would he be standing here right now if he were going for a bachelor's in creative writing?

"Cordero, you say?" Charlotte ventured, her eyes unfocusing for a moment as she ran through her mental database of anyone else with that name. "Are you one of Henry's boys?"

"No," Ren answered promptly, knowing for certain there was no way he and this woman would have any social connection outside of the girl he was already standing next to.

"Ren is an international student," Celeste continued for him, which somehow made it sound so much better than how he would have phrased it. He decided he should definitely let her continue to talk for him.

"Oh, how lovely," Charlotte replied, and now there were a few other women coming to join them, pulled in by Charlotte's brashness. "So where is it you come from?"

Ren looked at Celeste, but she gave him the tiniest half-shrug, letting him know he'd have to answer this one on his own.

"The Dominican Republic," Ren answered with only a slight stutter.

"You don't say? Isn't that interesting? Oh, and your English is just perfect; I'd never have guessed. Don't you think so too, Brenda?" Charlotte turned to one of her new companions. Ren noticed there were more of them now, not just ladies anymore, but a few of their husbands were closing in on the perimeter. He wanted to lean close to Celeste, not liking everyone being so focused on him. Was it because he was her boyfriend? Or just because they'd grown so tired of the same old faces at these functions that they were ready to grab on to anyone new?

"The Dominican Republic, eh?" one of the gentlemen standing behind his wife chortled. "How are you liking the winter, then?"

"Oh," Ren began, trying to think of some way to explain his thoughts about cold without hurting anyone's feelings about it. "The snow can be pretty if you're watching it from inside."

"And that's the truth," the man burst out mirthfully, nodding his head at Ren, who felt as though he'd gained some sort of ally.

"How long have you been living in the states, young man?" another woman questioned.

"What field of medicine do you plan to specialize in?" He heard the words, but now Ren wasn't sure on the direction. And they just kept coming. There were more voices, pushing and pulling on each other, the queries crowding in on Ren until he couldn't decipher one from the next. He tightened his hold on Celeste, not sure which or what to answer first.

"Now, now!" Celeste's father boomed in a tone that made it clear where he ranked in the room. "We'll pass around the boy's resume and business cards after dinner. Please take your seats; I believe the staff is waiting for our drink orders."

Like the closing scene of a play, the characters of this party returned almost automatically to their original positions, though one or two did continue to stare at Ren as they went. Ren forced himself not to slump in relief, hiding it by finally escorting Celeste to their table and pulling out her chair. The best part of that whole thing was it now didn't seem so daunting to be alone with Celeste's parents. Ren's heart rate slowed from "mortal danger" to "I didn't study hard enough for this test, and I woke up fifteen minutes late." Which, admittedly, wasn't much improvement, but still noticeable.

The table the Lyons had chosen pushed right against the large windows that covered the entire outer wall of the restaurant, and Ren had deliberately selected the seat closest to the window to protect Celeste against any chill that might come off the glass. Though now that he was standing next to it, he found himself frozen, not by the cold but by the view. Before, the inside lighting had obscured the glass, turning it into a mirror more than a window, but now he was standing right next to it, Ren could see out. See what it meant to be on the fortieth floor of the Chicago Stock Exchange.

Now he knew why they had named this restaurant Everest.

From this height, Chicago looked like it stretched on over the curvature of the earth, its streets laced over the land in elaborate patterns, bejeweled by lights of every color and brightness. Directly across, there were other buildings as high as this one, though there weren't many with lights on this late on a Sunday evening. The true spectacle was the moving cars beneath them. Red brake lights. Green traffic lights. Headlights of all sorts. Ren wished he could take a picture through this glass and have it come out anywhere close to the reality of what he was seeing. Though maybe it was for the best no photo would do this justice. Ren still didn't know how or if he could ever tell his family about tonight.

Ren moved his head slightly to change the perspective and was hit with sudden vertigo. He knew there was no possible way the building swayed, it was hard steel and concrete, rigid and steadfast, standing in this very spot since before he was born, but now that he could *see* how far from the ground he was, it made it feel as though it were moving. He could hear the other people in the room, talking and laughing together softly, the atmosphere cheery, a happy buzz on the outskirts of his dizziness, as though they didn't notice how high they were. How close they were to disaster.

"Ren, dear, are you all right?" Mrs. Lyons' sweet voice broke through the paralysis the window had caused him. He turned away from it, blinking, just now noticing how tightly he gripped to the back of his chair. He hadn't even pulled it out yet; he'd been held captive by the height.

"What?" he said, though he didn't know why. He had heard the question. "Yes," he responded quickly without making her repeat herself. "Of course."

"Sit down," Celeste invited, placing her steady hand over his. He registered out of the corner of his eye that Mr. Lyons was staring critically at him. Not a good sign, but he hadn't expected to get through an entire obstacle course of people only to be struck dumb and motionless by a window.

"Didn't seem that high going up the elevator," Ren tried to laugh off the last few seconds, tried to not be so stiff as he found his chair and scooted it close, grounding himself as much as possible. He deliberately faced away from the window, breathing in deeply as the building held still again.

"Should we move to another table?" Mrs. Lyons suggested worriedly, all her presence dedicated to helping Ren be comfortable.

"No, this one's great," Ren denied, trying to imperceptibly shake himself clear of the last couple seconds. "The view is perfect from *this* angle." Here he dedicatedly looked at Celeste, satisfied he'd made her smile. He heard Mrs. Lyons make an approving little coo, seated across the table from her daughter.

A waiter came, making suggestions on starters and wines. Mr. Lyons ordered for the table with brisk efficiency, and then the interrogation began.

It came, of course, in the guise of small talk, but Ren could feel it, nonetheless. Celeste's parents, understandably, wanted to know all about him. Ren answered best he could, begging for breaks as he inserted his own questions.

They asked about Celeste's and his relationship, so he asked them how they'd met and fallen in love. They asked about his future plans, and he asked about Mr. Lyons' company. Mrs. Lyons asked a hesitant question about his name that brought the smoothness of the conversation to a halt.

"Forgive me," she started, sipping from her wine glass. "But your name — I'm surprised."

Right, this question. Ren had heard it before, though usually it was thrown out there with much less tact. *What the hell kind of name is Ren?*

"It doesn't sound very Latino, does it?" Ren responded, trying to sound good-natured. She relaxed slightly in her chair as he put her at ease about possibly offending him. "That's because it's a nickname I picked up when I moved here."

"Ren is a nickname?" Celeste chimed next to him, and Ren wished the seating were different. He would have preferred Celeste across from him where he could watch her reactions better, where she could let him know if he were doing something wrong. She was almost out of his field of vision where she was, though she had started communicating with finger pressure on his knee or hand since direct eye contact was awkward. It felt like having a conversation in braille with audible words thrown in only here and there.

"My full name is Lorenzo," Ren told them, feeling Celeste press in shock and question into his leg. "With another four names in the middle, but the only person who uses all six is my mother when I'm in trouble."

"Really?" Celeste said, amazed, as Mrs. Lyons laughed lightly at the mention of Ren's mother. Ren suddenly wished he hadn't revealed that little-known-detail about himself. It made it look strange that he'd been dating Celeste for over a month, and she didn't even know his name. Fortunately, he was saved by a platter of fancy French dishes, and the conversation moved on as if nothing important had been uncovered in that moment.

They ate things Ren had never heard of, prompted by Celeste's excitement to share her favorites with him, and it was all delicious. He felt Celeste watching him from the side in fascination, and he knew she was enjoying this. She liked watching him experience these things for the first time.

Ren very pointedly did not look out the window again, though he could feel the chill from it on the back of his neck. He pulled his focus away, towards Celeste's parents, towards the words they were exchanging more than four hundred feet above the ground. He continued to answer questions long past dessert. He shook hands with strangers who came to their table to say goodbye before they began to make their way home. And finally, Celeste made a comment on the time and pressed against Ren's knee, a combination that indicated she was ready to go. Ren was more than willing to accommodate her.

He stood, perhaps too eagerly, and helped her scoot her chair away from the table. She and her parents embraced again, and Ren noticed her mother held onto her for a long time. He noticed her father's handshake with him was exceptionally firm, and he locked eyes with Ren fiercely. There was a silent communication happening here, but he wasn't sure what it was. In fact, it didn't hit him until they'd returned to the hotel room, and Celeste surprised him yet again with a bag containing new pajamas and a fresh set of clothes for him to wear in the morning.

She meant for them to stay in this hotel room. Together. Alone.

"You were marvelous," Celeste complimented him after handing over the clothes. He stood still, not sure what to do, watching her move around the room, setting her tiny bag on the end table beside the bed, lifting her hands to begin removing the sapphires from her hair. She moved casually at ease, completely in control.

"Celeste," he paused her, concerned. "What's going on?" He brandished the bag with the clothes in it. "Aren't you dropping me off at my place?" Because he thought she'd booked this room as a staging area, a place to get ready for her dinner so she wouldn't have to drive all the way out to Oak Brook and back. He thought when the event was over, they'd come back here, change, and then part ways for the night. He'd see her again tomorrow after work; they'd get coffee like always. Celeste let her arms drop, one cupped palm full of her hair pins. She stared at him, deciphering his body language, taking her time before she spoke.

"It's close to ten, Ren," she said with practicality. "You know how my parents feel about me driving home in the dark. Besides, I thought you wouldn't want to be alone tonight."

There was nothing but logic in her words; she said them calmly. And Ren did know how her parents felt about driving, winter, and darkness. But how did they feel about sharing a hotel room with him? Ren had to swallow hard before he could say anything, his eyes drawn to the bed dominating the center of the room. The single bed in the room. Had her parents known this was the plan tonight? Is that why her mother hugged her so hard? Why her father had practically glared at Ren?

"Celeste, do your parents know that —"

"I'm twenty years old, Ren," she said fiercely. Like she had made this point to someone else before. "I don't need my parents' permission to stay the night with my boyfriend in a hotel room."

She might not need permission, but Ren thought he might need to take out a better life insurance policy or hire a bodyguard if Mr. Lyons even suspected that Ren had slept with his daughter.

*Whoa, wait, hold on.* He hadn't just thought that. Was that her goal, though? Is that what she'd brought him here for? Planned the whole day just so it would end up here? Ren blinked, and suddenly Celeste stood right in front of him, slipping her arms around his neck, her hair unbound and falling in waves around her face. He didn't mean to, but he tensed. She backed down immediately, looking hurt. Ren quickly grabbed her wrist, needing to talk this out, clarify exactly what the expectations were. Because tonight was suddenly more serious than he'd thought, serious and delicate, and he didn't want to break something here that couldn't be fixed. Celeste looked at him expectantly, waiting.

"Today was wonderful," he started, holding her tight. "And before you showed up this morning, I thought it was going to be one of the worst days of my life. Thanks so much for setting it all up. But I just —"

*I just can't even **talk** about sharing that bed with you.* Ren took a deep breath. Celeste had her head tilted, focused on him, reading nuances in his body language, his tone, his hesitancy.

"I just feel like we've gone from five to five hundred in two and a half seconds," he tried to explain. "Last week, we could only manage to meet up for lunch twice, and today I learned you have a coat hook at the aquarium and a limo driver, and your parents regularly take you to dinners at one hundred and sixty-five dollars a plate. I just ... it's a lot, ok, and surprises are awesome, but if we're going to ... if that's going to happen ... I want to be ready for it. I don't want that to be a surprise. I want it to be something we plan together. Ok?"

He paused, waiting for her reaction. To his amazement, Celeste smiled, not the tight-lipped version he'd imagined for when she was angry. Her face was soft, though perhaps disappointed, and she went up on tiptoe to kiss his cheek.

"You're sweet," she told him, and he hoped she meant it favorably. He couldn't tell if he'd hurt her feelings. It wasn't like he didn't *want* to. Hell, did he want to? He did, and he didn't. He just wasn't sure, and he hadn't been expecting it. He'd imagined it, plenty of times, but somehow, he'd never dreamed something like this. The warm, low lights. The smell of lavender. Celeste Lyons. Hold on a minute, was he really turning down Celeste Lyons? Was he an idiot?

"I can call for a ride home for you," Celeste offered, breaking into his mental storm.

"Wait," he said before he knew what he was offering. He tugged her closer, easing his hand onto her waist, the plush of the velvet beneath his fingertips. "It is late," he agreed. "And you're right; I don't want to be alone tonight."

*I don't want to be alone ever.*

Celeste beamed, and suddenly they were separated as she released him, heading for her bathroom. "Get changed then," she told him, walking backwards.

Ren turned to do as he was told, rather weak-kneed now the decision had been made that, at least in some capacity, they were both going to sleep in the same bed. What would his sister Siara have to say about that? Denny? Alek? He knew what his brothers would do if he were home and he could tell them about this. They'd jab him in the ribs, make those jeering noises. His mother on the other hand — but then again, Celeste wasn't the only one who was old enough to make her own choices about things like this. And he wasn't doing anything wrong.

He still startled alarmingly when his phone rang halfway through changing out of his suit. He shook himself with a stern reminder that he hadn't done anything to feel guilty about. And he knew for a fact it wasn't his mother calling him.

"Justin?" Ren answered questioningly, as though he'd somehow mistaken the contact information his phone had helpfully supplied him.

"Hey," came the reply, over a thousand miles away. It made Justin's voice sound different, or that could just have been the time that separated their last meeting with this phone call. Ren wasn't the only one who'd had a busy day.

"How are you?" Ren asked, plopping down cross-legged on the bathmat, wearing only the pajama pants. He held the phone tightly, eager. "What was your first day like?"

"We haven't really started yet," Justin told him. "Today was just getting here and getting ready. I've got a bunk and a locker now. Zero week starts in the morning."

"Did they cut your hair?" Ren hadn't meant to ask that question, didn't know why it really mattered to him.

"Oh," Justin half-laughed, and Ren knew Justin was now self-consciously rubbing the back of his head. "Yeah. It feels weird to have it so short." Ren tried to imagine Justin with the practically shaved haircut of boot camp, but the only thing he could think of was that it would likely make Justin's eyes even larger. "The food is good, though."

"Huh," Ren exhaled, smiling, hearing again what Justin didn't say. He was in a secure place with a strict routine, with hot meals provided to him on a consistent basis. Though Ren had heard nightmare stories about boot camp, he thought it would be close to heaven for Justin. Good. He deserved it.

"What about you? You ate today, right?" Justin pressed him, making Ren remember the last time he said goodbye to his friends. How he'd run away to the ER for the entire day and only left because Justin and North dragged him out the door.

"I did," Ren assured, and suddenly the reality of what was happening hit him. He was sitting in a hotel bathroom wearing new pajamas. Celeste was similarly changing across the room. How was this his life now? "I think I ate duck."

"Duck?" Justin repeated.

"Uh, yeah. Celeste took me to dinner today. I met her parents."

"Nice," Justin said.

"Yeah," Ren responded, not quite sure.

"I've only got a minute," Justin explained, and Ren's heart sank. They hadn't had a chance to even talk. It was so good to hear Justin talk. "They let you have one phone call to tell your family you arrived on base. After this, I won't be able to call again. You could write me, though. If you wanted."

"Yes," Ren almost hissed. "What's the address?" He quickly switched the speaker so he could type it out as Justin gave it to him. They'd said goodbye to each other only that morning, and now Justin was twelve hundred miles away. So far away and not coming back.

"Ren, you ok?" Well, he thought he had been until Justin asked. He held the phone away so he could clear his throat.

"Sure," he lied. Justin had used his only phone call to contact him. What did that even mean? Justin had wanted them to do this Air Force thing together. He wanted Ren to write him. That was good. Except it was horrible. "Good luck, you know, with everything."

"Yeah, you too."

"I'll write you."

"Thanks."

Ren squeezed his eyes shut, held the phone tighter, though he could still feel Justin slipping away. He'd taken two minutes to tear something open in Ren, and now he was leaving again.

"See you, Justin," Ren said in parting, unable to tell Justin goodbye.

"Take care, Ren."

Ren didn't bother hanging up. He made Justin do it. Made him be responsible for closing their communication for who knew how long. Then he sat there on the mat with the phone in his hand, not a stranger to the emptiness that came with a conversation ended too soon, though this time it held a particular sharpness to it. Because unlike his family, Ren didn't know when he'd talk to Justin again. And he knew from experience that written letters were nowhere near as good.

He sat there longer than he knew he should. In fact, it wasn't until Celeste knocked on the bathroom door that he even tried to get up. She considered him curiously when he let her in, and he realized he was still shirtless, still holding the phone.

"Justin called," he told her, wishing he didn't sound like that was the end of the world. "He's on base now."

Celeste put her hand on his cheek, eyes shining sympathetically. She took the phone so he could finish dressing. She helped him hang the suit behind the door. Then she took his hand and led him toward the bed, tucking them both under the slippery sheets and snuggling up close to him.

"I'm sorry," Ren apologized to her, knowing his attitude wasn't acceptable. It wasn't fair to her. Not after all she'd done for him today.

"For what?" Celeste said softly. "For missing your best friend?" She surprised him with a cool kiss on his neck, under his jawbone. "I'd be shocked if you didn't."

Ren turned from his back to adjust their positioning, hating how Celeste didn't really understand. Hating how she was trying to make him feel better about it. He slid one arm underneath Celeste so he could pull her closer to him. She responded by draping an arm across his chest, placing her palm on his shoulder, resting her head just beneath his. He breathed her in, waiting for it to be real. She'd turned off the lamps; there was nothing but cold moonlight in the room now, reflecting off the white of her hair. He played with it, watching the glow shift in the dark.

*You are an idiot*, he told himself, because even as he held Celeste close, lifting locks of her hair and watching as the strands fell slowly when he turned his fingers, he still pictured Justin, rubbing the back of his neck where his hair used to be.

He had to figure this out; he couldn't exist in two places like this forever. At some point, he'd have to come into synch with what was real. It would just *have* to feel real eventually. Right?

"Ren," Celeste's voice again, a sweet purring he felt against his heart.

"Hmm," he hummed a response, studying the patches of light in the room, figuring out the new shapes of the furniture, determining what the shadowed lines were and what they meant.

"Tell me your names."

"You'll be asleep before I get to the end," Ren warned her.

"I can't think of a better way to fall asleep," Celeste returned, and it hurt. Ren hugged her, as tightly as he dared. He started reciting his names, a slow, rhythmic mantra meant more to ground himself than anything else. *Remember your name. Remember who you are, and where you are. Remember why you came, what you wanted to do.*

He brushed his fingertips through her hair. She asked him more soft questions. There began to be longer pauses between them, and somehow Ren fell asleep with Celeste in his arms. And even after he woke in the morning, he stared at her without really seeing her. Because how could she really be there?

But she was. Stirring awake, snuggling close to him. He kissed her forehead just as another test. He brushed her hair away from her face. She smiled at him.

"Good morning, Princess," he whispered to her. She kissed him under his jaw again, and something inside him tried to wake up. He ran his hand down her arm, coming to rest against her hip. *She's here. This is how it is now. It's good. It's gorgeous.*

"I could get used to this," Celeste whispered, eyes sparkling. Crystal and pure.

"I think I could too." And he wanted to mean it.

# 9
# MATRIMONY

For the next three years, Ren tried to get used to it. God, he tried. For her sake. For his sanity. They were so busy most of the time, it was easy to pretend that the getting used to it had already happened. He didn't have to think about anything too much, not anything past the next check on the list. Both Celeste and Ren excelled at making lists and keeping calendars. And they both had plenty to fill them with.

They got good at it, whatever this was. It felt a lot like playing house, except they weren't playing. In fact, it almost felt too serious. Ren knew he and Celeste were in a relationship, a dedicated one, but it seemed to progress without his knowledge or input, and he paused every so often as the revelation hit him that this was not his imagination, and he wasn't eight pretending to cook dinner with his *primas* in the mango orchard. This was really happening.

Not long after their stay at the hotel, Celeste added her name to Ren's contract and turned Ren's apartment into their home. She pranced through the door with a box of books like a certified Disney princess about to break into song. Alek's single remaining herb plant on the counter thrived under her care, though Ren had to sneak the ugly afghan and the camp chair out of her donation pile and into his closet. He didn't know why; they weren't even his or Alek's. But he didn't want them to leave the place.

Alek's room transformed into Celeste's; his yellow and black plaid bedspread replaced with her pale blue gingham one. His stacks of video games and electronic whatevers turned into neat rows of shoes and piles of books with hardcore titles. Ren enjoyed Celeste's room; the contrast of the soft feminine clothes and colors with the intensity and power of the literature amused him. And while Ren remained fiercely devoted to Alek, he had to admit the room smelled a lot better with Celeste staying there, equal parts lotion and bookstore.

As a couple, they spent time together when they could, as often as they could, but mostly they had rapid conversations over text or phone, or they would frequently shoot through the bullet points of a moment as they passed each other in the apartment, crossing paths between separate appointments. Variations on a never-ending theme.

"I'm on my way out. There are leftovers in the fridge from the auction last night. My mother sent them over. I think she thinks we're starving?"

"We kind of are? I'll try to make it to the grocery store tomorrow, but I'll be home late tonight."

"Me too. How did your anatomy test go?"

"Great. You've got the city council meeting tonight, right?"

"That's right. I'm speaking."

"You'll be fantastic. We're out of milk; are you still drinking that almond stuff?"

"Yes, but just get both. I know you don't like it. Don't forget we're meeting my family for the gala on the weekend. I put it on your calendar already, and your clothes are labeled in the closet for you, ok?"

"Sure. Thanks."

"*Bésame por suerte.*"

"Hey! *Bien hecho.*"

They had coffee at Hallowed Grounds between classes on Mondays and Thursdays, phone calls with his family on Sunday mornings, and dinners with her parents on Sunday nights. There were classes and lectures, labs and paperwork. He and Celeste studied together on the couch when it snowed, Celeste pausing Ren in his work often to share a particularly insightful quote she'd read. They took turns doing meal prep on Saturdays because neither of them liked to cook, and it was almost impossible to take time for it during the week. He let her pick out his clothes for whenever they went out together, a myriad of dinners, galas, and charity auctions. The rest of the time, he just wore scrubs.

While Celeste attended city council meetings and political rallies, Ren spent most of his time at the hospital. He divided his hours between the plasma center, Dr. Taneja on the third floor, and Dr. Delacroix in the ER. He assisted with emergency surgeries. He placed sutures. He trained with the Life Flight nurses and taught first-aid courses to university faculty and staff. He did an unbelievable amount of scrubbing up and taking vitals. And he threaded IVs like it was his calling in life.

And it was perfect. Except for how it wasn't real. How Ren felt like he was part of a sitcom television show where everyone seemed to know what was going on except him. He tried to explain it to Alek one night as they were on the phone together but couldn't quite find the right words. He staggered through the issue only to have Alek verbally shrug at him.

"I think it's called adulting, dude," Alek told him. "You'll get the hang of it; you're doing fine."

Then they talked about the Hubble space telescope, some man named Walt who did maintenance on it, and the methods they used for data collection, and Ren listened to all Alek said, but he couldn't stop thinking about how he was surrounded by people who seemed to be "adulting" so easily. Like Alek and Denny — they had bought a *house* together, for heaven's sake. Like, they had an address now that didn't have a second line to it. No Apt F or anything like that. Their backyard fence was completely obscured by bright pink and purple bougainvillea. Alek's counter herb garden was now an external kitchen garden complete with a lemon and kumquat tree. He and Denny were first authors on publications in peer-reviewed journals, and they complained vehemently about having to respond to reviewers and create annual funding reports instead of building astonishingly sophisticated robots and the computer programs to run them.

It was crazy. Insane how Ren could find himself in the ambulance putting pressure on a bleeding wound, hyper-focused and outside of time, and then suddenly, he'd be standing outside with Celeste on a balcony at twilight with a champagne glass in his hand *three months later*. As though his life weren't progressing in a linear fashion, more like his timeline was a ball of silly putty in the hands of a four-year-old who kept stretching it out between his fingers and then scrunching it up again without warning. Everything was slippery and just slightly foggy, as though he functioned on autopilot and only occasionally lifted his head to see where he was and what was going on.

But he didn't have much choice. Because dreams move forward in strange ways without a lot of conscious control. But he continued to try. Tried to slow it down, tried to focus. Tried to be *present*, an active participant in his own life. Tried to plan so it would feel as though he were at least *in* a boat as he was being swept down a fast-moving river. He practiced *looking* at things, forcing himself to attach emotions to what he saw, tried not to be numb.

He did like watching Celeste's hands as she put up her hair, or chopped vegetables, or did her makeup. The ritual of simple things. The movement of her finger across her lower lip as she concentrated on whatever she was reading. He paid attention to details like those, thinking things to himself about how lovely she was, how talented, how intelligent and driven. How lucky he was to have her. How they'd been together for six months or nine months or twenty. How he wished he appreciated her more. How he should probably talk to her. How he couldn't talk to her. How it was too late, and he didn't need to talk to her.

It didn't actually matter. The talking. Not about real things. Because Ren had developed an affinity for saying only and exactly what everyone wanted to hear, for writing his life the way it was supposed to be and not the way he perceived it, trying to force himself to believe what he said and what he wrote was the truth. He had plenty of opportunity to convince himself. It seemed he was always updating someone on what was going on. He called his family. Had regularly scheduled chats with Alek and Denny. Had almost daily meetings with Dr. Delacroix. He emailed back and forth with North. And he answered the same question over and over and over.

*How are you?*

"I'm great, Mom. We're getting ready for the annual Christmas party at Celeste's dad's company. Celeste said they're ordering shrimp cocktail for two thousand. Um, no, I don't know where they get that much shrimp; I guess they buy out Thailand?"

"Super busy, Denny, but you are too, aren't you? Did you ever resolve that formula you were trying to prove? What about that jerk who called you out at the last forum meeting? Did you make him cry when you dismantled his theory?"

"Life is good, bro. Your basil plant says hi. Celeste's taking excellent care of it."

"I'm fine, North; how about you? Have you heard anything from Justin? Seen him recently?"

Because while Ren sent hundreds of letters to Lackland Air Force base, the responses back were few and far between. At first, a letter turned up once a week like clockwork, stamped with an American flag postmark. Ren and Justin wrote pages and pages to each other. Ren talked about Dr. Delacroix and his training in the ER and about all the new places Celeste was showing him. Justin talked about training, and the food, and he wrote at length about the planes and how long it would be before he could touch one. Ren talked about Celeste moving in, about telescopes, about how Mrs. Lyons' Charity Aid ladies had all seemed to adopt him. How one of them was teaching him how to knit. Justin invited Ren to his training graduation. Ren desperately wanted to go but had to decline as he was acting as a TA for a biochemistry class, along with about fifty other commitments.

Ren asked if Justin were coming with North to the wedding, but North replied that Justin was sorry and wouldn't be able to join him.

The news crushed Ren. He'd been certain Justin would be there, especially if North came, and it seemed strange to have the event without him. Because, truly, the wedding would have never happened without Justin, though it had been far from anyone's minds at the time. Still, the day Justin was rushed to the ER, it introduced Officer Frederick Geisler to Doctor Angelique Delacroix, and their consequent romance was a surprise to everyone. Not that they weren't compatible or anything, just that, especially for Ren, Dr. Delacroix seemed to be a force that could only exist on her own. She burned too bright for anyone else to touch. The thought of her getting married unsettled Ren. He had always thought ER doctors could either be married or they could be ER doctors. The fact that Dr. Delacroix was going to be both shook him.

They were much closer now, Dr. Delacroix and Ren. He spent more time with her than he did with Celeste. During all her shifts, he remained at her side, and they often ate lunch together in the hospital cafeteria as they debriefed cases. Sometimes Geisler would join them.

After a year, Ren could anticipate the majority of her decisions and often handed her tools she needed without her having to ask. She finally started calling him Ren, and he started addressing her as Doña, a term of respectful endearment because saying her full name and title often took too long in the heat of the moment. She'd balked at first until Ren had a chance to explain to her what the word was and what it meant for him to use it. Then she seemed hesitantly pleased.

Ren seemed to be the only thing Dr. Delacroix was hesitant about. She seemed at odds about him — one day drilling skill sets into him so hard it brought him to the brink of tears and the next treating him as though he should be protected from the sight of blood. Sometimes when she snapped at him, she'd call him another name, not Ren or Lorenzo, but she would not talk about it when he asked her afterward. Ren noticed she was most gentle with him the days after she called him something else. She asked to see his hands almost constantly, frequently taking them in hers, turning his palms up and pressing her thumbs against the underside of his wrists. He grew skilled in making sure that whenever she did this, his hands remained steady. He learned how to keep eye contact. In those moments, it was a good thing to be numb. He did what he could, did his best to keep up with her, stopped asking about the name.

Ren noticed Geisler turned up for lunch more frequently, but even though Ren watched them together, watched how he kissed her, watched as her face lit up when she saw him — it was still a shock to learn they were getting married. She never talked about her life outside the hospital. She'd given no hint. In fact, he learned about the wedding when Angelique flipped an invitation at him on his way out the door, exhausted after a shift with her. She barely looked at him as she shot it into his hands; she didn't even break her stride. He had to follow her to her office to ask her about it.

"What is this?" he asked, unfamiliar with the size and shape of the envelope she had just given him. It wasn't a patient file, case study, or textbook. It did have his name on it, in a calligraphy script Ren knew for certain hadn't been penned by Angelique.

"It's a wedding invitation," Angelique told him brusquely, straightening the other paperwork on her desk in preparation to leave. This confused him. Why would she be giving this to him? Had someone stopped by the ER while he'd been busy and left it for him? But who? The only couple he remembered getting engaged recently was Sheridan and Noah, but their wedding date was set for the fall, so they wouldn't be sending out invitations this early, right? The envelope was sealed only by a golden sticker, so Ren opened it up for inspection, standing in the office doorway, shocked when he saw the names printed on the stiff card inside.

"You're getting *married*?!" he hooted at Dr. Delacroix without thinking, earning himself a glare.

"Is there a problem with that?" Angelique demanded. Ren internally retreated, though he struggled to picture her in anything other than scrubs and a white lab coat, tried to imagine her standing next to Fritz, exchanging vows and rings and everything. Though, really, why not? Why shouldn't they be happy together? Because you couldn't *be* in a relationship and be in the ER at the same time. It just didn't work. All the greatest doctors Ren had seen were either single or had broken romances. Angelique getting married seemed like a huge risk, and honestly, the only reason Ren and Celeste had lasted so long doing what they did was because ...

"No," Ren amended, abruptly switching his brain to another channel, staring at the card, trying to remember what the right words should be for situations like this. "No, it's great, Doña. Congratulations."

She softened more in that moment than Ren had ever seen her. Her smile was light and brilliance, and she turned her gaze downward to her desk. He realized he'd never seen her so genuinely happy before. It looked amazing on her. He suddenly wished hard for her to get everything she wanted in marrying Officer Geisler.

"I hope you'll be there," she expressed, scattering his thoughts. "We would have never met without you."

"And here I thought nothing good happened that day," Ren said lightly, though his memories of that time were tainted and strange. There'd been so much pain and fear then. And yet, Ren would have walked out of this office and back into that triage room with Justin in a heartbeat. Any time. His steps always slowed when he walked by it now, remembering the night he had spent with Justin inside.

And he wanted it back. To go back to that time, awful as it was. Just so he would have Justin so close again. Just so he could do it over. He knew it was a stupid thing to want, and he tried not to think about it.

But thinking about Justin must have been all over his face as he stood there with the invitation in his hands because Dr. Delacroix suddenly presented a second envelope to him. This one had Justin's name on it.

"It was a horrible day for him, but I can't say I'm sad it happened," she said quietly, as if she knew this was a delicate topic. "You know where to find him, I assume? Could you get this to him?"

"He's in the Air Force," Ren answered, his voice far away, still in the triage room years ago. He wondered sometimes if he'd ever really left. "I can send it to the address I have, but I don't know how long it takes to reach him."

This information seemed to confuse her. She tilted her head, reading his body language and tone. He forced his shoulders back, tried to hold eye contact with her.

"You two don't talk anymore?" she asked bluntly. "I thought you were inseparable."

"I mean, I write him," Ren defended, as though he wanted it clear that if they weren't close anymore, it had nothing to do with his lack of effort. "But I don't know where he's stationed right now, and it can take months for him to reply."

She softened again. Sympathetically this time. She reached for Justin's invitation, intending on taking it back, on not making it Ren's responsibility. He unconsciously pressed it against his chest, unwilling to part with it. He wanted to be the point of contact for Justin. He wanted it to always be this way — if someone wanted to find Justin, they would ask Ren where he was. Because he'd always know. Best friends always know. Or they should.

"I'll send it," Ren promised. "Maybe he'll come."

"Maybe," Angelique echoed, withdrawing her hand, though she sounded like she already knew he wouldn't. "These years, though;

they're so full. Both of you so busy learning who you are and where you fit in this world. Be patient. Don't rush."

Ren was certain there was wisdom in what she was telling him; he just wished he understood it. Be patient with what? With Justin? He was nothing but patient with Justin. But how was it not supposed to hurt when Ren learned that almost all his friends had more contact with Justin than he did? It came in conversations all over the place. As though messages from Justin had to come to Ren via other sources — paper-cut painful postscripts. *Justin says hi. Justin says good luck. Justin says he's fine.*

Ren took it. Better a P.S. than nothing at all. And he kept writing. Kept sending the letters to Lackland because he didn't know where else to send them. Kept talking about whatever random thing was happening in his life because he couldn't tell Justin any of the real things he thought about as far as they were concerned. The things he tried not to think or feel. *I miss you. I wish I could see you again, talk to you again. Do you still have my hoodie? Do you think of me when you wear it? Did you know I didn't want you to go? Did you know I was falling in love with you? Maybe I should have told you that. I'm still in love with you; I try every single day to not be in love with you; I think I've broken all my emotional response trying not to be in love with you. Would you hate me if you knew? I hate that it's too late now. I hate that you're so far away, and I don't even know where. I hate that you talk to everyone else more than to me. I hate how my life is perfect, and I don't even like it.*

Ren didn't say anything like that, but he continued writing all the other, less important things. About finals. About galas with Celeste and her parents. About books on anatomy and labs with cadavers. He kept taking and sending pictures. And just when he would be ready to give up on Justin all together, when he thought it was finally time to just break all ties because there was nothing there and never going to be, and he was just so tired of hurting and trying, and maybe it would all go away, maybe everything would be fixed, if he could just let this one thing go — *then*, as if on cue, something would turn up from Justin. Something tangible — a letter, a package

— and Ren's closure about their relationship would tear itself to shreds as he'd carefully inspect whatever it was Justin sent.

They always came to Ren battered, much like Justin himself, as if they'd traveled halfway across the world and passed through many hands to get to him. Ren hated that he liked that — the unintentional symbolism of it. They were forwarded through Texas, so Ren was never sure exactly how far they'd journeyed to get to him, and Justin never specified where he was, but that part didn't matter so much. The point was Justin hadn't forgotten him. The point was that even though Justin corresponded with Alek and Denny more often, and seemed to stay with North frequently, he never mailed anything physical to anyone except Ren. Never took the time to handwrite anything to anyone other than Ren, a detail that drove Ren insane. Still, whatever Justin's motives, Ren always took his time with the mail, treated each one with reverence. Reading the letters slowly, repeatedly, fingering the pages Justin had once handled, trying to guess where Justin had bought any of the things that he mailed him.

He sent Ren a small wooden box of exceptional tea that tasted of coconut and caramel. A CD from a pianist Ren hadn't heard of. Spanish copies of *A Tale of Two Cities* and *Jonathan Livingston Seagull.* A package of hard, scorched-rice flavored candy with Asian lettering on it that Ren loved so much he forced himself to only eat one piece a week to make them last as long as possible.

And each time he received a letter, he'd hug Celeste tighter the next time he saw her. Tried to do something extra nice for her during the days that followed. Because reading between the lines of Justin's words, slowly letting that candy melt in his mouth, felt like cheating on her. Like he was having some weird secret affair with a shadow or a memory or a wish.

She noticed; she'd comment. Say fly-away things like, "you're extra cuddly today," or "did I do something special to deserve this?" or the one that deeply cut into Ren even though she said it teasingly, "are you hiding something?"

He didn't want to be hiding things. He wanted to be what she thought him to be. What his mother and his friends all thought him to be. The person he'd left the Dominican to become. So, he read one more book Celeste recommended. Made one more meal she liked best. Learned to knit hats. Vacuumed the living room, cleaned the refrigerator, and pushed his feelings further and further under. And most days, it was fine. Most days, Ren was numb but moving. Sometimes, he was even happy in a complicated sort of way.

The day it all started unraveling began just like that. Happy in a complicated way.

Celeste came with Ren to the wedding, which took place on a Saturday at the beginning of May, three years into their relationship, and the day following Ren's monthly ambulance night shift. Celeste let him sleep as long as possible, but still had to wake him to get ready. By that time of the morning, his room was filled with warm sunlight, which Ren normally liked, but today the sun seemed almost painfully bright. The edges of his vision blurred as he went through the motions of getting up and shaving, and he couldn't tell if it was the bright sun or staying up all night causing it.

"Here." Celeste appeared while he was in the bathroom, presenting him with a mug of strong coffee.

"How'd you know?" Ren sighed, accepting it gratefully and groaning in relief as the hot liquid burned its way into his system. Celeste's coffee hit more like a shot than anything else, which made sense seeing as her only purpose in making or drinking it outside of being social was exactly why she was giving it to Ren right now — a caffeinated wake-up jolt.

Celeste leaned against the doorway of the bathroom with her arms folded, watching him finish cleaning the sink and his razor. "Well, three hours of sleep is hardly enough for anyone to face a busy day uncaffeinated — even you. I wish you could have traded someone for a better night."

"The only available night to trade conflicted with the union banquet," Ren reminded her, taking another long swallow of coffee. "It's all right; I don't know if a good night exists for this."

"How was it?" Celeste asked, concerned. She'd still been asleep when Ren came home early this morning. Ren shook his head, then leaned immediately on the sink when the movement made the room spin. *Wow, shouldn't have done that.*

"Ren?"

"We didn't lose anyone," he told her, blinking away the last few seconds. He hoped that was all the information she required. Her question had already started the flashbacks. Another overdose. An electrical fire in an apartment building. A fourteen-year-old girl whose parents discovered her bulimia because she accidentally got an entire spoon stuck down her throat trying to induce vomiting. Ren put down the coffee mug on the sink before Celeste could see it shake and took a step toward the doorway to grab her tight. *We didn't lose anyone, but that girl's eyes.* The mother's face as it dawned on her what her daughter had been doing to herself.

Celeste returned his hug, whispering an apology into his ear. "I'll stop asking," she promised, and for a few minutes, they stood silent as Ren struggled with his thoughts.

"You look nice," Ren changed the subject when he trusted his voice again, stepping back to admire her. She'd already put on a modest, white tea dress with a floral print. It swayed delicately around her knees when she moved and had gathered ruffles at the shoulder. She wore the rose pendant Ren had given her on her last birthday and styled her hair so that it somehow seemed loose but still stayed off the back of her neck. Her makeup was done the way Ren liked best, soft and barely noticeable. Every detail on her simultaneously soft and yet still clean and crisp. And she smelled amazing, as always.

"I've laid your cream suit out for you," Celeste told him, and he thanked her. They moved forward as if the last minutes hadn't happened. As if last night hadn't happened. They didn't have time to dwell on darkness like that. Not today. Today was supposed to be about Angelique and Fritz. Today was supposed to be happy, full of promise. Because even though Justin wouldn't be there, North would be. And even though Ren was tired, he was excited to finally intro-duce Celeste to Angelique. They'd never met before.

By this point, Ren could tie his own neckties, but he asked Celeste to do it anyway. She seemed to want to be near him, and his head was still foggy despite the coffee. She'd chosen the ocean-blue bowtie she'd given him at the hotel, that first night they'd stayed together, and he could tell she was remembering that day as she stood in front of him, smoothly pulling the fabric into place. Her eyes were tinged with nostalgia.

"It's amazing, isn't it?" she asked him, but he had no idea how to respond. "So many weddings. We're scheduled to go to *four* in June, Noah and Sheridan are in September, and Ella texted me last night that she and William just got engaged too."

"It's like everyone we know is getting married," Ren said, then abruptly shut his mouth as his own words shocked him still. He locked eyes with Celeste, noticing she seemed similarly stunned by what he'd just said. All their friends were getting married. The friends that had started dating at the same time or even after they had. Was she bringing it up because she thought that *they* should? But he hadn't even thought about it. How could he think about it with so much other stuff going on? How could he think about it when all this was just a dream anyway?

"I guess I'll have to brush up on my bridesmaid etiquette," Celeste commented coolly, breaking the tension. Ren sighed in relief, grateful all over again that she was the way she was. That they were not going to talk about this right now. "Are you ready?"

"All set. Do you want me to drive?" Ren asked her even though it was a complete joke. He still didn't have a license or a car and no real reason to get either since the only times he ever left campus involved going somewhere with Celeste or riding in the back of the ambulance.

"Maybe on the way home," Celeste responded, the same words they used every time, routine and familiar. One of a thousand little rituals they had for everything that safely defined the boundaries of their relationship. It felt comfortable to repeat the exchange, comfortable to get into the front seat of the Rav4. Today was just like the countless other events they'd already attended. Though today, Ren found it difficult to shake off the disquieting thought about everyone getting married, and he couldn't bring himself to look at the lake, a sight he normally enjoyed in the warmer months when they took this road. Today the sun was too intense on the water. Instead, he kept his eyes closed, his head leaned back on the seat, focusing on the softness of Celeste's hand in his while she drove. He could tell she looked over at him every once in a while, because periodically, she would tighten her hold — a momentary pressure.

"Oh, how charming," Celeste commented quietly, pulling away from the lake and into more shaded, secluded streets. "Such a sweet place for a wedding."

Now that they were under some trees, Ren thought it safer to look around. The wedding venue was located just off Lake Shore Drive, but you'd never know these quiet, sophisticated lanes were anywhere near one of the largest tourist hubs of the city. Angelique and Fritz had decided to take their celebration to the heart of Chicago's original Gold Coast, an elegant collection of fine, old houses owned by the once-famous of the city — Kimball, Coleman, Field, and Pullman among them. Most of the houses were still privately owned, though some of them were turned into museums and art galleries, and some were available to the public for events.

As they parked Celeste's car in the cul-de-sac reserved for the event and began making their way, arm in arm, into the house, Ren did his best to shake off the grogginess he still felt, especially when people started calling to him.

For the first half-hour upon arrival, Celeste and Ren toured the house, taking in the art and delicacy of the place, exchanging pleasantries and introductions with the medical staff who Ren knew, and commenting time and again how unusual it was to see them outside the hospital, so clean and dressed up. It felt more like one of the fancy places Celeste would take Ren to instead of the other way around, and Ren wasn't sure he liked being on this side of the introductions. Normally, he stood silent and smiling as Celeste did most of the talking. As they made the rounds of the house, Ren found himself wishing the ceremony could get started. His mind was still clouded, and all the movement and chatter of this place was making him disoriented. He felt slightly dizzy and almost sad. Which didn't make sense — it wasn't like he had any reservations about the event or the lovers participating in it. But as he looked around at the decorations, signed the guest book, and realized this was just the first of a long string of weddings he and Celeste had been invited to this year, he couldn't help but feel something almost like dread.

It helped when North found them. Ren hugged him as tightly as he wished he could hold Justin, relaxing for a moment against North's strength, delighted to see him after three years of separation. North didn't let go for a long while, but Ren still wasn't ready when he did. North stayed with them, catching Ren up on his latest news. He again expressed Justin's apologies on not being able to make it, though he didn't answer Ren's question of where Justin was. Ren figured it must be classified information, then worried about that. But North assured Ren that he was safe and doing very well in the program. He'd gained many new friends and the respect of both his superiors and peers. And Ren pretended to be ok with that.

Eventually, they all made their way to the back courtyard and found their seats in the hot, May sunshine. Celeste held to Ren's arm, looking at the plants around her, the bunches of lilac, the clean, white bows on the chairs, and the lights. She commented repeatedly on how beautiful everything was. She asked Ren for information he'd already told her about Angelique and Fritz, how they'd met, what they were like.

"It's so strange," Ren said quietly after he'd told her the story again, drowning in memory. "All of this because Justin almost died."

Celeste hugged his arm, and he could tell he'd tainted the elegance of the occasion somehow. He shouldn't have said that, but it was heavy in his mind. He found himself turning to North, meeting his gentle, black eyes.

"He really is ok?" Ren heard himself ask, though he'd already asked it. But North was sitting right next to him. His answer couldn't be cloaked by the anonymity of a text or an email, and Ren didn't know when he'd ever have another chance to ask him in person.

"He really is ok," North answered, the truth of it obvious on his face. Truth and something more. Something sad? Something secret. "He misses you."

Those three tiny words struck Ren above his left eye, a sudden flash of unbelievable pain. "I wish he could have come," Ren whispered unsteadily, recovering from what North had just said, putting his palm on his forehead.

North didn't respond. It seemed he might have been worried that he'd already told Ren something he shouldn't. Maybe Justin didn't want Ren to know he missed him, or maybe that part wasn't true, and North felt bad about lying to him.

"Ren?" Celeste said his name quietly on his other side, and he patted her hands reassuringly where they clasped around his bicep, reminding himself that she was here. That they were together and suddenly thinking about weddings. Because they were sitting *at* a wedding, and Ren should be nothing but happy about all of it. Justin was ok. The flowers were perfect. Celeste Lyons was sitting next to him.

Justin missed him. The sun was so bright. Ren was suddenly overwhelmed by torrents of things he'd been dedicatedly trying not to think about.

The pain hit again, and Ren swallowed, taking a couple deep breaths, confused and conflicted. What the hell was going on with him today? He needed to keep it together, though. So, Ren did his best to ignore the emotions that came when he thought about Justin missing him and what that might mean. Instead, he focused on small details like the ivy growing alongside the building and the petals on the walkway. Like Celeste and North's presence on either side of him. And he tried to shake away the ache that was settling into his heart and especially his head, a discomfort that continued to grow even as he dutifully tried to pretend it wasn't there.

He didn't have to try quite so hard when things finally got started and he could distract himself with the ceremony. He couldn't help but smile to see Fritz standing at attention at the altar, wearing a tuxedo instead of his uniform. Fritz looked blissfully foggy, as though he wanted to take in all that was around him, but he was somehow unable to. Like he was too happy to compute. And Ren watched him short-circuit as the bride's march began and Angelique appeared at the end of the aisle.

"Oh Ren, she's brilliant," Celeste whispered in a gush of amazement near his ear, and he had to agree. "You never mentioned she was so lovely." He hadn't, because he hadn't really thought about it. Angelique was grace and certainty, but now that he saw her outside of work, he finally noticed that, yes, she was also beautiful. All Angelique's braids had been undone for her wedding. Instead, her long hair was crimped and tucked under, and she wore a crown of flowers in place of a veil. She walked with strength and purpose, an emblem of feminine power and all of its intoxicating mystery, taking her place at Geisler's side where he accepted her with obvious honor.

They'd written their own vows, which somehow seemed appropriate for them. They spoke to each other of support and dedication, acknowledging that each of them led intense lives and they pledged to serve each other as each of them served the community. Celeste's hand felt soft and relaxed in Ren's; he almost forgot he was holding it. He found himself feeling inexplicably homesick, blinking more often than normal in the bright courtyard, every now and then raising his fingers to push against that place above his left eye. It was getting harder to ignore the pain that was gathering there, but Ren forced himself to focus only on his friends in front of him. He was no stranger to pushing away pain, after all.

Fritz and Angelique exchanged simple rings of practical silicone, owing to the nature of both their jobs, but there was nothing practical about their kiss. Fritz swooped all of Angelique and her gown up into his arms, holding her like she was a rainbow, and he didn't return her to her feet after their kiss ended. He carried her all the way down the aisle as easily as she carried her bouquet while his friends on the police force cheered and whistled. And Angelique didn't stop smiling the entire time.

Once they disappeared into the house, the guests also got up to relocate. Ren allowed Celeste to lead him out of the courtyard, his vision more than a little blurry now. Something heavy was tangled in his stomach, but he didn't know what or why. He heard Celeste speaking, talking about the elements of the ceremony she liked best, what sort of things she was going to pass on to her other friends about what they may want to include in their upcoming weddings, her favorite words of the vows.

The entire congregation shifted over to the Women's Park and Gardens where the pictures and reception would take place. It seemed more people had been invited to the reception than to the ceremony; the grounds were awash in dizzying colors and crowds. There was an enormous white tent and more lights, plenty of tables and chairs, and one long table where caterers were preparing to serve a luncheon. The cake was covered in violets and pansies and looked as though there was enough of it to serve not only everyone present but also half the population of Chicago.

They walked around the grounds as they had walked around the house, inspecting the decorations, looking at the gardens themselves, and making comments on what they saw. Ren didn't have much to add and mostly just listened, though he did keep moving. It was easier to keep moving. At one point, North placed an icy water bottle into Ren's hands.

After a while, the newlyweds joined their guests again, and a line quickly formed to speak with them and take a photo. It felt like forever before Ren, Celeste, and North made it to the front to offer their congratulations. North shook hands with Fritz, clapping him on the shoulder, while Angelique grabbed Ren without any of the inhibitions of professionalism that usually kept them at arm's length from each other. It threw him off balance; she'd never been physically affectionate toward him before.

"I'm happy for you, Doña," Ren murmured in her ear, his voice thudding hard above his eye despite the low volume. Angelique pulled back but kept the palm of her hand fondly against his cheek. He couldn't help but lean into it a little.

"Thank you for coming," Angelique said with sincerity. "I'm so glad you could be here."

They looked into each other's eyes for a moment, the gold in Angelique's shining out in the sun more vibrantly than Ren had ever seen. Ren thought his heart might break, or he might break, something was going to break apart any second now. He wanted to tell her all about it in that second, as he looked at all the love in her eyes. He wanted to drop to his knees on the grass and rest his aching head in her lap and tell her everything he was doing wrong.

He heard himself exhale in a manner that sounded more like a sob than anything, and he quickly held his breath so he wouldn't do it again. Because he absolutely could not break. Not here. Not at her gorgeous wedding — the happiest day of her life.

Instead, he blindly reached behind him for Celeste, who put her hand into his readily, and he pulled her into the circle, allowing the women to meet for the first time. He swallowed hard, staring at the ground, keeping himself balanced with a hand on the small of Celeste's back.

"Congratulations; you look so beautiful," Celeste gushed, clasping hands with Angelique. "I'm delighted to finally meet you."

"Likewise, love."

They went back and forth for a little while, talking about hair and dresses, flowers and a tiny bit about Ren. Soon, they also had Fritz's attention. He hugged Ren a little too roughly, then held out his hand to Celeste, giving Ren a side-long look as he did, as though he were confused.

"And who's this?" Fritz asked, as if it weren't completely obvious.

"My girlfriend," Ren responded, wishing his words were clearer. Fritz's hug had left him motion sick. "Celeste Lyons."

"Girlfriend?" Fritz repeated, a crease appearing between his eyes, and Ren could tell it was an effort for him to keep from frowning. "I could have sworn you were —" he cut off, as if realizing he was speaking out loud. "Good for you two. Thanks for coming," he amended brightly.

It was a relief that there were still many guests behind them waiting their turn. It made it more a polite gesture than awkward for Ren to pull Celeste away, allowing the next person in line forward to wish the bride and groom all the best. Ren hoped Celeste would take Fritz's words as a joke instead of what Ren thought he'd been about to say. But he couldn't forget the look on Fritz's face as he considered them together. Like he was expecting Ren to be there with someone else. And it bothered Ren. This entire day was getting to him, cracking something open, and he didn't think he'd be able to stop it this time. But, as usual, he was going to try.

The vague ache from earlier sharpened into an actual, stabbing pain above his left eye. As the hours went by, it became disorienting to shift his gaze, so Ren sat still at one of the tables, quietly drinking water, and listening to North and Celeste talk — to each other and sometimes to others who came up because they recognized North from somewhere. North seemed pleased to hear that Sheridan was getting along well, that she too was planning on getting married this year. Celeste's explanation of all that had happened with her friend seemed to pull their discussion forward to future events.

"So, Ren, you're graduating, aren't you?" North questioned him, and he summoned all his energy to answer.

"That's right, but it's not a big thing — it's just another step toward my M.D." He wasn't even thinking about his graduation because it was so far from being finished there didn't seem to be much point. "I have a quick week break, and then I'll start on the graduate studies portion."

"Give yourself some credit; it's still admirable," North said, not allowing Ren to be dismissive of all the work he'd already put into his education. Ren wished he could show more appreciation. It had taken quite a bit of effort to get as far as he had. And he was the only Cordero to have ever completed a secondary education, to go to college at all. North turned back to Celeste. "Are you graduating as well?"

"I am," Celeste replied modestly. "With my bachelor's in political science."

"*Summa cum laude*," Ren quietly supplied for her when it seemed she was going to be too humble to add it herself. God, his head hurt.

"Really?" North said, appropriately impressed. "Congratulations. That is quite an accomplishment."

"Yes, well, I'm not the only one," Celeste dismissed, though Ren knew she was extremely pleased. "Ren is graduating *cum laude* too."

"As hard as you two work, I shouldn't be surprised," North acknowledged. Ren felt his eyes on him but couldn't bring himself to lift his from the table. "So, what are your plans after graduation, Celeste? Are you starting a graduate program too?"

Celeste's pause went on so long it broke past the pained haze Ren was trying to breathe steadily through. He made the effort of looking at her, noticing the blush, how far away the question had taken her. Ren realized he'd never asked her that. He had no idea what she was going to do once she'd received her degree.

"I'm not exactly sure," Celeste finally answered. "I guess I haven't really given it much thought."

Ren's stomach dropped, a chill on his skin despite the warmth of the day. She was *lying*. He'd never seen it happen before, but he was one hundred percent certain. Haven't given it much thought? No way. Impossible. Celeste was so dedicated to having her life planned and perfect that she had an entire spreadsheet documenting what gifts she'd be giving her family and friends for the next ten years' worth of Christmases, birthdays, and anniversaries. She did not leave anything to chance, and she gave everything plenty of thought. It had taken her two weeks of research to decide what brand of *toaster* to purchase. There was no way she hadn't thought about what she'd do after graduation. So why was she lying? Sensing him staring at her, Celeste met his eyes for one careful second before shying away again. She looked guilty. Ren took another deep breath, focusing on not throwing up. He didn't know how much more of this he could take.

"I'm sure you'll figure it out," North assured Celeste, even though he was looking at Ren. "We all end up right where we need to be eventually. Look at them," he gestured with his robotic hand toward where Fritz and Angelique sat at the main table with their heads together. "He had to go through one unhappy marriage, and she had to wait almost fifty years for him, but eventually it all works out how it's supposed to." Ren wasn't sure how they went from speaking about post-graduation plans back to relationships, and stranger still was how North's words seemed to settle him, at least for the moment. But North had always been calming like that.

"And now, it's been great to see you again, but I need to get going," North was saying, changing topics, preparing to stand up.

"You're leaving?" Ren asked. Despite how hard it was for Ren to sit at this table right now, he hadn't even thought of leaving because he wanted to spend as much time with North as possible. It was the closest substitute for being with Justin, and he didn't want North to go yet. They had been together for the whole day, and yet, it wasn't long enough to make up for the time they'd been apart.

"Yes, I'm sorry. I have a flight to catch in a few hours. I'm due in DC early tomorrow morning." North was on his feet now, and Ren struggled to get up too.

"I'm glad you could find the time to come," Ren said. He felt like he could lose his balance any second, so he kept one hand on the table. North embraced him one more time, and Ren wished with everything he had that North could stay longer, that Ren had been able to concentrate more while they'd been together. That he hadn't wasted this precious time being distracted by a stupid headache.

"It'll all work out," North promised cryptically, an answer to a question Ren hadn't asked. Ren allowed himself to rest his head against North's shoulder, hating how weak his knees felt.

"Tell Justin I miss him too," Ren requested, and North patted his back in acknowledgment.

"I will," North promised solemnly before letting him go. He then hugged Celeste briefly and gently before making his way over to also say goodbye to the newlyweds. Celeste took Ren's arm before he could sit down again.

"I think I'd better get you home too," Celeste said. "You look like you're about to pass out."

"Home sounds good," Ren agreed, and he never meant anything more. Never wished harder that the apartment felt more like the home it used to. Celeste's sweet touches were nice, but what Ren really wanted was the cardboard boxes under the partial wall, the camp chair, the afghan. Alek laying out loaves of fresh-baked bread on the counter, and Denny and Justin sitting on the couch in the middle of slamming each other in a video game. He didn't acknowledge how much he missed that; it hurt too much.

Ren melted into the front seat, noticing that it was extremely uncomfortable. He twisted, eventually leaning his elbow on the center console and resting his forehead in his hand. He couldn't hold it up anymore, not while they were in a moving vehicle. It hurt so much it was making him sick, and Ren had no real reason to keep up any pretense anymore. Celeste kissed the back of his neck as she got behind the wheel, sending a shiver rippling uneasily through his stomach. He swallowed.

"You poor thing," Celeste said softly. "How much longer are you going to have to do ambulance shifts?"

"The rest of my life," Ren slurred, knowing Celeste was misreading his posture, thinking he was just overly tired from last night. And that might be part of it, but it definitely wasn't even close to all that hurt right now. He wanted to ask her about what she'd said to North. Wanted to ask her what she really had planned for after graduation and why she didn't want to say. But he didn't want to talk. Didn't want to hear his voice in his head. Now that he was in the car, he couldn't muster the energy.

Celeste put a hand on the back of his neck for a second, cool and surprisingly soothing. He sighed as she started the car. It wasn't a long drive home. Then he could get out of this suit and under his quilt, pretending it was just the exhaustion of the night shift that was bothering him. Celeste wouldn't question him. She hardly ever did.

Her phone rang before they were out of the cul-de-sac, a harsh sound that came through the car speakers. Ren winced without meaning to, curling into a tighter ball as Celeste pressed the button on the dash to answer.

"Hello, Mother," Celeste greeted Felicity. "Good timing."

"Hello, sweetheart," Mrs. Lyons said, her words piercing into Ren's brain. Felicity's voice was normally sweet and low, but tonight, coming through the car speakers, it seemed unnaturally shrill and loud. "Are you still at the wedding?"

"We just left," Celeste told her, navigating the route back to Lake Shore Drive. It wasn't all that late, but Ren felt like they'd been at that wedding for three straight days.

"Oh, that is good timing. Excellent. I thought, since you're already dressed up, you might like to come with us tonight? Your father is taking me to see Vivaldi's *Gloria* at Orchestra Hall, and we thought we'd get dinner at the Berghoff beforehand. We could meet you there in thirty minutes or so, if you'd like to join us."

Ren didn't mean to, but he heard himself make the tiniest groan at the idea of going anywhere else tonight. Especially if that anywhere else included eighty instruments all being played at the same time. Or lights. Or food. Or sitting up. Holy shit, what the hell was this? He'd never experienced a headache like this before.

"Thank you, Mother, but we're ready to just be home," Celeste declined smoothly, filling Ren with devoted gratitude. Then guilt as he realized she absolutely was the best girlfriend in the world, and he did *not* deserve her. "I'm sure it will be wonderful, but I think we're both too tired to appreciate it tonight."

"Perhaps another time then, dear. Tell me, how was the ceremony?"

Ren clenched his jaw, hating that Felicity wanted to chat right now. He lowered his head a little more as Celeste made a nauseating turn.

"It was so beautiful," Celeste related. "Dr. Delacroix used lilacs and ivy, and the entire courtyard was done up with lights and flowers. They wrote their own vows too, and he swept her off her feet and carried her down the aisle. They looked so happy."

"Princess," Ren whispered into the console, knowing he hadn't been loud enough. He wondered if he could just reach over and turn the volume down on the call. Every time Felicity spoke, anytime anyone spoke, it was like a gunshot above his eye. He wanted silence. And darkness. And he'd really like to get out of the car.

"That does sound nice. Remind me, what did they decide for the venue?"

"Celeste," Ren tried again, still too quiet. He didn't even hear himself that time. He swallowed as saliva flooded his mouth. *Shit. Really?* No, he just had a few more miles. He'd be fine. He'd lasted this long.

"The Keith House near the Women's Park and Gardens. That's where they set up the reception."

"Oh yes, I remember. That is a good choice for a small event. Of course, for you and Ren, we'll have to book somewhere with much more space."

"Mother!" Celeste squawked, the most ungraceful sound Ren had ever heard her make. But he didn't have any time to think about it because he wasn't fine, and he wasn't going to make it home. He had to get out of the car. He took a deep breath so he could speak loud enough to be heard.

"Celeste, pull over," he interrupted sharply, already turning toward the door handle as if he'd just leap out regardless of whether or not she stopped.

"Ren?" she questioned, looking at him out of the corner of her eye.

"Please," he begged, panting, suddenly way too hot. "Right now."

He heard Felicity asking increasingly frantic questions about what was going on, but neither of them answered her. Celeste obediently and quickly pulled to the shoulder along the long grassy stretch between the drive and the lake. Ren didn't have time for her to come to a complete stop; he barely had time to get the door open. He didn't even bother trying to stand up and get out properly; he nearly fell out of his seat and onto the ground where he threw up what seemed like everything he'd eaten in the past week. Each time he curled over, it increased the pressure over his eye until he thought his skull would split open. He kind of wanted it to happen. It would be a relief.

As it went on, Ren felt Celeste's hands bravely reach around him, unknotting his tie and pulling it clear. She even somehow managed to undo the top couple buttons of his dress shirt. Then she waited at his side, one hand on his shoulder, quiet and patient. She didn't fuss or freak out. Ren couldn't think to admire that at the time, but he did later when he was going over it in his memory.

"I'm sorry," he choked when he could speak again.

"You should be," Celeste admonished him, but she did it gently. Ren sat back a little on his knees but realized quickly that he didn't want to lift his head, so he curled up, one hand bracing him on the ground and the other pressed hard against his eye. He'd expected vomiting would help him feel better, but there was surprisingly little relief. His head was still killing him. "I thought you were just exhausted; why didn't you tell me you weren't feeling well? Why do you *always* pretend like everything's fine when it's —"

She stopped herself with a frustrated exhale. "Never mind. Do you think you can make it home? Or should we wait here a little longer?"

Ren wanted another minute, another hour, the rest of the night.

He wanted to fall to the side on the grass, close his eyes, and sleep. But obviously, he'd have to get up and get back in the car at some point.

Instead of answering, he painfully began moving toward the Rav4. If he rolled the window down and kept his eyes closed. If he braced himself on the door, kept his head resting on something. If Celeste didn't talk and neither did anyone else, especially not about marriage, then he thought he'd be able to make it to the apartment.

"Do you need any help?" Celeste asked next to him.

"No," Ren groaned, not wanting anyone to touch him. He just wanted to lie down and not think. He wondered what kind of pain medication he had at home that had the best chances of knocking him out for the next sixteen hours. Or longer.

He actually wasn't sure he wanted to ever wake up.

# 10

## POSTDROME

Celeste kept quiet. Ren also kept his mouth and eyes carefully closed, the pain now so bad it was sending creeping tendrils of stiff agony down the left side of his neck into his shoulder and jaw. Any movement of his head made it feel as though the entire world were rotating, so Ren dedicatedly locked all his vertebrae in an attempt to keep it still. He didn't want to throw up again. He wondered how he'd lasted so long, sitting up at that wedding table in the sunlight. He wondered if it wouldn't be so bad right now if he'd admitted something wasn't right a lot sooner.

Somewhere between the grass on the lake and the apartment parking lot, he weakly managed to tell Celeste what was going on. That this wasn't food poisoning or motion sickness or even exhaustion. It was just a headache, though admittedly the worst one Ren had ever experienced. He heard Celeste take breaths, the start of questions she swallowed instead of asked. Ren never opened his eyes as he got out of the car. Instead, he kept one hand pressed against his forehead and blindly let her take the other to lead him all the way from the parking area, through the front door, down the lobby, into the elevator, where he had to lean on her due to the queasy start and stop of it, down the hall, through the apartment, and finally, *finally*, into his familiar room.

He continued to put all his trust in Celeste as she helped him out of his suit. He didn't bother to see what she picked for him to wear afterward, though it felt like a pair of his pajamas as she smoothly pulled a shirt over his head for him. His headache was so debilitatingly distracting that he didn't even think about what she was doing, though he noticed she left almost immediately after tucking him in bed. Not just his room; she left the apartment. He heard the front door open and close and did have a moment of tired curiosity about what that meant. There was a fleeting, sinking thought that she might not come back, and he had been left alone.

But no, she returned after a short while. Or maybe a long while. Ren wasn't sure how long she was gone. He'd spent all of her absence with his throbbing head pushed hard into his pillow, surprised how lying down wasn't helping much with anything except the nausea. His jaw remained involuntarily clenched, his body tight without any conscious thought from him. Because the only thing he could think about was how much it hurt and how much he wished it didn't.

Celeste's cool hand on his forehead alerted him that she'd come back, though he hadn't heard her. His skin wrinkled beneath her fingers, and he groaned, a strangled sound of partial relief. The initial contact felt nice, but only for a couple seconds. Fortunately, Celeste had only touched him to get his attention and removed her hand once she knew she had it.

"Ren, can you sit up?" Celeste encouraged, her voice low and quiet, just barely above a whisper. Ren did what she said, struggling to open his eyes for her, noting gratefully that she'd left the lights off and pulled the shades, darkening the room. She took his hand as if he truly were blind and dropped a jumble of medication into his palm. He blinked at it, noticing tablets of Aleve, Advil, and Benadryl in the mix. He heard a sharp pop and lifted his head slightly to see Celeste had opened a can of Coke she must have obtained from the vending machines downstairs. *Huh,* he thought blearily. *All the ingre-*

*dients for a migraine cocktail.* Ren felt suddenly stupid for not even considering that; of course, that's what this was. Why didn't he think of it sooner? If someone had come to the ER presenting with these kinds of symptoms, Ren would have said migraine right away without thinking twice. But he'd never had one before. Never had to diagnose himself. Didn't know how *awful* they were.

"This should help," Celeste told him.

"You clever girl," Ren murmured appreciatively before shoving all the capsules into his mouth at once and taking the Coke from her. It took several swallows, but eventually he got them all down. As he took the medicine, Celeste arranged some pillows against the corner, a cushion Ren could lean into, resting his head while still staying upright enough to sip at the soda. Man, this girl was a miracle. And apparently experienced with migraines. He'd have to ask her about that. Later.

"I'm so sorry," Celeste whispered, a catch in her voice, and Ren wished he had the energy to address all that seemed to be in that apology. Starting with why she thought she had to apologize at all. He winced as a particularly sharp pain staked his temple. Took another sip of Coke.

Celeste disappeared once more, returning this time with a sewn flannel bag about the size of a textbook. Ren wasn't sure what was inside it, corn or rice or some other kind of grain, but he remembered it held heat. Celeste used it sometimes for cramps or to put over her feet on the couch when it was viciously cold outside. He let her position it over his shoulder, wrapping its heated weight around the back of his neck. It felt amazing and smelled of lavender. And it relaxed his tense muscles all throughout his neck and shoulder almost instantly.

"Is this any better or should I bring you a bowl or something?" Celeste asked him, standing at his bedside helplessly now that she'd apparently run out of remedies.

"No," Ren breathed, melting against the heat and the pillows. "This is fine." He didn't feel sick anymore at least, now he was still with his head supported. "Thank you," he managed.

She kissed him softly on the top of his head. "I hope it goes away soon," she wished for him. "I'll check on you later." She took his phone when she left, shutting the door, securing Ren in dark silence.

He drank the Coke. Then he settled and waited for the medication and caffeine to work, thinking about the wedding and all that had happened there. What everyone had said that Ren had questions about now. Like Justin missing him, and Celeste's graduation plans, and why Felicity was already booking spaces for — nope, he couldn't think about that one. Not yet, but he knew he'd have to go over it with Celeste soon. Time was almost up on not talking; Felicity had just made that clear, though deep down, Ren had always known, hadn't he? His breathing sped up, rousing the pain, so Ren forced himself to slow everything down, take only deep, ragged breaths, insisting his brain only focus on one hurt at a time, the throbbing gradually dying down as the Benadryl dragged him into unconsciousness.

Ren found himself drifting in waves of sleep for what felt like days. He'd surface to discover his surroundings still pleasantly dark, and he removed the heat pack from his shoulder after it returned to room temperature. He heard Celeste in the apartment, her voice but not her words as she spoke to someone on the phone. He thought she sounded upset, and he wanted to get up and comfort her but somehow couldn't manage. His eyes closed again almost against his will. It felt nice, so Ren just let himself drift, relishing the boneless comfort that sleep and drugs were providing him.

He opened his eyes, unsure what had woken him this time, focusing on his desk, noting his suit and the empty can were both gone from the room, or at least from his field of vision. Light tried to slip through the slits in the blinds, but for the most part, the room remained shadowed. Ren couldn't remember the last time he'd been this comfortable, and he thought about going back to sleep, but then he heard Celeste talking outside his door. When he realized she was speaking Spanish, he twisted on the bed, trying to pull himself awake enough to pay attention.

"*No estoy segura,*" Celeste mused, her voice quiet but her words clear. She spoke Spanish with the same clipped accent she had for English, an endearing mannerism to her speech. Ren lay still for a moment listening to her answers to unheard questions, trying to get oriented. "He's still asleep. I don't know, but sometime while we were at the wedding yesterday. He didn't say anything. He *never* says ... no, just the one time. I know he'd love to talk to you, but I don't think it's a good idea to wake him."

"*Princesa,*" Ren tried to call her, not even noticing he'd slipped into Spanish too. He paused to clear his throat to make himself more audible. His voice sounded as though he hadn't used it in a century. "*Ven acá, por favor. Puedo hablar.*" He said he could talk but knew he'd have to do a better job, or he wasn't going to ease anyone's worry over him. He tried to swallow some of the stickiness in his mouth. The residue of the sugar in the Coke felt disgustingly caked on his teeth.

"Hold on," Celeste said after a pause. "It sounds like he just woke up; he wants to talk to you."

Ren sat up carefully and rubbed his hands over his face, breathing deeply, trying to sort out if he was ok. His head no longer hurt, thank God, but his limbs felt weak, and he felt faded and shaky. Like he actually had been sick. Or maybe he still was.

Celeste wore a complicated smile when she came in the room, relieved he was awake and sitting up and doubtful he should be either of those things so soon. And something else. Something Ren squinted to see that was gone before he could. She dutifully handed over his phone so he could talk to his family, then patted him once on the shoulder and disappeared. Ren really had to talk to her. But first he needed to address the phone in his hand.

"Guys?" he asked hesitantly, bracing himself for their enthusiasm. Even though his head didn't hurt, he felt as though he were walking a fine line about it. It seemed it could start pounding again any second if things got too loud or bright.

"It's just me, *mijo*," his mother answered, her voice steeped strong in worry. "Are you feeling better?"

"I think so?" Ren tried to answer with conviction but failed miserably. He just hadn't been awake long enough to tell. And even though he thought he was ok physically, his soul ached, like something inside him was torn. "It was just a headache, Mom."

"Oh, honey, your voice. Are you sure you're all right?"

"I'm sure, but I promise to take it easy today, ok?" Ren assured and compromised together, eager to pacify her. It wasn't like she could do much to help him from where she was anyway. Ren was glad she couldn't see him right now, and especially not yesterday. He hoped Celeste hadn't gone into too much detail. But he didn't want to talk about that anymore; he was ready to switch subjects. "So where is everyone? Why are you alone?"

"I sent them out; I wasn't sure you could handle all of us at once."

"Is Luis with you? Marco?" Because he needed to talk to them, needed to ask them something. It was important.

"Yes, they're here. But don't push yourself. We can talk another time; I don't want to wear you out."

"No, please, call them in?" *I need my brothers.* Ren lifted his gaze, looking around for Celeste. He felt guilty about it, but she shouldn't hear what he was about to discuss. At least, not until he sorted out what he needed to tell her.

"Just Luis and Marco?" Eva checked, unused to requests to speak to specific family members and still sounding uncertain about Ren's wellbeing.

"Yes, for now. I need to ask them something." Need to wake up enough to listen.

"All right," Eva acquiesced, though she sounded confused. Ren didn't blame her; he knew this was strange. He heard her call to them, heard a door open in a church far away, then heard a muffled warning from his mother to her older sons. Something about being quiet. He wanted to roll his eyes but didn't dare chance it. Instead, he leaned his head back, waiting for distances to close.

"What's up, Enzo?" Marco came on first, his voice enthusiastic, quick. Ren smiled at the familiarity of it. Because Marco's idea of being quiet was nowhere near being actually quiet.

"You all right?" Luis joined in, more serious, mature.

"Yes," Ren wanted to skip over the part where he'd have to convince every single member of his family individually that he was ok. Especially since he wasn't all that sure. "I have a question."

"*Dinos,*" Marco invited. Ren opened his mouth and closed it several times, his lips still dry and sticky. He knew this discussion would probably break the glass that held his perfect universe, but they couldn't keep doing this.

"I was wondering," Ren forced the words out. "How long did you date Paloma and Isabel before you," *deep breath, Ren, this is stupid, it's not a hard word*, "proposed?"

"Ha!" Marco blasted, assuming the reason Ren could be asking this. Ren winced. "Way less time than *you!*"

"Not so loud," Luis warned him. "Can't you hear he's not ok?" Then he moved on to also answer the question. "Paloma and I were together for a year before we started talking about that. Then we waited another four months so I could figure out where we'd live."

"So you're slow, bro," Marco nagged in the background, though he was making more of an effort to gentle his tone. "In fact, I'm surprised no one's come and snagged her away from you yet. She is *perfection.*"

Ren knew that. He'd known that before he ever thought he'd have a chance to go on one date with her, let alone share his life and apartment with her. Now that they did share a living space, he knew she wasn't perfect, but honestly, that didn't damage her charm. If anything, her imperfections increased his affection for her. Which made this somehow harder.

"Everyone's different," Luis commented, picking up on Ren's unease. "But are you thinking of proposing to Celestia, Lorenzo? Have you talked to her father yet? You know you're supposed to ask his blessing, right?"

"No, I mean, yes, I knew that, but I haven't." Wow, what a conversation *that* would be. Ren and Alasdair did talk, but mostly about books and work ethic. He probably was expecting Ren to ask for his blessing at some point if Felicity was already looking at locations for the event. He couldn't believe this had never occurred to him. How long did he think he and Celeste could just go on doing what they did without anyone ever expecting them to do something more? Because really, that was the next step, right? That's what was supposed to happen. The future Mr. and Mrs. Cordero.

Ren swallowed; he felt dizzy again.

"Enzito?"

"How did you know?" Ren blurted out, closing his eyes, using his free hand to press against his forehead, reminding himself that nothing actually hurt. Even though everything did. "When it was … the right time, or the … right person?" He'd been about to say the right girl, but he couldn't get it out.

"Enzo, take a deep breath," Luis coached him, then paused while Ren maintained a slow inhale. "Why are you even asking us this right now when you can barely talk at all? Let's wait until you feel better, ok?"

"No," Ren denied. "I just need to know. I'm fine."

*Why do you always pretend everything's fine when it's not?* Why had she said that?

The glass was cracked already; he could hear it crunching all around him, a disorienting static. He was sitting still; he'd paused for too long and now the floor was dropping out from under him. The next choice he made *had* to be the right one, and not just for him. He had to do the right thing for Celeste too. And he needed his brothers to answer this question; he needed to hear what he was supposed to feel. He'd never manage to summon it on his own.

And it had to be now. Before Celeste came into the room or Ren went out to her. Because he knew she was going to ask, knew it was too much into their heads and needed to be addressed. It had to happen before they went to all the weddings in June. Before they graduated, and definitely before Felicity planned the entire thing without them even knowing. Ren did not want to get in a car and be driven to a chapel somewhere, his suit all laid out and waiting for him, all the particulars set in order on an *assumption*. This was more important than letting Celeste choose the color of his tie.

He had to wake up. Someone was going to get hurt if he didn't. Or maybe it was already too late for that.

"Ok, calm down," Luis cautioned. "I don't get it. What's the rush all of a sudden? You've been living together for years. What happened?"

Ren took another deep breath. "It's just ... it seems like everyone we know is getting married, and Celeste's mother mentioned picking out a place for ... for our wedding ... and we have been together a long time so that's ... just what you do, right?"

"No," Luis, and surprisingly Marco, said in unison.

"*Hermanito,* if you can't even say it without getting all breathless like that, then you are definitely not ready. And since when do *you* do what anyone expects you to?" Marco continued.

"This is too important a choice to let someone else make it for you," Luis added. "Besides," he went on. "You're telling me all about people who don't matter in this decision. What does *Celestia* have to say about it?"

"I don't think she said anything," Ren confessed, though even as he said it, he remembered the sharp way Celeste yelled at her mother about picking a venue. "We haven't really talked about it."

"Enzo, she's the only one you really should talk to about it," Luis scolded gently. "It's your life — yours, hers. It's no one else's business. Not her mother's, not even your mother, ok? So, if you're thinking about marrying her, you've got to be honest with yourself and ask some important questions."

"Questions?" Ren repeated.

"Like if you really love each other enough to want to spend the rest of your life together. You both have huge career commitments; do they even synch up? And are you thinking of proposing because it's something you want or if it's because you think everyone expects you to because it sounds as though you're being pressured. Do you love her?"

The question caught Ren off guard. That was something else he didn't think too much about. He knew he *should* love her. She certainly was lovable.

"Of course, I do," he answered. He thought it was the truth. They couldn't have stayed together this long if he didn't love her, could they? How could he not love her? Except, as he said it. The way Luis asked. No. No, how could that be possible? Three *years?*

"Wow," Marco drawled, one of the few English words he knew. Ren put a hand over his eyes, hoping he wouldn't start crying. He was sure that would start the headache thing all over again. He loved her; he must. Except he'd forgotten what it felt like.

"Look," Luis cut in. "We're not there, so I can't tell you for sure, but from what I can see in the pictures, everything looks right. You say the right things, and you wear the right things, and you pose just the right way. But I *know* you, Enzo, or at least I knew the Lorenzo who was more Dominican than he was American. *That* Lorenzo knew exactly what he wanted, and he did *not* hesitate in throwing all his effort into getting it. That's how you won the scholarship. That's why you're living in the US now. And unless something happened where you've completely changed from that Lorenzo I watched grow up, you're going to succeed in everything you've decided you want for yourself. But it has to be a conscious decision."

"Luis," Ren choked, not sure if he wanted his brother to stop or continue. He couldn't even remember that person. That passion. That certainty. Where was it now?

"I wish we were closer," Luis confessed. "I wish I could be there to help; it's so hard to hold onto a phone and listen to you when you sound like this. But I can't be there, so will you listen to me?"

"Yes," Ren promised, his throat closing around the word. *Yes, please tell me what to do. I'm just not sure anymore. My God, three whole years.*

"I don't want you to think about this anymore right now. You shouldn't make big decisions when you're feeling bad. When you feel better, have a talk with Celestia. An honest one. Think about where you'll be in the next five years. Ten years. I admit, I would be thrilled to hear she's going to be my sister-in-law; we all would love that, but mostly we want you to be happy no matter what you decide. And I want you to be sure about your decisions again. Understand?"

"I think so," Ren murmured.

"Good. Now focus on getting better, please. We love you, Enzo. We want you to be ok."

Ren stopped himself before blurting out an automatic, "I am ok." How had he gotten so off track here?

"Thanks Luis. Marco."

They only spoke another few minutes. Ren begged to have everyone come in; he wanted the room filled with the flow of their voices, their stories, their love. He assured them all he did feel better. He promised to send them pictures of the wedding but found he didn't have the heart or the energy to talk about it with them. He exchanged parting words of promise with his mother, telling her he'd take care of himself. They all wished him well. He told them he loved them. Streaks of sunlight were pushing themselves stronger against the closed blinds by the time Ren finished speaking with them. Part of him felt better after their conversations, but there was still an underlying dread. About what he had done. About what he had to do.

But Luis was right. He had to talk to Celeste. There were things he wanted to ask her, things he needed to say. He wanted to apologize for yesterday, or maybe for the last three years. He wanted to test himself on whether he could tell her he loved her. Because he'd never said it.

And he couldn't remember a single time she'd ever said it to him either.

He stayed in bed for one last minute, gathering his strength and his thoughts. He heard faint sounds coming from the kitchen and decided he would rather go to her than have her come to him. It was time to be present again. Make decisions. So he pulled off the quilt, testing his balance by standing up, satisfied it wasn't too difficult to be upright. The room didn't spin today. The light, well, it was a little too strong, but nothing like yesterday. If Ren took it easy like he'd promised his mom, he thought he'd make it through just fine.

Celeste was indeed in the kitchen as Ren walked from his bedroom to the living room couch, leaning heavily against the wall the entire way. The apartment smelled of strong coffee and frying eggs. Ren smiled sadly to see Celeste putting the finishing touches on a tea tray. He saw her as though he'd never looked at her before. How could he not love her?

"Hi Princess," he greeted softly, sinking cross-legged onto the sofa, glad it was a short distance from his bedroom since his legs felt strange and rubbery today, everything loosely put together. Or as though he was falling apart.

Celeste lifted her head from the tray, and her face broke into a sad smile of her own. There was an extra shine over her eyes, like she was holding back tears.

"I take it back," she told him, her voice solid, business as usual.

"What?" Ren asked, unsure what she was talking about. Of all the scripts he'd started in his room for what she'd be most likely to say, that wasn't one of them.

"All those times I was secretly mad at you and wishing your schedule would catch up to you like mine does. I'm sorry; I take them all back. I don't ever want to see you suffer another minute."

Ren found himself smiling at her confession. She'd thought that? But having her tell him, getting a more complete picture of how competitive she truly was, didn't damage his opinion of her. Whenever Celeste seemed human, that's when he found he cared for her the most.

She brought the tray over, setting it down on the coffee table before taking a seat next to him. Her body told Ren she wanted to talk, but her face said she had reservations about it. Like she wasn't sure he'd be ready for all she wanted to say, or maybe she wasn't ready.

"How is your head?" she asked him first, concerned. "I suppose you're looking a little better." She curled up on the opposite side of the couch, leaning against the back of it, considering him. She was wearing white linen capris today with a loose blue top that had small bunches of pink and white cherry blossoms on it. Adorable. Classy. Her hair was bound up in a thick ponytail. What the hell was wrong with him?

"It's good," Ren acknowledged, nodding, though he did it carefully. "Much better, thank you. How did you know what to do? You don't get headaches like that, do you?" If she had, he'd never noticed. He didn't think it could be something she could hide from him. Not for this long.

"No," Celeste assured, her eyes widening at the thought. "Luckily, no. But my mother used to get migraines often. How about you? Was that your first one?"

"Yes," Ren said, also leaning against the couch, resting his head, hating how Celeste's words reminded him that migraines, once they'd started, were usually a reoccurring thing. He'd have to start paying attention to this, have to start writing things down, looking for connecting scenarios that would reveal what his particular triggers were. Damn. "And hopefully it was a weird, one-time thing. How'd your mom get hers to stop?" Because Celeste said used to, which meant she didn't get them anymore. Which meant there was a way to prevent this from happening again.

"My father put a hard limit on how many things she could say yes to doing," Celeste answered, speaking casually, keeping things light. "And she quit eating chocolate and anything that has red dye in it. You know," her eyes were so sad when she looked at Ren, even though she was smiling playfully, "all things you're going to have a hard time doing."

"I could maybe give up red dye," Ren mused, trying to keep with the tone of their talk. He handed her heating bag back to her, frustrated how he could hardly handle the weight of it as he stretched his arm across the couch toward her. This migraine thing was a trip, even after it was done. "Thanks for letting me borrow that; it really helped."

Celeste took it from him only to lay it flat on the arm of the couch behind her. Her face changed, noticing Ren's weakness for the first time. "You need some food," she told him matter-of-factly, gently pushing the tray closer to him. He hadn't even looked at it until now, but she'd made him an intense breakfast. A sweet potato and sausage hash with onions and peppers in it, topped with a couple of eggs. Something they were more likely to eat for dinner than breakfast.

"Try it," Celeste encouraged. "It's good for migraine hangovers, and you look like you're going through a bad one. I can go downstairs and get another Coke if you think that would help?"

"No, that's ok," Ren assured before she could move. He wasn't sure he liked Coke, and he didn't want Celeste to leave. "This is perfect." As he said that particular word, he paused, staring at her. The girl he'd lived with for three years now.

*How could he not love her?*

"Celeste," he began, not touching the food yet. He wanted to get this started now that he'd decided it was the only way forward. He'd already stolen so much of her life. But which question first? It felt like he was about to start a verbal game of Jenga, each question he asked a block taken out of their relationship. Which one to start that wouldn't topple the whole thing? And yet, just like Jenga, Ren knew at some point, whether he meant to or not, everything was about to fall apart. He took a deep breath. "About what your mom said yesterday —"

"Eat," Celeste suddenly demanded, talking over him, plucking the bowl from the tray and physically pushing it into his hands. Then without any kind of pause, she was standing up and heading back toward the kitchen. Her reaction confused him, and he caught that sheen coating the crystal of her eyes again. What happened? Why didn't she want to talk about that?

*Because you probably hurt her feelings, idiot,* he realized as he held the warm bowl. Celeste moved with graceful purpose to the sink, turning on the faucet to wash up the dishes she'd used for cooking. How would it feel to have your mother mention getting married and then have your boyfriend leap out of the car to vomit? Bad timing. Really bad timing. How was he going to tell her? He didn't want to hurt her. But staying together would hurt her more in the long run.

He didn't want to eat, especially not after what he'd seen in Celeste's face, but she was right. He wanted her to know he appreciated her efforts, and he needed some energy for what he wanted to do here. They were so good at talking about grocery lists and chores and appointments. Fantastic at commenting about the weather and books and things that didn't matter. Ren had even forgotten the last time he'd ever asked her about the future. About what she wanted in life. They'd been drowning so long in their checklists, he wondered if either of them even knew what that was anymore.

Ren brought the bowl with him as he followed Celeste into the kitchen, just that short walk making him feel as though he'd run across campus. He hoped this sluggish exhaustion wouldn't cling to him too much longer. He had stuff to do. He'd already been still for too long. He leaned against the counter next to her, letting it prop him up. She avoided eye contact with him but stayed where she was, very studiously and carefully washing each dish as he started eating. The food tasted pleasantly wholesome to him, familiar, and he took a minute to consider how far Celeste had come since she'd started living with him. When she first moved in, she didn't even know how to boil pasta. Now she could do entire menus. It didn't take long for the taste of the hash to wake up Ren's appetite. He'd been much hungrier than he thought and for a few minutes, eating consumed his entire attention.

Celeste took his bowl when it was empty, keeping quiet, and Ren thought again about leaving it alone. It would be easier that way, no one's feelings would be hurt. She seemed to want to pretend yesterday hadn't happened. But Ren knew he couldn't do that. They'd never get back to the way it was. The only thing to do was talk it out and see what they could save.

If there was anything there to be saved.

Ren picked up a dish towel and began drying the skillet before putting it away. "Thanks for breakfast," he said to her, monitoring her expression. She only nodded, carefully avoiding his eyes, even when he leaned down to try and force her to look at him. "Thanks for always taking care of me."

His cleaned breakfast bowl slipped right out of her fingers, bounced against the edge of the counter, and shattered on the floor. Ren blinked at the pieces, surprised she'd dropped it and then even more shocked when he heard her start sobbing. He stood there stunned for a few seconds until Celeste began to kneel to clean up the fragments, her hands shaking hard enough he knew she'd cut herself on them. That made him move. He grabbed her arms and gently tugged her away, out of the kitchen, away from the broken glass, back to the couch, all his senses screaming at him to fix this. Fix it somehow. But how were they ever going to get anywhere when he couldn't even start?

"I'm sorry," Celeste apologized repeatedly, her whole body shuddering with anguish. Ren pulled her tight against him, and she eagerly curled against his chest, her fingers clinging to his shirt. "I'm so sorry, Ren!"

"It's just a bowl," Ren told her awkwardly, knowing whatever was causing this had nothing to do with the broken bowl. In fact, he probably shouldn't have said that. It made her cry harder. He let his head rest against hers, running his hand up and down her arm, trying to hold her together. He didn't know what to say, didn't even know what was going on. Everything was so messed up since yesterday. Although, the way she was crying cemented that something had been wrong a long time before that.

"It's ok, Princess," Ren soothed, hoping they could sort it out.

"No, it's not," Celeste denied, taking odd little hitching breaths around her words and tears. "Ren, I —"

*You're sorry, yes, I know. I am too. But what are you sorry for?*

"Celeste," Ren began.

"You're so perfect," Celeste cried, and he was shocked all over again. What? *He* was perfect? No, she was perfect. He was a mess. He kissed her forehead, wishing she hadn't said that, wishing she didn't think that. How was he supposed to tell her anything when she was already this upset?

"Celeste, you know I'm not," Ren whispered into her hair. "No one is," he told her, though it was mostly to remind himself. She shook in his arms, crumbling under the weight of a secret, or a lie.

"Take your time," Ren encouraged. "But I think this might be one of those things where you'll feel better if you can tell me what's wrong." The truth of what Ren just said smacked him hard at the base of his skull with all the force of three years of denial. Yeah, well, he was getting to it! He had to calm her down first.

"I've been trying," Celeste sniffed. "I've been trying *so hard*. I've been doing what I'm expected to do my whole life, but —" *That's it, Princess.* Ren waited, knowing her words would likely speed up as she went along, an emotional landslide that was just starting to flow. He mentally braced for it, unsure what would happen. Celeste's emotions were so carefully constrained; she kept them so rigidly in place. Even now she paused herself, tensing, as though she were going to retreat.

"I'm sorry," she apologized again. "I shouldn't be bothering you with this right now. You're still not —"

"No," Ren interrupted her, making sure she couldn't move away from him. "No, please, Celeste, keep going. Whatever you have to say is important, and there's no better time for it than right now. I'm listening."

"Ren, I lied to Mr. Kaplan yesterday. And to you. Remember? When I said I didn't know what I was going to do after graduation?"

"I remember," Ren said. "I wanted to ask you about it. It's not often that you don't have a plan."

For a second, he thought he'd ruined everything. She tried to laugh, but it came out strangled, and he was afraid she'd start crying again. A tear fell between them, but she shook herself back into semi-control.

"I have a plan," she whispered. Of course, she had a plan. She probably had more than one. And something clicked for Ren, a bit of sense slipping between their fingers. He tightened his hold.

"I'm not part of it, am I?" Ren asked her, making the only guess he had about why she wouldn't want to tell him that, and this time she really did start sobbing, bowing her head over their hands as if she were begging for forgiveness.

"Ren, you are the best thing that has ever happened to me," Celeste told him. "You've taught me so much. You're so sweet and respectful and encouraging. And I know everyone's getting married. My mother's already looking at buying baby clothes, and it just makes sense and everyone expects us to."

"It doesn't matter what they expect," Ren explained what his brothers had told him, and something tore free inside his soul. But it felt good. A pressure being released. He lifted Celeste's face, allowing her to see his, see there was nothing wrong with what she was saying. Nothing shameful about her feelings. "This is our decision," he assured her. "And the truth is I care about you a lot, Celeste, but I don't think we should get married."

There. He said it. It felt good to say it. Celeste looked as though something heavy had just been taken off her, and he knew she agreed with him.

"I wanted to tell you," Celeste confessed. "I knew I needed to. But there was always one more thing to do first. One more banquet. One more test. One more phone call with your family or one more dinner with mine, and time just kept moving forward, and it got harder and harder. I'm so sorry, Ren, for using you the way I have."

"I don't feel used," Ren revealed, hoping she understood him.

Though this felt like the first conversation they'd had in a very long time. "It's been a dream," he told her. "It's all been wonderful, every second of having you here with me, but ... I don't know, no matter how I tried, it just has never felt ... it's never been —"

"Real," Celeste supplied. He slumped in relief, smiling. She understood.

"Exactly," he agreed.

She dipped her chin, gently touching her forehead to his, and he felt closer to her in that moment than he ever had before. Which was strange since he thought they were breaking up right now. Except they were still holding hands. It was confusing. But at least nothing hurt.

"What do we do now?" Celeste finally asked, sounding drained, but clear. "Do you want me to move out?"

"No," Ren said quickly. "God, no. Not until you want to." Because he knew she was leaving. Probably soon after graduation. Celeste had places to go, and he didn't want to stand in her way, but he wasn't in any hurry. "Tell me your plan?" Ren suggested.

"I have three," Celeste divulged, and Ren's smile broadened. They may not be romantically compatible, but he still knew her well.

"That's my girl," he snickered, trying to be playful. It seemed to work. He watched some tension leave her shoulders as she sat up straighter.

Her eyes were shining again, but not in pain. Mostly gratitude. "Does this mean we can still be friends?"

"I think that's what we always have been. I think the only thing that changed here is we finally figured that out."

She threw herself at him, hugging him tight, and he squeezed her back, amazed how different it felt now. Fresh. True. It reminded him of how Denny used to wrap herself around his arm sometimes, how she'd toss her feet into his lap while they were watching something — the affection of a sister. A friend. And Ren realized he *did* love Celeste. Not the same way he loved Denny, or the way he'd love a girlfriend, but something similar. It felt so good to finally know that.

Somewhere shortly after she let him go, it seemed they both remembered about the broken glass on the kitchen floor. With all the cleansing drama of finally pulling up and exposing their true thoughts and feelings, they'd forgotten all about it.

"I'll get it," Ren offered, but he stood up too quickly. The room blurred around him as a sharp, oppressive buzzing drowned out all sound. Defensively, he dropped back onto the couch before he fell, raising his hand to his head, breathing heavily. Damn, he'd forgotten about that too. How long did the postdrome phase of a migraine last? Celeste pressed him securely against the couch, stabilizing him and keeping him in position as the buzzing gradually faded and his vision returned to normal.

"Take it easy," she cautioned him. "It'll go away faster if you do. I made the mess; I'll clean it up."

He didn't like it, but he knew she was right. But somehow, sitting still didn't seem like such a frightening thing anymore. Ren felt better than he had in a long time, postdrome symptoms and all. He felt at peace about Celeste. He couldn't be more relieved that she felt the same way. It was like a miracle. Ren suddenly wished he'd done it sooner.

Celeste's mother called as she was finishing with the floor, so Celeste paused, propping the broom into the crook of her elbow to speak to her. "Hello Mother, I was just about to call you. Thanks for checking on us. Yes, he's doing better now, but I'm going to keep him here and resting today. That means we won't be able to join you for dinner tonight, sorry. No, it's all right, don't worry about what you said about the wedding." Celeste turned to look at Ren for this, a pure smile on her face. "I'm glad you said it, honestly. It's given us a lot to think about. Oh, no, you don't have to — ok sure, we could probably do that. Thank you. I love you too. We'll see you later."

After she hung up, she returned to Ren's side, kissing him softly on the temple. "That's from my mother," she explained. "She says she hopes she didn't cause any trouble yesterday, and she wants you to feel better soon."

"I feel great," Ren said, never meaning anything more. "We probably didn't have to cancel." Though he was worried about what Celeste's parents were going to say once they learned Ren was not going to be their son-in-law after all. Celeste laughed.

"They offered to come to us," Celeste revealed. "Mother wants to bring dinner over instead."

"Oh," Ren said, even more worried. Celeste's parents had never been to the apartment before; it seemed to be an unspoken rule that they not impose on Celeste's new independence by invading her space. He wasn't sure what they'd think of it. After all, they lived in an enormous house on more acreage than the entire campus. Meanwhile, he didn't even have four matching dining room chairs.

"I can call her back and tell her you're not up for it," Celeste said, noting his expression. "But I think it could be a good thing."

"I think you're right," Ren agreed, letting it go. After all, the hardest part of his day was already over and had worked out better than he'd expected. It didn't really matter what Celeste's parents thought of his apartment, if they agreed or not with the choices he'd made with Celeste today. They were good people, and they loved their daughter. Ren felt sure they'd be supportive of whatever conversations took place tonight. And Celeste had said it herself; Ren's apartment was warm and felt like home. Though Celeste renewed her effort with the broom with particular vigor now that she knew her parents were coming over, and she continued to clean after the broken glass was disposed of.

Ren helped as much as he could, but mostly Celeste demanded that he simply sit and keep her company while she spruced things up to prepare for their guests. They continued to talk as she worked, going over their whole relationship again with fresh perspective now that they understood their true feelings about each other.

Ren explained how time had done strange things during the years they'd been together. He told her how he liked watching her hands, how much he enjoyed her room and her passions. Alternately, Celeste told him how amazing it had been to finally live independently, how that wouldn't have been possible without Ren helping her learn how to cook and vacuum and all the other details of maintaining a household that had always been done for her.

They talked about their favorite experiences together, what they liked most and admired about each other. Celeste expressed her gratitude on how Ren had taught her that it was ok to be flawed.

"You're the first person who really allowed me to be myself," Celeste told him seriously as she set their table. "It was ok with you when I messed things up. I feel so safe with you."

In fact, it was exactly that safety, that trust, that had given her the courage to pursue what she wanted to do. Ren found it rather ironic that he had built up the very talents and confidence Celeste needed to leave him. And it wasn't that she wanted to leave him; it was more that she wanted to go somewhere he couldn't follow. Like Alek and Denny — like Justin. Their dreams all led out of Chicago while Ren's had brought him to that one campus and wouldn't let him go.

Celeste had been accepted to graduate programs at Stanford and Columbia. She could also take up an internship position in the White House if she wanted. Ren didn't want to influence her too much about her decision, but he listened carefully as she went over each scenario with him, asking her questions about her ultimate goals and how the different places could best help her get there. She still had time before she had to commit to anything — most of her programs began in the fall.

Mr. and Mrs. Lyons arrived punctually bearing pizza, wine, and flowers. Ren eased into their visit when he noticed how hard they were trying to appreciate the apartment. Felicity hugged Ren first after she'd set the flowers on the table, taking his face into her hands and looking at him discerningly.

"You poor dear, how are you?" she asked him, and for the first time since that morning, Ren was reminded that something had been torn inside him. While he and Celeste were certainly ok with everything that had happened today, Ren remembered what Celeste had said about Felicity already picking out baby clothes. He hoped she wouldn't hate him after they explained. Then he remembered he'd have to tell Eva too, but quickly dismissed that thought. He had a week to prepare for that. One thing at a time.

"Much better, thank you," Ren replied, bowing down because Felicity was shorter.

"I'm glad to hear it," Felicity said, genuine and sweet. She let him go, but Alasdair was right behind her, ready with a handshake and also bearing wishes for Ren's good health. They'd barely said anything to each other before they were interrupted by a joyous exclamation from Felicity.

"Oh my goodness! Alasdair, would you look at the view!"

Because after making sure Ren could tolerate light again, Celeste had thrown the balcony curtains wide, opening the apartment and providing a view of the museum grounds and the lake. "Aren't you fortunate," Felicity clucked affectionately while Ren and Celeste smiled at each other. "The whole world out your window."

Things settled down more seriously then, pouring wine, serving the pizza. Ren had no idea it was possible to make pizza so fancy, but of course Celeste's parents had managed it. Not a single pepperoni on any of it, but Ren had to admit the combination of chicken, rosemary, and potato smothered in cream sauce and cheese was extremely delicious anyway.

They spoke a little about migraines and how terrible they were; Felicity offering her best advice for handling them in case Ren should ever suffer one again. They talked about preparations for the dual graduation party that Felicity and her Charity Aid ladies were all excited to put together, and Felicity again expressed her apologies for what she'd said about weddings. She emphasized clearly that she of course didn't mean to rush them. No offense meant.

And Ren was again grateful to Celeste because she took the conversation over after that. It made sense; they were her parents, but Ren couldn't help but admire the way Celeste spoke. So much logic and reason, with just the right amount of genuine emotion.

You'd never have guessed she'd been broken and sobbing in his arms on the couch this morning. The way she talked, everything had progressed smoothly and naturally to the only available conclusion. That she and Ren were and always would be close friends and compatible roommates, but neither of them was ready to commit to anything romantic or legally binding.

Alasdair sat nodding his head sagely as Celeste talked, complimenting them on their responsible maturity after she'd finished. Felicity was visibly disappointed but tried hard to hide it.

"I always knew you'd have to fly far before ever thinking of settling down," she acknowledged to her daughter, dabbing at her wet eyes with a napkin. "There's so much of your father in you." Then she smiled at Ren, reaching over to pat his arm. "And please don't feel you aren't still welcome anytime," she pleaded. "You are a part of our family now, and I cannot bear to think of you not coming to our events anymore. The ladies would be devastated if you disappeared. No matter what happens, please be sure to at least keep the Christmas auction and the Midsummer luncheon on your calendar, won't you?"

"Sure," Ren promised, wondering what it would be like to go to either of those things without Celeste picking out his clothes, without leading him around arm and arm. He wasn't sure about what he was saying, but he thought he'd be willing to promise Felicity anything to try and make up for upsetting her plans.

They chatted for a short while longer about those usual, comfortable subjects. The pieces of light and nonsense that had no bearing except to pass some time on a warm, May evening. They took a tour of the apartment, a monumental event that lasted all of two minutes to peek into every nook and cranny of the place, and then they all made their way to the door again to say their goodbyes.

"That went well," Celeste ventured when it was over. They had returned to the couch, the rest of the chardonnay split between them.

"It was all you," Ren complimented, raising his glass to her. "You speak so elegantly. You are going to be so impressive as a leader. I'm looking forward to seeing it."

"Ren," Celeste said, blushing hard, sipping at her wine to hide it.

"Seriously, I'll vote for you when you run for president," Ren told her, and it sounded like a joke when he said it out loud, but he hoped she knew it was true. "Well, I mean, if I could vote, I'd vote for you. I'll tell everyone who can that they should vote for you." She smiled.

"But what about you?" she pressed, obviously ready to change the subject, and there was some weight to her question. "What are you going to do?"

"I think I'll move in with your parents," Ren said teasingly.

"Oh honestly," she chided him. But he didn't want to think about that. He'd happily accepted Celeste into his life because he needed something to fill the aching hole his friends had left in him when they moved. That's why he let them go on so long too; he just couldn't imagine being alone. Though with the career path he'd chosen, there didn't seem to be any way out of it. He was tied to this place and this program for another decade at least.

"I'm going to medical school," he finally said, his voice solid, surprisingly cold. "My plans haven't changed."

"I feel terrible about leaving you, though. You'll be all right on your own?" Celeste checked, and Ren remembered Sheridan. Remembered Celeste had faced a choice like this before. She could have gone to Columbia already, years ago, but she'd stayed behind because Sheridan needed Celeste's support at close distance. Now she was looking at Columbia again but feeling restrained because of Ren. He didn't want her to feel guilty for going. Just like he hadn't wanted that for any of the others who were already gone. This had been his choice. No one else should suffer for it. He'd already taken so much of her time.

"I'm not going to have any time to think about it," Ren quipped, desperate to keep this light. "I think Dr. Delacroix has the next ten years all booked out for me. Plus, I'll be calling you and Alek and Denny and my family and sending pictures and keeping the Charity

Aid ladies happy. And I'll be emailing North and writing —" Shit, he'd been doing so well too. Celeste turned to look at him, her features sharp, gauging what had tripped him up. "Writing Justin," he finished, though it was too late to be smooth about it.

"Ren, are you feeling ok?" she asked him, noticing the atmosphere of the room had changed drastically in the last couple seconds.

"Yeah," he assured her half-heartedly. *Damn it, Justin.*

"You know," she started. "I've always wondered." She spoke hesitantly, as though she knew she probably shouldn't bring up what she wanted to say, but since they were going over all their secrets, she was going to go ahead and do it anyway.

Ren couldn't look at her. Instead, he kept his eyes down, looking at his wine, at the intense colors of the slow-moving sunset through the open balcony door, spinning rainbows on the coffee table.

"I've always wondered," Celeste repeated, taking her time. "You know, it was such a relief when we started dating. I was so happy to have photos of us on my phone and something true to say to all those idiots. Sorry; I have a handsome, smart, and successful boyfriend. I couldn't be less interested."

"I imagine you got asked out a lot," Ren allowed, wondering where this was going.

"Daily," Celeste burst out, annoyed. "I've heard everything, I think. Being asked on dates is fine. It's all the other things I was asked to do. Things I had yelled and whistled and written to me. It was revolting. I was completely disgusted by even the thought of being in a relationship with someone. Before I met you, I'd gained a pretty solid reputation of being a cold-hearted bitch to be honest. And I was ok with that even though I hoped it wasn't true. I just hated that every single one of them seemed to only want to be with me for one thing."

Ren remembered the hotel room, a new tenderness in his heart now he understood exactly what Celeste had been offering him then. What it had probably taken for her to leave herself vulnerable that way. It gave him some satisfaction in how he'd handled it, how he'd treated her. The fact that they hadn't done anything. How Ren might be the only one who hadn't wanted that from her.

"Then I met you at the donation center, and you were so pure. I was relieved when I realized you liked me and I liked you back," Celeste confessed. "I was so happy I'd finally found someone who truly respected me, who didn't just want to have sex with me. At least, it was like that until I started to wish you wanted to."

"You wanted me to?" Ren broke in, surprised, his head swimming at this abrupt change in topic. Well, no, it wasn't a true change in topic, but it felt darker somehow, and Ren felt sad for Celeste. For how she'd been objectified because of her beauty. For how he hadn't noticed she might have wanted to be more physical with him. But they'd been so busy. He'd had this amazingly strict, Catholic upbringing. He hadn't really thought of it. He'd watched her get dressed, and he'd tucked her into bed, and he'd kissed her a million times, but he'd never once thought of doing anything more. And it hadn't hit him until just now how strange that must have seemed.

"I thought I did, for a while at the beginning," Celeste clarified, as if to make it clear that Ren hadn't disappointed her and they were ok in that area. "But it never seemed that you did. And sometimes when we kissed it felt like you were ... forgive me, but it felt like you were trying to force yourself. That you wanted to get it right even though you weren't sure what right was supposed to feel like."

"That's astonishingly accurate," Ren complimented her, whispering, wondering what her point was in bringing all this up.

"And so, I started to wonder if maybe ... well, if maybe you might be more attracted to Justin than to me."

Ren had to shut his eyes; the room had started spinning again. Here he thought he'd hidden it so well. He'd worked so hard, and she knew anyway. She'd noticed. Sure, she'd noticed. She was so smart, *summa cum laude* indeed. She reached across the couch to take his hand, and he gripped her hard, unable to answer her.

"Ren, it's ok," Celeste assured him quickly.

"It's not," Ren denied, eyes still closed. One problem solved, but there was always that last one. The one that had followed him for years. The one he didn't think would ever go away.

"Why?" Celeste urged, and all the reasons came to Ren in a dizzying rush. Because his mother didn't know. His brothers couldn't know. *Justin* could never know; it would kill Ren if he knew. If he pushed Ren away because of it. "Ren, you were the one who taught me how to be comfortable with who I am. To be honest with myself about what I want. You're not going to allow yourself the same thing?"

"It's not what you think," Ren told her.

"I'm sorry, but are you sure?" Celeste pushed, and Ren didn't know if they were talking about the same thing anymore. "It's just, well, you should see how happy you are when a letter comes from him. It's obvious you care about him a lot."

"I love him," Ren heard the confession slip out of his mouth before he could even think what he was saying. "I've known what I am for a long time, Princess; that's not the problem." What a weird day. He couldn't believe he was talking about this. Talking with *Celeste* about this. But like before, it was a release to give voice to these things. Celeste's hand remained sure around his, supportive and kind.

"You don't think he could feel the same way?" Celeste guessed, and Ren felt himself fold up inside, his ribcage crushing, squeezing the air from his lungs. He almost wished he could be numb again, that this had never come up.

"Justin's not like that," Ren said determinedly. Celeste took several breaths, contemplating what she wanted to say.

"How do you know?" she finally asked. "Have you ever talked to him about it?"

"I don't even know where he is," Ren said dejectedly.

"You don't need to," Celeste suggested quietly. "You have his phone number."

"Justin has never, ever, not once answered the phone when I

called him," Ren explained violently, but it was the truth. On rare occasions, they sometimes texted in real time, and Justin called Ren once on his birthday that first year after he left, but for Ren to call Justin? Forget it. Pointless. Ren had given up on it.

"I think you should try," Celeste prompted, which sparked something like terror in Ren. He quickly diverted it to anger.

"No," he protested, shaking his head. "I don't want to lose him."

"So, you're never going to tell him?" Celeste asked, sounding inexplicably sad.

"No," Ren exclaimed, shocked she wasn't understanding this. "Do you realize he went over to talk to you at the coffee shop that day as a thank-you gift to me? He brought us together, Celeste. Why would he do that if he were interested at all?"

"Oh, I can think of several reasons," Celeste shot back, quick and fierce, bringing Ren's next point up short.

"Wha ... really?" Ren said, suddenly conflicted.

"Weren't you the one telling me this morning that it's better to say these things out loud rather than let them weigh you down forever? Ren, think about it, he probably stepped out of your life for the same reason you're not asking him now. You'd both rather hide and suffer in silence to not risk your friendship by bringing it up. I'm sure this is the basic plot of every star-crossed love story in history."

Ren cocked his head at her. "When was the last time you read a star-crossed love story?" he challenged.

"Why do I have to read it?" Celeste responded coolly. "I'm *in* one."

Ren rolled his eyes. He had to admit, he liked talking with Celeste like this. He'd rather they were talking about *her* love interests, but the freedom of the back and forth felt good and real. Even if the subject was awful and terrifying. Or maybe it felt hopeful? Celeste had a way of making things sound so logical; Ren wasn't sure he could trust it.

"You really think?" Ren questioned Celeste, the girl he'd shared his life with for three years. The girl everyone thought he was going to marry. His newest and closest friend. She smiled at him.

"There's only one way to know," she told him with conviction. "Call him."

"What — right now?" Ren demanded. They'd just barely broken up, and now she wanted him to call Justin? A shudder ran over him, cold and lonely and frightened.

"Oh my God," Celeste gushed, a curious twinkle in her eye. "Yes, now. It seems a good day for confessions, don't you think?" She gave a little huff, shaking her head. "Look at you; you are so in love with him."

"I'm so sorry," Ren apologized, realizing what that probably meant for her to realize this. He'd been her boyfriend for so long. But she didn't look upset.

"Don't be," Celeste dismissed. "It's nice to see you like this. The Ren I met. It's good to have him back."

"Thank you, Princess," Ren said, grateful for all she was. She leaned forward, setting her empty wine glass on the table, piercing him with her crystal gaze.

"You're welcome," she accepted graciously. "Now call him."

"Ok," Ren accepted, though he wasn't sure what he'd say. He couldn't even breathe. But Celeste was sitting there on the couch, looking sweet and certain and just a little bit smug. He thought he could borrow her courage. It was just a phone call.

Just a phone call, but his hands were shaking as he dialed Justin's number. He wondered where he was. Was it the middle of the night? Was he in training? It must be far; it was taking forever for the number to connect.

Celeste took his hand again. He couldn't believe he was doing this. He closed his eyes as the phone started ringing.

<h1 style="text-align:center">11</h1>

# INCOMPATIBILITY

Ren didn't know why he was nervous. It wasn't like Justin was going to answer. He was just proving a point for Celeste, that's all. The phone rang once, then again, three times. Ren was in the process of pulling it away from his ear to hit end on the call, ready to shrug at Celeste in a defeated, "just like I said" sort of way, when he heard a click on the line.

Nerves hit Ren too hard to stay seated on the couch. He jerked to his feet, began pacing from the balcony window to the partial kitchen wall, his heart thundering hard. Denny's huge all-caps confession flashing into his memory. Was he really going to do this?

"Justin!" Ren blurted out, running a hand through his hair. *Be cool,* he lectured himself. Yeah, but how? What was he even supposed to say? *Hey, Justin, I know you say we're best friends, but I can't stop thinking about you, and I know I've been in a relationship with a girl for years, but the person I'm really in love with is you. What do you think?* That was *not* smooth at all! How would Celeste do it?

"Hello?" came the faraway voice on the line, and Ren paused, fingers still threaded in his hair, suddenly confused. That wasn't Justin's voice. He checked the phone, reviewing the number. No, it was right. Or it had been. Did Justin not have this phone number anymore? Because whoever had answered was definitely not Justin. The voice was pitched low, but it belonged unquestionably to a woman.

"Hello?" she repeated. Ren saw Celeste gesturing for him to say something from the couch, her whole body engaged in what she was watching. How he wished he could trade spots with her. She didn't understand how everything had just tangled up in this plan of hers.

"Um, hi," Ren said, trying to regain his mental balance. "I'm sorry; I think I have the wrong number."

Celeste tilted her head; her eyebrows drawing together, also confused. Yeah, now what? Now Ren didn't know where Justin was, *and* he didn't have his phone number. And just because Denny had written confession on a paper, that didn't mean Ren wanted to write any of this in a letter and then wait three months for a reply. That would be a new and creative kind of torture. Possibly even worse than what he was experiencing now.

"Who are you looking for?" the unknown voice in the unknown location asked him. She sounded sharp; her words cut. Her method of speech reminded Ren of Kelly, Justin's lawyer.

"My friend, Justin," Ren told her, too intrigued to not answer. "This used to be his phone number."

"It still is, but he's unavailable right now. Is there a message?"

Um, no, not a chance. Ren hadn't called to wish him happy birthday or ask his advice on how to fix an alternator in a car. He'd called for a very specific purpose, and that certainly did not transfer well through a stranger. So, no messages, but Ren had a million questions suddenly curling around his tongue. He thought it might be rude to ask about half of them but then decided he didn't really care.

"Why are you answering Justin's phone?" Ren demanded. "Is he ok?"

"He's fine," she replied smoothly. "I take it at night to make sure no one bothers him. He sleeps like shit as it is without people forgetting about time zone differences." Ok, who was this girl? "Are you one of the astronauts?"

"Astrophysicists," Ren corrected automatically, his heart growing heavy. They called Justin? He took their calls? They had spoken to this person? "And no, I'm not."

"Right, you couldn't be. They never screw up the time zone." Holy shit, what was with this girl? How many people called Justin? Could it be he was actively ignoring Ren? It wasn't like he called him all the time; he hardly ever tried. Wait a second. Alek and Denny never screwed up the time zone. Did that mean they knew where Justin was? Did everyone know except Ren?

"Where are you exactly?" Ren asked bluntly, suddenly irritated he seemed to be the only one out of the loop. She sighed.

"Currently? Japan. Which is GMT plus nine for future reference."

Ren was starting to feel hostile towards this strange woman and incredibly left out of Justin's life.

"Ok, noted," Ren quipped, then decided if he wanted to get anywhere with this girl, he'd have to keep tension out of his voice and be polite.

"So, did you have a message, and if you aren't one of the NASA guys, who should I say it's from?" It sounded like she was trying to make an effort to be polite too. Ren was doing his best not to hate her. No, actually, that wasn't true. He wasn't trying at all.

"There's no message," Ren said, abandoning the plan. If she didn't know who was calling, it was because Justin hadn't even put Ren into his contacts. This whole thing had been a crushing, horrible idea. "I was just hoping to check in with him. It's been a while. I didn't know he had someone screening his calls now. Who —" *Yeah, Ren, go ahead. It's none of your business, but you'll probably never call this number again.* "Who are you exactly?"

"I'm Harlow," she returned, sure of herself, though not quite arrogant, and Ren frowned at the phone, doubting that could be her real first name.

"And you're Justin's secretary?" Ren prompted, needing her to say it, his voice defensively sarcastic.

"Partner," she said flatly. "For about six months now if that was your next question." Partner. *There you go, Celeste. Like I said. Justin's not like that.* And even though Ren had known that before, this news stung hard. Justin had never mentioned her. And Ren had received at least one letter in the past six months, so it wasn't like it was lost in the mail still. It just seemed that Ren wasn't important enough to know where Justin was or for Justin to answer his calls or to let him know he had a girlfriend now who had to have slept with him enough to know it might help to take his phone away at bedtime. Shit.

*You can't be hurt about this, Ren,* he lectured himself. *You've had a girlfriend for three years.* Yeah, but Justin had set them up. He'd meant for them to get together. And he knew about them from the start.

"He failed to mention you," Ren stated, and he knew he sounded cold, but damn it, Justin. *You could have at least let me know. So much for being best friends.*

"We told everyone who needed to know." Yeah, ok, he hated her. Time to get off the phone before he said something stupid.

"Well, good for you guys. Look, sorry I bothered you."

"You're sure there's no message?" *Thanks for the olive branch, Harlow.* Ren wanted to growl at her.

"No. In fact, you don't even have to tell him I called." Because he knew he wasn't calling again. He didn't want to ever have another conversation with Harlow, knowing she was with Justin right now, looking at him in the dark, lying next to him, touching him in ways Ren had only fantasized about long after the chance had been taken away.

How had he let Celeste talk him into this?

"Take care of him," Ren said in parting, making it sound almost like a threat. But maybe it should. Because how could she know what a precious thing it was to be with Justin that way? To have the freedom to touch him, trace her fingers over his scars, hold him as he slept. How could anyone possibly appreciate it correctly?

"I do," Harlow said resolutely. Ren shook his head, unable to respond. He ended the call without another word, realizing he was still standing paralyzed near the coffee table. Celeste sat watching him with a thoughtful, questioning expression on her face.

"Well, now we know," Ren forced out, failing completely at keeping his voice free of tears. No, he was not crying about this. No way. He'd said at the beginning that he was going to be happy for all of Justin's successes in life, and that specifically included any relationship he chose. If Justin was attracted to that harpy of a woman, then Ren was going to get behind it.

Even though it hurt like hell.

"What do we know?" Celeste prompted, reminding him that she had only heard half of that conversation. Ren swiped his wine glass off the coffee table, draining it in a rush.

"That Justin's *girlfriend* keeps his phone at night so no one bothers him while he's sleeping," Ren replied acidly. *Chill out*, he told himself. *It's not Celeste's fault this went horribly wrong. It's yours because you knew it would before you started, and you tried anyway.*

"Oh, Ren, I'm sorry," Celeste apologized quickly, but the last thing he wanted right now was sympathy. Or really anything but a one-way ticket to Japan so he could stare down that bitch and demand to have an actual conversation with Justin about all the ways he'd been keeping things from Ren for the last three years.

"It was a good thought," Ren allowed, not wanting to unleash any of his pain onto Celeste. But he couldn't stand her looking at him like that either, so he hurriedly placed his wine glass in the sink and started heading toward his room. "I'm going to go study. Finals, you know."

"Ren," Celeste called after him, but he was already past the couch, almost to his door. "Ren, wait."

"I just want to be alone for a while, Princess," he called over his shoulder, shutting himself in.

"You *never* want to be alone," Celeste reminded him. It was true, but the one person Ren wanted to be with was completely inaccessible, fourteen time zones away across the date line and, oh yeah, in a committed relationship. Didn't Celeste understand that he was trying to protect her from having to see him broken? He was supposed to be her boyfriend, had been her boyfriend forever; he didn't want her to see this.

"Ren," Celeste called from the other side of the door. He closed his eyes, leaning against it, biting his lip so he wouldn't cry. *You already knew*, he kept reminding himself. *You knew before he left*. But the letters. The gifts. There'd always been that margin of ambiguity. That little sliver of hope. "Ren, listen."

"Celeste, it's fine."

"You had a girlfriend, too, Ren," she explained, speaking as though she weren't talking about herself. "I know it never felt that way to us, but it was true. You had a girlfriend for the same reason I had a boyfriend. Because that's what you do. That's what you're supposed to want. You just have no idea how much Justin respects you, but I have seen it. He wants your approval, Ren; I know he does. He raised himself out of the ashes because of what you showed him about his true character. Because you're so good at seeing the good in people. And if watching you gave him the impression that a successful life meant a solid career, a wife, and a family, then that is what he is going to copy, no matter his true feelings."

"Celeste, you are not responsible for making this right for me," Ren half-begged her. Because she was doing it again. With her logic and her reasoning and her elegant speeches. He hated how she was making him want to believe, the contradicting proof still fresh in his mind.

"You know, you didn't actually talk to Justin."

"Celeste!"

He heard her sigh, knew she was leaning her head against his door. Knew she felt guilty for her suggestion, and she did indeed desperately want to fix this for him. Because it had been her idea, and because she was struggling with the fact that she'd be leaving him alone. Even though it was nothing like that. His choices were his own.

"Please don't give up on him yet," she said softly. Ren closed his eyes, feeling wet on his cheeks. *Don't worry*, he thought. *Even if it tears me to pieces, I don't think I can. Damn it, Justin.* "Give him more time."

She left him then, as he'd requested, and he stayed in his room for another twenty minutes, pacing, wiping furiously at his eyes, replaying his conversation with Harlow; he was never going to get over the ridiculousness of that name. How could Justin date someone with a name like that?

But soon the flare of disappointment had smoldered down to just an ache, one Ren was familiar with. He shook his head, picked up his anatomy book, and headed out to the living room again. Celeste sat at the dining room table, reading. She looked up when he came out, but wisely didn't say anything, didn't even smile. He pulled a chair close to her, also opening his book. They didn't say a word, but they held hands under the table.

And thankfully, they did not speak about Justin again throughout the remainder of Celeste's time at Stony Island. It was easy not to; there was a ton to get ready, and it was customary at this point to slip into that unthinking routine. There were finals to take, books to pack, and the graduation party to finish coordinating.

Ren and Celeste played their ongoing roles as the perfect couple during their graduation party for Felicity's sake. Celeste held to Ren's arm as they moved over the grounds, smiling and thanking everyone who wished them congratulations. They looked knowingly at each other when the sweet ladies made subtle and sometimes extremely forward suggestions about settling down. They pretended they were too innocent to understand. Though when someone brought up the subject of having children, Celeste hit a snapping point and confessed she was headed to New York. This came as a shock, of course, so Ren jumped in quickly with his full support and admiration for her decision. The ladies looked dubious but quailed under Ren's lavish praise of Celeste's plan.

She buried her face against his arm after that, and he patted her reassuringly. "It's no one's business," he told her. "No one gets to tell you what to do with your life except you. Don't give it another thought."

But Ren did. He wondered if he were really making the right choice. Especially now that he knew for certain about Justin. He allowed himself one last imagining of what their life would be like if he did marry her. What their children might look like, what it would feel like to hold them, real and breathing in his arms. He'd always wanted children. He knew they didn't love each other like that, but maybe they could learn to?

Celeste seemed to have the same thought. She pulled him to the side at dusk, as the party ended and the catering staff began to tear everything down.

"I have an idea," she said.

"Does it run along the lines of us promising to marry each other if we're both still single at thirty-five?" Ren guessed. Her eyes widened for a second, but then she smiled, lifting one shoulder.

"You knowing exactly what I was going to propose just solidifies the fact that it is indeed a perfect plan," she said, her bearing full of the majesty that made him call her princess in the first place.

"Then I agree," Ren said to all of it. Celeste put forth her hand, pinkie finger extended, and Ren wanted to laugh. They were going to pinkie promise on this? Yeah, sure, why not? There was no way Celeste would still be single at thirty-five unless that's what she really wanted. Ren locked little fingers with her, shaking his head.

And he held her one last time as he stood by her shiny, blue Rav4 one week later when it was time for her to start driving to New York, after stripping the apartment of any trace of her except for some of the books and the clothes she had purchased for him.

"You were the best boyfriend," Celeste told him, pressed against his chest.

"I was your only boyfriend," Ren reminded her, playing with her hair.

"The fact that these details are not mutually exclusive is irrelevant," she shot back, and he smiled at her. Ran his hand over her hair and opened her door.

"You're going to be fantastic," he assured. The corners of her eyes crinkled. She stood on tiptoe, lightly kissing the corner of his mouth, soft and cool as a snowflake, their first and last kiss exactly the same.

"Take care of yourself, Ren," she instructed firmly. He nodded and watched her drive away. This time without him.

Then he went upstairs and pulled the afghan and camp chair from his closet, placing them carefully in their previous positions. The afghan on the back of the old couch. The camp chair next to the door even though it was May and there would be no coats stacked on it for months yet. Ren made a bookshelf out of the partial wall, setting up the titles Celeste had left for him. They took up about three quarters of the space, so Ren also shifted the basil plant to take up the rest. There. A shrine to the past residents of Stony Island. But filling up the small counter did nothing to fill the big empty place in Ren's heart. If anything, it just emphasized the loss, but Ren left everything where he'd put it. Even though the memories pained him, he didn't want to lose them by removing all the reminders either.

*It's ok*, he told himself. *When you came here, you were excited, and it had nothing to do with any of the people you met when you arrived. You were driven, remember when you were driven? When all you could think about was becoming a doctor. That's what you wanted, more than **anything**. Remember that. That's who you are. And you're going to be good at it.* Ren opened the balcony door, stepping out into bright sunshine. He looked out to the lake, how it sparkled when it was warm. *It's ok.* He gripped tightly to the railing, staring as far as he could past the museum, as far as he could see over the water. *You're a doctor. That's what you wanted to be.* He tried to hold tighter to the gritty metal under his hands. Grounding himself to his decisions. *It's ok.*

Ren then threw himself into grad school with all his energy. What else could he do? He needed to fill all those empty places, all those wounded corners, and the med program graciously complied by pouring information, duty, and responsibility on him. Things began to shift as Ren reconciled himself to his new, singular identity.

For one thing, Ren's scholarship ended when he obtained his degree. As a grad student, he had tuition remission and a stipend. He had to update his visa status. And he had to finally admit that he could no longer keep up working at the plasma center, even part-time. There weren't enough hours in the day, or at least the right hours. He would have gratefully continued if the center could stay open past eight in the evening. But in the end, he had to resign. And all these financial changes meant he had to downgrade his Stony Island contract, which made the second bedroom available to the Resident Dean to rent out as he saw fit.

Which didn't seem like a big deal to Ren. It just meant he'd be getting a new roommate. And that was good because the absolute worst times of Ren's day happened when he was home by himself, surrounded by ghosts and memories and emptiness. He tried to shove it aside. He played music as loud as he dared. He read Celeste's books. He wrote constant letters and emails and cleaned the kitchen counter probably more than all the other kitchen counters in the building were cleaned all together, but even then, he'd find himself sitting on his bed, or on the couch, or in the bathroom, shaking like crazy. At first, he thought it was just the delayed panic response Angelique had gone over with him when he'd sat at her desk sharpening pencils. But as it continued, as it got stronger, he wasn't sure anymore. The only thing he knew was he hated it, and he would do just about anything to distract himself.

He tried making phone calls. He called Celeste. He called Alek and Denny. He tried to close his eyes and pretend they were here. He called and desperately begged them to tell him what was going on. Drown out the emptiness of his life by filling it with the details of theirs. And it worked for a little while. Until he noticed that they were busy. Unlike Justin, however, they always answered him. They always took that time to speak with him, but they always needed to leave before Ren was ready for them to go. Not only that, they started picking up on Ren's strained, cheerful tone. They started asking him questions he didn't want to answer. Like if he was ok. Like if he was lonely. He stopped calling so much.

Somehow, he drudged up the courage to ask North about Harlow and felt vindicated to learn he'd been right; Harlow was her last name. His triumph didn't last long when North went on to confirm that she and Justin were indeed partners and never left each other's side. They flew together, bunked together, trusted their lives to each other. Ren despised it, even though he had been the one to ask. He wanted to ask other questions too. Like how come no one told him about her before? How come Justin answered phone calls when they came from everyone except Ren?

North didn't seem to want to talk about Harlow much, treating the conversation carelessly. Like it wasn't killing Ren to know. Like it didn't make it excruciating to keep writing letters to Lackland, knowing they were really going to Japan. But Ren did keep writing them. Because of Celeste. *Don't give up on him.* Ren wrote, but he didn't remember what he said afterward. He was a shark, needing to keep moving so he wouldn't drown. So his hands wouldn't shake. So no one would know he was struggling so much. Because he was going to be a doctor and needed to be certain and quick.

The migraines continued. At first, it felt as though they showed up at random, like Ren was being stalked by some sadistic archer who knew exactly the worst possible time to shoot an arrow into Ren's brain, always directly above his left eye. Ren kept a journal about it. Dates, times, durations, and symptoms. He learned he could work through the slowly developing ones that increased in severity over the course of many hours. If he kept moving, he could keep up the appearance that nothing was wrong until he made it back to his room and could collapse in a painful heap onto his bed, but if he woke up with one, there was nothing much to do except try to sleep it off or take way more medication than he should to try and shake it before he had to go to work or class. He set his alarm earlier than he needed specifically to give himself time for medication to work. He felt like a stroke victim. He felt like the left side of his face was melting, bones and all, and he frequently had to run his fingers around his left eye socket to make sure it wasn't sagging since it truly felt as though it were crumbling away.

In addition to the journal about the headaches themselves was the other section where Ren tried to figure out why they happened. Because there didn't seem to be a common denominator anywhere, but he had to figure it out simply because he didn't have time to be stuck in a dark room so much wishing he was dead. It took him numerous painful episodes before he narrowed it down. Sleep deprivation. Interrupted sleep. Sudden changes in barometric pressure. Stress. Ren stared at his list of triggers and thought it would be easier to give up chocolate. He was a grad student in med school. There was no way he could eliminate stress and sleep deprivation from his life. So, he compensated.

He started bringing Excedrin and knitting with him everywhere, his pain relief and coping mechanism. The Excedrin kept his headaches at bay so he could finish his shifts, and the knitting kept his hands steady. It kept him from thinking too hard about blood or screams, silence and loneliness. Justin and his stupid girlfriend.

People misunderstood his need for knitting socks. He got teased frequently for sitting slumped in the break room or the hospital cafeteria, his elbows tucked close to his sides, head bowed over a project. Didn't he have enough to do without adding another time-consuming hobby? Wasn't it only old ladies who did things like that? Hey, could Ren make a stethoscope cover? He ignored it all. He was careful never to let Dr. Delacroix see him knitting. He knew people told her, but he never wanted her to see how bad it really was. Because he was a doctor, damn it, and this couldn't keep happening. He'd made a decision.

But it was hard. And it grew increasingly more haunting as Ren spent more time in the ER, taking Excedrin more often than he liked, and beginning to realize just how many things could happen to a human body. The sheer horrifying variety of it. Tens of thousands of ways to break bones or tear through skin. Those weren't so bad, though. Ren could cast broken arms all day. It was the outliers. The strange or brutal or tragic cases. The two-year-old who had pulled a pan of hot oil down from the stove, a millisecond of a mistake that cost her half her face and weeks of scorching pain. Ren visited her often during her recovery on the third floor. He knit her a soft orange cat that had similar broken patches of color on its face so they could be twins. He held the mother's hands in the hallway while her tiny daughter slept under the influence of heavy painkillers, the cat tucked up under the unburned part of her little chin, allowing the woman to sob out all her guilt for not being there in that tragic second.

There were more. They never stopped coming. Ren knew he shouldn't let them bother him so much, which somehow made them bother him more. They followed him home, the only things waiting when he got there, an ever-growing crowd of faces and moans and suffering that sounded the same as the pain in his own heart.

So, when he got a notice from the Resident Dean that a new tenant would be joining him, Ren breathed a sigh of relief. Finally. The summer had dragged on so long. He was so ready to welcome a new roommate. To assimilate whatever this person would bring to the apartment, twist it up together with the books and the video games and the balcony. There was no reason not to be excited, and Ren was thrilled to not be alone during those horrible dark hours of the night.

Spencer Whitman came with his parents early in the afternoon on a Saturday. Ren had been anticipating his arrival all day. He'd brewed iced tea, scrubbed every corner of the apartment. He'd made fish tacos and rice for them to eat as their first meal together. He didn't know much about Spencer, just that he would be arriving from Ypsilanti, Michigan, as a new freshman.

When he'd run out of things to do with himself or the apartment, Ren picked up his knitting and sat on the couch. It was too hot and humid for knitting, and his fingers stuck to the stitches, but he had to do something, or his nerves would overtake him and being a twitchy, shaking mess is no way to make a first impression.

Without knocking, Spencer avalanched into the apartment midafternoon, his parents following in his wake. Ren hurriedly tucked the hat he was making into his backpack, surprised at the sudden arrival.

"Hey, you made it," Ren began, ready to welcome him. He'd been ready since May to welcome someone.

"Yeah, great," Spencer muttered as he pushed past Ren with his enormous suitcase, heading directly for Ren's room.

"Uh, actually that one's mine," Ren said, following him. Spencer rolled his eyes and headed for the second bedroom. Alek's room. Celeste's room. The bed shook under the weight of the suitcase as Spencer threw it on top of the mattress.

"Did you want some help with the rest of your stuff?" Ren offered as Spencer turned from the bed to find Ren standing in the doorway. Ren watched his eyes open wide, as though he were just seeing Ren for the first time. Ren forgot what he'd picked to wear, but the way Spencer looked at him made him want to check himself. Spencer was wearing torn jeans and a band T-shirt.

"Dude," Spencer said, but not the way Alek did. In fact, the tone was unmistakably, "back off," and Ren realized he was probably overbearing. Just because he'd been waiting for this all day didn't mean Spencer was ready for it. Right.

So, Ren backed off, allowing Spencer to return to the front door. He would have gone to his room then to hide completely, but Mrs. Whitman seemed to want to talk to him at least while Spencer and her husband made trips up and down the elevator. She accepted a glass of iced tea.

She told him all about their four-hour drive and all about their family. Spencer was the youngest. He had two older sisters, one of whom was a teacher in Detroit and the other a cosmetologist in their hometown. Then she asked Ren questions about the nearest stores and what student life was like and how long he'd been there. She seemed nice. Protective. Meanwhile, Spencer's dad lugged in a drum set, which wouldn't fit anywhere except by the balcony door between the couch and the television. An electric guitar followed. Well, that was new. Ren had never hung out with musicians before. Spencer shoved the coffee table into the corner to make room for a big, black box with several dials on it that Ren recognized as an amp. Ok. They'd have to talk about that.

He had zero kitchen stuff. Not even a coffee mug. Because, as Mrs. Whitman explained, Spencer had a meal plan since he probably wouldn't have much time left over from his schoolwork to do much cooking.

"So, Ren, is that right?" Mrs. Whitman continued as Ren watched with growing concern all the new changes taking place to his apartment. *It's not your apartment, Ren; it's his apartment too. He's paying half the fees here. It's not like you've never had to adjust to new people living with you.* Yeah, but this time it felt different. Less a moving in and more a hostile takeover.

"Yeah," Ren said, trying to pay attention and not worry too much about the speakers that were moving past them into Celeste's, no, Spencer's, room.

"You seem to be, um, well established here. Exactly what have you been studying that's taking so long to finish?"

Ren stopped looking at Spencer, who was combing the long hair at the top of his head over with his fingers. The sides were buzzed short. Ren had seen this haircut on a lot of the younger students. It seemed to be in fashion right now, but unfortunately only about fifteen percent of the guys could pull it off. Spencer wasn't one of them. Ren wanted to look directly at Mrs. Whitman when he answered her question. He wanted to make it clear he was not just a professional student who didn't have any direction. He had a *solid* direction, the only thing keeping him together, and even though he knew it shouldn't matter what she thought of him, he wanted her to understand.

"I graduated in May," he explained. "I'm in medical school now working toward my M.D. I'm being mentored in the ER." He said the words formally, but he still knew she didn't get what he was saying. Didn't know he'd fought his way here from the Dominican Republic for this, gave his all for this. She didn't know that Dr. Delacroix did not mentor students or that Ren was the first one in years. But he stopped himself from going any further. He knew what he was. He had no need to impress anyone. Not that it was working anyway.

"Well, that's nice," she told him, smiling politely. "Spencer is so lucky to have a veteran like you to help him."

Ren and Spencer locked eyes across the room. Ren's blue to Spencer's muddy brown, and something like a cold understanding slipped between them. Mrs. Whitman was kidding herself. Spencer was not about to accept any guidance from Ren about anything, and Ren wasn't so sure he wanted to offer. A wedge tapped between Ren's ribs. He'd been looking forward to this?

The Whitmans all declined the fish tacos, which Ren expected by this point. They said they wanted to take Spencer out for one last family dinner before driving back to Michigan. Did Ren maybe know a good place? Like, nothing like tacos or Mexican, but a good place?

Ren was internally rattled. He felt oddly old and clumsy, misunderstood. His apartment felt weird, even worse than when he'd been here by himself. *It's just new*, he told himself. *You don't know this guy; you'll get used to each other. It's going to be fine.* He told the dread creeping up on him that it was being premature and overly dramatic.

"Everest is probably my favorite," he suggested, knowing full well most people did not spend that kind of money on dinner, even special, we're-dropping-off-our-only-son-at-college dinners. But he was feeling defensively snarky right now, so he said it anyway. He'd put a lot into those tacos; Alek would have been so proud. Ren would have been fine with the whole last celebratory meal thing if they hadn't made it a point to insult his food. "The chef there is really good, and they have the best selection of Alsatian wine in the city."

The Whitmans were all blinking at him, and he liked that. Kind of. Except for the part where he knew he was being a jerk, but he just couldn't stand it. *You people have no idea*, he thought. *I've lived a life beyond this apartment. So, so far.* But even in the apartment, there had been so much. They'd contacted the space station from this room. Ren and Celeste had kissed on this couch. Justin. Justin had almost died here. Ren felt a moment of bitterness for the life he'd enjoyed. All the things that were gone now. And he felt something like regret for how he was handling this interaction. He wasn't sure what it was about this boy that made him feel like this, and he didn't like it, but he also didn't seem to be able to stop it either.

"Or I think there's an Applebee's or IHOP if that's more your thing," he finished, pulling his phone from his pocket like he had better things to do. Because this certainly wasn't working out. And he wanted to get out of this before he said anything else he'd feel ashamed about later. What he'd already said was enough. He thought about dialing Justin's number, but the Whitmans were thankfully out the door before he could start calling anyone.

He stared at the phone for a minute, anyway, watching it tremble slightly in his hand. He wanted to call Justin and tell him so much. How he had been looking forward to a new roommate, but not an hour after meeting him, he was having serious doubts about that. Wanted to ask Justin if he liked being in the Air Force, or if he ever wondered if he'd made the right choice. Wanted to tell him he was lonely, that his head hurt too often, and his hands shook too much, and he was getting tired of hiding it from Angelique, but he'd rather die than have her dismiss him. *And I have to keep going, no matter what, because this is what I chose to do, and I hate your damn girlfriend and her stupid name. And I love you.*

Ren dialed the number, the tone of it a sad little song to him now. An incomplete song because he didn't hit send. He'd stopped trying for that. His thumb knew the sequence and could run through it rapidly, pausing after the last digit, hold for three breaths, dismiss. He put the phone in his pocket. He ran his fingers along Spencer's cymbal, giving in to the urge to gently tap it, hear the shivering ripple of it rattle through the room. He didn't know then how much he would come to hate the sound. Then he grabbed his keys and headed out, toward the bright lakeside. Because it was still summer, and the lake was vast and sparkling. And Ren knew the warm days were running out.

When Ren had lived with Celeste, time had been a slippery thing. Brushing up against him in vivid detail at some points and then dancing away for weeks before it came back into view. A minute could last an hour, but then an entire month could be blinked away in a haze of lists and books.

Spencer's arrival into the apartment smashed every clock from the walls. Time was never fleeting anymore; no minute dropped from Ren's notice. The atmosphere of his home cooled, darkened, itched in the space between Ren's shoulders, and clenched his back teeth. Spencer living there became an assault on all Ren's senses, different from anything he'd experienced before.

The boy didn't talk, but he made a lot of noise. His *presence* dominated the place. He grunted at Ren. They had awkward meetings in the hallway near the bathroom where they tried to pass each other without words or eye contact. Ren discovered a new migraine trigger — the scent of whatever gel Spencer used in his hair.

Ren did try to make friends, for his own survival more than anything. He hated the awkward silences when they were both at home. He asked questions about Spencer's classes, how he was settling in, was he finding everything ok, searching for a conversation sweet spot. Most people had one. A vocal nerve that if stimulated would prompt them to volunteer everything they knew on a particular subject. Ren tried asking about the drums, the guitar, Spencer's intended major, the boy had to be passionate about *something*. Though Ren was starting to believe that Spencer's only interests were styling his hair, playing those instruments at inconvenient moments that seemed intentionally timed to break Ren's sleep or concentration, and pretending Ren wasn't talking to him. Ren had never seen anyone with this little personality. He didn't know what to do with it.

So, he started taking walks. He'd bring his textbooks with him, studying along the way, noticing the sun setting earlier as summer faded. Ren felt as though he'd been living this way forever; he couldn't believe how slowly time moved now.

Spencer started bringing people to the apartment. One of them, a mousy boy with acne that Ren thought was named Wes, played Spencer's guitar; another guy who gave Ren the creeps brought over a bass. Spencer talked to them, a language that seemed to only make sense among themselves, full of slang and innuendo. They laughed together, but they always grew quiet when Ren was in sight, pausing as he made himself coffee or a sandwich, all of them staring at him with the same expression. It was like they all wanted to pretend he wasn't there.

Ren did what he could to oblige them. It wasn't like he was home much anyway. He spent a considerable amount of time in trainings and classes. He started doing his homework in the hospital cafeteria. It was easier to think there, less distracting, less hostile. Angelique questioned him about it, told him he looked tired, told him to go home and rest.

He assured her he would, but then just relocated to one of the campus libraries until it closed, making sure Angelique never caught him at the hospital at an unassigned time again. Because he just didn't want her to know. Didn't want her to question him, his resolve, his focus. He never wanted her to feel like she'd made a mistake in taking him on. Because if he couldn't be a doctor then he had nothing left. He had to prove he could handle it.

And he could, truly. Sometimes it was the only thing that made sense. Being in the hospital, actively engaged in the ER, was the only time Ren ever felt briefly ok. The only time he felt in control. There was a comfort in the routine of it; something in Ren's life that hadn't completely changed. Straight, simple lines of sutures. Plain grayscale images of X-rays. Angelique's strong, positive voice and guidance, provided Ren could keep her suspicions low enough where she didn't ask him personal questions. Luckily, they had enough external patients Angelique didn't usually go farther than to ask to see his hands, turning the wrists upward and pulling up his sleeves to search for tremor from his fingertips to his elbow, all while he focused on the streaks of gold in her braids. She asked if the knitting was working for him. He replied that it honestly was, though he kept to himself that it only worked *while* he was doing it. Then he smiled and knit her a scarf in lilac wool. She seemed satisfied by his answers, his activity, and his performance. Ren was grateful she only saw him in the places where he was normally at his best, and by the time he started breaking down, it was either time to go home or could be passed off as simple exhaustion.

It was a strange sort of balance. Ren stayed at the ER as long as he could, hyper-focused to the seconds he spent there since they were so effective at blocking out everything else in his life. But it took its toll throughout the day, wearing him out, wrenching his insides, the trauma stacking up on his heart. So, he fled to his room, where he shook uncontrollably in the aftershock and tried to block out the sound of Spencer and his drums, Spencer and his friends, Spencer and whatever the hell he was doing out there. Ren stayed hidden in his room as long as he could stand it, sleep if he could, and then he'd get up and head back to the ER with his pills and his wool.

September closed in on him, chilling the evenings. Ren took his coat out of the closet again. He didn't need it during the heat of the days, but the early morning walks to the campus hospital and the drudging path back to the apartment were both getting colder. Winter again. Ren despised the winter.

Spencer seemed to grow increasingly more comfortable at Stony Island, as evidenced by all the crap he left everywhere. Empty Mountain Dew cans, half-eaten pizza slices. Ren didn't think he ever rinsed the sink after shaving, leaving streaks of foam and tiny hairs stuck all over the basin. The sharp smell of hair gel never left the bathroom, so Ren started brushing his teeth in the kitchen.

And they could never talk about anything, though Ren tried. He tried to politely ask that Spencer just leave the mail addressed to Ren in the mailbox; he'd get it. Please pick up after your band practice sessions. Please don't eat my food; you have a meal plan, and my budget is tight. I have to be up and out of the apartment long before you're awake, so could you at least use headphones for your music after midnight? The list went on and on.

"Spencer, come on," Ren would implore sometimes when he could get Spencer alone. It was bad enough that Ren had to bring it up in the first place; he didn't want to have to do it in front of Spencer's friends. They already seemed to hate him. "I'm not your mother —"

"You sure?" Spencer quipped.

"And I'm not cleaning up after you; I don't have time. Could you at least keep the mess confined to your bedroom? And *stop* using my dishes if you aren't going to wash them."

"Whatever," Spencer said, which didn't sound anything like compromise or agreement. And nothing changed. No, that wasn't true. It got worse. Time slowed down even *more*. The weekend lasted half a year with Ren, twitchy and on-edge, attempting to get through the necessary chores that would minimize his time at the apartment for the rest of the week. He took his homework to the laundry room, sitting on the floor with his back against the rumble of the washing machine. He simplified the meal prep so he wouldn't have to be exposed in the open area of the kitchen for very long. He started keeping bread and peanut butter in his room for those nights he'd come home, starving and exhausted, only to find that someone had helped themselves to his clearly labeled, carefully prepared meals in the fridge. When he called Spencer out on it, he was met with shrugs. Ren started making less appetizing stuff in the hopes that he'd be able to eat it himself.

And even though Spencer was an obnoxious, spoiled little shit with bad manners, he wasn't the worst. The biggest problem was Damien, the creepy guy who played bass. Ren could tolerate Spencer rolling his eyes but having Damien stare at him whenever they were in the same room was unsettling. He was much bigger than Spencer, bigger than Ren. He wasn't even a student; Ren had no idea where Spencer had found him or what Damien saw in Spencer that kept him coming over. Until one day when Damien caught Ren in the hallway and brought it all out in the open.

"Hey," he said, blocking Ren's entrance. "Spencer says you work at the hospital — that true?"

Damien had a large face, a big nose, too-big lips, and a forehead that folded into his eyes like a bulldog's. His voice was as deep as the bass.

"Yeah," Ren responded, eager to get into his room. It had been a bad day, and he wanted it over. He folded his arms tight against him, not expecting this conversation to be anything good.

"So, like, where?"

Ren watched, confused, as Damien carefully checked the hallway to make sure they were alone. What the hell was this about? He doubted Damien had any real interest in Ren or his job unless he wanted something from ... oh.

"I'm not stealing medication for you," Ren told him flatly. He was too tired for this. He just wanted to get inside, make himself a peanut butter sandwich, put on his headphones and his own music, and pretend life was normal. Sometimes he could still do that.

"Now hold it," Damien said, not quite threatening, but not far off. He took a step closer to Ren, which forced him to back against the opposite wall. Shit, he could not let this guy corner him. "I wasn't gonna just take 'em. I thought we could cut a deal. Do you know the street value for oxy right now? I'd split it with you. We could make bank, man."

"Yeah? Still not interested." Ren didn't care how broke he got, he was not risking his visa status and his career on something like this. It was ridiculous. It wasn't like he could just walk up to the pharmacy and take something either. There were lists, counts, locks, a record of each and every dose, where it went, when it was administered and by whom. Even if he wanted to, there'd be no way.

"Come on, man, think it over," Damien pleaded, putting an unfriendly hand on Ren's shoulder. "Don't be so close-minded. This could be good for you."

"I don't think so," Ren maintained, ducking out from Damien's touch. He shot past him into the apartment and then locked himself in. Spencer looked up from the couch, his face twisting into confusion.

"What the hell do you think you're doing?" he asked, looking at the locked door. Damien knocked, hard.

"I don't want him here," Ren told Spencer, wishing his opinion mattered. He wondered if Spencer was in on this whole making a profit from illegally obtained drugs thing. The way Damien caught Ren in the hall made him think not.

"You're such a freak," Spencer said, his lips curling around the word.

Ren went to his room as he'd intended. He knew Spencer let Damien in the second Ren left, though thankfully no one followed Ren to his room. He knew Damien would keep coming over no matter what Ren said. He would keep staring unnervingly at Ren. And now Ren knew why.

He picked up a pen to start a letter, hoping to push away the last few minutes by doing something routine. Who's turn was it for a letter today? Denny? Celeste? Maybe Justin. But what was he supposed to say? *My spoiled roommate's creepy friend is trying to get me to steal meds for him, and it's freaking me out when he looks at me. I'm writing from my room now, but it feels like a cage. Hey, sorry there was no letter last week; I started one, but my hands were shaking so badly even I couldn't read what I was writing, so maybe we'll just stick to email for a while until I figure this out.*

Ren didn't think he was ever going to figure this out. Instead of a letter, he pulled up his email. He'd send one email to everyone today, just a few lines. *Hey guys, hope you're doing well. Not much going on here, just more classes and studying and hours in the ER. I watched Dr. Delacroix do an emergency bypass today; it was crazy. Mostly my job was to hand her things. It took five hours, but I think the patient is going to be ok. Let me know what you guys are up to, all right? Send me some pictures of the beach, Alek; it's pathetic you live so close, and you never go. I'm mailing you some more socks, Celeste; I know it's getting colder where you are. I'll be here if you need me. Night.*

He sent the email and then stared at his phone, needing more. Needing something. He dialed Justin's number. Didn't finish connecting the call. He had half the conversation in his head anyway. *Justin, what do I do? I thought I was a pretty easy guy to get along with, so why is it I have five friends in the whole world, and none of them are here?*

Ren plugged in his phone, took some Excedrin out of habit more than anything. Then he pulled his quilt over his head, forgetting he hadn't eaten. The drums started in the living room.

The next day Ren petitioned the Resident Dean for an apartment switch. He just couldn't do it anymore. He'd put more than enough energy into making it work, but it simply wasn't possible. He and Spencer were incompatible, and Ren didn't want to see Damien again.

The office told him that all the room assignments had been made, which he knew already. They seemed hesitant on making an adjustment, and Ren understood that too. They couldn't accommodate everyone who didn't get along with their roommate. Otherwise, they'd do nothing except play musical chairs with the tenants. They told Ren they'd see what they could do, but it could take a while. Ren figured that meant he was out of luck. He'd have to ask around himself to see if he could get someone to switch. But how was he going to persuade someone to do that? He had nothing to offer, and he couldn't think of a single person who would voluntarily put themselves into the hell Ren lived in every day. He wondered where Wes lived, the kid with the acne who played the guitar. Maybe Ren could take over his contract, and then Wes and

Spencer could drown in Mountain Dew cans as much as they wanted.

"Ren, did you sleep?" was Angelique's first question as he joined her at the nurse's station in the ER. He had, but not well. There were drums, drugs, and loneliness that kept him up for a lot of the night. He'd woken with a migraine, and while it was mostly gone now, he was still in that postdrome weak part where all he wanted to do was sit still and sip coffee.

"My roommate plays the drums," Ren admitted, his voice flat and lifeless. Such a simple sentence for such a huge problem. But if he didn't give her some reason why he looked the way he did, she would start pressing. And he'd cave, and then she'd know how weak he truly was.

"Ah," Angelique acknowledged, as though she knew all about it. "Get some earplugs." Ren nodded carefully. That would take care of the *external* noise. "And I think I'll have you help with paperwork this morning until you perk up a little. Unless you need to go home?"

"Paperwork sounds perfect," Ren responded, forcing himself to lift his head and smile at her. She nodded, checked his hands, and then began a round of the triage rooms. Ren remained at the nurse's station, answering the phone, sorting through the filing. Making it tidy and putting it away. Papers were so nice. They had a certain order and a place where they should go.

By ten that morning, Ren had enough control of the little energy he'd mustered that he could follow Angelique. They took an X-ray of a kidney stone. Set a broken arm. Put five stitches in a hand for an accident involving a kitchen knife and an avocado. An easy sort of day and Ren breathed it in deep. This was as much rest as he could hope for.

When he returned home, he marched straight through the apartment, holding his breath and looking ahead to his door. He heard Damien call to him, something about reconsidering that he ignored. He heard someone tell him to fuck off as he closed the door behind him. He looked at his phone and wished he could call someone. Call someone and tell them. Call someone and beg to be rescued. He wanted to go home, but he didn't know where home was anymore. He longed for the Dominican, but not really. He longed for the *feeling* of the Dominican, the sands, the scent of his mother's cooking, the buzz of the mango orchards. He wished someone would call him. He wished someone knew how much he was hurting without him having to say anything. He wanted someone to notice even though at the same time he was dedicating all his energy into keeping it secret. It didn't make any sense, but he was stuck in this holding pattern and didn't know what to do about it.

Ren went through the motions of spreading peanut butter on bread but then only ate half of it. The peanut butter was too sticky in his mouth; his throat too tight to swallow. *I've got to get out of here*, he thought. But didn't know where to go. So, he sat at his desk and opened a book, looked at the list of trainings and tests he would be responsible for in the next few days. He emailed a couple pictures to his family. Sent another check-in email to the group instead of individuals. Plugged in his phone and curled up under the quilt, feeling the sort of apathy that accompanies someone who knows they're stuck. And somewhere in there, even with the band in the living room, he fell asleep.

Something woke him in the deepest part of the night. Something abrupt that jolted him awake and raced his heart. At first, he thought it was a nightmare he had no memory of that had pummeled him to consciousness. It felt the same. Cold sweat. Dread. Palpitations. But no, it was his phone. Ringing. His phone was ringing?

Clumsily, more shaken than groggy, Ren reached over to the desk for his phone, his mind flipping through his list of contacts for who could possibly be trying to reach him right now. He knew that no phone calls coming at this time of night could be good. He swiped at the screen to answer, registering the name with equal parts hope and fear. Justin. The person Ren had most wanted to contact, but not in the middle of the night.

"Justin," Ren greeted, forcing strength into his voice. What did he need? Surely, he must need something if he was calling Ren now. Calling Ren at all. "What's up?"

The heaviest silence dragged at Ren's wrist to the point where he had to bring over his other hand to hold up the phone. Was there a connection? Had the call dropped between the miles that separated Justin from Ren? "Justin?" Ren called again into the nothing. He checked the phone where a tiny timer ticked off the seconds of the call. Still connected. "Justin, I can't hear you."

Where was he? What was the scene on the other end of the line? Why would Justin call and not say anything? Unless there was something wrong with the call. That happened sometimes when Ren called his family. It usually fixed itself by hanging up and calling back. But Ren didn't dare do that; somehow, he felt if he hung up now, he wouldn't be able to get Justin back. Besides, it wasn't completely silent on Justin's end. Ren could pick things up now. There was an alarm going off in the distance. Breathing. Heavy breathing — had Justin even meant to call him?

"Justin, can you hear me?" Ren tried again, still holding the phone with both hands.

"Ren."

Oh, no. Something was wrong, very wrong, too wrong. Ren hadn't heard Justin say his name like that for years, not since the day he'd collapsed in Ren's living room. His voice was different this time, grating instead of breathless, but just as full of pain.

"Justin, what's wrong?" Ren demanded. "Where are you?"

"My plane," Justin murmured, though it didn't sound as though he was answering Ren's question. He said something else, but Ren couldn't understand him. He thought he caught the word 'eject,' and there might have been something about Harlow. It was garbled in blood, dark, and distance.

"Justin?" Ren had way too many questions. Had Justin said he had to eject from his plane? What did that mean? Was Harlow there too? Was she as hurt as Justin sounded? Where were they? Did someone know where they were? Was help on its way? Was help too far away? Fine, forget it; let's just assume it was all up to Ren for the moment. But how was he supposed to do anything? "Justin, are you safe right now?" Because if he did eject from the plane, did that mean that someone had shot the plane down? Something malfunctioned in it? And who knew where Justin would have come down?

"Ren," Justin said again, and Ren knew he was losing him. Knew he couldn't answer any of these questions even though Ren really needed him to.

"Justin, stay with me," Ren demanded, getting to his knees on the bed in agitation that he was just too far away to do anything useful. "You've got to give me something to work with here. Are you hurt? How do I help you?" *Where are you?*

But the silence returned to the line. The breathing, not so heavy anymore. The alarm in the distance. "Justin!" Ren shouted into the phone, hoping to rouse him, starting to panic as a thousand different ideas about what could have happened or what might happen started splashing around in his head. "Answer me, Justin!" Because he couldn't lose him. Despite everything that hadn't happened and couldn't happen between them, Ren was not willing to continue in a world that didn't have Justin in it. *"Justin!"*

Ren jumped as sound exploded from the wall next to him, an annoyed pounding from the other room.

"Shut the fuck up!" Spencer, woken from sleep. Ren slammed his own fist against the wall. He'd be as loud as he wanted to be. Justin might be dying on the other side of the world, the most important thing in Ren's life, and he was listening to him fade, helpless in this room. It made him furious and terrified.

"Justin, hang on!" Ren continued to shout, ignoring Spencer. "I'll find you." Yeah, but seriously, how? The breathing broke, something that sounded like choked amusement. Like Justin were trying to laugh.

"That's good," Justin breathed, thankfully still conscious. Still alive. "Could use you right now." The words were hesitant, but understandable. They were also the last Ren could get Justin to say, despite his frantic yells into the phone. Despite Spencer's pounding on the wall. After a few more seconds of begging on Ren's end, the call dropped.

"No," Ren said to the screen where the exact time of the call blinked at him. So few minutes. Not near long enough. It *couldn't* be the last time Ren talked to Justin. He tried to call back, but of course, it yielded nothing. That couldn't be it. Just absolutely no.

Ren started dialing another number, no longer caring about time. First, he'd call North. And somehow, some way, they were going to find the phone number of someone who knew where Justin was. Find someone who could help him. Find someone who could bring him back to Ren.

He should have never let him go.

# 12

## COPENHAGEN
## INTERPRETATION

Ren wasn't surprised that North didn't answer the first time he tried his number. It didn't deter him from dialing it again. And again. Ren hit redial a fourth time. A fifth. He'd continue pressing that button until dawn if he had to. As the phone rang incessantly, Ren paced, but discovered his room was too small to do it properly, so he left for the larger area of the living room. He had to do something. He was too far away to do anything. He picked up a soda can from the coffee table, a burst of need, anger, and desperation exploding in his chest. He crushed it in his hand and then paced down the hall and slammed it as hard as he could against Spencer's closed door, letting it fall to the floor. It felt kind of good. Good enough to go get another one. Spencer had left a considerable supply.

It took about half a dozen cans, two sweatshirts, and an empty pizza box before Spencer appeared, looking disheveled and pissed, staring bewilderingly at the growing pile of trash and clothes in front of his door. Ren threw a can that wasn't completely empty through the opening. It soared past Spencer's head and landed on a bunch of papers on his floor, spilling the remainder of its contents.

"What the actual fuck?" Spencer demanded.

"Yeah, you are," Ren snapped at him, knowing that didn't make sense but also knowing Spencer would take it as an insult regardless. "Clean up your crap."

"It's four-thirty in the morning, asshole!"

"By all means, take your time; I'll just leave it all here for you," Ren said bitingly. A small flicker of caution told him he'd better knock it off. There could be serious repercussions from this, but he ignored it. He didn't care right now, and it was too late. He went to get something else Spencer had littered the apartment with — ah, perfect, an empty Starbucks cup. Spencer ducked, slamming his door closed as Ren drew his hand back to throw it. It tapped softly against the door, joining the pile. Ren found that he was panting. Also, that someone was talking to him from the phone. North. Finally.

"Ren, I'm sorry — I don't have time to talk right now. There's a situation."

"I know. Just tell me if you found Justin yet." Ren jumped right in. *Don't you dare hang up on me, North. Not without telling me something.* "Is he ok?"

The urgency in North's voice didn't diminish, but it did change. He seemed to pause, as though he had also been pacing with the phone.

"How?" North started to ask, but Ren didn't want to waste time.

"He called me," Ren explained quickly, eyeing the hallway. He'd moved away from Spencer's door, focused on North. "Less than ten minutes ago. Where is he, North? What happened?"

"He called you?" North repeated, trying to catch up, sounding as though that were extremely surprising. Well, it kind of was. How often did Justin call? Oh, wait, let's think — *Never.*

"He could barely talk, but yes, he called me," Ren said firmly, as though asserting that it wasn't that weird, they were still friends, and Ren was entitled to some information. He glanced at the hallway again, though it seemed Spencer was going to stay in his room. Just as well. "Someone's on their way to help him, right?"

"There's a med and extraction team en route right now, but I can't tell you where he is, Ren. I can't really tell you much of anything."

"Fine, I get it." *I hate it, but I get it.* "How do I help?" *Because Justin called me for help. He knows he can still count on me for that.* North breathed, a frustrated sound. As though he had been asking himself the same question.

"Are you a religious person, Ren?" North asked him, and it brought Ren to a crushing halt. What sort of question was that? How bad was this "situation?"

"I used to be," Ren said, deflated, all the energy falling from him. He hadn't thought about that since he was a kid. "My mom is."

"Pray for him, then."

"North," Ren said, almost a whine. *That's it? That's all you're going to tell me to do? There must be something. **There must be something!***

"I know," North commiserated, though it didn't help Ren feel better. "I promise, I will update you when I can. Can you keep your phone close?"

"Yes," Ren affirmed, ready to do just about anything. He couldn't lose Justin. Not now. Not ever. What had his last words to Ren been? *I could use you right now.* How could he live with himself if those were the last words Justin ever said to him if he didn't try to be in any way useful?

"I'll be in touch," North said, and if it had been anyone else, Ren would have doubted the truth of it. But Ren trusted him. They had been through this before. "I know it's hard but be patient. Justin ... he's resilient. You know that. There's no reason to think he won't come back from this."

He didn't sound as though he were lying, but Ren wasn't sure. It was hard to reconcile the pain in Justin's voice with this partial assurance from North. And coming back wasn't the same as coming back whole. What if he lost an arm, like North had? What if something worse happened? There just wasn't enough information. And it sounded as though it could be hours, maybe days, before they'd find out. What was Ren supposed to do?

"Ren, trust me, the best thing to do is whatever you were going to do before he called. Understand? It'll drive you crazy if you don't. Now I've got to go. Tell me I don't have to worry about you too?"

"I'll be here," Ren promised. "Just help him."

"You know I will."

Ren didn't want to, but he let North go. *There's someone en route,* Ren assured himself. *A whole, specialized team.* He wanted to tell himself it would be all right, but he wasn't there yet. The call from Justin was too fresh, too frightening. How was he supposed to just wait around for someone to update him?

The truth was he couldn't. He didn't even think knitting would help calm him this time. So, at four-thirty in the morning, even though he swore he would never do this again, Ren found himself deep cleaning his apartment. He continued his trend of throwing all Spencer's stuff into the pile at his door, but he stopped hurling soda cans at it. That rage had passed, and Ren honestly didn't want to disturb him again. Didn't know what he'd do if he had to see him or speak to him before he had a chance to calm down. So, he didn't tempt fate and kept everything quiet, doing what he could to eliminate Spencer's presence and scent from the bathroom. He took his own hot shower, made coffee, and then decided to get ready to go.

He started packing. He packed his old suitcase, the one he'd brought with him from Cabarete. The one that had been enough at the time to hold all his worldly possessions. He packed it now with the idea that he might be leaving the country this afternoon. He didn't know how that would be possible, but if Justin ended up somewhere overseas, some medical base in some mysterious location, and if he wanted Ren to sit at his side as he recovered, then Ren would be ready. He'd done it before, hadn't he? Helped Justin through his darkness. Nothing had changed about Ren's willingness either. When he was finished, he placed the suitcase in the space between his door frame and his dresser. Ready for him to grab and leave at a moment's notice.

Then he packed up the kitchen. The dishes he didn't want Spencer to use, the coffeemaker. Celeste's fancy salt and pepper shakers she'd left behind. He took the books from the partial wall, the afghan off the couch. Everything in the apartment that Ren considered his went carefully into his room. If he were leaving today, he wanted it safe from Spencer and Damien. Or at least as safe as he could make it.

At his accustomed time, Ren locked his bedroom door. He took a moment to look around the vastly improved, though noticeably empty, apartment. This would be what it would look like if Ren didn't live here. Well, no, Spencer would trash it in less than two days, but that too would be a testament of Ren's departure. This place. It held no warmth for him anymore. He zipped up his coat and grabbed his backpack, ready for the chilly pre-dawn walk to the ER, checking his phone the entire way.

The hours of anxiety from the moment Justin called hung heavily off Ren by the time he reached the nurse's station. There is only so long a human can hold to that type of stress, and Ren was running out of energy before his day even started. Yet he couldn't let go of it. The questions wouldn't stop. Had they found Justin? Was he ok? Where were they taking him? When would North know more, enough to merit calling Ren with an update? How long had it been since that phone call? Did Ren have his volume up enough so he would hear if a call came in? He checked for the three hundredth time. Yes, still up all the way. It's just no one had called.

"Morning, Ren," Dr. Delacroix greeted him as usual, her voice and pace brisk as she joined him from her office, as if this were just another day. Ren still held his phone, and he found himself unable to lift his eyes from it. He'd been thinking so hard about what could be happening where Justin was that he hadn't prepared for what he was going to tell Angelique. And now that she was standing in front of him, his throat cinched up so tightly he wasn't sure he'd be able to say anything.

"Morning," he managed, deliberately easing his phone into his scrubs pocket. *The volume is all the way up*, he told himself. *You don't have to check again. You will hear when North calls. And he will call. Now it's time to focus on something else. Focus so you don't collapse.*

"Ren." Angelique turned his name into a demand, suddenly on high alert. "What is it?"

He shook his head. Dr. Delacroix had better things to do than listen to him whine about his problems. Especially when there wasn't anything to be done for them. Justin was halfway across the world. Ren couldn't get there in time, maybe couldn't get there at all. He hadn't slept enough, and he was certain he'd dramatically increased the hostility in his apartment, but what else was new? None of these issues were hers. They had other things they needed to pay attention to. But he did need to ask her permission to keep his phone, which meant he'd have to tell her at least part of it. Which meant he'd have to say it out loud. Without breaking down. He could already feel exhausted tears stinging the corners of his eyes. This was going to be a challenge.

"Lorenzo," Angelique repeated, unused to him not answering her. "Tell me what's wrong."

An extremely painful challenge. Justin's name felt tangled around Ren's heart, clamped around it like barbed wire. Trying to say it just clenched it down. "Justin called me early this morning," Ren got out in one rushed breath. Then he had to inhale and steady himself for the next awful sentences. "He's … hurt." God, this was so hard. One more breath should do it. Angelique stood patiently quiet, which was good. If she said anything, it would break Ren's resolve. "I'm waiting to hear if he's ok. Can I keep my phone with me?"

Now it was Angelique's turn to take a breath, a very audible one as she considered how she wanted to proceed. Ren still couldn't look at her. He knew he'd just put her into a difficult position. He wasn't supposed to have his cell phone while he worked. Nothing should distract him from the intensity of the ER. But maybe he could do paperwork. Maybe he could stock cabinets. Hell, he would gladly scrub every nook and cranny of this place with a toothbrush if that's what it took. But two things were certain. Ren needed his phone, and he needed something to do.

"Let me see your hands," Angelique insisted before she answered him. Obediently, Ren put them forward, and this time he didn't try to hide the tremor. His entire soul was shaking; he couldn't hide it today. Ren knew he wouldn't be able to pay attention to anything else. Not the way he would need to pay attention. He knew it, but he also knew he wanted to stay right here in the ER, in Angelique's sure and protective shadow. He wanted to be near her certainty, her strength. Needed to borrow it for a while.

Angelique sighed as she pressed her thumbs into the undersides of his wrists, a gentle and familiar touch. Ren waited for her judgment with his head bowed, wishing he could beg her for things she could not give him. Ren glanced at the triage room, the one he'd stayed in with Justin, the one that slowed his steps when he passed it even now, years later. Angelique noticed the shift of his gaze.

"Does he know?" she asked him quietly. "That you've dedicated yourself to him so completely?"

"That doesn't matter," Ren responded, voice many times stronger than before. That was a choice Ren had made. *It's not Justin's fault he can't respond. But I'm still his best friend; he said so himself. And when he's in pain, he knows I will fix it.* Except this time. He went too far. Ren couldn't reach him. "He has to be ok," Ren whispered, the prayer North had asked for, all the energy and faith he had left going into the words.

"Come with me," Angelique invited, gentler than Ren expected. She tugged on the sleeve of his scrubs, but he'd learned a long time ago to follow her without question. She led him through the ER doors, giving a quick explanation to one of the nurses that she'd be back in a few minutes and to page her if necessary. The route she took through the hospital corridors was a new one to

Ren, which surprised him. He thought he knew everything about this place.

Similar to the ER, a security guard manned the entrance to the wing where Angelique led them, but he accepted Angelique's credentials and allowed them both through the doors. Once on the other side, Ren knew where she'd taken him. The pastel murals painted on the hallway walls gave it away. Angelique had brought him to labor and delivery, which they marched past quickly on their way to an even more secure part of the hospital with another set of locked and guarded doors. The NICU.

"Wait here," Angelique said firmly, physically placing Ren out of the way of the door but not fully into the room. He did as he was told, though he did gaze around at all the incubators and bassinets. The massive amounts of equipment it took to recreate the environment of a womb. Why had Angelique brought him here? He watched carefully, trying to pin his attention on what was going on, as Angelique addressed the nurse in charge.

She wore petal pink scrubs and had a streak of bright pink in her otherwise dark brown hair. She had her glasses resting on top of her head, looking like the kind of matron who would cuff you on the ear one moment and then hug you too tight the next. She seemed to recognize Angelique, joining her easily in the center of the room. They stood close to each other, the NICU nurse with her hand around Angelique's waist as she leaned in so Angelique could explain what she was doing here.

After a minute, Angelique leaned back to beckon Ren over, and he wearily went to her side. He lacked the energy to even be truly curious as to what was going on. His thoughts were far away. On the sands where Justin might have lost his plane. Angelique took his wrist securely in one hand. She held hands with the NICU nurse with the other, as though physically bridging a gap between them.

"Ren, this is Connie Pierce," Angelique introduced them. "Connie, this is my grad student, Ren Cordero. He may have to leave unexpectedly today, so I don't want him to get trapped in the ER, but while he's here, I thought maybe you could use him for touch therapy."

"We'd be glad to have him," Connie responded, her voice and eyes full of kind understanding. Full of what Angelique had whispered to her before she'd called Ren over.

"Excellent," Angelique said, as though they'd just sealed an agreement. She turned her attention to Ren, still holding his wrist. "If you do need to leave, please come see me before you go. I'd also like an update." She squeezed him gently, her tiger eyes as fierce as they always were, but as Ren looked into them, he could see all she wasn't saying out loud. Which shocked him. He didn't think he could do that anymore.

*This is the best I can do for you*, she told him with the pressure of her fingertips, the gold of her eyes. She'd brought him here, where he would need to be calm and restful. She'd brought him to a place where he could be still and focus, where he could give and receive comfort. *This is the only way I know to help you through this.*

"Thank you, Doña," Ren whispered.

She nodded, breaking eye contact, as though Ren had somehow overwhelmed her. She moved toward the door, lifting her hand and resting it momentarily on his shoulder on her way by. There was another message in the touch. She wanted Ren back. Because even though she didn't teach classes and made students cry, despite the many rumors about how merciless and brutal Dr. Delacroix could be, she had chosen Ren. And Ren heard what she said to him a long time ago in her office, the day he'd come in the ambulance with Justin. *It would be a shame to lose you.* She looked as though she thought he might be gone already. He didn't want to be responsible for that. He'd have to try harder.

"Doña," he called after her. She looked over her shoulder, waiting, but he didn't know what to say. "It'll be fine," he forced out, more a wish than a reassurance. She gave him a sad, long-suffering smile. Like she was remembering something that pained her.

"I'm sure it will be," she acknowledged, and then she was gone.

Ren wanted to follow her almost as badly as he wished he were at Justin's side right now. But he knew he'd just be in her way today. Her solution seemed the best. At least she hadn't sent him home.

Connie had Ren scrub up as though he were about to perform brain surgery. Once he was clean, he was directed to a rocking chair and told what he could and couldn't do with a baby in his arms. Then she brought over a three-pound baby girl. Born at twenty-nine weeks, doing well but still needing to gain weight and learn good feeding skills before she could go home. Her name was Elle.

Ren arranged her against his chest, careful of her feeding tube taped against her cheek. Connie draped a blanket over them and then left to take care of her numerous other duties. Ren tilted his chin down to look at Elle, at her cloudy, cross-eyed gaze and her inability to control the muscles of her mouth. It made him want to cry. And laugh.

At first, Ren didn't know if he could handle this, rocking slowly, allowing warmth to build between his and her bodies. Ren's imagination kept throwing dark and terrifying images at him of where Justin might be, what he might be going through right now. They were so strong that Ren's muscles would cramp up in the chair, and his sudden stiffness would disturb Elle. He had to relax for her comfort. So, he closed his eyes and focused on her softness, the scent of her head that was biologically engineered to prompt him to hold her closer. It worked. He snuggled her securely, breathing her in, and she lowered his blood pressure. Angelique was a genius.

Hours went by. Ren held Elle, then Jaden, Antonio, Amelia, and Simone. Four pounds. Two pounds, ten ounces. Feeding tubes. Breathing apparatus. Monitors for oxygen and pulse and temperature. Cannulas and crocheted lace blankets. Strong, hummingbird-fast hearts thumping against his chest. Life.

Ren stroked their heads, gently touched their tiny noses, let them grip his little finger, stared into their miniature faces, and he thought about Justin. Prayed for Justin. Wished for Justin. The stillness of the rocking chair, the flow of the nurses, promoted an environment of peace and logic. An atmosphere where Ren could think clearly. Ren remembered that no news was likely good news. If North hadn't called, it meant Justin was still alive. He may be in surgery. He may be in transport. But he was still alive. And suddenly the phone not ringing wasn't such a terrible thing. As long as it didn't make a sound, Ren could tell himself that somewhere on the earth, Justin was still breathing. His heart beating just like the ones against Ren's ribs. The heartbeat Ren had monitored the most. Fighting, certainly, but Justin had always been a good fighter.

Connie asked him if he needed a break, if he wanted to go eat something, but he shook his head. Before, he'd wanted to run, move as fast as possible. Now he didn't want to break the spell of quiet this chair had granted him.

"Let me know," Connie told him. He watched her move around the room, taking vitals, administering formula and medications, taking notes on her clipboard. Parents came in with soft voices and whispers. They sat beside the bassinets and gazed with worried adoration at their children. It was sweet to watch. Familiar to Ren to see how pain and love mingled in their gestures, how their eagerness to touch conflicted with the hesitation that something could break if they tried. He watched the practiced movements of the nurses stepping in to assist in those transitions, picking up babies with all their attached equipment and placing them into ready embraces.

Ren was holding a petite, blonde baby recovering from heart surgery named Madison when her mother came in. The woman arrived in a protective, guilty storm, and she eyed Ren suspiciously. He wanted to jump up and trade spots with her, but he'd been given strict orders to stay still. *You do not stand up with an infant. We will come to you.* Madison's mother washed her hands while Connie smiled through the explanation that Ren was here to volunteer, wasn't that wonderful, to give Madison the soft touch she needed while her mother was taking care of her older children. And even though the mother also smiled and thanked him, Ren could tell she wasn't happy about it. Ren understood completely.

He gave up his rocking chair to Madison's mother, the stiffness in his legs and back as he stood letting him know he probably should take a break. Take a quick walk. Get a drink. Maybe see what Angelique was doing. See if *she* was ok. Tell her thank you again for what she'd done for him. Not just this morning either.

"Headed out?" Connie asked when she saw Ren removing his protective gown and mask.

"I think so," Ren said slowly, as though he were waking up.

"Thanks for your time. You're on our volunteer list now, too, so feel free to come back whenever you like. We can always use a good cuddler in here."

"Thank you," Ren responded, grateful for this invitation. Did she even know what she was giving him there? The way she smiled indicated she might. Ren wondered what Angelique had told her.

He wandered through the hospital hallways, slowly at first but gaining speed and resolve as he went. The phone remained silent in his pocket. When he returned to the ER, Angelique was in the middle of treating a preschooler who had fallen from some playground equipment. From the looks of it, he'd made a mess of his face, but head wounds bled a lot, so it would take a good cleaning before the actual injuries and their true severity became apparent. He was also screaming in terror, so that didn't help. Ren hesitated briefly in the hall before inviting himself in to assist. He was ready now.

Angelique glanced at him, so he quickly showed her his steady hands. She nodded him forward to take her place so she could move on to the next thing. Ren quickly put on some gloves along with the biggest smile he could manage and soon had the little boy laughing as he finished cleaning his face. He hadn't knocked out any of his teeth, or broken any bones, and it seemed a couple of butterfly bandages were going to do the trick on the worst cut on his forehead. Angelique checked Ren's work before she let the boy and his mother go home.

"Justin's ok then?" she asked him in the quiet moments that

followed, placing the file for the boy on the desk at the nurse's station to deal with later.

"I haven't heard yet," Ren said, something inside him cracking slightly as he allowed himself to think about it. *He's still alive*, he told himself. *North would have called by now if he wasn't. He's alive, and he's going to stay alive, and you're going to keep moving.* As if those things were related somehow.

Angelique studied him, eyes scanning him up and down as though checking him for injury. Like she wanted to ask him if he were ok but knew better than to damage the control it had taken him four hours in the NICU to find. She didn't look as sure as she normally did, and Ren thought he understood her hesitancy. He'd shown her weakness. If that continued, she could take away the only thing he had keeping him together. He knew she was thinking about it.

And even though he knew he was a horrible person, Ren was grateful for the student who showed up to the ER at that moment presenting with symptoms of spontaneous pneumothorax. It broke past whatever Angelique might have wanted to say. They spent the remainder of Ren's strange shift repairing the collapsing lung and sending the patient to recover on the third floor, a line of stitches down the side of his chest. Of course, it had all just postponed the conversation. As soon as they were finished, they were once again standing at the nurse's station. Though Ren felt as though he'd just proved a point. He could be worried about Justin and be alert in a triage room at the same time.

"Well done, Ren," Angelique complimented him on his work with the lung.

"Thanks," he said, the triumph of the successful treatment fading. It was time to go home. His least favorite part of the day. He wished she'd ask him to stay, wished something else urgent would walk through that door and demand their attention. It made him uncomfortable to wish for someone else's suffering like that though.

He shouldn't want to inflict pain on a stranger just so he could distract himself from his own.

"Ren," she started but then snapped her mouth shut. She breathed in a quick little huff of impatience and then went forward as if she'd just won a battle with herself. "You call me, understand? For anything. It doesn't matter what time it is; I want to hear from you. Will you do that?"

"Ok," Ren agreed, and even though he was used to her ferocity, she'd put him off balance with the intensity of her request. "I'll call as soon as I get some information."

"No, Ren," she shook her head. "Don't get me wrong; I do want to hear about Justin. I am concerned about him, but I'm more concerned about you. Call me for *anything*. All right?"

"Yeah," Ren said, though he couldn't see himself doing that. Not to Angelique. He needed her respect. Needed to make sure he lived up to the standard of being her first grad student in a decade. He got asked about it daily. Other grad students, undergrads, sometimes even staff or faculty. They always came at him with the same expression, the same questions. *Hey, they say you're Dr. Delacroix's student, is that true? No! Isn't she mean? Doesn't she scare you? How'd you do it? She never takes students. Did you hear what happened to the last one?* He tried to ignore all of it. The crude suggestions of what he might have done to ingratiate himself in her favor. The praise of what his skills must be like to have gained her attention. Whether the comments were good or bad, none of what they said mattered. But Dr. Delacroix's opinion of him mattered more than anything. He didn't know what he'd do if he disappointed her enough to reconsider. Which meant he would call with an update on Justin and keep his other problems to himself.

So, he forced himself to stand straight after putting on his coat and backpack. He promised her again that he would call her, and then he walked out of the ER as though he had no dread at all in his heart.

But just because he couldn't stay at the ER didn't mean he had to go home yet. Ren didn't want to think about what might be waiting for him. *Idiot,* he chastised himself. *You really thought you'd be leaving the country this morning, didn't you? Honestly thought you'd go pick up that suitcase and you'd be with Justin tonight.* It had seemed the only natural thing to do; Ren had been so sure that's what would happen. The fact that the sun was on its way down and he still hadn't received a phone call only emphasized how stupid that hope had been.

Ren walked in the direction of Stony Island, but with no intention of going there yet. He passed Snell-Hitchcock where he'd first found Justin. He walked through the quad and past the turnoff he'd normally take when he'd meet Celeste at Hallowed Grounds. He hadn't been there once since she'd left. He walked past his own apartment building, glancing up to where he knew his bedroom window was, remembering a cold January night where Denny had stood in this same spot, looking up at that same window. The light had been on then.

He continued walking east, past the closed museum grounds, and all the way toward the lake. It wasn't too cold or dark yet that he was outside alone; there was still the occasional runner or dog walker on the path that paralleled the shoreline. In the summer, this area was full of life. Bright green grass, well-tended trees, multitudes of people on the paths and on the water. But this was mid-September, and the evenings carried the promise of winter. The lake was no longer sparkling; it churned in grayscale, chilling the shore. The grass was turning brown, patches of dead leaves everywhere. Despite the coming night, Ren sat down on a bench anyway, looking out into the darkening waves.

He thought about contacting Alek and Denny, letting them know what happened. But wouldn't that be cruel to share the incomplete information he had? Or maybe they already knew. It always seemed Ren was the last to learn about things happening with Justin. He could call Celeste, but he didn't want to bother her either. So, he simply sat and stared at the lake, comparing it unfavorably to the beaches of his childhood. He sat with the phone in his hands, not calling anyone, not moving.

Hunger clawed at his insides with almost more intensity than the worry in his throat. He hadn't eaten anything today, just some coffee this morning. But the thought of a peanut butter sandwich wasn't all that enticing either. Nor was the idea of getting something while he was out. Ren wanted a very specific thing, craved it, yearned for it. That want deadened his desire for everything else. So, he stayed where he was.

The sun went down, and it grew cold enough Ren finally determined that he'd rather hide in his warm room than remain on this bench. He was in the process of standing, of sliding his arms through the familiar straps of his backpack, when his phone finally rang.

He stared at it for a second, confused, North's name appeared bright against the new dark. Once it registered, Ren hesitated one more ring, debating on whether he could handle bad news right now. By the third ring, he'd reconciled that even if North had the worst news, it wouldn't help to wait for it. He'd been impatient for this call all day, and now he had to accept it.

Resigned, Ren plopped back onto the bench sideways, drawing his knees up to his chest, taking a breath as though he were going to jump into the frigid lake.

"North?" he asked, amazed at the hope and terror in his voice, especially since it had been so many hours since he'd last made a sound.

"He's ok, Ren," North told him immediately, knowing exactly what Ren would need to hear. Except Ren could detect something in North's tone. Something that made him unsure. Not a lie, just something he wasn't saying.

"What does ok look like?" Ren returned, not demanding, but had North forgotten that Ren had spoken with Justin this morning? He'd heard he wasn't ok. What North meant was Justin was alive, and Ren would definitely take that, but ok was a stretch. "Where are you? Are you with him? Can I talk to him?"

"I'm with him, but he's sleeping. We're in Germany; it's a little after one in the morning here."

"What happened?" Ren pressed, wanting to get a clearer picture. North didn't seem able to answer, emphasizing Ren's suspicions about what ok meant. "North?"

"A lot of what Justin does is classified, Ren," North gave the frustrating disclaimer. "I won't be able to answer many of the questions you probably have."

"Got it," Ren acknowledged, his voice trembling. His hand wiped at his eyes before he even knew there were tears there. "Well, thanks so much for the update. Maybe we can chat again in a couple months if you think you can find the time." He knew he sounded bitter, but he couldn't help it.

"Calm down," North chastened, sounding more like a soldier than anything else. Also tired. Ren knew he was being uncooperative and selfish, but he'd spent all day waiting for this call. Spent all day trying not to succumb to terror. Spent a lot of his nights wondering why Justin didn't talk to him. "I'm sorry you felt ignored, but this is the first chance I've had all day to contact you."

"I'm sorry," Ren apologized, knowing North didn't deserve anything he'd just said. He wrote Ren regular emails, gave him updates all the time when he could. Probably gave him more information than he was technically supposed to. North and Celeste were the best at maintaining contact. Justin was the worst. "I ... it's been a long day."

"For all of us; I know," North soothed while simultaneously reminding Ren that he'd also had an exhausting and worried day. Just on the other side of everything. The way Ren had been the first time they'd gone through something like this with Justin, and North had been the one in the background waiting for updates. He'd handled it much better.

"So," Ren gently inserted, trying to switch the topic back to Justin, make amends for his outburst. "What does ok look like?"

"I don't understand what you mean," North responded, sounding edgy, frustrated.

"I mean I know he was hurt so what are his injuries?" Ren clarified, keeping his voice soft, undemanding. Or at least trying to; he could feel his words starting to catch flame as they left his mouth. "If you can't tell me what happened, can you at least tell me that?"

"Are you sure you want me to —"

"Yes," Ren said firmly before North could finish. Yes, he wanted all those details. Heart rate, blood pressure. He wanted North to get Justin's chart and just read it all to Ren. If he had that information, he could put together for himself what had happened.

"Right — forgot who I was talking to," North said, defeated, and Ren could hear how much he didn't want to repeat the damage to Justin's body. But how else would Ren even have an idea of what happened? What sort of recovery Justin was looking at? How long and in what capacity he could return. North took a preparatory breath. "They're being careful with his spine and neck, but nothing looks broken on the X-rays. They're worried since he carried ..." North paused, as if reconsidering giving Ren that information. Ren had to let it go as North moved on. "They had to give him a unit of blood and treat him for shock and heat exhaustion. And he has ... when they ... he's just a mess, Ren. Nothing life threatening or anything, but they had to put in over sixty stitches." North paused to recover, and Ren squinted, trying to imagine what all those stitches could be for.

"Explosion debris?" Ren guessed. "Broken glass?"

"Yes," North confirmed, sounding relieved Ren had put that together on his own. "He's pretty torn up, some places deeper than others. He ... I think he'll have at least one scar on his face."

"Like yours?" Ren prompted, remembering the line across North's chin, the small gash that dipped into his eyebrow.

"Worse than mine," North responded. Ren nodded, accepting that. Not really caring about scars. So long as Justin was breathing, Ren would never care what he looked like. But if debris and broken glass had shot into Justin's face, that was a concern for other things.

"What about his eyes?" Ren pushed just a little more, assembling these facts into a picture of Justin sleeping on a military hospital bed in Germany.

"His eyes are fine; no injuries," North answered quickly, as though happy to give at least a little good news. Though, really, it all sounded ok. Blood loss, stitches, probably swelling and bruising, but no broken bones. Possible whiplash or exposure. Injuries that would take a few weeks to heal in a safe environment with ready access to antibiotics. Weeks. Not months. Not years. It made Ren wonder why North sounded so gloomy. Unless there was something he was leaving out. Or maybe he was just tired. He likely hadn't planned on an emergency trip to Germany today.

"Are you all right?" Ren asked him, hearing the drooping heaviness on the other line, shame creeping in on him as he remembered lashing out earlier in their conversation. Now that he was secure about Justin, Ren could focus on other things, enlarge his capacity for sympathy. North tried to laugh, but it came out too forced.

"I just wish Justin hadn't been so good at being a pilot," North confessed, and Ren immediately understood what North meant. The best pilots were rewarded with the most dangerous missions. Ren suspected Justin was part of the Air Force elite. And he hated that even as he was extremely proud of him. Because with Justin it was nothing but conflicting emotions all the time.

"Well," Ren replied, sad. "I don't know how it could have been any other way. He always wanted to be just like you."

"God save him," North muttered, not accepting the attempted compliment, then made a shushing sound. Ren tuned in, immediately attentive. Because he could hear Justin now. Still sleeping, but not well. His mind working through the trauma of what happened to him during the only moments Justin was unguarded enough to process outside his will. Ren curled up on the bench as he listened to Justin cry, helpless and desperate.

"Ren," North began, and Ren knew he was about to be cut off.

"Let me talk to him, North," Ren requested fiercely.

"Another time," North said, as though he were in a hurry to free his hands to soothe Justin.

"No, wait, North," Ren begged quickly, rushing to get the words out before North disconnected the call. "Please, let me help."

"I don't think," North sighed, stopping again before completing some distressing truth or secret Ren wasn't supposed to know. Ren stood from the bench in a frustrated jerk, gripping the edge of it hard, his back hunching over. Don't think what? That it will work? That it's a good idea? How would they know if he didn't let Ren try? Justin had called him. He'd reached out to him this morning first. Ren discovered he hadn't fully let go of his anger about this yet. How he was always the last to know, the p.s. on the email.

"North, what's the big deal? Why are you protecting him from *me*?" Ren demanded, not even sure where that question came from until it was past his lips. But it was a release to say it. Because he did feel that way. As though Ren were being deliberately separated from Justin, and not just right now. Ren had always blamed the military for this, for making Justin practically impossible to find and contact, but maybe that wasn't true. But then what was all that talk at the wedding? About how people end up where they are supposed to be, with the people they are supposed to be with? But that was all philosophy and conspiracy theories for another time. Justin needed him. Before North hung up.

"Put me on speaker, North," Ren said once more, as though he had any power to prevent North from leaving Ren stranded by this bench with just the strength of his voice an entire ocean away. "He called me first."

"Ren," North sounded as though he wanted to tell him something important but couldn't. Some inarticulable secret. Some forbidden wish. Something else Ren would ponder during the nights that followed, the nights he couldn't sleep. The nights he wished he could disappear into the waves that blacked out his vision if he looked out over them, hearing their motions but unable to see.

"You can hang up on me if it doesn't work," Ren told him coldly. "But at least let me try. I've done it before."

"All right," North caved, and while he didn't sound angry, there was something defensive in the tone. Ren didn't understand, but he knew North had devoted himself to sparing Justin any kind of pain. And somehow that included keeping him away from Ren. Which didn't make sense, but at least Ren had gotten past the barricade today. "Go ahead."

Ren changed his grip on the phone, loosening it, cradling it. He remained bowed over the bench, but this time more reverently. Everything in him softened as he prepared to comfort his friend.

"Justin," Ren began. "Calm down, now; you're safe. I'm here with you. You're going to be fine. You can rest now."

Ren continued in Spanish, knowing Justin liked hearing him speak his own language, knowing neither Justin nor North would understand a word of it but could drift on the lilt and tone. The waves. The truth. He could tell Justin the truth.

"God, I miss you," Ren told him, keeping his voice in a lullaby cadence. "I call you all the time, but never let it go through because I know you're busy. I know you're really far away even if no one ever tells me where. I shouldn't have let you go. I should have told you everything. Denny said I'd regret it. She's always right, you know?"

He continued pouring his heart out to the boy he loved most in the world. The boy he could never tell any of this to if he were awake, in a language he could understand. But would Ren's life have been different if he had said these things? If he'd said the words he was saying now? Or would Justin have shied away, fled from him faster and farther. Ren couldn't forget why he'd held back in the first place. That doubt. That fear. The risk. Better to have it this way, right? Where Justin sent him letters, however infrequent, considered them friends. Better this than nothing.

"Sleep now," Ren told Justin, his heart emptied of all it had been holding. His hands were shaking, but this time Ren wasn't sure why. "Get better. Call me tomorrow so we can talk when you're awake, all right? I'd really like that."

His voice was breaking, his body weak now that he had finally managed to give voice to all the emotions he'd been repressing. It felt good to say them. It hurt to say them. Hurt enough that Ren didn't think he could continue. Fortunately, it seemed he'd succeeded in his intentions. North came back on the line, whispering, satisfied.

"Thanks, Ren," North acknowledged quietly. "I don't know what you said, but he's still now."

"Call again if you need to," Ren prompted, his voice shaking along with his hands, tears on his face. "Don't worry about the time or anything. Now that we know it works, I can talk him down again if he needs it." *Whenever he needs it. Every time he needs it. I'm not going to hurt him, North. I thought you knew that. He's safe with me.*

"Get some rest, then," North recommended. "Keep your phone close."

"You too," Ren returned. Because they both sounded ragged and worn, frayed at the edges.

"Copy," North said in farewell, leaving Ren where he'd started. Alone on the edge of Lake Michigan, the night surrounding him. Ren took a deep breath, holding the phone close to his chest. *Well, Denny,* he thought, *I did it. Told Justin exactly how I feel about him.* He tried to snicker as he imagined her rolling her eyes about the lie in that truth, but it came out much closer to crying. Ren looked west, where his apartment waited two miles away. He gave one last longing look toward the cold waves, wishing they were different, that everything was different, before finally gathering himself enough to begin the walk back.

He remembered halfway there that he'd promised to update Dr. Delacroix. He sent her a text instead of calling her, not trusting his voice. The night pierced him with chill, which followed him all the way past his front door.

The apartment itself was warm, but the welcome Ren received

was not. Normally, Ren and Spencer did their best to ignore each other. As few words as possible. No eye contact, even when they were practically on top of each other in the hall, tripping over each other in the kitchen. But that had been before this morning when Ren had changed the dynamic. Had apparently given permission for open warfare instead of simmering hostility.

"Aw shit," Spencer whined the moment Ren was through the door. "You came back."

Spencer exchanged a gaping, arrogant smile with Damien, who was tuning his bass without any real enthusiasm. They both glared at Ren, who was trying to keep his posture straight as he walked past them, trying to pretend he didn't hear or see them.

"You're late, freak," Spencer informed him, as if Ren didn't already know that. Though he was surprised Spencer took note of his presence enough that he could tell. "We were hoping you'd moved out and weren't coming back."

"Looks like neither of us is getting what we want today," Ren muttered, almost past the living room, one more step to the end of the couch. Something heavy smacked him between his shoulders, and he felt a rush of something sticky and wet splatter against his coat and the back of his neck. An open soda can dropped to the floor, and Ren took a second to glare behind him at Spencer and Damien. He wasn't sure which of them had thrown it; they looked equally vicious and pleased with themselves. Ren wanted to murder them both.

"What? You mad now? I thought you were into throwing stuff?" Spencer challenged, but it was Damien who had his hands tensing into fists. Ren turned away without comment.

"That's what I thought. Go on. Go hide in your room," Spencer dismissed, since both of them knew there wasn't anything Ren could do about what just happened. Not with Damien here. "No one wants you here anyway."

Ren swore at them in Spanish, tainting his voice darker than he ever had before. He wished Justin were here. Wished he had a fraction of Justin's courage. Spencer looked as though he wanted to retaliate but didn't know how. Ren disappeared into his room before anyone could say or do anything else. Though he'd have to sneak out later and clean the soda from his coat and backpack.

Spencer started drumming, the pace and violence of it a message to Ren more than a beat. Ren rested against his closed and locked bedroom door, insisting to his racing heart that he was safe and there was no way they were going to fight right now. Though he wanted to. He took off his backpack and coat, inspecting the damage. Just a splash, but the idea that Spencer was now brash enough to throw things at Ren's head was a problem. Ren probably should have given it more thought when he was slamming trash against Spencer's bedroom door this morning.

Dr. Delacroix texted him back, her words quick and efficient. She was glad to hear Justin was ok. She emphasized again that if Ren needed anything he should give her a call. She said she would see him in the morning. She repeated North's instruction to get some rest. Ren sat on his floor, braced against the side of his bed with his coat in his lap, staring at his phone. She'd said to call her, but what would he even say? What could he say that wouldn't make it seem like he was a whining child who couldn't figure out his own issues?

He didn't remember falling asleep, but he woke in the dark slumped to his side on the floor with his phone still loosely clasped in his hand. He was stiff, sticky, and starving. His phone helpfully supplied him with the time, four-thirty in the morning again. But with Spencer still asleep, it gave Ren the opportunity to wash his coat and clean up his backpack, take a shower to get the soda out of his hair and off his neck. He set up the coffeemaker on his desk and started it brewing. He looked at the packed suitcase, thinking of putting things back where they should go, but he decided against it. There was no need to unpack; he was still leaving. He may not be flying to Germany, but he had to shift the living arrangements. He wanted to be ready to go the second something became available. He had to find something.

The only bright spot of the morning arrived when Ren was on his way out. He'd left way earlier than he needed to, but he didn't want Spencer to catch him outside his room. He walked slowly down the hall, down the stairs, thinking about maybe ducking into the lounge for a while, maybe closing his eyes for a bit before heading to the ER. Because he needed to look fresh and ready, needed to look as though he had rested.

He did end up in the lounge, to give himself some privacy to answer his phone, which started ringing just as he hit the ground floor. It surprised him. So many calls in such a short amount of time. And he couldn't help but smile when he saw who it was, forgetting all the darkness of the previous night, the discomfort of the morning.

"Justin," Ren breathed, sounding too relieved but too happy to care. "Hey, how are you?"

"I'm good," Justin answered automatically, and just like with North, Ren could hear there was more to what he said than his words. He did sound all right, properly dosed with pain medication. "Is this a bad time? I didn't wake you up or anything, did I?"

"No, but don't ever worry about that," Ren insisted. "Call me whenever you want." *Really. Call me. Please.*

"Sorry about yesterday," Justin apologized, his voice going low and soft. Ren didn't want to think about yesterday. "Or was it the day before yesterday? Anyway, sorry."

"Don't be," Ren assured. Two tiny words when he wanted to slam Justin with questions. *Why did you pick me to call? Why did you only think to call when you thought you were going to die? Why don't we talk more? Why does North think he has to keep me away from you? What would you do if you knew how much I love you?* "I'm glad I could be there for you."

"You always are," Justin admitted, and Ren sagged against the couch, part of him content that at least Justin knew that, even if he didn't always act on it. The other part of him was fixed on Justin's tone. Something was wrong here, but Ren didn't understand it. All Justin's words made sense but the emotions behind them were skewed. Like they were having two extremely different conversations.

"Justin, what is it?" Ren asked directly, needing to figure out the disconnect. Justin coughed slightly.

"Ren, can I ask you something?"

"Of course," Ren replied, wondering about Justin's hesitancy, ready to be whatever Justin needed.

"It's about Harlow."

Ren closed his eyes, exhaling shame and hurt. He'd forgotten all about her. But she was important to Justin. Ren had to swallow his true feelings to keep his tone neutral. There was always something, wasn't here? Always something wedged between them. Distance. Scholarships. North. Girlfriends.

"Yeah, where is she?" Ren asked, because that was a fair question. Justin was hurt, and North had flown immediately to Germany. But where was Harlow? Why was this the first time Ren had heard about her during all this crisis? Why wasn't she at Justin's side? The silence after his question grew uncomfortable, drawing out way too long. "Justin?" Ren checked, wondering what he'd done. Or maybe he hadn't done anything; maybe something else was wrong. "You all right?"

"We went down together," Justin wheezed out, overcome with the kind of pain morphine doesn't touch. Oh, no; she hadn't been killed, had she? Ren didn't like her, but he wouldn't wish for anything like that. "Her jet was the one hit. She wasn't responding. I, well, basically I caught her plane with mine to try and control the descent a little bit. But there was a lot of smoke. I couldn't really see. We still ... we came down hard."

"Justin," Ren said his name in a desperate, tiny breath. He should be over there. Should be with him right now. Ren didn't know if he should shush Justin or allow him the painful release of continuing. And what did he want to ask Ren about? Everything was over; there was nothing Ren could do. Except listen. Ren wanted to tell Justin how amazing that had been — because what kind of skill would it take to catch an out-of-control jet with another and bring them both blindly to the ground? He had no idea Justin could do anything like that. But he didn't think Justin wanted to be congratulated, so he kept quiet, waiting.

"Her plane was on fire," Justin went on, telling Ren all the things North had kept from him last night. Ren was no longer sure he wanted it. Even here, in the light of a new day where he knew Justin was all right, it made Ren shudder to hear all the ways it might not have turned out so well. "I didn't have a choice. I had to move her. I had to get her out."

Oh, that's what Justin needed. He didn't want to ask Ren anything. He needed to hear that he'd made the only decision he could. Because something had happened. After the crash and the fire. Something that hadn't come out yet.

"I carried her," Justin continued, and Ren remembered North saying something about that. *They're being careful with his neck and spine.* Because he carried Harlow. "I pulled her out and carried her to where they could get us. Two miles on my shoulders." Because what else could he have done?

"You saved her life, Justin," Ren explained, affirming the truth of it. He wondered how many times he would have to do this for Justin. Help him understand he'd done the right thing.

"I ruined her life," Justin lamented, his voice dark and empty, like the burned-out cockpit of Harlow's plane. "They said her back is broken and her hip. And I *carried her.*"

"Justin, listen," Ren started, wondering how much detail he should go into. He hadn't seen her injuries. He couldn't be sure.

"They won't tell me everything," Justin went on, not ready for Ren to offer an opinion on the events as he knew them. "They won't tell me what I did to her."

"Justin, you *had to* move her," Ren insisted, wanting to help him feel better even though he hated how much Justin seemed to care about this girl. "That's how critical situations work. We train on the order of operations all the time. First, you ensure your own safety.

Next, you remove the patient from immediate threat. When I come to the scene of a car accident, the first thing I do is get everyone out of traffic. Then we look at the damage. You didn't do anything wrong, Justin."

Though there would be complications from what had happened. The jostling might have knocked loose bone fragments into Harlow's bloodstream, the potential for an embolism. She'd be watched close for blood clots or any kind of blockage. There may be swelling or even severing of the spinal cord. All injuries that could have happened before or after Justin moved her. There would be no way to determine for certain what extra damage Justin had inflicted, if any. But he seemed intent on blaming himself.

"She won't fly again," Justin said, as if that were the worst thing that could happen to a person. Maybe for Justin that was true. "Might not ever walk either."

"She's alive, Justin," Ren reiterated. That was the important thing. *She's alive and you didn't kill yourself trying to help her stay that way.* That was all Ren needed. Now if he could just get Justin to see it, though he knew he wouldn't. Not until she could absolve him herself. "She's probably not awake yet, is she?"

"No, they're keeping her sedated," Justin said, defeated. "She looks awful. Ren, what do I do? How do I help her?"

*Don't ask me that!* Ren wanted to yell at him.

"Just be there for her," he heard himself advise, knowing that Justin needed a job, understanding what that felt like. "Don't forget you need to recover too but stay with her. Watch her vitals; talk to her. And when she wakes up, you make sure she remembers what you did for her."

"She's going to be so pissed," Justin lamented.

"Good," Ren said. Because anger motivates so much better than despair. "Use it to help her. Challenge her." Because Harlow seemed to be the sort of girl who thrived on challenge.

"All we do is fight now, Ren," Justin confessed, and Ren had no idea what to do with that.

"That didn't cause this, Justin," Ren emphasized, more passionately than he would have thought possible, wishing the answers to his own problems came to him as easily. "And yeah, she's going to be pissed. She's hurt and terrified and maybe a huge piece of her identity has suddenly been cut out of her. But you did not do that. And no matter what she says to you, because people in pain say all sorts of crazy things, you don't listen to that. You did the only thing you could. You saved her life."

"Ren, I —" Justin breathed unsteadily into the phone. Ren was almost panting too. "Thank you."

"Anytime," Ren promised, eyes closed, his head hanging as he sat crushed into the corner of the couch. The same place he'd been when Denny had told him Justin was on trial for manslaughter. *Anytime, Justin. I'll be here if you need me.*

"And how are you doing?" Justin asked, almost as an afterthought, desperate to change subjects. "Feels like we haven't talked in forever." Ren almost broke. *That's because it has been forever.* He remembered the feel of Justin's hair in his fingers, his heat, the scent of him on Ren's pillow. All the memories he carried like Justin's stitches. They held him together. They could prove fatal if they grew infected.

"Just staying busy," Ren forced himself to say, though not as lighthearted as he'd imagined he should sound. Justin was focused on so much right now. His own recovery. Harlow's much longer and harder recovery. Their relationship together. Ren didn't want to give him anything else that could weigh him down. That's not what his role was supposed to be.

"I had a dream about you last night," Justin told him, and Ren couldn't help but smile. "I couldn't see you, but you were there. Speaking Spanish."

"Sounds accurate," Ren acknowledged, wondering if he should tell Justin the truth. *You were crying. I was there. North didn't think I could, but I comforted you. You responded to me.*

"You said," Justin began, and Ren held his breath. Ren had said nothing Justin had understood. Right? But Justin paused, reconsidering. "No, I don't remember. Dreams."

"Yeah," Ren agreed, though he didn't know what he was agreeing to.

"Anyway, I'll let you get back to your day. I know you've got a million things going," Justin went on.

"Call me later," Ren begged. "If you need anything. Or even if you don't, you know, just ..." *Ren, you are an idiot.* "It was good to hear from you."

"Thanks, Ren," Justin said again. Then he left Ren alone in the lounge, and he had to scramble to get to the ER on time.

# 13
# DISTRACTIONS

Part of Ren loved becoming Justin's new coping mechanism. He loved that Justin now called him almost every day. They talked in the morning; Ren leaving his apartment early so he could slip into the privacy of the lounge, curl up on the couch there and close his eyes so he could focus entirely on Justin. It was the connection he'd missed for all their years of separation, and he reminded himself constantly that it was good.

He just wished they didn't have to talk about Harlow quite so much.

The break in her hip couldn't be pinned, so there was nothing to do except stay extremely still. The good news was she had feeling below her waist, the fracture in her back had not damaged her spinal cord or connected nervous system. But that meant she had to endure the excruciating pain of her recovery. The military doctors kept her heavily medicated, certainly, but there are limits to how many doses can be administered in a twenty-four-hour period. They could not give her enough to keep the pain at bay indefinitely, short of putting her into an induced coma. Which might have been nice but not an appropriate treatment for her. They were already on high alert for blood clots. Justin kept watch at her side through all of it.

And also through all of it, or at least for a half an hour or so every morning for the past ten days since the crash, Ren would sit on the lounge couch with his eyes closed and his head in his hand, patiently translating all the doctors had said. What signs were good and what embolism meant. Justin sometimes asked Ren how long it would take before she could move? Walk? Ren made his best guesses, reminding Justin that he was still a grad student and nowhere near the expertise level of the Air Force trained medics. And even if he were a licensed MD, his studies revolved around the ER. Ren would have been a great resource at Justin's side for when the planes went down, pulling Harlow from the cockpit, immobilizing her on-scene in preparation for transport. Keeping her vitals up until she could be secured. Assisting with Justin's bleeding and shock. But on this side of the incident? Ren was barely any better than Justin.

But it was obvious Justin needed him. Or at least needed something. Justin may not have been in as bad of shape as Harlow, but he was just as trapped. Denied his normal releases of missions or training, denied his plane and the freedom of the sky. Broken from his routine. Tethered to the medical wing of the overseas base by both his own wounds and his guilt. And there wasn't much Ren could do to help him.

Except answer the phone, every single time, no matter what time it was or how many years or days or hours it had been between calls. Ren would always answer the phone when Justin called, and he would listen.

Listen to how broken Harlow appeared in the bed. How long she slept and what her voice sounded like when she woke. Listen to all the doctors said to her and about her. And listen to all the terrible things she said to Justin in those moments of consciousness. When she was awake but had to wait for her next installment of pain meds that would knock her silent again. When she was hurting the most. She poured out her fear, pain, and blame on Justin. And Ren knew that despite his constant assurances, Justin believed every word that came out of her mouth.

She raged that Justin had ruined her career. He'd always been jealous of her. The only reason he ran point on missions instead of her was due to the sexist decisions of their superiors. He should have waited for the med team to come before trying to be a fucking hero. He should have listened to her on how that mission should have gone in the first place. And she couldn't believe he was standing near the bed, walking so easily into her room.

And then she'd flip it around instantaneously, and suddenly it wouldn't be Justin's fault anymore. But it also couldn't be something she could return from. She wished for death. She begged for it. Pleaded with Justin to explain why she was still alive, why she was forced to stay that way even as Justin begged her to relax, be patient, please eat. She cried. Justin cried when he thought she couldn't see him, and when he thought Ren couldn't hear it in his voice.

Ren despised it. He hadn't been a fan of Harlow from the start and listening to what she said to Justin was not helping his opinion. He knew he should have more charity about it. After all, he'd seen what suffering helplessness does to people. It makes them vicious. Makes them snappy and short. Hell, he'd seen it in Justin the very first time they'd ever spoken to each other. He knew anger was another symptom all on its own. He just wished Harlow didn't have to say it *all*. He wished he could stand by her bedside, smack her upside the head, and tell her to shut up. She should be nothing but grateful. She had promised Ren that she would take care of Justin, and guess what, bitch, *tearing him down is not how to do that.* He wanted to tell Justin to leave her alone if she couldn't behave herself; he didn't have to stick around. She was full of pain and poison, and Justin would be fully justified in cutting her off. Ren wanted to assure him he would never treat him that way, no matter what.

But he knew Justin blamed himself for her pain, that he felt the need to punish himself somehow for what had happened. His injuries weren't sufficient, so he was almost using the emotional damage Harlow inflicted to make up the difference. He felt it wouldn't be fair if he didn't sit by her side and share in her suffering. But when it got to be too much for Justin, he'd slip away for a break and call Ren, who would then painstakingly unravel all Justin's nerves.

*She doesn't mean it*, Ren would soothe, as though he didn't hate her and what she was doing. He knew he was only doing it for Justin's sake but defending her made Ren's chest hurt. Made him want to scream. He defended her anyway. *She doesn't know what she's saying. She's scared. She's hurt. It has nothing to do with you. You know it's not true. Keep being patient; you're doing great. It'll get better.*

It wasn't enough. Not for any of them. There weren't enough drugs for Harlow. Ren couldn't find the right words for Justin. And for Ren, well, he didn't know anything could hurt the way this did. Didn't think there could be anything worse than talking to Justin every day and telling him everything except the one thing he really wanted to say. Trying to help Justin fix his relationship with his girlfriend when Ren wished he could beg him to leave her, leave all the dangers of the military, and come home to him. But he couldn't do that. Especially not now. So, he kept answering the phone, kept getting up before dawn so he could be in the lounge and ready for the call to come in. It might not be enough, but Ren would take whatever he could get.

Besides, they didn't *always* talk about Harlow. Ren would demand reports on Justin's recovery too, gaining a small sense of pitying amusement as Justin grew increasingly cagey as he healed, as the stitches began to itch like crazy. He knew it was hard for Justin, but it comforted Ren. It meant at least Justin was improving steadily and well.

"I'm going to rip them out with my teeth, Ren, I swear to God," Justin growled.

"You know that wouldn't help, right?" Ren replied, calm, relaxed on the couch for these parts of their conversations. The Harlow-free minutes of their talk that he lived for. "It's your *skin* that itches, not the sutures holding it."

"They're still in my way," Justin returned.

"Don't mess with them; they'll get infected," Ren cautioned, using his doctor voice. "Find something else to do." He realized he'd made a mistake as soon as he'd said that. There wasn't much Justin *could* do right now, and Ren hadn't wanted to remind him how stuck he was. Ren plowed quickly ahead to clarify. "They've got to have some kind of rec area or therapy room in the med bay, don't they? A ping-pong table or something?"

Justin huffed indignantly, letting Ren know he was right. There were resources and activities available. Justin just hadn't been taking advantage of them. Because he was hell-bent on punishment.

"Seriously, Justin, go get North and play some ping-pong. Take a short walk outside if you can; get some sunlight and fresh air." Though Ren knew all too well that even if that helped, it was a temporary kind of relief. Distractions only lasted so long. Sooner or later, he had to go back, trapped in that room. But still. Distractions served a purpose.

"North's not here," Justin revealed, surprising Ren. "They flew him back to D.C. three days ago."

"Really?" Ren checked, not that he didn't believe Justin was telling the truth, but it surprised him that the Air Force would take North away from his wounded son. That North would have agreed to leave Justin alone.

"He's coming back," Justin assured, and Ren remembered Justin on his bathroom floor, staring after North, always afraid when North left that it would be the last time Justin would see him. Sounded as though that fear hadn't fully dissipated. "Less than a week, he said."

"That's good," Ren acknowledged, though now he felt the sudden weight of being solely responsible for Justin settle on his back. With North missing, Ren no longer had a man on the ground to help Justin in person, no one monitoring him in the night. Which meant that

Ren would have to make their phone conversations as bolstering as possible. And he really needed to get Justin better help than a thirty-minute call with Ren every morning. "Who else is there?" Ren asked, earnest now. *Who can look after you since you decided to put an entire ocean between us and there is no way I can get to you?*

"I'm not that into ping-pong, Ren," Justin began his dismissal of Ren's suggestion, but Ren wasn't talking about that anymore.

"Ok," Ren allowed, moving on. "Don't play ping-pong, but do something, Justin." *Do something besides sit next to Harlow trying not to scratch open your stitches.*

"You sound like Major Grimes," Justin said, and Ren could tell it wasn't meant as a compliment. "He's always after me to participate in all that weird therapy shit they've got going over here."

"Perfect!" Ren pounced on that. It was better than nothing. "I concur with my esteemed colleague Major Grimes; participate in the weird therapy shit."

"You seriously want me to go learn basket weaving?" Justin asked, not sounding opposed to the idea, just surprised that Ren had such a fierce opinion about it.

"Yes, I *strongly recommend* you go learn basket weaving," Ren said firmly. "Dr. Delacroix says the same thing. I know it sounds stupid, but it's actually really good for processing trauma. Which *you have been through* no matter what you say. And it doesn't have to be basket weaving, any small, repetitive task with your hands will work."

"Like knitting?" Justin said quietly, not snidely, but definitely with more insight than Ren wanted, making him wish he'd kept his mouth shut.

"Yeah, I guess knitting or crocheting would fall into that category," Ren answered, trying to make it sound as though he'd never made the connection before. Make it sound as though that wasn't the reason he'd learned how to do it or the reason all his friends had a steady supply of mittens, sweaters, socks, and hats.

"Ren," Justin started, way too serious, and Ren knew what he was about to do. He was going to ask Ren questions about trauma and why he'd need help processing it. But they weren't talking about Ren. Ren made it a point that they would never talk about anything consequential in his life. He'd tell Justin the random funny story about memorable patients in the ER or they'd laugh about whatever scientific exploit Alek and Denny were currently obsessed with, but Ren made sure to never burden Justin with any of his problems. That wasn't the purpose of the calls; he was supposed to be supporting Justin, not dragging him down like Harlow was doing. He was not going to be responsible for that. Not going to be anything like her.

"Just pick something to distract yourself from your stitches," Ren interrupted. "Something fun."

"What do *you* do for fun?" Justin challenged, in his direct way that made Ren wonder how Justin could be so perceptive about Ren's emotions and still not have any clue how Ren felt about him.

"*I* am a grad student," Ren defended. This conversation was getting difficult. He was going to have to cut out of it soon or risk completely breaking down on Justin. "I sold my soul to Dr. Delacroix, remember? You were the one who told me to do it."

"How about this," Justin said, as though he were about to start a lecture. There was a weight to his tone Ren didn't hear often. At least not from Justin. He sounded like North. "I'll go to therapy if you go do something fun."

"I just got done telling you I don't have time," Ren tried to protest, but Justin had taken up a crusade and shot him down before he'd started.

"You've got time. If you didn't, I wouldn't have half a dozen pairs of hand-knit socks."

Ren drooped on the couch, hiding his face in his hand. *Damn it, Justin.*

"You don't like my socks?" Ren put out as a desperate attempt to deflect what Justin was trying to insist on him. "I'm offended."

"Your socks are great; I'm wearing them right now. Stop changing the subject." Justin plowed through his weak defenses, not even allowing Ren a moment to cherish the fact that Justin was wearing the socks. "Tell me what you do for fun. And don't say knitting because we both know that's not why you do it."

"I," Ren paused, wracking his brain for something to say. He hadn't done anything fun for months. Not since Celeste left, and even then, he wasn't sure if what they'd done together had been for fun or if it was just something else they thought they needed to do. He thought he might have forgotten what fun was. He scanned the lounge, searching for inspiration, his eyes settling on the bulletin board on the wall opposite the fireplace, which was covered with fliers and handwritten advertisements. A car for sale. Math tutoring services. And the magic golden ticket.

The UChicago Ballroom and Latin Dance Association. Wednesday nights from seven to ten. Perfect.

"I dance," Ren answered Justin, as though he'd actually gone. As though he'd been a regular on Wednesday nights for ages. "Ballroom and Latin ... you know, when I can."

"You have never mentioned doing that — ever," Justin responded, insinuating that he knew Ren was lying. Ren wanted to snap back that it wasn't exactly as though Justin had been very involved with him for the past few years. He'd missed *plenty* of details.

"I just started," Ren answered. *As in I made the decision five seconds ago.* "And I did take a couple ballroom classes during my undergrad." *I skipped that class twice to take care of you, but that's something else you don't know about me.*

"What does Celeste think about it? She's ok with you dancing with someone else?" Justin asked, and Ren realized he'd also never told Justin that he and Celeste broke up. He figured that everyone just kind of knew, what with her going off to New York and everything. At the very least, he figured Alek and Denny would have told him. God, was Ren going to have to confess to everything today? Though he'd noticed that since they'd started talking about Ren and his life, Justin seemed lighter. More engaged and animated. As if talking about Ren might be helpful for Justin. Ren had become the distraction.

But still. There were some things Ren was not willing to talk about. Which meant he'd better gloss over the whole Celeste thing pretty quickly.

"Celeste and I decided we're better as friends," Ren muttered. "I think she's dating a prince or something right now." Not that it was going to last; the guy might be set to inherit a small kingdom Ren had never heard of, but no one she'd dated so far could keep up with Celeste for very long. Ren took a certain pride that he held the record, and he wasn't even straight. Though he suspected that was the very thing that had allowed them to last so long.

"Huh," Justin said, slowly processing this news, sounding stunned. "I thought you were still together."

"Not since she left for Columbia," Ren said flatly.

"So, who do you go dancing with?" Justin pressed. Asking Ren questions he didn't want to answer. "You don't go by yourself?"

"That's the *best* way to go," Ren argued.

"If you say so," Justin said, apparently unconvinced. "But you *do* go?"

"Justin, come on. What's with the interrogation? You don't believe me?" *Does that mean you can tell when I'm lying to you? As in every time I've lied to you or is this a recent talent you've developed in the past week and a half?*

"Send me a picture," Justin requested, apparently aware that Ren was lying but completely oblivious to the torture he was putting him through by calling him out on it.

"I don't have a picture," Ren confessed, voice muffled because he'd buried his head between his knees. *Shit.*

"Uh huh," Justin responded, as though he knew it all along. It forced Ren into a rapid and entirely made-up-on-the-spot explanation.

"It's dark in there," Ren said, not even knowing if that was true.

"And I need both hands when I'm dancing, you know. I didn't realize I'd have to prove it because my *best friend* doesn't believe me."

"I didn't say I didn't believe you. I just want to see a picture," Justin said smoothly. "When are you going next?"

"Tonight," Ren gritted out between clenched teeth, rocking slightly.

"So, take some tonight," Justin recommended, as though it would be the easiest thing in the world. Ren exhaled petulantly.

"And then you'll do the therapy?" Ren pushed back, intending on at least a small victory. If that's all it would take for Justin to get some help, he'd sacrifice one evening at least pretending like he was having fun.

"I'll mail you pathetic, misshapen baskets for the next month," Justin promised, and Ren felt some of his muscles loosen. Ok. Fair exchange. At least then he'd know Justin was with someone else besides Harlow, doing something besides getting emotionally ripped to shreds in her room. Ren could accept that.

"Deal," Ren agreed, hoping Justin really would bury the apartment in baskets. Wouldn't that just piss Spencer off though?

Arrangement in place, they let the call end. Ren always found himself sitting still for a few seconds afterward, staring at the screen, at the little blinking number indicating the time they'd spent talking. Still too few minutes when compared to how long it had been since they'd last seen each other. And every time Justin hung up, Ren's soul dropped. Because despite how Justin had called consistently for the past ten days, there was still that apprehension of loss. Justin stared after North every time he left, keeping him in sight as long as possible. Ren stared at his phone.

But he couldn't stare long. He had to meet Dr. Delacroix in the ER where they spent their day alternating between incoming patients, filing, and Ren running through imaginary scenarios while Angelique watched him critically. She seemed pleased with his progress, definitely happy that Ren was no longer arriving at the nurse's station in obvious distress. Once his hours were up at the hospital, he went over to the library to study for a lot less time than he normally did before he realized he was going to have to get ready for this dancing thing. And he probably shouldn't wear his scrubs if he was going to send the picture to Justin. Which meant he'd have to go home early.

*Justin, I swear if you only knew half of what I put myself through for your sake.*

By the time Ren was close to the apartment, he was already sick with dread. He'd made it a point to interact as little as possible with Spencer, and he knew this was probably the worst time for him to draw any attention. It was easy to avoid him in the mornings; Ren was always long gone before he was even awake, but the moments where Ren was exposed between the door to the apartment and the door to his bedroom in the evenings were another story. Ren had learned to hate those moments the most.

Spencer hadn't thrown anything else at Ren, but he'd grown ruder and more confrontational when he realized Ren had taken the coffeemaker and had no intention of bringing it back into the kitchen. Ren made a very cold point that the appliance didn't belong to Stony Island; it was Ren's personal coffeemaker. That he had purchased. With money he had earned. And he wouldn't be opposed to reinstating it on the kitchen counter if Spencer could prove he was deserving. As in there would need to be some severe improvement on the upkeep of the place before Ren would be willing to share anything of his again. He'd gotten used to having it in his room now, liked how he didn't have to clean Spencer off it every single time before he could make fresh coffee, and it was pleasant how the scent lingered in the small space, blocking out the less than desirable smells that dominated the rest of the apartment.

If Spencer didn't like it, he could buy his own. Except he didn't. Instead, the number of empty, disposable coffee cups littering the space at either end of the couch increased dramatically. The trash overflowed until Ren realized either he would have to take it out himself, despite contributing practically nothing to it, or the apartment could be written up and fined for breach of contract. He was just grateful Alek and Denny would never see it looking like this.

Ren successfully ran the gauntlet to his room, not bothering to even glance at Spencer, though he could feel his eyes follow him as he went. Ren knew he wasn't used to seeing him this early in the day, but Ren didn't speak to him at all before locking himself away in the corner of the apartment that was still exclusively his. Though even here, things felt different. Ren thought it mostly had to do with the fact that he had never unpacked. He'd carefully removed all his posters. The dishes waited in boxes on the floor of his closet. The suitcase still sat ready by the door, though Ren removed his toothbrush and things like that every day to use them, still brushing his teeth in the kitchen, before carefully replacing them as though he still felt he'd be leaving here any minute. He knew it didn't make sense, but he couldn't bring himself to put his things back. Not just because he didn't want Spencer using his kitchen stuff anymore. He just didn't belong here, and he couldn't spread his things out, even in this room. It felt vulnerable. Unsafe and uncomfortable.

Ren's hands were already shaking as he started searching through his dresser drawers, his body wracked with the unused adrenaline it had produced for a potential confrontation with his roommate. And they didn't steady much as Ren continued to paw around the few not-uniform-related articles of clothing he owned, trying to figure out what he should be wearing for a picture Justin was going to see. The suits Celeste left him seemed a bit too much. He finally decided on jeans and a blue button-down in his closet that Celeste liked. Celeste said the color looked good on him. Though it didn't feel like it fit him the way it used to. He wanted to go check himself in the bathroom mirror, but he just didn't dare. And what did he care what he looked like anyway?

*What are you even doing, Ren? Trying to impress Justin? Getting all dressed up for someone who won't even be there? Who won't notice the effort? This whole thing is so dumb. What are you wasting your time for?*

*It's better than staring into the lake,* a small voice deep inside him whispered, surprisingly sounding like Denny.

Ren paused, sitting on the bed, holding his head in his hands, trying to get himself under control. Trying to figure out what was wrong with him anyway. *It's ok,* he assured himself. *It's not a big deal. This is to make sure Justin participates in something wholesome while he heals, something that will help him since North's gone, and you are too far away.*

*Besides,* Denny continued to whisper at him, *what's the harm? You really haven't done anything fun in forever. This could be good for you. You won't be hiding in your room, avoiding eye contact with Angelique. Maybe you'll even meet someone.*

That thought put Ren on his knees on the floor, one hand clinging to the quilt on his bed. *Meet someone? You've got to be kidding.*

*Still,* the persistent Denny voice pushed. *You did like dancing once.*

Ren really hated how he was always one tiny thought away from crying lately. But it was true. He had enjoyed dancing. Quite a bit. The music, the movement, the flexibility within the pattern of the steps. But would it still be like that now?

*One way to find out* — this time it was Celeste clicking logically into his brain. Ren had a wry thought about when his sister Siara was going to show up too and complete the set. *Go on, Ren,* Celeste encouraged in his memory. *It's ok to take a break.*

Ren checked his hands, still trembling but not near as badly. Maybe this could be fun. Conflicted, hesitantly hopeful, Ren put his phone in his pocket and took a deep breath to leave. He always took a deep breath when he exited his room, and he usually held it as he passed through the apartment as though it would help him stay invisible.

He kept his head down, moving quickly. *Avoid eye contact. You don't want to get into another shouting match with idiots tonight. Don't ruin the mood you're trying to make by having the same conversation about soda and noise ordinances and trash fines that didn't sink in the first three hundred times you mentioned it. Just walk right on through.*

"Oh hey, are you Spencer's roommate?"

Whoa, wait, just a second. Ren slowed, even though he knew he shouldn't, but that was definitely a new voice. A *girl's* voice. How on earth did Spencer convince a girl to come home with him? And how wasn't he dying of embarrassment that he'd brought her home to this disaster? And why was she talking to Ren?

Curiosity claimed him, paused him directly in front of the door, but he kept his hand on the knob, ready to flee at any given moment. He lifted his head, turning cautiously to the side.

There *was* a girl here! Wow. Ren blinked at her silently, assessing. She had pulled the camp chair closer to the drums and was sitting in it with her legs crossed, her skirt so short that for a second Ren wasn't sure she was wearing one. She was prettier than Ren expected her to be with fair skin and hair just past her shoulders that was somewhere between brown and blonde. It looked as though she'd taken a long time straightening it. Taken a long time on herself in general — she was wearing an entire cosmetic section on her face and enormous gold hoops in her ears.

"You are, aren't you?" she continued, smiling at Ren, who had forgotten the original question in his surprise to discover someone besides Spencer, Damien, or Wes in the living room. Someone who was speaking to him directly. "Wow, I can't believe I've never seen you before!"

"That's because he's a vampire," Spencer volunteered blandly from where he sat on the couch. "He only comes out at night." He had a notebook today instead of his guitar. Ren rolled his eyes, tightening his grip on the knob, ready to go, regretting that he'd paused in the first place. He should have known it would be a bad idea.

"I'm Lindsey," the girl volunteered, ignoring Spencer, shifting in the camp chair, perching on the edge of it as though she intended on standing up. "I'm doing the vocals for Spencer's band. We're working on a new song."

*That's unfortunate,* Ren wanted to say, but decided against it. He was too tired for this. Whatever this was. Instead, he nodded mutely at her, pulling the door open. Ren didn't think any of the music could be saved by the addition of vocals. *Good luck with that.*

"Want to hear it?" Lindsey asked quickly, as though she wanted to get the question out before Ren stepped into the hallway. He just barely noticed Spencer's head whip over to her, his lip curled in disgust that she would invite Ren to participate in anything they were doing together. It almost persuaded Ren to stay, just to piss him off, but he didn't want to encourage any interaction with any of Spencer's friends.

"Nope," Ren replied brusquely, moving quickly and intentionally out the door. *I don't want to listen to you or him for so many reasons. Nothing personal.* Ren smiled bitterly as he closed the door behind him. *No, come to think of it, it's extremely personal.*

Still, it wasn't Lindsey's fault she was under the impression that Spencer had a band or was in any way talented. Ren still wouldn't have taken the time to listen to her sing, but he didn't have to shut her down that hard. And yet, he couldn't really pull together the capacity to feel sorry. He let the picture linger in his head for another couple seconds. Lindsey, bubbly and hopeful with too much makeup and not enough clothes, trying to spark up anything that wasn't purely hormonal in Spencer. Ren felt a rush of goosebumps lift along his arms. Spencer — ick. Ren was just shocked that Lindsey was still sitting there trying. Any sensible girl would have looked at all the empty cups on the floor that had Spencer's name on them and promptly turned around never to return. The fact that she'd stayed indicated they might just deserve each other. Another round of shivering disgust. Ugh. Ok, time to get all of that out of his head.

He had something more important to do.

The UChicago Ballroom and Latin Dance Association held their sessions in various locations throughout campus. Today's dance was scheduled in the large reception hall of the Ida Noyes building almost a mile's walk from Ren's apartment, almost, but not quite all the way to the University Hospital on the same street. Ren's struggle to find something to wear, his strange interlude with Lindsey, and his own hesitancy to participate brought him to the entrance almost fifteen minutes late.

Which meant he spent another few minutes outside, listening to the familiar rhythm of a Latin beat just beyond the doors, which paused every forty seconds or so for the instructors to teach or correct a step. He wasn't sure he wanted to go in. He hadn't been exactly social for a very long time now, and even before, he'd had Celeste on his arm for this kind of thing. He never showed up alone anywhere. And it wasn't like he could just slip inside, stand alongside the wall, snap a photo, and then leave. He knew Justin would expect to see him actually dancing, or it wouldn't count. Which meant he'd have to at least talk to someone. He remembered when something like that had not been a huge deal.

So why was it so hard now?

And if he didn't go in, where would he go? The walk to the lake was getting colder, the sunset earlier. He'd brought nothing with him to work in the library. If he didn't go inside now, he'd have to return to the apartment. He wouldn't have a picture to send Justin, who then might not engage in the therapeutic group activities on base. Which meant he'd spend more time with Harlow. That thought resolved him.

Riding the flood of sudden determination, Ren pushed open the main doors, not exactly ready, but not giving himself the option of turning back. He paused at a table manned by two students to pay the entry fee. They smiled at him, welcoming, like there was nothing unusual about him turning up. In fact, they thanked him for coming. Then they ushered him forward into the reception hall and told him to have fun. Right.

There were more dancers than Ren anticipated, maybe fifty or so couples and dozens more on the sidelines, loners like Ren. He shifted to stand near them, unaffiliated, but watching. He wondered at all the other motives collected in the room, what had drawn all of these people here tonight. He figured he was likely the only one here just to get a picture so the boy he loved wouldn't hang out with his girlfriend so much. *God, Ren, this is really your life.* What the hell happened?

"Hello?"

Ren jumped at the voice right next to him. He'd been thinking and watching the routine so hard he hadn't noticed that he'd been ganged up on by three girls. He took a step to the side, turning toward them, resigned. *Here we go.*

They stood in a tight formation, but it was clear which of them had spoken. The other two had come over for emotional support. He'd seen clusters like this before, though he was surprised to discover nothing had changed much in the years since he'd been in a class. There was the lead girl, the one who said hello, dark-haired and petite. Then behind her would be the girl who didn't want to be here but came because the other two had forced her (she wore over-alls and long braids), and the last would be the girl who also wanted to dance but would faithfully remain in her friend's shadow, letting her go first. In this incarnation of the archetypal trio, the last girl had thick, auburn-ish hair and a massive number of freckles.

"Would you like to dance?" the lead girl asked him, smiling with all her teeth. Ren scanned the girls again, this time assessing height.

"Yes," he answered her, but forcefully made eye contact with her friend, the ginger girl, extending his hand to her where she stood in that unseen shadow, intent on pulling her forward. "If you'd be so kind?"

He watched panic and pleasure ripple rapidly over her face. She glanced at her friend to study her reaction, see if this would be allowed. Ren also looked at her momentarily, noticing the shock that Ren would deviate from social normalcy this way. She didn't know Ren did stuff like this all the time. Or he used to. It was nothing against her, really. She was just too short to dance with comfortably, and her friend had several inches on her. An easy decision with dramatic consequences.

"I'm Heather," the girl told him as he led her by the hand to join the couples in the center of the room. *Right. Dance small talk. Justin I'm going to kill you.*

"Ren," he responded without much emotion, thinking he should probably tell her he'd asked her based on nothing else other than how tall she was. He didn't want her to get the wrong idea about any of it. *It's just a dance.* He pulled her professionally into position, his body automatically lifting, some muscle memory intact for this. She followed his lead rather sluggishly, her form too loose and too far from him. Not much experience then. Whatever. It wasn't important. It wasn't like Ren was an expert or anything. He wasn't being graded anymore.

The instructors called for attention to give directions on a new step, which Ren attempted to perform with Heather for two minutes before everyone was asked to switch partners. Ren made eye contact with someone else on the sidelines without actually looking at her, holding out his hand, which she came forward to take eagerly. Five minutes later, he switched again, exchanging nothing more than names, hardly even looking at his partners. This was supposed to be fun? He used to like this? And how was he supposed to get a picture when he didn't know anyone here, and things kept changing every few minutes?

They played a game, one of those rapidly exchanging partner ones that was more about drilling the step into your subconscious than anything. Ren appreciated that. The quick pace warmed his blood in almost the same way as responding to an emergency in the ER did, just without the stress. He could mess up here, often, and nothing bad would happen. He could opt out for a few minutes to catch his breath, and no one would care. No one would die if he forgot what to do next.

Yeah, all right. This was kind of fun.

The instruction segment ended, and the main lights went out. Couples parted, some going back to their actual dates, relieved to be reunited after dancing with strangers. Ren envied them. There was something special about knowing your partner, trusting them, getting familiar with their particular style and movement. Knowing you belonged with someone.

Ren had danced with Celeste, on those rare occasions when the event called for something like that. She had plenty of grace but too much reservation, and she didn't take all that much enjoyment from it. It didn't help that usually when they danced together, they were watched by way too many people. Ren had never brought her to anything like this. Maybe he should have.

He still needed a picture, something that had suddenly become harder to obtain with the lower lights. Ren paused on the sidelines, watching the floor, registering the contentment of established couples who had been doing this a long time and how it contrasted with the rather desperate hunger of those who had come here alone, hoping to find someone. Ren felt strange that he was in the middle, no dedicated partner but no desire for one either. It was a lonely place if he stood still long enough and thought about it.

So, he chose not to be still. It was easy here where the ratio was tilted so far in his favor. He danced a foxtrot with a girl named Jamie, then broke away from her to start the cha cha they'd learned earlier with another girl named Tanya. And after that Ren gave up on trying to remember all the names, the faces, the features. He never lacked for a partner, and most of them he never truly looked at, a negligence that was encouraged by the dark atmosphere. Because it wasn't about the partner. It was about the movement and the music, letting go of every thought except what step came next in the beat. Ren allowed himself to get lost in that; it felt good to put everything down. He hadn't noticed how tense he'd grown carrying it. Hadn't noticed how much he missed the touch of another human being, even a stranger, just holding someone alive in his arms for a few minutes of contact was rather renewing. It felt nice, a warm palm on his shoulder, a hand in his hand.

He did focus enough that he managed to get a couple pictures, and one slightly blurry video. He used another cluster of girls to help him with it, said he needed it for a class, though he didn't specify any further than that. He took the tallest girl of the group again, forgot her name almost instantly after he'd asked for it, lost it in the music. He trusted his phone to her friend, who agreed to Ren's request only if he'd dance with her next. Something Ren could say yes to immediately; he did not care who he danced with.

Before he knew it, the lights came on again, the atmosphere broken. He thanked his last partner, releasing her hand, bewildered it was over. Couples and clusters began taking their coats from the stage at the end of the dance floor, preparing to leave. Ren looked at his phone, confirming it really was ten at night. He noticed the girls who had taken the photos for him had thoughtfully also added themselves to his contacts, sent texts to their own phones to get his number. He shook his head, remembering a time when something like that would have made his entire week. *Where were you before?* He thought of the girls, all of them who had approached him first tonight. *Where were you when I was nineteen and thought I wanted you?*

*You could call them,* Ren's brain suggested, but he stamped it down quickly. *No. Not going down that path again. It's not for me. I'm emotionally unavailable. If I tried being with anyone else, it would just be Celeste all over again.* Except worse. With Celeste, Ren had started dating her with the intention that eventually he'd get over Justin. Now he knew better. Celeste had been an amazing sport about the whole thing, and it was a miracle they'd come out of it still friends. But Ren couldn't date anyone else now; it wouldn't be right or fair.

Dancing, on the other hand, didn't carry any sort of commitment outside of the song. He could dance with every girl in the room, and nothing would happen past that. Until Ren somehow let go of Justin. But Ren dismissed that thought even faster than the idea of calling any of the new contacts in his phone. He'd never let go of Justin. Even if it meant he stayed alone.

Ren followed the other dancers out of Ida Noyes, walking unsteadily, the broken gait of someone exhausted from carrying something heavy. Like someone slipping in and out of consciousness. But that was how distractions worked, and he'd known that.

Temporary. So very temporary. No matter what, the lights always come back on. The dream ends. No one spoke to him on the way out, or at least not that he noticed. He took the long way home, deciding not to cut through campus, but instead to follow 59th Street all the way east until it connected to Stony Island Ave. He knew he probably shouldn't; it was already long past his normal bedtime for someone who was planning on getting up at four-thirty. He'd probably regret it in the morning, but regret seemed to be the default setting on his life, so he continued to walk slowly, waiting to cross paths with his own street.

The air carried the chill of autumn, here at the beginning of October, and most of the trees had already lost their leaves. Piles gathered in the gutters of the streets and on the dead grass, giving a haunting look to the already dark appearance of the college. Ren sighed, letting the cold sweep over him, battered as helplessly as the paper-fragile leaves at his feet. This was not his favorite time of year; the whole planet growing darker and cold, seeming smaller somehow for that.

The natural high of movement and music that Ren had enjoyed while dancing bled itself completely out by the time he reached the hallway outside his apartment, blown off him all along his walk like the leaves off the trees. He leaned against the wall beside his door for a second before going in, gathering himself. He could hear the drums inside, Damien's bass. No one was singing, though, which meant maybe Lindsey had gone home. Ren took a deep breath, preparing for the quick, focused march to his bedroom. Eyes forward, move fast.

"Hey!"

Damn. Spencer paused in his drumming, Damien following his lead, zeroing everyone's attention to Ren as he shut the door behind him. But he was used to that. Hated it, but he was used to it. He didn't have to respond to anything. In fact, it was safer if he didn't. He kept walking to his room as though Spencer hadn't called to him.

"Hey! I'm talking to you!" Spencer continued, disentangling himself from behind the drum set.

"Unnecessary," Ren shot the word defensively behind him. *There is no need to engage. We **ignore** each other; follow the protocol.* Ren almost made it to his room before Spencer caught up with him, catching him by one shoulder and swinging Ren roughly around. Ren brought his fists up, surprising even himself. What did he think he was going to do? Spencer took a half step back, eyeing him.

"Stay away from Lindsey," Spencer commanded him. "She's out of your league and off limits; you got it?"

Ren couldn't help it; a weird, uneasy laugh burst out of his mouth. This kid. He seriously thought he had to warn Ren about that? Out of Ren's league, huh? *If it were worth my time, I could show you what that really looks like,* Ren thought bitterly, his heart hollow and worn. Lindsey and Celeste might as well be different species. Out of his league. Whatever.

"She's all yours," Ren allowed, knowing his smile was condescending but not caring. "I'm not interested."

Spencer looked undecided about whether he should be satisfied that Ren had given in easily or offended because Ren didn't think his girl was worth stealing. Ren drew some cold amusement watching both emotions crawl slowly over Spencer's features.

"Keep it that way," Spencer threatened one more time before heading back to the living room where Damien waited, glaring at Ren from the edge of the couch.

Ren lowered his fists, then stared at his hands for a long time after he'd let himself into his room and locked the door behind him. So many memories zipped through him, each one tearing his heart a little as it passed. Justin's startle reflex. The way he had also stared at his hands in shock, like they weren't even his. *Were you really going to hit him?* Justin asked, an echo of the time he'd asked North the same question after the verdict hearing.

*No,* Ren answered the shadow Justin in his head. At least, he didn't think so.

Ren woke up with a migraine. He staggered through getting ready, pausing a lot to rest his head against anything that was available. The kitchen counter. The shower wall. He even knelt on the floor of his bedroom and leaned against the mattress, halfway through getting dressed, breathing as deeply as possible, trying not to throw up again. He kept his eyes closed after he left his apartment, making his way down the familiar path to the lounge on touch alone, collapsing onto the couch in the cold silence of the very early morning. No, not quite silence, he could hear the wind outside, blustering in common autumn force. He leaned his head back, resting it, and waited for Justin to call.

There were a few texts already; they'd come in late last night from Alek and Denny. Ren hadn't bothered to write them an email after coming home, so they were checking on him. He curled up on his side on the couch, one eye open against the glare of the phone, texting them quickly that he was ok, just had a late night. He sent them the dance photos to prove he'd gone out and done something. Let them figure that out.

Celeste had also emailed him with pictures of her own. She'd just got back from Sheridan and Noah's wedding in Hawaii. She'd reminded Ren weeks ago that he was still invited, but Ren had declined her offer to take him. He'd wanted to see Celeste again, sort of. He wanted to see her, but he didn't want her to see him, even though he knew that made no sense. But he knew she'd take one look at him and *know* he was crumbling on the inside, that he'd been lying to all his friends for months now. He didn't want that, didn't want anyone to see how poorly he was handling being left behind. He didn't want to drag everyone down. They had their own lives going on.

Ren scrolled through the photos of Celeste and Sheridan on the beaches in their formal wedding attire. The sun, the spray — all the smiles. Noah wearing the same expression as Officer Geisler at his wedding, like he couldn't believe how lucky he was. Celeste looked majestic; the waves of her bright hair untamable in the humid, salty air near the ocean. Her smile spread easily across her lovely face as she hugged Sheridan tight for the picture. Ren missed her. It had still been a distraction, a denial all its own, but it had been better. He'd never felt the need to lock himself in his bedroom.

He tried to text her, at least to say welcome back. But he couldn't say welcome back without also thanking her for the pictures. And he couldn't thank her for the pictures without giving her his opinion on how great she looked in them and how happy he was for Sheridan, and suddenly that seemed too much to type out on his phone while he was lying on his side on the couch at quarter to seven in the morning, so he shut everything off and closed his eyes. He'd get back to her later. When his head didn't hurt anymore, and he could sit at one of the library computer stations and type properly. Tonight would be soon enough.

Justin called right on schedule, and for a little while Ren forgot about his headache, successfully hiding all his pain from Justin. They talked about the dance photos and the video; Justin expressing his surprise that Ren actually could dance. He asked about the girl Ren was dancing with, hesitant, probing questions, but Ren had forgotten her name.

They talked about Harlow, of course, but Ren tried to turn the topic as quickly as possible. He was tired of talking about Harlow; plus, there wasn't much else to be said. Her recovery was going to be slow and long, and for a lot of it, no one would be able to see much progress. But Ren still had to allow Justin to get everything out of his system, reassure him again about the correct inevitability of his choices, and how he wasn't responsible for hers, untying the same knot he'd untangled yesterday. The same knot he'd work on again tomorrow. The day after that. Every day for the rest of his life if that's what Justin needed. Ren did notice it didn't take as long as it used to, which was a comfort.

Justin also shared the good news that he'd gotten half his stitches out earlier that morning. The other half were scheduled for removal in a couple days depending on how the wounds looked. Ren cautioned him against doing too much too soon, because half the stitches was not the same as all the stitches. He reminded Justin about their deal, and Justin acknowledged he was signed up to do a group session in an hour. He refused to send Ren pictures.

"You'll get your proof," Justin promised cryptically, forcing Ren to be content with that, even though he wanted to point out how not fair Justin was being. Ren had gone to a lot of trouble to get those dance photos. He'd expected Justin to return the gesture. He'd been looking forward to at least a small glimpse of what Justin looked like now, military haircut, years after they'd last seen each other. It would have been nice and probably painful. Like normal.

"Thanks, Ren," Justin said suddenly.

"For what?" Ren responded, wondering if he'd missed something.

"Too much to list, really," Justin answered vaguely. Ren sat up, holding his head in his hand, urging Justin to keep going. "Pushing me into therapy, writing me all those letters even when I wasn't writing you back very much, listening to me every day even though it's so early where you are. Just everything."

"That's what friends do," Ren affirmed. *It's also what lovers do, Justin. If you could be open to that. If you could let go of Harlow enough for me to even suggest it. We could be so good together, Justin, if you'd just give us a chance to try.* Ren pulled the phone away from his mouth, exhaling shakily, new aches joining the old ones in his throat, tensing his shoulders. "Hey Justin?"

"Yeah?" Justin encouraged, waiting expectantly.

*Hang on, Ren, what are you doing? Don't say stupid stuff just because your medication hasn't kicked in all the way yet. Pay attention.*

"When are you coming home?"

"To the states?" Justin guessed, missing Ren's meaning. "Pretty soon, I think. North said he'd take me back with him. Not sure when though. I won't be on active duty for a few more months."

"No," Ren interrupted, knowing he should be grateful that Justin had missed the point of the question. He swallowed the tears out of his voice, unwisely continuing. "I mean do you think we'll ever see each other again?"

"Oh," Justin grew quiet. "I don't know, maybe? Is that something you want?"

*Are you kidding?!*

"Oh my God, yes," Ren blurted out, then realized he'd come across too eager. "It'd be great to get everyone back together, wouldn't it?" He tried to ease his outburst. "You, Alek, Denny, all here like old times. Remember?"

"A little," Justin acknowledged, forcing Ren to recall that not all of Justin's memories from that time were good. "I wouldn't say no to a chance to eat Alek's cooking again."

"Right?" Ren agreed quickly, glad Justin hadn't read too much into what Ren had just done. *Don't get too comfortable,* Ren chastised himself. *If you want to keep talking to him every day, then you'd better keep your emotions in check.* "Alek's cooking is the best."

"It really is," Justin continued, and Ren pressed against the back of the couch, crushed by memory, knowing he'd never get that back again. Even if they all flew into Chicago this weekend, it wouldn't be the same. And they'd leave again. It might make the separation worse. Plus, they'd see the apartment, see what Ren's life was like now, which would be an atrocity. Perhaps it was best they make these imaginary plans stay imaginary.

"It's a fun idea," Ren sighed, the frenzy of hope fading as the reality of making it happen settled between them both. "Practically impossible, but fun."

"Yeah," Justin said softly. "Hey, Ren?"

Oh, it'd been so long since Ren had been asked that question. The one that began and ended with his name. The one he was certain had more to it that Justin never vocalized.

"Yeah?" *What is it? What have you been wanting to ask me so long? Is it the same thing I've been wanting to ask you?*

"How is it going?" Justin eventually settled on a question, and Ren knew that was not what he'd been wanting to say. Knew it and wanted to push back. *Come on, Justin, let's have a real conversation.* Except once they did, that would be the end. No more pretending afterward.

"What do you mean?" Ren repeated, thrown off. "How is what going?"

"You know, your life? Is it what you wanted it to be? I know you had a solid plan when I met you. I just wondered if that was still working out the way you wanted it to."

Ren pulled the phone away, shoved his face against the couch. *What kind of question is that, Justin? Why ask me something like* **that**? *I got everything I ever said I wanted. It's my own damn fault it turned out like this.*

"I guess so," Ren said, wishing he sounded more certain about it. *Don't you dare drag him down, Ren. Get your voice together.* "Everything's on track." *And I should probably remind myself about that more.*

"Good," Justin replied. "That's good to know."

"What about you?" Ren pushed, not wanting to be the only one who was forced to answer the question.

"Well, I never had much of a plan in the first place," Justin admitted, making it light. "Still, it's been different than I thought it would be. A lot of it is better."

"And the part that's not?" Ren wondered.

"Can't have everything," Justin retorted, as though he were quoting something. *So very true,* Ren thought, but then wondered what it was Justin wanted that he thought he couldn't have. Ren wanted to know what it was. Wanted to give it to him.

"Justin?" Ren began.

"Yeah?" Why did he sound like that? What was in his voice that made him sound like that? *And what are you doing, Ren? What do you think you're going to say here?*

"Have a good session, ok? Let me know how it goes?"

"I ... sure. Talk to you later?"

"I'll be here."

Forever.

Justin hung up, and Ren curled over, holding himself as tightly as possible, squeezing the air out of his lungs, breathing in little pants, the pound of his headache back in force. What the hell was that about? How was he supposed to keep talking to Justin if this was how their conversations were going to go?

*You could just tell him;* the suggestion attacked him in multiple voices in his head at once. Denny. Alek. Celeste. *Just tell him.*

*I could,* Ren answered them hesitantly. Maybe that would be better. To finally know. It would hurt, but maybe after it was done, Ren could pick himself up. Start to put himself back together. Move on from this never-ending loop. *Ok,* he thought shakily. *Tomorrow. Tomorrow when Justin calls, I'll tell him.*

Except Justin didn't call. Not the next morning. Or the morning after that. Ren waited in the lounge almost too long. He tried Justin's number but couldn't get him. He texted him several times, asking if he was ok. If Harlow was ok. No response.

It was like Justin had completely disappeared.

# 14
## CATALYST

Ren made a list. Then another. He bought a brand-new bag of coffee at the Walgreens closest to the apartment. He walked to the lake in increasing layers of warm clothes. He knit cheerful, rainbow-striped hats for the preemies in the NICU and rocked them gently for hours in the evenings. He went dancing again. He wrote emails and played the CD Justin had sent him. He patiently listened to Alek and Denny vent about the varied and numerous challenges for putting together a one-day symposium, murmuring sympathetic encouragement at expected intervals during each conversation. He took pictures and sent them to his family and friends. He religiously attended his classes, labs, lectures, and ER schedule. He studied in the library and the lounge and the laundry room. He started carrying an umbrella everywhere he went as October began its annual tradition of pouring rain in frequent and lengthy intervals.

For a week, Ren strung every positive activity he could think of onto his routine, every distraction, anything he had ever liked, he even started cleaning the apartment again. Some things worked better than others. The NICU was better than the lake. Dancing was better than studying. The ER was the best of all, though it carried its own challenges.

And he waited for any of it to *help*.

When Ren had lived with Celeste, everything had been routine. The food they ate, the clothes they wore, even what they said to each other. He wanted that back, that cycle of knowing what was coming next that was so predictable entire months could just drop out of his memory. He was so tired of consciously dealing with every single second of his life. So tired that there were so many since he couldn't stop waking up at four-thirty every day and spent way too much time flat on his back at night, staring at the ceiling. Staring at the lake. Staring at words on a page he knew he'd read twelve times already but still couldn't remember.

He was tired of endlessly checking his phone. Tired of coming up with answers to questions, of making conversation, of pretending.

*You've got to get used to it,* he told himself. *This is your life. This is just how it's going to be from now on. You've done everything you know how to do. So, the only thing left is to just keep going.* It wasn't enough, but it was all he had. And then it was morning again. Or time to meet Angelique. Or time to send another photo. Answer another phone call that wasn't the phone call he really wanted. And he was fine, thanks for asking, but please could you also stop asking?

Mostly everyone accepted Ren's answers. Alek and Denny were too busy to notice if Ren was being quieter than normal. Celeste was easy to distract if Ren asked her the right kinds of questions. His fellow classmates were drowning in their own stress and hardly ever glanced at each other. And Justin? Well, they'd have to have some kind of working relationship or communication in the first place for him to ever notice it was different, wouldn't they?

The conversation with Ren's family that week was hard. He put up a good front, talking about the weather, the upcoming dark and cold of winter, the rain. They talked about dancing and babies. The ones Ren held in the NICU and Marco and Isabel's new little girl. The first granddaughter ever. They'd named her Amayah. Ren tried to pretend that didn't bother him, but inside he felt betrayed. Amayah might have been Marco's sister too, but she belonged to *Ren*. It felt as though she'd been taken away from him somehow, even though he knew that was petty. But what if Ren had wanted to name his daughter Amayah? *Except*, he thought sadly, the congratulations barely out of his mouth, *you probably won't ever have a daughter at this rate.*

His mother brought it up shortly after, what with all the talk about babies, asking pointedly if he'd met anyone, gone on any dates. He countered that he was too busy. She expressed regret that he and Celeste had broken up. He reminded her they were headed in two very different directions and were better as friends. She then suggested a myriad of local Dominican girls she'd shown Ren's pictures to. She wondered if she could give Ren's phone number or address to them.

"No, Mom, don't do that," Ren protested.

"Why not? They're nice girls, good families," Eva persuaded.

"I'm sure they are, but how would that work when I'm not even in the country?" Ren pointed out, feeling this shouldn't be something he'd have to make obvious. But that one argument suddenly boiled over a topic that had apparently been brewing for a long time, and Ren was in no way ready for it. And once it started, it all came out at once. He should have just said yes to the phone numbers.

"But you're not going to be gone forever, are you?" Eva said pleadingly. "You are planning on coming back. Soon, right? It's been years, *mijo*. I thought you'd be back to visit at least once."

"It's hard," Ren began.

"You would have figured it out if you'd wanted to," Ren heard Marco say teasingly in the background. Except not really teasing. There was a bitterness in it. Marco now had two children Ren had never seen in person. Luis' son, Mateo, was thirteen years old. Ren was missing everything and had to be told all the highlights once a week from a church office. There was more than just distance separating them. And he could tell from this conversation that they all knew it. Felt it. The ocean between them was wider than it measured on a map, the gulf growing every year.

"Marco," Eva threatened, but her voice had changed. There was new doubt in it. "You do want to come home, don't you, Enzo?"

Ren curled up on his bed, on top of the quilt Eva had made him. Such a complicated question, though honestly, he shouldn't be surprised it had finally been asked. He hadn't visited. Hadn't even tried. And he wasn't sure why. He didn't have an answer. He wanted to see them, but then he'd have to leave them again, and he didn't really know if the Dominican Republic could be home for him anymore. There was a lot about America he'd grown used to. He no longer saw himself living near the mango orchard, marrying a local girl, opening a practice. Hell, he couldn't think past the end of the *day* anymore, let alone any kind of future. Why'd they have to ask this now?

"It would be great to see you all again," Ren told her truthfully, though he wasn't sure he could stand looking at his old house, the mango trees, the ocean. Would they even be the same? Would it hurt him or heal him? Did he even belong there anymore? Did he belong anywhere? "But I can't leave here yet. I'm not finished."

"Are you sure this is something you still want?" Eva asked him seriously. "It's been so long since we've been together. And you don't sound happy anymore."

"It's what I want," Ren said quickly, trying to be firm. "Now where are my boys?"

His nephews. He wanted to talk to them. They never got tired of hearing about America, hearing what their *tío* was doing. They still had admiration and excitement in their voices when they interacted with him. He needed that. Except even those conversations were different. They still asked him for peanut butter and ketchup, and Diego shyly requested crayons after one of his older cousins prompted him. Because Diego was four but had only ever heard from Ren as a voice on a phone, so he just didn't have the same relationship with him that the older boys had. Or used to have. Ren promised them everything, amazed and sad that all the things they asked for that were next to impossible to obtain on the island were easily accessible for Ren from a corner store two blocks away. How? How could he go back? Now that he'd been here so long? Now that everything was so different?

Ren spent most of his Sunday morning after the phone call simply lying on the quilt, looking at all the different fabrics in it, trying to see if he could still remember where each patch had come from. The piece from his childhood blanket. The cotton of his father's work shirt. His mother's best Sunday dress. The green print with roses on it that had been Amayah's. They were all faded now, worn, soft in that fragile way that reminded Ren that nothing really lasts forever. He pulled on another sweater and headed to the lake, wondering how he was going to handle the next conversation.

Because as difficult as talking on the phone could be, it was nothing compared to the in-person scrutiny Ren received at the ER. In the world of avoidance that Ren was quickly building out of carefully wrapped half-truths, Angelique's tiger eyes remained sharp and fixated on him. She watched him as he mopped up triage rooms. She stared at his hands while he wrote down stats. She followed the motions of his fork when he forced himself to eat lunch, publicly visible, in the hospital cafeteria.

And it didn't take her long before she started asking him questions that had nothing to do with case studies.

*Ren, are you with me? How is Justin doing? Your family? What are your plans for the weekend? Ren, how have you been sleeping? Did you get earplugs and figure out the roommate situation? How are things going with your classes?*

Ren kept forcefully giving her the correct answers to all these questions, relieved when her attention would be diverted by the next incoming emergency. Though she would be right on top of him again immediately after it was over.

"Connie tells me you've knit a hat for just about every baby in the

NICU right now," Angelique mentioned, too pointedly to be casual, as they sat together in the break room.

"Babies need hats," Ren quoted, speaking around the bite of beef stroganoff he'd been chewing for the last two minutes, trying to get it to the consistency he thought he could successfully swallow.

"True, but who needs the hats more, Ren?" Angelique asked, the question a dart into his psyche. "The neonates or you?"

"Am I doing something wrong?" Ren asked her, his voice still, his eyes on the pile of napkins stacked between them.

"No," Angelique reassured, and Ren was able to swallow. He wanted her to say it again. But maybe this time without looking at him like that. "But sometimes that can be a problem all on its own."

"I'm fine," Ren insisted. *I don't have real problems. I have no good reason to feel the way I do.* "Hats that small don't take long."

"Let me see your hands."

Ren relaxed slightly. He'd studied for this test. He tucked his fork in his mouth, feigning nonchalance, freeing his hands so he could obediently hold them out to her. *She said you didn't do anything wrong.* The remembrance of that gave him the courage to make eye contact with her for the few seconds she needed to gauge him. *There are twenty-seven bones in the hand.* Ren listed them off to himself, getting to the sixteenth before Angelique gave up looking for whatever she was trying to see.

"Eat," Angelique commanded testily, and Ren gratefully continued, more than eager to please her. He'd do just about anything for that. To stay near her competence, to have her guiding him, telling him what to do. The structure of the ER was the most comfortable part of Ren's day, though sometimes it followed him into the night. Visions of blood and screams. Justin's stitches. *He'll probably have a scar on his face.*

Ren walked slower and slower to the apartment in the evenings. Now that he was keeping it clean, more people were turning up regularly. Lindsey was a constant fixture on the couch or in the kitchen, her eyes following Ren whenever he darted through the living room, always calling after him to stay and have some pizza, stay and hear the song. *What's the rush? Don't be so shy!*

"You know the worst part of the day is when you get home?" Spencer asked him once. Ren didn't particularly care, but Lindsey was standing in the hallway to his bedroom, which slowed him down.

"Excuse me," Ren finally said to Lindsey, who seemed rooted to the wall, blocking the hallway. She blinked at him, her eyes appearing much larger than they were due to the make-up. Ren wondered how long that took her to do every day. Celeste had never been that dramatic in her application.

"Don't go hide in your room," Lindsey pleaded. "Stay with us. I'm making popcorn, and we're going to watch a movie." Ren could feel Spencer glaring at him behind his back.

"I've got stuff to do," Ren told her, hoping he wouldn't have to touch her to get past.

"It's just a movie," Lindsey returned, pouting in a way she must think was irresistible. "Do your stuff after."

"I'm calling my girlfriend," Ren blurted, and Lindsey's eyes widened in surprise. "She's expecting me."

"Bullshit," Spencer coughed behind him.

"You really are," Ren shot the insult without turning to look at him, noticing it made Lindsey smirk. It lasted barely a second before she was grilling him for information.

"I didn't know you had a girlfriend," she admitted. *Of course, you didn't*, Ren thought. *None of you know a damn thing about me.*

"That's because he doesn't!" Spencer jeered from the kitchen. Frustrated, but sensing that if he didn't show some proof, he wasn't getting past Lindsey, Ren brought out his phone and pulled up the pictures he kept of Celeste. He pointedly flipped the screen to Lindsey and started scrolling through them. He and Celeste together at the wedding. At the aquarium. Selfies over dinner. Cuddled on the couch. Photos of her when he'd caught her just going about her day, looking lovely. Reading standing up because she was too engrossed in the subject to notice she hadn't sat down yet. Smiling at him in the snow in her white peacoat. Lindsey's eyes widened even more.

"Yeah," Ren said, probably harsher than he needed to, but he was trying to set some boundaries and make a point. *See? You can quit trying so hard. There's no way you come close to comparing with her, so leave me alone.* "Now let me by."

She stepped into the other hallway, the one leading to the bathroom, subdued. Ren heard Spencer making some asinine comment but couldn't decipher the words as he hurriedly unlocked his door and shut himself inside. He took a second to look through the pictures himself, going back farther in time until he got to the one where he sat in the middle of the couch, Celeste on one side of him and Justin on the other at Alek and Denny's going away party. The last time they'd all been together. He stared at it for a very long time, at Justin's face, at the arm Ren had over his shoulders. And he never called Celeste at all.

Days continued to pass in slow, painful rhythm as Ren struggled to keep it together. *This is your new normal,* he kept telling himself. *You'll get used to it. Keep going.* But thinking that way didn't exactly comfort him. In fact, it filled him with dread that he was stuck in this cycle for the rest of his life, and he wanted to scream. He'd swallow it down and do something trivial. Take out the trash, take a deep breath, start knitting a sweater with really intense cables to make it impossible to think of anything except the stitch count, there's only a few hours left of today. *Tomorrow will be better. You knew a long time ago this choice was going to isolate you. You knew you'd end up alone.*

One by one, Ren began dropping things from the schedule as his energy started dwindling. He skipped dancing on Wednesday. He stopped walking to the lake as the weather continued to deteriorate. It seemed like it rained all the time now. Ren couldn't remember the last time he'd seen the sun. He couldn't think of anything to say in an email or a reply to a text, so he kept them short or remained silent. And when Sunday came around again, when the three rings chirped from that familiar number in Cabarete, Ren stared at his phone and watched the number disappear, the little symbol appearing at the top of his screen to indicate he'd missed another call. He just couldn't do it.

He sat cross-legged on the floor, locked in his room, afghan over his knees, and his head resting against his bed, listening again to the piano CD Justin had sent him, the last piece of the scorched-rice candy in his mouth, wondering what he was going to do, scrolling through pictures and unanswered texts.

*Ren, where are you?*

*Didn't hear from you at all yesterday, you ok?*

Ren cautiously entered the apartment late Sunday night after spending most of the day at the library, relieved to find it dark and empty for once. He wandered around the living room and kitchen, turning on all the lights, inspecting the damage. Not too bad. Looks like Spencer had actually thrown some of his own trash away the last couple days. Or maybe Lindsey had. They hadn't done all of it, but still. The table was clear enough that Ren noticed a distinct pile of papers resting on it. Unsorted mail.

Ren picked it up, knowing already that most of it was advertisements. Stuff addressed to current resident that Spencer always just left on the table, or the counter, or the floor. Too lazy to mess with it any further than to drop it wherever he happened to be. Ren started going through it. Coupons for Burger King and pizza and coffee. The sales of the week happening at the grocery store and Walgreens.

And one small manila envelope addressed to Ren from Lackland.

Ren rapidly scanned the rest of the stack to make sure there was nothing else, then left it all on the table almost exactly as he'd found it, taking the envelope with him to the sanctuary of his room. Because even though he was alone in the apartment, he wanted to make sure he opened this without interruption. Ren sat at his desk and checked the envelope carefully, but as usual there weren't many clues as to where it had come from before it had re-routed through Texas. The Air Force seal partially covered the stamps. Ren analyzed Justin's handwriting on the address. His scrawl was worse than ever.

*I'm still here, Justin*, Ren thought, clutching the unopened envelope. *All these years. Still here. But where are you? Where the hell did you go? Why did you disappear? And if you had to disappear, then why are you still sending me stuff in the mail? Don't you know it'd be easier if you just stopped?*

But even as he thought that, Ren knew he didn't want it to happen. Didn't want Justin to ever really be gone. He took a pair of scissors from his packed box of desk items and just barely cut the edge from the envelope, knowing he was going to keep it for no other reason than Justin had written his name on it. He reached inside, pulling out something narrow, pliant, and textured along with an index card.

*Here's your proof.*

That's all Justin had written on the card, along with a simple dash and his messy signature. Ren opened his palm, staring at the woven bracelet Justin had sent him. No, that Justin had *made* for him in the medical wing in Germany. He'd used embroidery floss in a brilliant red, complimented by black, gray, and white, the colors repeating themselves in steep Vs for several inches and ending with braided strings on each side for Ren to use to tie onto his wrist. Clumsily made, but so much better than a basket. What did it mean?

"Damn it, Justin," Ren breathed, hunched in his chair, clinging to the threads. He checked the postmark date on the envelope again. Just a couple days after their last phone call.

Ren lay his arm on the table, attempting to knot the strings with only one hand and failing miserably. He tried to use his teeth but didn't trust the shaky result to stay in place, especially since Ren would be putting on and removing gloves most of the time. No, he couldn't lose this. He'd have to get some help securing it. He went through his list of people who could assist with something like that, coming up surprisingly short. In fact, he could only come up with one.

"Doña, could you help me?" Ren asked Angelique timidly, first thing Monday morning when they met at the nurse's station. At first, she looked stunned, then softened into eager acceptance, as though she'd been waiting for Ren to ask.

"Certainly, Ren, what is it?" she invited, and Ren held up the bracelet. Justin's bracelet.

"Could you tie this on for me?" he requested quietly, unable to look at her. Because he was so confused and lost and didn't want her to see it. But he needed it on his wrist, next to his pulse. Needed to know Justin hadn't forgotten him.

"Oh," Angelique said, and Ren knew she'd been expecting him to say something else. "All right."

Ren once again braced his arm on the desk, wrist turned up, and Angelique bent over him, slipping the bracelet underneath, and bringing the ends over to begin a strong knot.

"Starting a collection, are you?" Angelique asked pleasantly as she worked, her fingers moving efficiently, giving small, sure tugs on the strands.

"Sort of," Ren answered, watching her carefully, keeping his hand still. Was that knot going to work? Could he trust it? "My nephew made the blue one for me right before I left home. I've never taken it off." Never broke that connection even though it feels broken anyway. If only all the bonds could be that strong. Ren felt something in his chest hitch, loneliness hitting him hard. "Doña, can you make it tighter? I really don't want it to come off. I can't ... can't lose it."

She paused at his intensity, at the slight tremor in his voice that he hadn't been able to control, standing straight and staring at him, her face inscrutable and focused, and Ren pressed his lips tightly closed, knowing he'd made a mistake.

"All right — enough. Come with me," Angelique instructed suddenly, clamping one sure hand around his wrist, over both bracelets, and tugging him toward that familiar office near the ambulance entrance. Ren tried not to panic, though he knew this couldn't be good.

"We need to talk," Angelique said, but then she didn't say

anything. Ren waited as they both stood facing each other in the small office, surrounded by medical clutter. She took his hands, her index fingers extended so they rested against the pulse points on his wrists. "The truth now," she demanded. "How are you doing?"

"I'm fine," Ren threw out quickly. *Why do you always pretend everything's fine when it's not?* He held his breath, locking eyes with his mentor, beginning to name the bones of the hand slowly in his head, waiting for the test to be over. He'd just wanted to make sure the bracelet stayed on. What was so wrong with that?

He got to the twentieth bone. The twenty-third. Angelique stared at his face, his eyes. He wanted her to stop. He wanted to twist out of her grip. He wanted something to happen outside this room that would break the tension before he cracked under this quiet pressure. He felt his eyes beginning to fill with tears. His hands were going to start trembling any second. *Doña, let me go. You aren't supposed to see this. You aren't supposed to look at me so hard for so long.*

She continued to stare, not saying a word, and somehow the silence made it worse. Ren tried to focus on something, anything. The gold in her eyes. The ticking of the clock on the wall. He listed all the bones up to the shoulder, and he heard himself exhale in a desperate little rush. Then he inhaled even faster to cover for it, but it was audibly shaky, and one tear dripped guiltily down his face. He ripped his quaking hands out of hers and dropped into the chair at the desk, hiding his face and panting. What the hell was going on? She'd said she wanted to talk.

"Doña," he pleaded, his voice muffled and tiny. But he didn't know what he wanted from her. *Let me try again. I can keep it together. One more chance.* Except he couldn't say anything. He had to hold his breath, or he really would break.

Angelique went to her knees on the floor in front of him, graceful, strong. He couldn't look at her anymore, though he knew she was trying to catch his gaze.

"Ren, it's ok," she told him, her voice professional. "This happens to everyone in the field at some point. Sometimes more than once."

For some reason, that made Ren want to laugh, knowing Angelique had no idea what she was saying. He very much doubted his classmates were dealing with the same kind of shit that he was right now. He felt unique and isolated in his suffering. "The first year of medical school can be a hard adjustment."

"What?" Ren asked, suddenly confused, trying to keep up. Medical school? She thought he was cracking under the strain of medical school? What would it be like if it were really that simple?

"I think it would be best for you to take a break," Angelique continued.

"*What?*" Ren checked. Was she sending him away? No, no, don't do that.

"Ren, you've been struggling for a long time now. I know you think you've been hiding it, but I can tell it's getting worse. I'm sending you home, and I'd like you to stay there for at least two weeks."

"But, no, did I do something wrong?"

"No," Angelique answered, and Ren could tell she'd almost called him something that wasn't his name. The way she talked to patients. She'd only barely stopped herself. He hated that she saw him that way. She took a breath before calmly continuing, no judgment in her tone, but Ren felt judged anyway. "But the way you've been going, it's only a matter of time. This isn't a punishment; it's meant to be preventative. You understand?"

"No," Ren denied. *Don't take this away from me. It's all I've got left.*

"You're pushing too hard," Angelique diagnosed while Ren started shaking his head. "You're exhausted, Ren. Physically, emotionally. You need to catch your breath and your balance before you do make a mistake. Before you hurt someone, and that includes yourself."

"Doña, please," Ren started, even though he knew he'd never change her mind.

"Listen," Angelique ordered, and Ren was programmed to obey her, though he was certain he wasn't going to like anything she was going to say. "Consider this time as a special assignment if that makes it easier for you. Eat real food and enough of it. Catch up on sleep. Hang out with your friends. Get your priorities in order, and please get some rest. All right?"

"Can I still go to class at least?" Ren asked bitterly, wondering why she was asking him if it was all right when he obviously didn't have any choice.

"Yes, but don't go to the NICU. I've heard from Connie how much time you spend there, and while it's certainly admirable, I want as much distance between you and the hospital as possible for a while."

Ren sat stunned in the chair, feeling abandoned. A failure. He'd tried so hard to make sure this wouldn't happen. That she would have no reason to kick him out. And even though she flat out said he hadn't done anything wrong, it had happened anyway. Because Justin had sent him a bracelet he didn't want to lose.

"Ren, I'm trying to help you. I want you to succeed," Angelique continued to talk to him, as though she felt she needed to explain herself. Like she knew he was hurt and angry and didn't want that between them. "You're doing so well, you really are. I know what people say about me, and I know I can be harsh and demanding, but I have been where you are, I know what it's like, and contrary to belief, I don't actively try to break my students. There are limits, and you've hit yours. Please trust me."

"You don't understand," Ren heard himself murmur, though he regretted it instantly.

"Then you help me understand," Angelique invited. Ren shook his head again. No. There were some things he couldn't talk about, wasn't ready to share, especially to her. He knew he'd failed her now, and he didn't want to lose any more of her respect. There was nothing for it except to do what she said and then never show her weakness again. He stood up, though found it impossible to lift his head. He really was tired, but not in a way sleep could fix. Angelique stood with him, monitoring him still too closely.

"Two weeks?" Ren double checked.

"As long as you need," Angelique corrected, and Ren did his best not to shudder. He knew that wasn't supposed to be a threat, but two weeks was already too long.

"Ok," he accepted. Not that he had much choice. His voice was calm, but inside he was reeling. What the hell was he supposed to do? Where would he go if he wasn't in the ER? The NICU? How would he fill all those hours? For that many days? He turned to go before he made it worse. Could this get any worse?

"Ren," Angelique called after him, and he paused with his hand on the doorknob. *Now what, Doña? What else can you possibly do to me?* "Who gave you the bracelet?"

Ren's hand tightened suddenly. "Justin," he said, surprised but relieved that there was no emotion in his voice as he said it. He hadn't even meant to tell her the truth.

"Oh, Ren," Angelique said, and suddenly his name sounded like all the terms of endearment she always used. There was pity in it and exasperation, and Ren was thirteen kinds of finished with this conversation. He couldn't handle one more discussion about Justin.

"Guess I'll see you in two weeks," he tossed off, his tone now openly laced with sarcasm, and he pulled the door to escape into the hallway. He heard her try to call him back, but she'd already done enough damage for one day. She did send him a text, letting him know that if he needed someone to talk to, he could call her. She asked that he send her daily updates, just to keep in touch. Ren stuffed the phone in his coat pocket angrily. Why on earth would he talk to her? She'd just ruined everything.

Except she hadn't. He had. And he knew it, but damn, it hurt. He wanted it to be someone else's fault. He wanted to blame her for messing up his carefully constructed routine. Wanted to blame his family for not understanding what he was doing here, for not accepting it. Wanted to blame Harlow for Justin not calling him again. He just didn't want it to be his fault. His failure.

But he still knew it was.

Alek and Denny started texting him more frequently during his probation, asking him all the questions he wanted to ask Justin.

*What's going on? Even you can't be that busy.*

*We called you eighteen times yesterday, when are you going to call us back?*

*You know we could have sent a message to MARS and got a response by now?*

*Hello! Earth to Ren! You're still alive, right?*

*Lorenzo! Where are you? Are you mad at us? It's the symposium, isn't it? If you start calling again, we promise not to talk about how it's control-ling our life. Not one little whisper. Send us an email, a photo, a text.*

Then some came in just from Alek.

*Come on, buddy, call me back. I think I know what this is about, and you and I should talk. He's not ignoring you, all right? It'll go better in person, just call me. Or better yet call him.*

But Ren no longer wanted to. Couldn't handle the disappoint-ment of another failed attempt. They just had no idea. And he didn't have the energy or desire to explain. Even when Alek arranged for Thai food to be delivered to the apartment in the hopes that feeding Ren would persuade him to call, Ren just ... he just couldn't do it.

He received an unexpected email from Siara.

*Dear Enzo, what happened? We missed your call on Sunday. You never miss a call, and you didn't send us any emails either? Mom's worried. I think we hurt your feelings last time we talked, but you know we didn't mean to. We just miss you so much. You're ok, right? Everything's ok? Don't be mad at us. Get in touch soon, please? I'll make sure they don't pressure you about coming back home. I understand why you can't, but since you already have to stay far away; please don't disappear. Love, your sister.*

Why did they all think he was mad at them? He wasn't mad. He just didn't want to talk. Not about the Dominican Republic or symposiums, radios, or weather. Especially not about Justin and his motivations for vanishing off the face of the earth.

He stared at his ceiling, the piano CD playing softly, harmonizing badly with the rain on the window. It had repeated itself five times now. He ran his fingers over the red bracelet, then the blue one before letting his arm flop across his eyes.

He read the Spanish version of *Jonathan Livingston Seagull* that Justin had mailed him and thought about it a lot. The bird who had given up everything, all his relationships, his entire identity, to fly faster than any other seagull. To fly faster than a falcon. And in the end, he'd done it, and the book made it seem like such a great thing. But Ren couldn't help but notice that in the end, Jonathan had to die to obtain his goal. It made the book less inspiring than Ren knew it was supposed to be.

Ren stared at the other book on his desk. The one he'd purchased for Justin when they'd been talking every day. He'd bought him the dual language version of *La Vida es Sueño*, the Spanish and the English next to each other on the pages. The story of dreams and reality, of preordination and prophecy. Of choices. He'd written in it. Marked the page that held the soliloquy that Justin requested Ren to recite so often.

He'd addressed the envelope to Lackland. Justin's birthday was just around the corner, but Ren hadn't sent the book yet. Didn't know if he should. Didn't know if Justin would want him to. Did he want him to? Or did he want Ren out of his life now? But then why send him the bracelet? Did it mean anything other than Justin had promised him proof, a fair exchange for the dance photos? The indecision kept the book on Ren's desk.

He survived through Friday. Five very long days of frequent unanswered texts from Alek and Denny, some from Celeste. Constant glares from Spencer peppered with sarcastic comments about what Ren was doing home in the middle of the day, didn't he have to put up with him enough already? Ren ticked off the days like a prisoner, carefully wording his daily updates to Angelique to give the illusion that she'd been right, and this was working, careful of the pacing so it would look as though he were healing gradually right on schedule. Too fast of an improvement would expose his lies.

Though he wasn't sure it would help him even when he was allowed back into the ER. Because if she'd seen it once, how was he going to hide it from her when he returned?

Spencer threw a party Friday night. Ren had no idea he knew that many people. Didn't want to know where he got all the beer. Lindsey tried to coax Ren out of his room for the first ninety minutes, tempting him with alcohol and food. He wrapped himself up in the afghan and wished he'd left before it started. He could have slept better on the couch in the lounge. Now he was trapped. The music vibrated the floor long into the night, and guests constantly tried to open his door, mistaking his room for the bathroom. It went on forever. The shouting, the laughing, the music. Alek and Denny called him a few times, but there was no way he could answer. He wished he could shut himself off as easily as his phone.

Ren was shaky when he woke the next morning, like he'd gone through something traumatic. The apartment was quiet, but he didn't know when everyone had finally left. Didn't know how he'd managed to fall asleep, though he suspected it was some defensive shut-down maneuver of his subconscious. He got dressed, then cautiously opened his door around noon, not sure what he'd find.

The bathroom was a catastrophe. It looked like several people had vomited in the bathtub and then left it to dry. Ren's towel was on the floor, wadded up and stained with more than one kind of bodily fluid. He'd need BSI gloves to even start cleaning this up. God, it'd take hours. But then again, he had all the time in the world, didn't he?

He made his way through the hallway, into the living room, relieved that no one had punched through a wall or broken any furniture. Almost. Someone had knocked the basil plant off the kitchen counter. The pot was shattered, and dirt had been tracked everywhere. There wasn't much left of the plant. Ren was surprised that he couldn't really muster much emotion about that. It just went on the list, one more thing.

It was pretty much how he'd expected it to be. Food containers, paper plates, empty beer cans, not-quite-empty beer cans. It looked like someone had crushed an entire bag of chips and then tipped it upside down over the couch. And then Ren saw something he really didn't expect. Lindsey was still here, passed out on the floor between the coffee table and the couch, completely naked.

Now disgusted even more than when he'd been in the bathroom, Ren began hunting down her clothes. Where the hell were her clothes? He found her skirt and panties stuffed between the cushions of the couch, and her flats were in the regular pile by the front door. Her shirt was missing, so Ren returned to his bedroom and searched through the drawers, coming up with the extra-large, long-sleeved T-shirt the Red Cross had handed out for a service project he'd volunteered for some time ago. He'd never worn it and didn't care if he ever got it back. It would work.

He heard Lindsey retching as he closed his bedroom door, heard something splatter and worried he'd have to clean vomit out of the carpet too, but when he peeked around the corner, he saw she was using an empty bucket of KFC chicken to puke into. A shiver of revulsion zipped up Ren's back.

"Here," he said to her softly, coming just close enough to put the shirt on the pile of her clothes on the couch. "You can wear this."

He politely left her alone to cover herself, returning to his room to make her a peanut butter sandwich and then carrying it out into the kitchen where he filled what he hoped was a clean, red plastic cup with one of the last containers of Gatorade he kept in the fridge. She sat, stunned and miserable, legs folded on the floor when he put both cup and sandwich in front of her on the coffee table. The shirt was way too big on her, it fell off one of her shoulders. All her carefully applied makeup smeared almost comically on her face, her lipstick so high up one of her cheeks it looked like half a Glasgow smile, and her eyes were caked so dark they could have been bruised.

Her face took on an alarming green shade as she noticed the food, and Ren could tell she was fighting hard not to throw up again. "Small mouthfuls," he ordered her. "It'll help."

Then he ignored her for a while as he did what he could about the apartment. He filled four trash bags and took them downstairs, swept up the very last piece of Alek that had been in the apartment, and entertained wild and satisfying fantasies of murdering Spencer in his own bed. Lindsey rested her head on the coffee table, nibbling at the sandwich, taking small sips of the Gatorade. Her face grew pale instead of green. Ren gave her a warm, wet dishtowel to scrub over her face. It took some of the makeup off but didn't improve her appearance all that much. Spencer stayed in his room the entire time. Which was a very good thing. Ren didn't know what he'd do if he saw him right now.

After a while, Ren ran out of things to do in the front of the apartment. At least things that didn't require him to turn on the vacuum cleaner, and he thought he'd better get Lindsey out of here before he made that much noise. He went over to her, sitting on the floor across the coffee table after making sure he wouldn't be sitting in anything disgusting. He noted that Spencer had carefully put a protective cloth over his drum set. Covered his drums but left his girlfriend naked in the living room. Real classy.

"Better?" Ren asked, surprisingly furious. He didn't know he could still get this angry about anything Spencer did. It was stupid.

Lindsey stared at him, and he noticed how young she was, her face full of shame and regret. She folded her arms across her chest protectively, seemingly unable to say anything. Not even a nod.

"Are you hurt?" Ren asked another question. "Did anyone hurt you?" Because no one deserved that.

"No," she said groggily. Ren wasn't convinced. "I don't remember." Yeah, that figured. He'd be surprised if she did.

"Look at me?" he requested, and she obeyed him. He quickly checked her eyes, their focus, seeing nothing wrong except the obvious hangover. "You should probably go to the ER," he suggested, knowing the tools they had there for girls like Lindsey. He'd never been permitted to perform those particular procedures, but he knew about them. "They can, well, they can make sure no one —"

She started to cry.

"They'll be gentle," he tried to comfort her. "I work there; I know them all."

"I just want to go home," Lindsey said, eyes downcast again. She shuddered, and Ren couldn't imagine how she must feel. "Can you take me home?"

"I don't have a car," Ren confessed. "But I can walk you if you want. Might help you feel better to walk anyway."

"Ok," Lindsey whimpered. He made her finish the sandwich first, making sure she kept it down before letting her get up and put her shoes on. They found her coat behind the balcony curtains. Ren opened the door and let her lead them outside. He had no idea where she lived.

They walked without speaking; Ren monitoring her steps, which were unsteady but not concerningly so. Sometimes, she'd grab onto his arm, and all his muscles on that side would stiffen up until she let him go. He brought her all the way to the entrance of her dorm, letting her know she'd be good on her own the rest of the way. He had no intention of following her inside.

"You're nice," Lindsey told him, subdued. She had his arm again, pinning him there on the sidewalk in front of the door. He couldn't wait to get away from her. "You're the nicest person I've ever met."

"Then you should probably upgrade the people you hang out with," Ren suggested, still mad and having a hard time masking it. He wasn't nice; he'd never really been nice to her. He was just being decent. Couldn't she tell the difference?

"I would, but you always ignore me," she countered, and now Ren really wanted to get away from her. *Don't you do this to me*, he thought. *Don't you dare. I've got enough going on.*

"I have a girlfriend," Ren reminded her, sticking to his lie.

"Yeah, you used to," Lindsey sighed. "But whoever that was in the pictures you showed me, she's not your girlfriend now."

"Yes, she is," Ren maintained, wondering why he was even bothering to take the time to argue with a nineteen-year-old girl who couldn't remember what she'd done last night.

"You know, the sooner you get over her, the better off you'll be," Lindsey suggested, and it hurt that she made sense, even though she had no idea what she was talking about.

"I have to go," Ren said quickly, pulling his arm away from her with difficulty. He really, really had to get away from her. Now.

"Kiss me?" Lindsey requested.

"No," Ren denied her, immediate and harsh, but then couldn't stand how hurt she looked at the rejection. The mirror of it. His stomach twisted. "Is there someone home at your place? Someone who can look after you?" *Because I can't.*

She bit her lip, eyes downcast, but at least she nodded. Slightly. Enough for Ren to figure it was a nod.

"Ok. Go on in then. Have them help you. I've got to go."

He walked away from her, leaving her at the door with her makeup all smeared and wearing his shirt.

"You're going to end up all alone."

What? Did Lindsey say that? Had Ren heard her say that? Or had those words come from somewhere else? The knot in his stomach tightened. He needed more distance.

He walked away and then started running as soon as he was out of sight of her building, ran as fast as he could, right past his apartment, all the way to the lake even though it was cold and overcast. He curled up on the bench and pushed his shaking hands against his face. Alone.

*I can't do this. I can't keep doing this. I can't take another day of this, let alone another week.*

He pulled out his phone, rather desperately dialing Angelique, not knowing what he was going to say, but then her voicemail came on asking him to leave a message, and he took a huge breath and suddenly everything was coming out at once. Destroying all the careful planning he'd put together for her the entire past week in a weird fit of lonely hysteria.

"Doña, I can't do it. Please, you have to let me come back to work. You said yourself I didn't do anything wrong. It's all I've got left. My friends are so far away, and Justin's not talking to me. I don't even know where he is. I *never* know where he is, and my roommate is a jerk, and I haven't seen my family in years because I gave up *everything* to be a doctor, and they hate me for it, and I don't even know if I want to go home anymore because I know it's different, and I'm too different, and I don't think I belong there. And the only place where things make any sense, when I feel like myself, is when I'm with you in the ER. I'll do whatever you want me to do. I won't touch anything or do anything except stand next to you and watch, just please let me come back. I can't —"

The message cut off, the automated system telling him he'd exceeded the time limit, jolting him back to reality. He suddenly realized what he'd just done and thought about calling her back and trying to fix it, cancel out his whole emotional confession, but he knew no matter what he did at this point, it would just make it worse. One more thing he'd just messed up because he wasn't thinking.

He sat there on the bench, his body too heavy to move, looking at the waves, looking at the old pictures in his phone, hearing Lindsey repeat her recommendation to him. *You're going to end up alone. The sooner you get over her, the better off you'll be.* Except it wasn't her. It was him. And damn, getting over Justin sounded so liberating right now. But the only way Ren could even try would be to throw himself into his doctorate. And the only way to do that was to somehow get back to the ER. And he'd probably just ruined his chances.

The clouds darkened, the afternoon drawing to a close. Ren grew stiff and cold during his hours on the bench; there weren't any joggers or dog walkers out today. He'd have to start moving if he didn't want to get soaked. There was probably a chapter of something he needed to study harder, something he should reread. Or since it was still only Saturday, maybe he'd just go to bed early, pull the quilt over his head, and pretend things would be different in the morning.

He walked slowly, the wind picking up as he went, blowing its way toward the lake, pulling the storm forward. Ren could sense the pressure changing, knowing what it was going to do to him, and the idea of just tucking himself into bed when he got back to the apartment started to sound like the best one. If he took his meds early, it might help prevent the debilitating pain he knew was coming. The familiar bottle was at home on his desk. He just had to get there. It was already so dark.

Ren half-heartedly checked the mailbox in the lobby before going upstairs, though he knew even if there had been anything for him, Spencer would have already taken it and left it somewhere. Ren remembered as he dragged himself up the two flights to his floor just how bad the apartment had been when he'd left earlier with Lindsey. He knew Spencer didn't know how to vacuum, but he'd likely wanted to take a shower if he were even half as hungover as Lindsey had been. Which meant he probably had at least attempted to do something in the bathroom. It needed a heavy decontamination before it could be used, but hopefully Spencer had made a start.

As usual, Ren stood in front of his apartment door, thinking of anything else he could possibly do before going inside. Preparing himself for what might be in there. Obviously, band practice was happening; he could hear the drums already from this side of the door. Drums. Damien's bass. Wes's guitar. No Lindsey tonight, but honestly, Ren hoped she'd never come over again.

He stood in the hall, gathering himself, just as exhausted as Angelique said. He checked his phone one more time, but she hadn't sent him anything yet. Maybe that meant she hadn't checked her phone messages. Maybe he could send her an update, just like normal, and tell her not to worry about it. That might work. He'd have to figure out exactly what to say. It would have to be enough to acknowledge the message without making her curious to listen to it.

He'd do a couple drafts in his room beforehand to make sure it was just right.

The phone went into his coat pocket, and his keys came out of it. He took the coat off and just stood there, leaning against the wall for one more second, preparing to march through to his room. The two bracelets on his wrist were just visible beneath his sleeve when he reached forward to open the door. Ren couldn't help it. He smiled when he saw them and breathed in some strength. Time to go in.

"Where have you been?" Spencer asked the second he walked in the door. Which was odd. Spencer never cared where Ren was. They both liked it better when they didn't have to look at each other. The music stopped; he could sense everyone's eyes on him. He took another breath, starting to walk toward his door, making it past the couch in about half a dozen steps.

"You didn't clean the bathroom yet," Spencer threw at him on his way by, and Ren made the mistake of pausing. *All you have to do is unlock your door,* Ren told himself, but there was a tight ball of rage in his chest, and it burned all the way up his throat.

"I already maxed out my quota for cleaning up after you today," Ren shoved at him. "It was your stupid party; you clean it."

Spencer made a dismissive sputter. "Yeah, don't think so. Cleaning bathrooms is your thing. So, chop chop," Spencer actually snapped his fingers at Ren, who stood motionless near his door, too furious to move. He felt his hand slowly curl around his keyring. Did he really just snap his fingers?

"I'm not doing it," Ren said, emphasizing each word. He turned his back on Spencer, trying to fit the key into the lock. His hands were shaking again, making it difficult.

"Yeah, you will," Spencer told him coolly. He snickered unexpectedly. "What else are you people good for?"

What? *What?*

"Shut your mouth, Spencer," Ren threatened, a growl he'd never heard from himself before. It didn't have much effect. Spencer seemed to be enjoying how he was getting to Ren, and Ren knew better than to engage. He really did. But you people? If Spencer meant what Ren figured he meant, that was taking things way too far, even for an idiot.

"Oh, come on," Spencer jeered, his voice far too superior for a short, spoiled kid from Michigan. "We both know you're going to do it eventually. So *andale* your ass in there."

Ren watched Spencer's eyes suddenly change, widen in shock as his mouth dropped open, and it took Ren a second to realize it was because Ren had roughly shoved him against the wall and punched him in the gut with the hand that still held his keys between his fingers. Spencer grunted, wincing, and Ren drew back his hand to deliver another blow. He'd been fantasizing about beating Spencer to the ground for a while, and now that he'd started, he had no intention of stopping. Pieces of his anatomy book flew through his mind, giving him suggestions on the best place for his next hit. He could slam Spencer against the temple, possibly knocking him out. He could crush his windpipe or his nose between his fist and the wall, leaving him sputtering and *speechless*. His muscles tensed up with contained momentum. Spencer whimpered, pinned against the hallway wall.

Something barreled into Ren from the side with the force of a freight train, and he did a mental pivot to figure out what was happening. He found himself thrown violently to the floor, something heavy and abrupt bashing into his torso, momentarily blinding him with pain. It happened several more times before he scrambled to his feet, standing curled to the side, a hand on his ribs, looking up to find Damien bearing down on him. Oh shit. How the hell had Ren forgotten about Damien?

Ren knew he couldn't fight Damien. His only way out was escape. But Damien had torn him away from Spencer and into the living room, and both Damien and Spencer were blocking Ren's path toward his still locked bedroom door. Ren didn't even have his keys anymore. Where were his keys? They'd been knocked out of his hand when Damien threw him down. Going to his room wasn't an option.

Damien grabbed Ren's shoulder and cannoned his fist into Ren's side, the same place he'd just been kicking him. Ren fought the urge to drop, knowing that would give Damien too easy of a target. He had to stay standing, and he had to get out of here. He pounced for the door and grabbed at it desperately, managing to get it open before Damien laid into him again, his fingers snagging into the fabric of Ren's sweater and using that hold to push him hard, out of the apartment and into the wall opposite his front door, Damien's arm pressed intensely on the back of Ren's neck as he flailed uselessly against the wall.

There was yelling now. Spencer, egging Damien on. Wes screaming at them to stop. Other doors started opening as Damien got in more hard punches against Ren's lower back. More yelling. Some of it from Ren. He felt Damien lean away for a stronger hit and took the opportunity of the relieved pressure to drop downward and shoot toward the stairs.

He flung himself past several of his neighbors who had come out to see what all the shouting was. They flattened themselves against the wall as he clawed his way past them, staying pressed to the sides as Damien bulldozed through right behind. Ren raced for the stairs, just grabbing to the railing to go down when Damien caught up to him again, snagging Ren's bicep and wrenching him around, his opposite hand near his ear, ready to punch Ren in the face.

Ren ducked, jerking his body as far as he could away from Damien at the same time, trying to break his grip on his arm. The punch didn't land, and Ren had successfully torn free from Damien's fingers, and all that would have been great except for how he'd been standing at the very top of the stairs. He made a clumsy grab for the rail as he began to fall, feeling his foot slip out from under him when he tried to catch himself, and then there was nothing he could do except try to protect his head and neck as he went tumbling down the entire flight of steps, landing in a tangled, painful heap at the entrance to the second floor.

He didn't take any time for self-assessment once he'd come to a stop, just gathered his legs together to get up and get out. The yelling continued, but underneath the chaos, Ren could hear Damien's heavy footfalls on the stairs, coming for him.

Ren half jumped down the last flight of steps, heart beating hard at the prospect of falling again but he was still more afraid of the danger coming after him than what he could do to himself racing forward. He hit the lobby without incident and then catapulted out the front entrance. And even then, he didn't stop. He kept running, never once looking back to see how far Damien followed him.

He was halfway to the hospital before he ran out of breath and had to slow down. Pausing on one end of the quad, panting with difficulty, Ren looked around and found himself alone. He rested one knee on a bench but didn't dare sit down. He just wanted a second, just needed to catch his breath, figure stuff out. His throat burned, too dry and ragged. Thankfully, it didn't seem that adrenaline had allowed him to run on any broken bones; everything seemed sound enough even though he'd fallen down a flight of stairs.

Shit, an entire flight of stairs. Ren tried to pinpoint injuries from that, but nothing was distinct to him right now. All the cells of his body were screaming at him for something, but Ren didn't think he was truly hurt. *That could have been so much worse*, Ren told himself, starting to shake now that he was holding still and thinking about it. *You are so damn lucky.* He heard himself start laughing and covered his mouth tightly with his hand, horrified. *You are so screwed.*

He curled over, his palm resting against the coldness of the bench, other hand still over his mouth. *What are you going to do now?* His mind went still, as though waiting for something external to answer that question for him. *No, seriously, what are you going to do? What's the plan?*

Call the police? Except Ren had started the fight, and that thought made him feel cold. He had attacked first, hit Spencer first. That made all this his fault. Shit. How had he messed up like that? Lost control of his anger that way? Let that stupid boy goad him into violence; he was better than that.

*Apparently, you're not.*

And he had no idea what the true consequences of that were going to be. Not just what Damien could do with his fists, but what Spencer could do with the American legal system. Could that one thoughtless second get Ren kicked out of med school? Out of the country? Had he fucked up his entire plan with one unsatisfying punch? *Shit.*

*All right, one thing at a time, focus a second.* Obviously, going back to the apartment right now was not happening. Which sucked because Ren had dashed out without his coat, keys, wallet, or phone. All that stuff was now at Spencer's mercy, in a pile in front of Ren's bedroom door.

Ren started walking again, slowly. Even though he wasn't sure where he was going, it felt better to be moving. Made it feel like he was in control of the situation. Even though it was all a lie.

*Where are you going to go?* He asked himself continuously but came up with nothing. This was all his own fault. He couldn't ask for help with this. His injuries were too minor to justify going to the hospital, and he was still on probation. Anyone seeing him there would just send him home, or worse, call Angelique. He'd already done enough damage to that relationship today. No need to make it worse by making her think he was trying to sneak into the ER behind her back. And now that he couldn't text her his daily update, she was for sure going to listen to that phone message. Ren let his head hang, his arms curling around his sore ribcage, astonished at his complete lack of judgment today. He gave himself a little shake; he couldn't sink into dejection yet. He needed a plan. *Think.*

But he couldn't go to his apartment. And he couldn't really go to the hospital. Ren unconsciously made his way toward the library, but then didn't go in. All the buildings looked strange to him in the October dark. Everything looked colder, taller, packed tight against each other. Ren kept walking, no longer thinking of where he was headed, where he could go. His mind was too full of mistakes. How he'd hit Spencer first. How he'd called Angelique and said all the wrong things. How everyone thought he was mad at them. How he couldn't talk to anyone anymore.

*Where are you going?* He thought from time to time as he moved, but still didn't have an answer or any desire to stop. He couldn't stop, not now. Ren kept walking, away from campus, following the easiest path of the streets. His vision got weird, blurry. Ren wiped at his face, but there were no tears. *Where the hell are you going?*

He didn't know, but he knew he wasn't there yet.

# ABOUT THE AUTHOR

Karin Mallard has loved writing since the second grade when she would race through her schoolwork so she could ask her teacher for a piece of paper with a sticker on it as a writing prompt. These "sticker stories" were later replaced with random paragraphs woven into her math and Spanish notes, whole notebooks full of terrible poetry, and a run in the early 2000s dedicated to fan fiction.

Karin earned a bachelor's degree in English with an emphasis in creative writing from Brigham Young University - Idaho. Currently, she lives in Orem, Utah, with her husband, Richard, and their three children.

In addition to writing, Karin also enjoys reading, hiking, knitting, freelance editing, and rewatching movies.